Daughter of
Dragons

PRAISE FOR THE PILLARS OF REALITY SERIES

"Campbell has created an interesting world… [he] has created his characters in such a meticulous way, I could not help but develop my own feelings for both of them. I have already gotten the second book and will be listening with anticipation."

–Audio Book Reviewer

"I loved *The Hidden Masters of Marandur*…The intense battle and action scenes are one of the places where Campbell's writing really shines. There are a lot of urban and epic fantasy novels that make me cringe when I read their battles, but Campbell's years of military experience help him write realistic battles."

–All Things Urban Fantasy

"I highly recommend this to fantasy lovers, especially if you enjoy reading about young protagonists coming into their own and fighting against a stronger force than themselves. The world building has been strengthened even further giving the reader more history. Along with the characters flight from their pursuers and search for knowledge allowing us to see more of the continent the pace is constant and had me finding excuses to continue the book."

–Not Yet Read

"*The Dragons of Dorcastle*… is the perfect mix of steampunk and fantasy… it has set the bar to high."

–The Arched Doorway

"Quite a bit of fun and I really enjoyed it. . .An excellent sequel and well worth the read!"

–Game Industry

"The Pillars of Reality series continues in *The Assassins of Altis* to be a great action filled adventure. . .So many exciting things happen that I can hardly wait for the next book to be released."

—Not Yet Read

"The Pillars of Reality is a series that gets better and better with each new book. . .*The Assassins of Altis* is a great addition to a great series and one I recommend to fantasy fans, especially if you like your fantasy with a touch of sci-fi."

—Bookaholic Cat

"Seriously, get this book (and the first two). This one went straight to my favorites shelf."

—Reanne Reads

"[Jack Campbell] took my expectations and completely blew them out of the water, proving yet again that he can seamlessly combine steampunk and epic fantasy into a truly fantastic story. . .I am looking forward to seeing just where Campbell goes with the story next, I'm not sure how I'm going to manage the wait for the next book in the series."

—The Arched Doorway

"When my audiobook was delivered around midnight, I sat down and told myself I would listen for an hour or so before I went to sleep. I finished it in almost 12 straight hours, I don't think I've ever listened to an audiobook like that before. I can say with complete honesty that *The Servants of The Storm* by Jack Campbell is one of the best books I've ever had the pleasure to listen to."

—Arched Doorway

PRAISE FOR THE LOST FLEET SERIES

"It's the thrilling saga of a nearly-crushed force battling its way home from deep within enemy territory, laced with deadpan satire about modern warfare and neoliberal economics. Like Xenophon's Anabasis – with spaceships."

—The Guardian (UK)

"Black Jack is an excellent character, and this series is the best military SF I've read in some time."

—Wired Magazine

"If you're a fan of character, action, and conflict in a Military SF setting, you would probably be more than pleased by Campbell's offering."

—Tor.com

"... a fun, quick read, full of action, compelling characters, and deeper issues. Exactly the type of story which attracts readers to military SF in the first place."

—SF Signal

"Rousing military-SF action... it should please many fans of old-fashioned hard SF. And it may be a good starting point for media SF fans looking to expand their SF reading beyond tie-in novels."

—SciFi.com

"Fascinating stuff ... this is military SF where the military and SF parts are both done right."

—SFX Magazine

PRAISE FOR THE LOST FLEET: BEYOND THE FRONTIER SERIES

"Combines the best parts of military sf and grand space opera to launch a new adventure series ... sets the fleet up for plenty of exciting discoveries and escapades."

—Publishers Weekly

"Absorbing...neither series addicts nor newcomers will be disappointed."

—Kirkus Reviews

"Epic space battles, this time with aliens. Fans who enjoyed the earlier books in the Lost Fleet series will be pleased."

—Fantasy Literature

"I loved every minute of it. I've been with these characters through six novels and it felt like returning to an old group of friends."

—Walker of Worlds

"A fast-paced page turner ... the search for answers will keep readers entertained for years to come."

—SF Revu

"Another excellent addition to one of the best military science fiction series on the market. This delivers everything fans expect from Black Jack Geary and more."

—Monsters & Critics

ALSO BY JACK CAMPBELL

THE LOST FLEET
Dauntless
Fearless
Courageous
Valiant
Relentless
Victorious

BEYOND THE FRONTIER
Dreadnaught
Invincible
Guardian
Steadfast
Leviathan

THE LOST STARS
Tarnished Knight
Perilous Shield
Imperfect Sword
Shattered Spear

THE GENESIS FLEET
Vanguard

THE ETHAN STARK SERIES
Stark's War
Stark's Command
Stark's Crusade

THE PAUL SINCLAIR SERIES
A Just Determination
Burden of Proof
Rule of Evidence
Against All Enemies

PILLARS OF REALITY
The Dragons of Dorcastle*
The Hidden Masters of Marandur*
The Assassins of Altis*
The Pirates of Pacta Servanda*
The Servants of the Storm*
The Wrath of the Great Guilds*
The Servants of the Storm*

THE LEGACY OF DRAGONS
Daughter of Dragons*

NOVELLAS
The Last Full Measure

SHORT STORY COLLECTIONS
Ad Astra*
Borrowed Time*
Swords and Saddles*

*available as a JABberwocky Edition

Daughter of Dragons

The Legacy of Dragons
Book 1

JACK CAMPBELL

JABberwocky Literary Agency, Inc.

Daughter of Dragons

First paperback edition in 2017 by JABberwocky Literary Agency, Inc.

Published as an ebook in 2017 by JABberwocky Literary Agency, Inc.

Originally published in 2017 as an audiobook by Audible Studios

Cover art by Dominick Saponaro

Map by Isaac Stewart

Interior design by Lisa Rodgers

ISBN 978-1-625672-73-5

To
my niece Alison McMahan Sevier

For S, as always

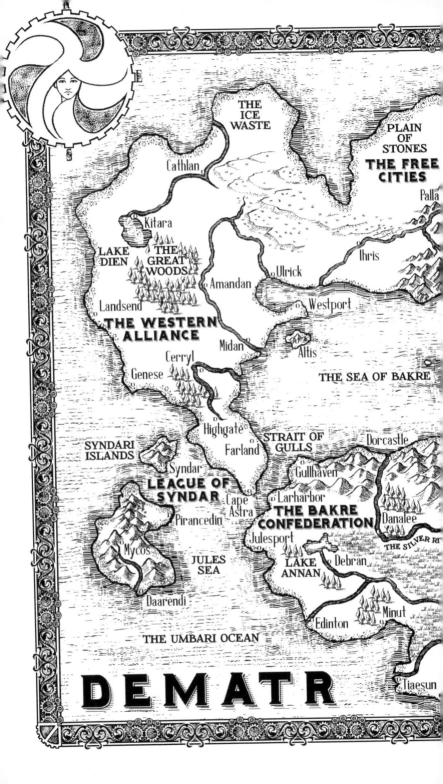

ACKNOWLEDGMENTS

I remain indebted to my agents, Joshua Bilmes and Eddie Schneider, for their long standing support, ever-inspired suggestions and assistance, as well as to Krystyna Lopez and Lisa Rodgers for their work on foreign sales and print editions. Thanks also to Catherine Asaro, Robert Chase, Carolyn Ives Gilman, J.G. (Huck) Huckenpohler, Simcha Kuritzky, Michael LaViolette, Aly Parsons, Bud Sparhawk and Constance A. Warner for their suggestions, comments and recommendations.

CHAPTER ONE

The Mages of the world of Dematr sometimes see visions: glimpses of the future or of a possible future. But understanding those visions can be very difficult. The future rarely happens as people expect, and even those people with the firmest belief in what their future will hold can be very mistaken.

Especially when that person is the daughter of the two greatest heroes of her world.

Kira of Pacta Servanda was six years old the day she stood on a battlement in Dorcastle, staring up at a statue of her mother while surrounded by bodyguards who fenced Kira off from the nearby crowds. As the morning sun cast the shadow of her mother's statue over Kira, she had felt both invisible and an object of curiosity, and had realized that she would spend the rest of her life in that shade.

Kira was still six years old when the world of Dematr learned that a new kind of ship had left the far-distant world of Urth. The ship would take only ten years to cover the immense distances between stars. Of all the colony worlds, the ship was coming to Dematr. Because of Kira's mother.

When she was ten, Kira's father, the wisest of Mages, discovered that she had inherited some of his abilities as well as her mother's skill with machines, something thought impossible. But that one thing that might have made her special had to be kept secret from others, a source of worry rather than pride.

Kira was sixteen when the ship from Urth arrived, and she discovered that her world still needed heroes.

Outside, birds sang to greet the early morning. Inside, the irresistible force and the immovable object confronted each other.

"I don't want to go," Kira said to her mother.

Master Mechanic Mari, also known simply as Lady Mari but most often as "the daughter," stared at her own daughter in disbelief. "Why wouldn't you want to be there? This is the most important thing our world has experienced since…"

"Since you saved the world?" Kira asked. "Go ahead and say it! Everybody else does!"

Her mother sighed. "I had a job to do. I did it."

"And my job is to follow you around so people can see the freak."

Mari stared at her, shocked. "Freak? Who calls you that?"

"Everybody!" Kira said. "Oh, they don't say it out loud. Usually. There she is! The daughter of the daughter! The girl whose mother died years before she was born!"

"I didn't die."

Kira shook her head, feeling frustrated at the same answer Mari always gave when someone brought that up. "Mother, I've talked to some of the healers who were there. They were all eager to tell me how you died and then Father came running in and brought you back."

"Your father will tell you that as far as he could tell I was still there," Mari insisted. "He just helped heal the bullet wound in ways my body couldn't manage on its own. Haven't we talked about this?"

"No, *we* haven't. Father and I have. *We* never talk about anything."

Mari looked at her, her sadness so obvious that Kira felt angry at herself. "Dearest…it's hard to speak about some of the things your father and I went through during the war. Even so long after the war the things we had to do, the things we saw, want to stay locked inside. I know it's difficult for you to understand."

Kira shook her head, trying to sort out her feelings. "I don't— It's just—" She clenched her fists. "I can't talk to you."

"I have the same problem." Her mother raised her voice. "Alain, come try to talk to our daughter!"

As Kira's mother left the room her father came in, calm and composed as he almost always was, his Mage robes contrasting with the shirt and pants Kira wore. "What is it, Kira? Why are you angry?"

He could read anyone's emotions, and seemed particularly good at seeing what lay inside Kira. She blurted out the truth. "I don't know. Except that it's so hard. It's bad enough being somewhere alone, and I'm almost always alone, except for the guards."

Her father looked at her, openly saddened. "I know a girl your age should have friends. Many friends. I do not…"

"I know, Father, I'm sorry," Kira said. Her father hadn't had friends growing up. Literally none, since the Mage Guild that had taken him from his family did its best to erase the very concept of friends from the minds of acolytes. "It's not your fault. It's just too hard. Anyone who wants to visit here has a hard time because of the security, and if I want to go somewhere I have a hard time because of the security, and then we found out that anyone I made real friends with might get targeted by Mother's enemies, and how could I do that to anyone? So I've got guys like Gari way off in Danalee and girls like Devi way off in Tiaesun, but…that's not it, Father. Not today. Everybody is going to be there today, and when I'm with Mother everyone looks at me and thinks—" Kira clamped her mouth shut, staring toward the nearest window at the open country around their home.

"You look very much like your mother did when she was younger." Her father said that in a way that made it sound like the greatest thing ever. Kira felt combined affection for him and irritation at the comparison.

"Do you know what they say?" Kira asked in a low voice. "Some people say that because Mother died once she couldn't have a child the normal way, so you cast some spell that made a baby copy of her. Me."

"You should not listen to such nonsense," Alain said.

"Why do I have to go?"

"We think it could be important to have you there," Alain said.

"We're going to look primitive, aren't we?" Kira waved around to encompass the room and the world. "They have all those amazing things, and we have…steam locomotives."

"I thought you liked steam locomotive creatures."

After all this time her father still thought of locomotives as being like Mage creatures rather than Mechanic devices. That managed to get a smile out of her. "I do. They're cool."

"Kira," her father said, "if these people from Urth believe they are better than we are because they have Mechanic devices better than ours, they are fools. We intend to show them the sort of people we are. We do not know what sort of people they are."

"You're…concerned about them?" She had started to say *scared*, but that was ridiculous. Nothing scared her father. "Why would you want me there, then?"

Alain studied Kira for a moment before replying. "It is important that you be there. You have a role to play in what will happen."

She felt a chill. "Father, is that foresight? Did you see something about the future involving me?"

He paused again, this time considering his words. "Yes. It is time you were told. The vision came before you were born. Its meaning remains unclear. But you were there."

"Before I was *born*?" Kira stared at her father in shock. "And nobody mentioned this until *now*? What was I doing? What am I supposed to do? What—?"

Her father held up one hand, halting her burst of questions. "I do not know the answers to those questions. I do know that you will be equal to whatever challenge arises."

Kira inhaled deeply, trying to calm herself. "I'm not you. I am not *her*. Just because I look like Mother—"

Her father came closer, his gaze intent. "You are very like her in more ways than you realize."

"Father, I can never be anything like—"

"Have I ever lied to you?"

"No." *The word of a Mage* was still common slang for something worthless, but when she was younger Kira had gotten into more than one epic fight with peers who thought that saying applied to her father. "All right. I'll go."

"Quickly. Please," her father added. The word *please* still sounded slightly stilted, a legacy of his early Mage training, when he had been forced to think of all others as merely shadows deserving of no notice. He had only learned to see other people as real again thanks to her mother.

There was absolutely nothing in the world that was not about her mother, Kira thought despairingly.

Kira ran up the stairs to her room, her thoughts tumbling over each other. Foresight about her? And this ship from Urth? *I know who the heroes in this family are. My mother and father. Not me. Am I fated to mess things up somehow?*

She knew that a lot of people believed she lived in some grand estate. It had been so long since Kira had been comfortable trying to have friends visit, especially after that disastrous surprise twelfth birthday party where Kira had barely known any of the boys and girls who had been invited, that she wondered if anyone she had known remembered the truth. Lady Mari could have had a great house for the asking, but had refused to accept anything other than a decent place with a house, the barn, and the small workshop, as well as enough open land around it to make it easier to protect her family. They wouldn't even have had any of the still-rare electric lighting if her mother hadn't needed the power for the long-distance far-talker her responsibilities required.

Kira ran a finger over the broken portable far-talker she had been fiddling with. Her mother, her aggravating and impossible and difficult mother, had given the valuable device to her immediately when Kira asked if she could try to fix it.

Her uniform as an honorary officer in the Queen's Own Lancers caught Kira's eye. If there might be trouble, that gleaming chest armor and helm could be useful. But Lady Mari had to be totally impartial in disputes between countries. If Lady Mari's daughter showed up in a uniform of Tiae's military at a very public appearance with her mother, the world would notice and not in a good way.

She kicked off her boots, pulled off trousers and work shirt, yanked on her nicest slacks, slid into her calf-high leather cavalry boots, buttoned up her nicest white shirt with the frills along the front, and topped it off with her fitted dress coat that came down just below her hips.

Her eyes came to rest on the pistol hanging in its holster. Looking like Lady Mari was not just aggravating. It could be very dangerous. Not everyone had been pleased when the Great Guilds were overthrown. Many of the Senior Mechanics who once controlled the Mechanics Guild that had controlled the world hated her mother for destroying their power. The Dark Mechanics who had exploited their knowledge for crime also hated her. There were Mages who, while never admitting to an emotion like hate, had never accepted being forced to follow the same laws that other people did. The list didn't stop there, Kira knew. Some of those people still wanted revenge, as she was frequently reminded. And her father, of all people, was worried about today.

Yanking off the dress coat, she pulled on the shoulder holster, checked the pistol to be sure the safeties were set, then put the coat back on and made sure it concealed the holster straps.

She eyed her small collection of jewelry, then plucked out the Roc earring—a jeweled depiction of one of the giant Mage birds dangling as if in flight—and fastened it on her right ear. Mage Alera might be there today, and Kira had always liked the shy older woman and her Roc Swift.

As she hurriedly brushed her short hair, raven-black like her mother's, Kira paused to look at herself in the mirror, seeing a younger version of her mother. So did everyone else. She could have put on Mage robes or an Imperial legionary uniform and people still would have looked at her and seen Master Mechanic Mari of Caer Lyn, the woman who had held the last wall of Dorcastle against impossible odds, who had fulfilled the long-ago prophecy of the daughter of Jules to free the world from the grip of the Great Guilds, and since then had used her moral authority and vast popularity to help resolve disputes and prevent more wars.

Kira's hand went to the hair above her temple, where on her mother a bright streak of white had remained since the day her father saved Mari's life, nearly dying himself in the process. "Why couldn't I have looked like somebody else?" Kira asked her reflection. "Isn't it hard enough to have a mother who's so famous and did so many amazing things? Who is ever going to look at me and see *me*?"

As usual, her mirror offered no answers.

Downstairs again, Kira saw to her dismay that her mother, who rarely wore any ornamentation besides her promise ring, was wearing a Roc earring similar to hers. At least her mother was wearing her dark Mechanics jacket rather than something matching Kira's outfit.

The country of Tiae was far enough south that it rarely got cold, but the weather this morning had enough bite to it that Kira was glad for the covered coach waiting for them. Twenty cavalry from the army of Tiae waited to ride escort in front of the carriage and twenty more waited behind, the breath of the horses forming small clouds in the chilly air. The cavalry were all from the Queen's Own Lancers, their commander saluting. Feeling self-conscious, Kira returned the salute along with her mother.

Her parents sat in the back, facing forward, and Kira sat in the front, facing them. She kept her eyes out the window as the driver flicked her reins and the coach's horses started forward, straining to get into motion a coach rendered heavier than usual by the armor plate in the sides.

The coach, accompanied by the alert cavalry, rolled past the small plot of land with a low fence around it and a single stone marker. Kira gazed at the place where her little brother Danel had rested since dying soon after his birth, feeling the same old sense of loss. She looked at her mother, who was also gazing that way. "I'm sorry."

Mari nodded. "It happened."

"I wish you could have had more children."

"What, are you lonely?" her mother asked, trying to make a joke of it and failing. "Yes. That would have been nice. But I can't complain. I have you."

Kira looked away again, emotions swirling inside. "They still can't do anything about it? Even for you?"

"No," Mari said. "The things that went wrong inside me can't be fixed. Not by healers. Not by your father." She rubbed her face. "Let's talk about something else."

"We always do," Kira said.

Her father leaned forward. "Do not judge."

Kira nodded wordlessly, wishing that whenever difficult topics arose they didn't get shunted aside, but not wanting to get into that old argument again.

"There's something important we need to ask of you," her mother said to Kira.

"About the foresight thing?" Kira said, letting her voice grow sharp and a little accusing.

Mari glanced at Alain. "Yes."

"Because it sure would have been nice to have a little time to *prepare*."

"Kira," her mother said, her voice taking on an edge, "we've been preparing you for things like this your entire life. Here is what we need from you. While we're dealing with the people from Urth, keep your eyes and your ears open. Since you're still young, they might underestimate you and say something they wouldn't in front of Alain or me."

"Like when we meet with the Imperials?" Kira asked.

"Yes," Mari said. "Just like that. We really don't know what's going to happen. The Urth peoples' messages to us have been friendly and peaceful, but also frustratingly vague, and your father and other Mages have had visions that imply some sort of threat."

"How dangerous is this?" Kira asked, suddenly more aware of

the pistol resting under her arm, its weight both reassuring and disquieting.

"We don't know. You have a role to play in what's going to happen. We don't know what that is," her mother added, "but your father and I will be with you."

That was reassuring despite the worries churning inside her. Lady Mari and her Mage had defeated the most powerful forces on Dematr when freeing the world, and surmounted every challenge since then as well.

"Your father has been teaching you how to spot when people aren't being truthful," Mari continued. "Are you confident you can do that?"

Kira nodded. "Yes. Maybe not with a Mage, but with most people I can tell."

"That's my girl." Her mother smiled at Kira. "Don't worry. I'm sure we can handle whatever happens."

Kira managed to smile back instead of pointing out to her mother that she had just said she could tell when someone wasn't being truthful. She glanced at her father, who gazed back with a clear message not to call her mother on it.

Kira leaned back in her seat, pretending to sleep as the coach and their cavalry escort headed down the road toward Pacta Servanda.

Pacta Servanda, once only an old town, nowadays popularly known as the city the daughter had built.

The field where the ship from Urth would land lay outside the city and was already surrounded by an immense crowd, kept back by large numbers of soldiers. As the coach swept through a lane kept open in the crowd, Kira huddled back into her seat, embarrassed by sharing the privilege of Lady Mari. It wasn't like *she* had earned such treatment. "What exactly is landing here?" she asked her mother to distract her thoughts. "Not the whole ship?"

"No," Mari said. "There is some big part that detaches and can land here while the rest, including their main engines, stays above the world. Your Uncle Calu explained about the relative thing, right?"

"Yes," Kira said. "Relativity. Even though it took the ship ten years to get here, time passed at a different rate inside the ship because of the way it was traveling, so to them it only felt like a couple of months."

The coach came to a halt, the cavalry riding onward to join the nearby honor guard. Kira followed her mother and father out, to find Sien waiting for them.

Queen Sien of Tiae wore a uniform similar to that of her cavalry, sword by her side, but with a single bright emerald in a gold band on her brow instead of an armored helm. Kira stood by, feeling worried and unnecessary, while Sien greeted her old friends and allies.

"And you, Kira," Sien said, coming over to surprise Kira with a hug. "You look so much like your mother the first time I saw her."

Kira tried to smile politely and hide her frustration at the comparison. "Good morning, your majesty."

"So formal!" Sien said, then looked closely at Kira. "They told you?"

"Yes," Kira said, not surprised that Sien had been informed of her father's foresight, but also annoyed that yet one more person beside herself had been told.

"Good. If you need something and can't get to your parents, Tiae is at your side," Sien said.

Kira blinked in amazement. The Queen of Tiae had just promised her full backing. To her? "I...I promise I will not ask for that without the best reasons," Kira faltered. She looked around, trying to think of anything else to say. There were other groups of dignitaries nearby, leading figures from the various countries and independent cities, including a cluster in the unmistakable fine suits and uniforms of the Empire that ruled the eastern portion of the world. "Is that Camber?" Kira asked, startled.

"Yes," Sien said. "The Emperor's closest advisor. Only something like this could have brought him to Tiae. The Imperials are not happy that the Urth ship is landing here rather than in Imperial territory."

"The Imperials don't have the daughterness living there," Master Mechanic Alli remarked as she came up, grinning.

Kira caught the annoyed look from her mother and had to suppress a smile. "Hi, Aunt Alli. You know Mother doesn't like you calling her that."

"That's why I do it, to keep her head on straight when so many other people are telling her how great she is." Alli studied Kira. "How are you doing?"

"All right. Are you going to come by the place? There's a tree stump that needs blowing up. I could set the charge and do it myself, but it's more fun with you."

"Mari raised you right," Alli said. "Of course, I'm the one who taught you how to blow up stuff."

"And how to shoot," Kira said, grateful for the distraction from her thoughts about what might happen with the ship from Earth. "Will I ever get to fire a dragon killer?"

"Maybe the next time you're up in Danalee. Hey, Calu," Alli called to her husband. "Come say hi to Kira and these other important people."

All too soon, Mari and Alain beckoned to Kira. "We have to make some more courtesy calls," her mother said.

Kira balked when she saw where they were heading. "Do I have to meet the Imperials? You know they're going to want to talk about that again."

"Surely today they wouldn't—" Her mother made a face. "Who am I kidding? Since your first birthday they've been trying to get us to betroth you to a prince in the Imperial household. Of course they'll bring it up. Your Aunt Bev is over there. Why don't you go talk to her?"

"Thanks." Kira left her parents and walked quickly over to where Mechanic Bev was standing alone, as she often was, watching everyone else.

Bev smiled when Kira came up. "Hi, my favorite crazy honorary daughter. Not eager to talk to the Imperials today?"

"Was it that obvious?" Kira asked. "I've heard all about how advantageous it would be for me to become engaged to a prince of the Imperial court so that East and West could be bound together by ties of family and blood and blah, blah, blah. I know Mother and Father have never encouraged them to think I'd agree to be traded like some prize horse, but it's still so creepy."

"You'd probably work your way up to Empress," Bev observed with a wink.

"Yeah. Sure. Don't want."

"What's got you so tense?"

Kira bit her lip, looking around. "Something is supposed to happen."

"Foresight?" Bev's posture shifted, ready to protect Kira. "Some danger to you?"

"We don't know. But some Mages have been getting worrisome visions about the ship from Urth. Bev, a long time ago you told me there are no secrets between us. You didn't know about Father's vision before I was born? That something would happen involving me and Urth?"

"No. And right now I'm a little upset about that!"

Kira smiled with relief. "Ever since I was little you've been a bodyguard, and my self-defense teacher, and the sort of friend I couldn't find elsewhere because of being my mother's daughter. I would have hated it if you'd known and not told me."

"If I'd known," Bev said, a stormy look appearing on her face, "you wouldn't be within a million lances of this place."

That was why her parents hadn't told Bev, Kira realized. Bev had devoted her life to protecting kids from the sort of things that had been done to Bev when she was young, and she wouldn't have agreed with Kira running unknown risks. "Mother and Father will be keeping an eye on me."

"Just don't forget everything you've learned," Bev said, her gaze on Kira growing sharp. "Mages have had visions? What about you?"

"Me?" Kira asked, pretending that she didn't understand the question.

"Don't play dumb with me, girl. I'm one of the few who know you have minor Mage talents, remember?"

"I haven't—" Kira hesitated, uncomfortable. "I've never experienced foresight," she mumbled. "Why did this happen to me?"

"Everyone who knows would like the answer to that," Bev said, her eyes concerned. "Mage talents require seeing the world in a totally different way than Mechanics do. Not even traces of Mage talent should be possible alongside Mechanic skills. You having both is inexplicable and…"

"Scary," Kira finished. "One more example of me being a freak."

"You're not a freak."

"Then why are Mother and Father being so different the last few years? I can't explain it, but I can feel it. The way they look at me sometimes these days. It's like they think I'm a bomb that could explode at any time."

"I imagine most parents of teenage girls feel that way," Bev commented.

"Bev, I'm not *her*. I'm never going to change the world."

Bev sighed. "Everybody knows you're not Mari."

"No, I'm not!" Kira looked down at the grass, misery rising in her. "I'm sixteen. When my mother was sixteen she qualified as a full Mechanic. Youngest person ever. And when she was eighteen she qualified as a Master Mechanic. Youngest person ever. You know what everyone is already thinking. Every time they look at *me* and see *her* they think it. Soon they're going to start saying it. Asking me when I'm going to slay some dragons and raise an army and free the world like she did! Asking me what I'm going to do with *my* life that could match that!"

Bev looked down as well, grimacing. "You know that your mother and father never thought of themselves as heroes. Still don't. Your mother doesn't spend time remembering doing great things. She remembers her mistakes and the people who got hurt. The last thing she wants is for you to experience anything like that."

"I wouldn't know," Kira said, hearing the resentment in her voice. "She never talks about that stuff with me."

Bev's sigh carried a lot of weight. "Kira, it's hard to explain. There are some things that are very hard to talk about, even a long time later. Your mother still has nightmares."

"Yeah," Kira said, upset with herself. "I hear her sometimes at night. That's one of my earliest memories, waking up, hearing my mother crying out and wanting to help."

"I'm sorry. Being in battles, having lots of people trying to kill you, seeing people die, that stuff doesn't just go away." Bev tapped her head. "It stays there, and sometimes it feels like it all just happened. Trust me on this. Your mother wants to tell you how it was. She can't. And she knows how being her daughter has made your life hard. She was really upset when we had to put you into private teaching when you were ten, but after we stopped that plot to blow up the school to get at you in order to hurt Mari, it was just too dangerous for the other kids to keep you there."

Kira nodded, catching a glimpse of new arrivals. "There's Mage Asha and Mechanic Dav."

Bev looked that way and waved. Asha, still dazzlingly beautiful, gave them a smile while Dav, leaning on his cane as he walked stiffly, waved back with his free hand.

"Aunt Bev?" Kira asked. "Why does my mother blame herself for Uncle Dav's limp? I've asked and all Mother will say is it was her fault."

Bev sighed again. "She thinks she's responsible. His pelvis couldn't heal right after he took an Imperial crossbow bolt in the hip. She and Dav were fighting legionaries on the deck of the *Terror*. They got the deck cleared, but he got hit, and your mother got him down below even though she had been hit, too."

"Mother?" Kira switched her gaze back to the figures of her parents where they were talking with the Imperial delegation. "Wounded? You're not talking about when she got shot at Dorcastle?"

"No, this was months before that. She got hit in the arm."

Kira covered her face with one hand. "That big scar. I saw it when I was little and I asked what it was and Mother said she'd gotten hurt once, like it was no big deal. Ever since then I've thought some piece of Mechanic equipment clipped her in an accident."

"What would you have wanted her to tell her little girl? That most of an Imperial legion had been trying to kill her and didn't quite succeed?"

"I'm not a little girl anymore."

"No," Bev agreed. "You're not. I'll talk to Mari. She needs to try to tell you a few things. I think that will help her as well as you. Look, whatever this thing with Urth turns out to be, you've got a lot of good women and men at your back." She looked around. "It's almost time. You'd better get with Mari and Alain. And tell them we're going to have words about that foresight I wasn't told about."

Kira hastened to rejoin her parents, once more feeling out of place as she stood by them. The small groups of dignitaries were forming into a row, each beside the others, Lady Mari and Master of Mages Alain making up their own separate group between Queen Sien on one side and the Imperials on the other.

People everywhere were gazing at the sky. Shouts erupted as a bright spot appeared, becoming a silvery object that seemed to be plummeting toward them and growing rapidly in size as it came nearer. Kira felt a surge of anxiety that it would hit them and turned to look at her mother.

Mari had a disdainful look as she gazed upward. "They're trying to throw us off balance, like one of those riders who charges up to you and swerves their horse aside at the last moment to make you flinch."

The ship, or the part of the ship that was landing, was shaped like a flattened sphere, the height of a three-story building and perhaps twice as wide, an eerily beautiful iridescent sheen playing over the silvery exterior. There was no external sign of whatever propelled it and allowed it to fly. It came to rest on the grass not more than twenty lances away from where Kira stood with her parents. She saw the ground beneath the ship compressing from its weight, forming a shallow bowl that held the craft steady.

Kira felt as if the entire world was holding its breath, waiting for something extraordinary, torn between hope and fear.

After a long pause, an opening the size of a large door suddenly appeared in the side of the ship near the ground. A ramp extended downward, and a figure came down the ramp.

Kira hadn't really known what to expect. But she had definitely not anticipated seeing a tall, thin woman in a black pantsuit. Something about her felt strangely uncomfortable to Kira, a sense that the legs were too long, the feet too small, the breasts too large, the face too finely chiseled. The woman stopped at the foot of the ramp, looking over the waiting people, then began walking straight toward Kira's parents. Kira felt her inner tension rise with every step the woman took toward them. The background noise from the crowd had vanished, everyone silent as they watched, the only sounds the faint sighing of the wind and a snort from one of the cavalry horses.

The woman stopped less than a lance length away. "You are Master Mechanic Mari? Good. The low-res faxes through your Feynman Unit didn't offer enough detail. But you're exotic. That's very good."

Kira saw her mother blink in surprise at the odd greeting. "I am Master Mechanic Mari. This is my promised husband, Master of Mages Alain, and our daughter Kira. You are...?"

"Oh. Talese Groveen, Senior Executive Vice President for Research and Development at Universal Life Systems."

"Universal Life Systems? That is part of the government on Earth?"

"No, no! ULS is the largest corporation in the Solar System. Now, since you run things here—"

"I am not in control of this world," Mari interrupted. "I only help resolve conflicts. These are the leaders of the governments on Dematr," she added, gesturing to either side of her. "Queen Sien of Tiae, whose land is where we are now. Camber, representing the Emperor who rules the Empire in the east. President Julan of the Bakre Confederation—"

"Yes," Talese Groveen said with a quick flash of a smile that Kira thought remarkably bright and insincere looking. "There will be plenty of time for introductions. I have people who will conduct interviews and collect information. Now, this Alain, your husband. He can perform actual magic? And your offspring? Does she have that gift as well?"

Kira stared at the woman, her tension momentarily forgotten in astonishment at the Urth woman's rudeness. She remembered what her mother had told her about the Senior Mechanics who had ruled their Guild and the world with iron fists. This woman from Urth seemed to share that level of self-assured arrogance.

Now the woman wasn't even looking at anyone, just gazing intently at a spot in space just before her face, her fingers held at waist height and moving slightly as if manipulating something unseen. "Do you mind if I do some scans?"

Kira's mother frowned. "I'd rather not agree to anything until I know what it involves."

"Oh, it's nothing. It would save time if we can get this done right away."

"Not now," Mari said, her voice taking on that steely quality that Kira knew from experience meant trouble.

Apparently that penetrated the woman's self-absorption. Looking annoyed, she said something inaudible to the air in front of her face, and a moment later other men and women came out of the ship.

Kira watched them approach, getting the same uneasy sense that they weren't put together quite right. Certain qualities of their bodies seemed to have been emphasized oddly while other features were lessened. Even worse, there was a disquieting sameness about many of them. Kira realized that those who looked to be about the same age all bore very similar physical characteristics.

Except for one—a teenage boy who looked haphazardly natural, right down to the sullen scowl with which he regarded the world of Dematr and every person in sight.

Like the first woman, most of those from the ship appeared to have their attention focused on something invisible just in front of their noses, their hands and fingers moving slightly at waist height. Kira tried not to stare as she wondered why someone visiting a new world for the first time would not look around at it.

"These are my people," Talese Groveen announced. "They'll begin their interviews while I continue to speak with you, um, Lady Mari, and your husband. Oh, your daughter. *Jason!*" The name came out like the crack of a whip.

The teenage boy shambled up to them, looking as if he was being dragged into a room full of torture devices. "Yeah?"

"This is my child, Jason," the woman said, flashing that meaningless smile again. "Perhaps your child could entertain him for a few moments while we adults discuss important matters?"

Kira, already wondering at the restraint of the dignitaries around her, felt herself go into a slow burn at being dismissed as a child. At the moment she would have much preferred discussing marriage prospects with the Imperials to "entertaining" that boy. She looked at her mother, who returned a meaningful glance. Kira sent back a look of reluctant agreement paired with an implied expectation of reward for her sacrifice. "Certainly," Kira said in a bright, cheerful voice. "My name is Kira of Pacta Servanda."

Jason turned his sullenness her way, shifting to surprise and nervousness as he looked at Kira. "Uh, hi."

"Hi." Kira smiled politely at him and began walking off at an angle, moving slowly enough for Jason to catch up. Surely this wasn't what her father's vision had been about? That she would need to be here to keep a sullen boy occupied?

The boy from Urth stared around and at the ground as if he couldn't quite take in everything. Kira warmed to him slightly because his reactions seemed so natural. "Can we go that way?" Jason asked, pointing to an open area away from the ship.

"Sure." They walked off through the grass, staying away from where the crowds some distance off were held back by a double row of soldiers. Kira felt self-conscious again, knowing how many of those people must be staring at her as she and the boy walked their way. Grateful to be away from the odd woman from Urth, she also felt isolated from her parents and their friends. The bulk of the pistol under her coat did little for her peace of mind. Aunt Alli always insisted that weapons should be used only when absolutely necessary. This boy didn't walk with the assured movements of someone with much martial-arts training, so Kira had no doubt that she could take out Jason with her bare hands if need be. But what good would her pistol do against that ship from Urth?

Jason, like the others from Urth, had something he apparently could see before his face as his fingers made small movements in front of him. But he kept looking away from that, staring at the world with a wondering expression at odds with his earlier sullenness. "Is it all like this?" he asked Kira.

"Do you mean our world?" Kira asked. "Different places are different, but it's all Dematr. I think Tiae is beautiful, but other places are nice as well."

"It's hard to find something like this on Earth," Jason said. "You guys are so lucky."

She didn't know what to say to that. "Was the trip hard?"

"Huh?" Jason stared at her as if puzzled that she would ask.

"Was the trip to this world hard?"

"For me?"

"Yes," Kira said. "For you."

"Oh, uh," Jason fumbled. He seemed unused to having people express interest in him. "It wasn't too bad. Boring, I guess."

"Are you the only person your age on the ship?" Kira asked, trying to find something to talk about. "I know how hard it can be, surrounded by older people with no one close to your age to talk to."

"Yeah," Jason said, his gaze on her astonished. "Why are being nice to me? Why do you care?"

"You're a guest," Kira said, trying to understand his attitude. "And you're a person. I care because everyone matters."

"Who told you that?"

"My mother and my father," Kira said, getting a little annoyed at the tone of the last question. "Sometimes they don't understand things, but they do know stuff. And you are a guest of our world, so I am trying my best to be polite and welcoming even though I'm really having a hard time figuring you out."

"Huh. Um…your name's Kara?"

"*Kira*," she replied. Did he have to emphasize her irrelevance by not even getting her name right?

"Okay. How old are you?"

"Sixteen."

"Sixteen? Your years must be close to Earth Standard. What do you guys do for fun here?"

She gave him a skeptical look, trying to judge whether the question was sincere. "Read, ride, walk, talk, sail, work on hobbies, fight wars, blow up things, and slay dragons."

"Yeah, games are fun, right?" he replied.

"Games?"

"Yeah. Virtual games." Jason laughed. "You can't blow up stuff for real!"

"I do," Kira said. "Aunt Alli taught me how. What's a virtual game?"

He stared at her. "You don't— You've never— How do you—"

"I'm doing my best to keep this conversation going," Kira said, getting irritated. "But you're not helping."

"Is everybody here like you?" Jason blurted out.

"No. Everybody is different."

"But you're here." Jason seemed to come to some decision, his fingers dancing on the air before him. "That's enough. Okay. They can't hear us."

Kira frowned at him. "What are you talking about?"

He jerked a thumb back to indicate behind them. "Keep looking forward. Don't let your face be visible to the ship when you talk to me. If they can see your lips move, they can analyze the video to tell what you're saying." He indicated his belt buckle and the insignia on his chest. "These things have monitors in them."

"Monitors?" Kira asked, keeping her head pointed away from the ship.

"They're supposed to be primarily for monitoring our health status, but they can provide audio feeds to the ship's central data core, as well as visual of whatever they face."

"Audio feeds?" She had seen those terms. In the once-banned tech manuals. "That's like a far-talker, right? You mean they can listen to anything you say wherever you are?"

"Yeah. But I have an app that can fool the feeds. It blocks them from actually hearing us and substitutes a few words of conversation every now and then. That's why I had to get you to talk a little bit." He grinned triumphantly. "I'm not supposed to have the app. But it comes in handy."

Kira gave the boy a measuring look out of the corners of her eyes, wondering if she should reappraise her first assessment of Jason. "Why?"

He looked ahead for a moment as if steeling himself. "My name's Jason."

"I know. We were introduced. I'm Kira, just in case you still don't remember that."

"Uh, sorry." He swallowed nervously. "There's something I have to tell you. I didn't know if I would tell anyone. But if there's even one person in this world like you who can talk to me like I'm worth talking to, I have to let you know."

Kira thought she recognized the behavior and braced herself. This didn't look like a prelude to danger. It looked more like Jason was about to…what? Ask her out? "Look, I don't know you, and—"

"You have to tell your parents and everybody else here not to agree to anything my mom or the others on the ship ask you to do or say yes to."

CHAPTER TWO

Having expected some totally insincere declaration of romantic interest, Kira found herself thrown off balance. "Why not?"

"They want to cheat you," Jason said in a rush. "Don't look at me! Keep looking forward! I have to say this fast because I don't know how long it will take for the ship's monitoring routines to suspect the feed from me isn't real. It's like this. Universal Life Systems is the biggest outfit in Earth's solar system, with major influence on Earth and Mars, all the colonized moons, and every orbital habitat. They sell designer genetic packages so parents can be sure their kids are free of defects and look like whatever the latest trends are."

"Wh-what?" Kira demanded. "You can design children?"

"Yeah, of course we can. The important thing is, getting something new to sell has become pretty hard." Jason glanced at her again. "You, this planet, your mother and father, are all new. Mom wants you to agree to something that will look like no big deal, but in the fine print it will grant full control of all of your genetic material to ULS."

"Full control of our genetic material?" Kira asked. "Why?"

"So they could put it into designer packages. Especially cosmetic genes. They're going to want girls that look like your mother. I mean, lots of people back on Earth are interested in colony-world blood because they think it's going to be more pure and strong and other nonsense. They'd pay my mom's company to create kids for them that have mostly their genes, but are nearly identical external copies of your mom, and you I guess, cleaned up internally with some colonial genes left in to make it look cool."

Kira stared straight ahead, feeling both horrified and confused. "Girls on Urth. Babies. Made to look like my mother? And me?"

"It would be a thing," Jason said, sounding disgusted. "Really fashionable. That's why Mom was so happy to see that you and your mom looked exotic. That'll increase demand. There'd be hundreds of thousands of people paying for their babies to match you, even at the huge prices ULS would charge."

"*Hundreds of thousands?*" Kira inhaled deeply, calling on her father's Mage teachings to calm her mind. "Who look like me and my mother?" The idea was too weird.

"And they're not only going to get the rights to your genetic material, they're going to cheat you," Jason continued. "You won't get money or knowledge out of the deal, just some cheap toys that they think will really impress you."

"But we thought your ship would bring us some devices and information to help our world recover from what was lost," Kira said.

"No," Jason said, looking unhappy. "We know you've got the survival technology manuals from the colony ship, but even if my mom and her company wanted to provide extra stuff, they couldn't because we're legally restricted from giving you anything important."

"*What?* Why?"

"There are a lot of people back home who think you need to be protected because you've got this unique culture that shouldn't be 'disrupted.' Nobody asked you whether or not you wanted to be disrupted, right? But my mom and her company don't plan on giving you anything worthwhile anyway. They just want to cheat you."

Kira put her hands to her mouth, trying to think, her mind focusing on one word. "What exactly does exotic mean?"

"Uh, unusual, different, exciting. You know."

"My mother? Me? You think we're…beautiful?"

"No," Jason insisted. "Exotic. That's not the same thing. Beautiful is easy. Just select for widely admired appearance traits. Exotic is a sort of random thing, where features come together in unexpected ways."

Features coming together in unexpected ways. That didn't sound like a compliment, even though Jason apparently thought it was. "Why would anyone want to look just like me?"

"Uh, not like you," Jason said, sounding apologetic. "Your mom. Lady Mari. Back on Earth there have been vids and books and stuff. I'm sure the details are all wrong, but the basic thing is, your mom is really famous and sort of a folk hero."

Kira heard someone laughing and realized it was her. "My mother is so famous *on Urth* that people want to make their children copies of her?"

"Yeah."

"Oh, that's just so…awful." Kira managed to stop her bitter laughter. She had spent her life worrying how she could ever live up to being the daughter of the daughter. But her mother's shadow extended out to the stars. Even on Urth people would look at Kira and see simply a copy of Lady Mari, a copy who could never match the original.

She had to fight off the urge to scream.

"They want your dad's genetic material, too," Jason continued, unaware of Kira's internal turmoil. "That Mage stuff has them stumped, if it's true, but there must be some genetic component. There's something about the Mage thing that has them excited, but I don't know what it is."

Kira's felt an odd tingle cut through her distress as if trying to focus her attention. "They want to know a lot about Mages?"

"Yeah. And they figure that you're a hybrid," Jason said, "so they want your genetic material as well. That's why she asked if you could do Mage stuff."

"A hybrid?" Kira asked, hoping that her voice wasn't trembling. "Like a farm animal?"

"Well, genetically, sort of. The term just means—"

"I know what the term means!" *Think, Kira. What would Mother and Father be doing now? Trying to learn more.* "Why are you telling me this? Why are you working against your mother and her company?"

"I don't want her to win," Jason said, hostility simmering in his voice. "Not her company, which I think is way too big and too powerful but hey I'm just a kid so what do I know, and especially not her."

"You don't like your mother?"

"Don't like? Yeah." Jason stopped walking, gazing into the sky. "I don't want to bore you with my hard life story. But I guess I have to explain. My parents got divorced even before I was born. They decided they hated each other before their honeymoon was over," Jason said, trying to sound sarcastic. Kira heard something else in his voice, something sad and deep, but didn't interrupt. "That's why I look different. They couldn't agree on a genetic package, so to spite each other they mix-and-matched me."

She barely managed not to look at him in horror. "How could anyone—"

"I'm just a weapon for them to use against each other," Jason continued. "They only keep me for the visitation periods because they think it bothers the other one. And they constantly tell me how messed up I am because I supposedly take after the other one. Just a useless, worthless parasite, that's me."

"Jason, I am so sorry—"

"Hey, I don't need pity. It's my life. I'm just explaining," Jason said. "Why do you think I'm here? Because I was on a six-month visitation with my mom. So, technically, she could take me on this trip and be gone for twenty years Earth time, but only have me with her for about four months on the ship. What a great way to mess up my ties with my dad, huh? Actually my dad would be really happy not to have to deal with me for twenty years, except that he never wants her to win, so he's probably raising a big legal fuss back on Earth." Jason inhaled slowly. "Yeah. It's great to be wanted."

"You're telling me all this to get revenge on your mother?" Kira asked.

"Well, yeah. I mean, I made up my mind when you were nice

to me. But what they want to do to you sucks." His glance at her was challenging. "That matters. I mean, not wanting you guys to get messed over. There's nothing wrong with that. I can worry about it and want to help, can't I?"

"Of course you can," Kira said, wondering why Jason sounded like he thought he had to defend caring about what happened to others. "What about—"

"The app!" Jason was looking at the space in front of his face, his fingers moving before him. "I've got to kill it. Don't say anything about what I said. Just talk about dumb stuff from now on. Okay?"

"All right." Kira waited until Jason made a small, unhappy hand gesture toward his ears. "Uh, I've been wondering. A lot of us have. What exactly does oh-kay mean?"

"Huh?"

"Does it stand for something?"

"I don't know." Jason squinted at her as if trying to see if she was serious. "It means okay. Like, uh, good, fine, sure, all right…"

"It means all right?" Kira managed to smile naturally at Jason despite her inner turmoil. "That's what I guessed."

"Okay." Jason turned and began walking back toward the ship, very awkward now that his burst of information had been exhausted. He had seemed lively and engaged for a brief while, but once again appeared sullen and unhappy.

Based on what he had told her, Kira wondered if Jason was ever happy. "What's Urth like?"

"Boring. You people have funny accents, you know."

"How nice of you to point that out," Kira said, trying not to sound too resentful.

He must have picked up on her tone, though, giving Kira a worried glance. "I say stupid things like that all the time. I'm not too smart, I guess."

"You seem smart enough to me," Kira said, wondering if Jason was now making excuses or seeking sympathy. "When are people going to get to see the inside of your ship?"

He shook his head, his unhappiness deepening. "They're not. We were told none of you get to go into the ship. Too dangerous and, uh, disruptive."

Disruptive. There it was again. Kira, too shocked at the disrespect toward everyone on this planet to be angry right away, fumbled for something to say.

Jason looked over at the cavalry, standing next to their mounts in a long row, the horses shifting position slightly and occasionally trying to nip at each other. "Those are cool. Are they real?"

"Nothing is real," Kira said, unable to resist the chance to lighten the mood.

"Uh…what?"

"That's what my father says. Everything we see is an illusion created by our minds. But those cavalry are part of the illusion, yes."

To her surprise, Jason laughed. "You got me. Yeah, the observer effect and all that. From what we've heard of your, uh, Mages, scientists on Earth have speculated that their magic involves some sort of quantum-level manipulation."

Kira shrugged. "My uncle Mechanic Calu figured that out twenty years ago."

"He did? That's not in any of the background materials. Oh." Jason snorted disdainfully. "It figures that some person back on Earth would claim credit for the idea. 'Plagiarize! Let no one else's work evade your eyes!' " he said, singing the words. "Anyway, the soldiers there with their horses. Are they reenactors of some kind? Or would they actually go to war like that?"

"Sure they would," Kira said. "What's a reenactor?"

"It's somebody who dresses up like someone from history," Jason explained. "Like, a hobby."

"Someone from history?" Kira shook her head, puzzled. "But that's just like somebody now. Except for the new Mechanic weapons. The uniforms and the armor haven't ever changed."

Jason looked baffled. "Huh? I mean, like, centuries ago."

"Yeah. That's how soldiers have always looked."

He got upset, for no reason that Kira could understand. "If you don't want to talk about it you don't have to."

"I did talk about it. What's your problem?"

"Everybody knows that things don't—" Jason paused, frowning. "They've always looked like that? For centuries?"

"That's what I said." Kira glared at him. "Why is that confusing you?"

"Wow." Jason stared around as if he had just stepped from the ship for the first time. "No change. That stuff about the, uh, Guilds? That controlled your world?"

"Yeah, the Great Guilds," Kira said, not understanding what he was getting at but hoping that she wouldn't have to talk about Her Mother The Hero.

"They didn't allow change. That's what you guys have told us." Jason stared at the cavalry again. "But I didn't realize— What's that like?"

"What's what like?" Kira demanded.

Jason looked away. Was he embarrassed by something? "I'm not making fun of you," he mumbled.

"Then what?"

"It's just…on Earth, and everywhere else, things change. All the time. The uniforms soldiers wear are different from century to century and even decade to decade. But you guys were frozen. Not your fault! I'm just having trouble getting my head around the idea."

Kira decided it wasn't worth getting her back up over, especially since Jason seemed genuinely worried that he had said something wrong. "That was how things were. We don't know anything different. The world is changing now, but it all takes time."

Jason nodded quickly. "So, those guys would really fight? With those weapons?"

"Yes," Kira said. "If Tiae went to war, the cavalry would scout and fight. You see they've got my Aunt Alli's carbines at their saddles, but we also still carry lances and swords."

"We?"

She shrugged, trying to sound as if it was no big deal. "I'm an honorary officer in the Queen's Own Lancers. I train and drill with them sometimes."

"Really?" Jason was surprised enough to drop his attitude, gazing at her with open admiration. "You mean you ride the horse and use the sword and everything?"

"Yeah," Kira said, smiling despite herself. "I've got a uniform just like that."

"No way." He stared at the cavalry. "The armor, too? Real armor to use in real fighting?"

"Yeah. The cuirass is sort of heavy but most of the weight is carried on your shoulders, so the part that feels the heaviest is usually the helm."

Jason, from a world where designing children was apparently no big deal, seemed astounded by the sight of working steel armor. "There's this junk called MORGs. Sims using VR and stuff. I've played those, but it's not real. No matter how good it is, it's not real." He looked at her, puzzled. "But you are."

"Why do you think that's weird?" Kira asked, not having understood most of what he had said.

Jason didn't answer for a moment, looking back down at the grass as they walked. "Back on Earth, a lot of stuff isn't face to face. You meet people and do things through links, and on the links it's easy to look like whatever you want to be. Most people spend a lot of time trying to look like something different than what they are. I mean, I know guys who show themselves in uniforms with swords and all, but it's just an act."

"You're not used to people who really are what they look like?" Kira asked, perplexed.

"Yeah." He shrugged. "It's how people on Earth do things."

"What are you really, then?"

He smiled crookedly. "A jerk."

"Why do you do that?" Kira asked. "It's like you want to insult yourself."

"Saves time," Jason said with another shrug. "Can I ask you something else? Why are you just an honorary officer in the cavalry? Is it because you're a kid?"

"A kid?" Kira asked, offended until she realized that Jason must also consider himself a "kid." "No. I mean, partly. But even when I get older I can't join Tiae's military. It's because of my mother."

"She won't let you," Jason said sourly, as if confirming his own worst suspicions.

"No," Kira insisted. "It's because of who she is. Lady Mari is supposed to be as impartial as possible, not favoring any group or country. If I became part of Tiae's army, people would think she was favoring Tiae. They already worry about that because everyone knows what good friends my mother and Queen Sien are."

"How do you know that's the real reason they won't let you?"

"Because Mother and Father sat down with me and explained it several years ago," Kira said.

"And you believed them?" Jason said with an edge of scorn in his voice.

"My parents have never lied to me," Kira said. "Never."

He stared at her, then at the ground. "I should hate you."

"It's a free world now. Go ahead," Kira invited him.

"I don't want to." They had reached the vicinity of the ship again. "Um…see you."

"Yeah," Kira replied in a noncommittal voice. She watched him shamble away, shoulders hunched, head down. It made her want to call a better goodbye, but she decided not to. Jason's problems weren't any of her business.

She looked around, seeing that Talese Groveen, from her expression and body language, was apparently saying something harsh to a group of her "people." Where were Mari and Alain? She finally spotted her mother talking to the Imperials again. Why did it have to be the Imperials? Gritting her teeth, Kira walked to them, trying not to look like she was in any hurry.

"Kira?" her mother said, not completely hiding her surprise that she had joined the group. From the looks of everyone, the conversation they had been having was not a happy one.

Kira feigned embarrassment. "There was something I needed to, uh…" She leaned close to her mother's ear, cupping her hands around her mouth as she quickly summarized what Jason had told her, including the warning about the ship being able to read lips. She saw Mari's eyes widen when she got to the part about thousands of copies of her, but otherwise her mother didn't reveal that anything unusual was being said.

Her mother nodded at Kira when she was done. "I'm sorry you don't feel well, dearest. Maybe if you sit in the coach for a little while you'll feel better. I'll send some people over there to keep you company. Your father is over that way speaking with other Mages. Tell him…I need him back over here."

One of the Imperials appeared ready to speak to Kira, but Camber stopped him, eyeing Mari and her with an appraising gaze. "I hope it is nothing serious," he said, adding extra meaning and a veiled extra question to his words.

"Hopefully nothing we can't handle," Mari said. "I'll let you know confidentially, for her privacy."

Kira walked toward the coach, now trying to look like someone who didn't feel well. She glanced back, seeing her mother in a huddle with Camber to pass on the warning as the other Imperials formed a protective wall around them.

Kira found her father and gave him the same message, earning herself a measured look and a nod of approval. She reached the coach and paused before getting inside, looking back. The Talese woman was in the act of brusquely waving Jason into the ship.

"Are you all right, Lieutenant?" a cavalry trooper asked, riding up.

Kira smiled at her. "Yes. Thank you, Sergeant Bete. You can let the others know I'm fine. Just, um, a little lightheaded."

"Next time, wear your helm when the sun's out," Bete advised with a grin, turning her mount to ride back to the rest of the lancers.

Kira sat in the coach, out of sight of the ship, as various people came by, expressing authentic-sounding condolences and then being told Kira's warning. Asha, Mage-solemn, touched Kira's hand in thanks as Mechanic Dav shook his head ruefully. "Uncle Dav? Can I ask a hard question?"

"You? Of course."

"Do you blame my mother for your limp?"

Dav smiled at her. "If not for your mother, my bones would have been resting on the bottom of the Sea of Bakre for the last twenty years. I've never felt anything but gratitude toward her. The one responsible for this," he tapped his hip, "is the legionary who fired a crossbow at me. And whoever he or she was, they were just doing their job."

"You don't even blame the Imperials?"

"I would if they tried again. Hey, our girls Devi and Ashira are wondering when you'll visit. You're always welcome in Tiaesun."

"I need to get down there again," Kira said. "Sien wants me to visit, too."

A long time passed, the slant of the sunbeams through the windows of the coach shifting down and toward the west, before her mother finally joined Kira in the coach. "Ugh," Mari said, checking to be sure she couldn't be seen from the ship. "That Talese woman kept pressuring us to approve things, and saying none of them were all that important but we should go ahead and say yes. Thank you for your warning, Kira."

"I just did what you asked me to do," Kira said, uncomfortable with the praise. "What did the Imperials say?"

"Camber was expecting that sort of thing. The Imperials see the Urth people not as welcome visitors but as rivals. And Sien badly wants to hurt that Talese woman, but she restrained herself. Everyone was warned, and even the Syndaris appear to be worried so much about being taken that they'll refrain from trying to make their own deals with the Urth people."

Kira realized that her mother was sharing diplomatic details with her just as if she was one of those who had worked with Mari ever since the war. The realization emboldened her to ask a question. "Mother, why didn't you ever tell me where the scar on your arm came from?"

Mari gave her a surprised look that shaded into guilt. "There never seemed to be a good time."

"Was it really bad?"

"No. Your father wrapped a bandage around it to stop the bleeding. When we made it to the *Pride* the healer stitched it up. Hurt for a while, that's all. Um, I did have trouble using that arm for…part of the battle in Landfall's harbor."

"Were you scared?"

Her mother met her gaze. "A little. We were all exhausted. Physically and emotionally numb. At the time I was mainly worried that we'd lose the tech manuals."

"Have you *ever* been scared?"

Mari looked away. "Sometimes I've been so scared I couldn't breathe."

Kira didn't ask any more questions, thinking her mother's answer couldn't be true, that no one could be scared and do the things her mother had done.

Mari also didn't say anything else until Kira's father entered the coach. "Is everything all right, Alain?"

"Perhaps." He sat down, frowning slightly. "Before I received Kira's warning, I did demonstrate a small spell at the request of some of the Urth people. All I did was create the illusion of mild heat above my hand. I did not agree to anything, even though they did ask for approval for something. I only demonstrated."

"Hopefully that's all right. Kira, did you actually say the Urth people were planning on making thousands of girls who were…me?"

"Hundreds of thousands," Kira said.

"Truly a frightening idea," her father said.

To Kira's surprise, her mother started laughing. "Yes, it is. I'm not exactly an easy person and I wasn't easy growing up. Think of all those poor mothers!" Mari sobered, still looking slightly dazed. "But I'm more worried about something else. What exactly did that boy tell you about Mages, Kira?"

She concentrated, trying to remember the words. "He said some of the people on the ship from Urth were very interested in Mages. He didn't know why, but he thought it was important enough to bring up while warning me about the genetic things."

Her father looked closely at Kira. "Was there something else?"

"No, I…" Kira paused. "When Jason mentioned the Mage thing, I felt an odd sort of tingle. It was weird."

"A tingle? As if something was trying to get your attention?"

"Yes." Kira stared at her father. "How did you know?"

"Foresight, in its simplest form." Alain looked at Mari. "The talent has emerged in Kira. It tells us the interest of the Urth people in Mages is what we have been warned against."

"Foresight." Looking distressed, Mari leaned forward to hold Kira's chin and gaze into her eyes. "So your Mage talents are getting stronger. Are you having any problems with Mechanic tasks?"

"No." Upset at her mother's reaction, Kira leaned back and away. "I'm fine."

"Can you—"

"*I'm fine!*"

Mari sat back as well and gave Kira's father an exasperated look.

Alain leaned forward slightly, his eyes on Kira. "I was once taught to forget that the idea of help even existed. I was once badly punished for helping another in need."

Kira gritted her teeth. "I know."

"Just as you would help those you love, do not reject help when it is offered by those who love you."

"This one understands," Kira mumbled, using the traditional Mage response in part to admit to her father that she knew he was right and in part to provoke her mother a little for making such a big deal out of things. "I'm sorry. But I'm fine."

Mari closed her eyes, moved her lips as she counted to ten, then looked at Kira again. "All right. We'd better get moving." She signaled to the driver and the coach surged into motion, the cavalry once more escorting it.

Kira hunched back again as the coach passed through the crowd of onlookers who were calling out to the daughter. Mari always insisted that Kira's father had been her equal in all things, had been right there beside Kira's mother the whole way in changing the world. But to the people Lady Mari was the daughter, the leader, the one who trailed myths and legends like a brilliant garment. And Kira, measuring herself against her mother, had long ago miserably realized that the myths and legends were not far short of reality.

Her mother, after taking some deep breaths to brace herself, leaned out the window and waved and touched hands with people as the coach passed them, the crowd calling her name over and over again. Mari kept it up until they had cleared the crowd, then sagged back into her seat.

"Why do you do it?" Kira asked her mother. "I've always been able to tell it's hard on you."

"It's important to them," Mari replied, looking worn out. "They deserve attention and concern. Just like everyone. Except this world, apparently. The people from Urth aren't going to share anything with us?"

"Nothing important. Just stuff that Jason called toys. Partly because they want to cheat us, and partly because of some law to keep our culture from being disrupted."

Her mother glared out the window of the coach. "At least now we know why the technical questions we ask Urth rarely get answered in any useful way. Yet these people seem very interested in learning our secrets."

Alain nodded. "You showed Mechanics and Mages what could be done when they worked together."

"*We* showed that," Mari corrected him. "When we survived all of those attempts to kill one or both of us. But if the Great Guilds had ever cooperated that way, this world could never have been freed. We're being warned that Urth's pursuit of knowledge about Mages holds danger. We have to find out why. Especially since they're withholding their own secrets from us. The Great Guilds kept us from changing so they'd remain in control. Why is Urth doing it?"

"From the way Jason talked, it sounded like they think they're protecting us or something," Kira said.

"As if we're children?" Her mother looked at Kira. "And, yes, I know how much you've chafed against the limits put on you in the name of protecting you. But the goal wasn't to keep you unchanging. It was to help you grow, with the certainty that the day would come when you would make all of your own decisions."

Kira sighed. "Mother, I'm sorry about earlier. Even though we've argued sometimes—"

"Sometimes?" her father asked, keeping his voice even.

"*Sometimes*," Kira repeated, "you haven't been cruel to me like Jason's parents have. I know I complain about things. But I can tell the difference in how he has been treated. Jason was pretending to be all tough about it, but he's not all that good at hiding how he feels. I heard some real hurt."

Mari wrinkled her face in revulsion. "How can parents do that to a child?"

Alain gazed at Kira. "The boy Jason only wanted to get back at his mother? He did not have any other motivation?"

"He said something about it not being right, about wanting to help. But he wouldn't talk much about that." Kira made a face. "It was like he expected me to make fun of him for it. Just like he expected me to insult him. It was sort of sad. I hope he's all right."

Her mother glanced at Kira. "You care what happens to him?"

Kira felt suddenly awkward and uncomfortable . "Yes. A little. What's wrong with that?"

"Nothing's wrong with that. From the way you described him the boy doesn't seem like he has a lot of friends."

"I'm not his friend," Kira muttered.

"I didn't say you were. I just think it's nice that you care about him."

"Mother! I don't care about him! Not that way!"

Mari held her hands up in a calming gesture. "I'm not implying anything. I just wanted your impression of him."

"He's a teenage boy," Kira said. "He doesn't seem to like himself, so how could I like him? I don't care whether I ever seen him again.

Maybe he'll be all right when he gets older. But he's not my responsibility. I don't have any interest in trying to fix everything that's wrong with him."

Neither of her parents managed to completely hide their relief at her words, which irritated Kira enough that she spent most of the rest of the trip staring out her window and saying little.

Master Mechanic Mari, once "of Caer Lyn" and now simply "of Dematr," stood in her home looking out of a south-facing window toward the distant shoreline. She had wanted a place closer to the water, but that would have also been close to assassins trying to reach her or her family by sea. Queen Sien had been understanding of Mari's desires to hear the ocean, but also insistent on the need for safety, and Tiae did after all supply most of the troops that guarded Mari's home. Besides which, Sien was one of the few people on Dematr who could be more stubborn than Mari.

"You are there again," Alain said.

Smiling sadly and apologetically, she turned her head to see him. "I'm always there. Part of me will never leave Dorcastle. But, yes, standing here, looking out at the water, I remember that talk we had on the sixth wall."

"It should be a good memory," he said, coming to stand by her. "You were certain you would die, but you are here with me."

"I try never to forget how lucky I am." She grimaced. "But right now I need to be thinking about other people. Like our daughter."

"I did not expect foresight to develop," Alain admitted, his brow barely wrinkling in thought.

"She should be like Asha and Dav's kids," Mari said. "Devi is doing fine with Mechanic training and Ashira is showing signs of Mage talents. But Kira can somehow do both. How can one mind hold two such incompatible visions of the world? Alain, I keep hoping one of the talents will fade. I don't care if Kira ends up a Mechanic or a Mage, as long as she's one of those. But if both sets of skills keep strengthening…" Her voice trailed off.

"We do not know what will happen," Alain finished.

"And now this mess with the ship from Urth." Mari sighed, feeling anger and disappointment mingled. "We had such hopes. But Urth turns out to be not all that much different from our world."

"The people of Urth do look different," Alain said.

She shuddered. "Designing children. How do we find out more about what they intend? The only one of them who gave us any real information was that boy who talked to Kira."

"If he will speak to Kira—" Alain began.

"I will not use our daughter as bait! I know a little bit about how that feels, remember?"

He took a moment to reply. "We could ask Kira. She said he was unhappy. Suppose that Kira asked him to come out here, so she could speak with him again? There would be no risk to Kira with us nearby."

"What if that boy tried to kidnap her? To force us to agree to those genetic things?"

"I think he would find that Kira is not easily forced to do anything," Alain said. "She is much like her mother."

"That's your fault! You're the one who wished for a girl who took after me!" Mari exhaled slowly, thinking. "I hate doing this, but…I'll ask Kira."

"I can—"

"No. I have to be the one who asks." Mari shook her head. "I complain about how hard it is being the daughter, trying to keep this world from blowing up, but raising my own daughter is a bigger challenge than that."

"Before you speak to her," Alain said, "we should talk of foresight. I have spoken with other Mages, and there is something we are all beginning to sense."

"Kira?"

Working at her desk in her room, Kira heard the tentative note in her mother's voice and braced herself for either bad news or being told to do something that she didn't want to do. "Yes?" Kira replied, trying to mimic her mother's tone.

From the look on her mother's face, she must have succeeded a little too well. "This is hard enough, Kira. I have to ask a big favor of you."

"This isn't about the Imperials again, is it?"

"No. It's about that boy you met. The one from Urth."

"Jason?"

Mari gazed steadily at Kira long enough to make her nervous. "Yes. Jason is the only person from that ship who has told us anything. We need to know a lot more."

"I told you everything that he told me," Kira said.

Her mother took a deep breath. "Maybe he would tell you more if he had another opportunity. To talk to you. Here."

"Why would he come here?" Kira asked, confused.

"If you asked him to visit—"

"What?" Kira leaned back abruptly in her chair, staring at her mother. "You want me to ask an insufferable boy from Urth to…go on a *date* with me?"

Mari spoke with forced calm. "Kira, it's not a date. You won't have to go anywhere. We'd have him come to this house, give you two some time alone—"

"Some time *alone?* I cannot be hearing this! Why should I agree to that?" Kira demanded.

"Because he told you some very important things the last time you saw him," her mother said. "But we need to know more."

"I am not—" Kira began, her temper flaring.

"*Listen!*" When her mother used that daughter voice, even Kira stopped talking. "Your father has been talking to other Mages. The foresight about the ship from Urth is increasingly warning of great danger to this world *and* to Urth. Whatever they are doing or planning to do could cause great harm." Mari paused again, looking at Kira. "I can't tell you to do this. But I am asking you."

She looked back at her mother, guilt flooding her. Kira knew of the sacrifices her mother had made for others. What was this compared to what her mother had gone through? "All right," Kira said. "It's not like you're sending me to slay a dragon."

"Thank you, dearest," Mari said, smiling at her. Kira felt her face warming from embarrassment as her mother continued. "You know that you didn't have to."

Kira looked at the floor. "You didn't have to save the world. This isn't anything like that, and you need me to do it. So it's sort of like a job, isn't it? And, judging by my mother and my father, people in this family aren't very good at saying no when they're needed to do a job."

"No, we're not. I'm proud of you."

"Why? I'm not… I haven't…"

"Kira." Her mother leaned close, gently touching Kira's face. "I know how hard it is living with…that person who is also me. The daughter of Jules. I can never get away from her, either. Don't let that make you think less of who you are."

Kira looked back at Mari, staring into her mother's eyes. "I don't know who I am."

"Who do you want to be?"

Kira sat at her desk after her mother left, frowning at her reflection in the room's mirror. Who did she want to be? She'd never be her mother. Just like now. Her big, important job was a date with a very awkward boy. Her mother had slain dragons, and she went on difficult dates. "That pretty much sums it up, doesn't it?" she asked her reflection. "Mother saves the world, and I try to be nice to an obnoxious guy so he'll tell us a few more things."

Kira spun her chair about, gazing out the window, wishing that she could fly away to some place that had never heard of Lady Mari or the daughter.

How could Urth be in danger from something on Dematr? What kind of danger did the strange people on the ship pose to this world?

If she could help answer those questions, she'd have to try. Kira realized that in that much, at least, she was her mother's daughter.

CHAPTER THREE

Kira had decided that the definition of awkward had to include calling a ship from another world on a far-talker, while her parents hovered nearby, and asking to speak with a boy she barely knew to invite him over. She wondered how much harder it would have been to fight a dragon instead.

Standing outside as night fell, Kira thought that for something that wasn't supposed to be a date, it felt suspiciously like a date. "If he tries to touch me, I am going to hurt him," she told her mother.

"Don't do any permanent damage," Mari replied.

"I won't." Sometimes her mother was almost cool. "Remember not to say anything about what he told me until he indicates it is safe," Kira told her mother and father.

Something that resembled an egg the size of a large coach came into view in the sky, flying straight for the house. The egg stopped directly overhead, then dropped to land gently not far from Kira. As with the bigger Urth ship, an opening suddenly appeared in the side, this time revealing Jason seated within.

He swaggered out of the egg. "Pretty cool, huh? I, uh, brought you something." Looking both worried and bashful, he offered her a small package.

A gift? From a boy she hardly knew? Kira glanced at her mother, who indicated it was up to Kira. Resigning herself to the inevitable, she accepted it.

Forcing a smile, Kira pried open the box, which at least was reassuringly just a box rather than some amazing technological device. Inside was an earring identical to the one she had worn the day the Urth ship arrived. Kira stared at it, then at her mother. "It's…it's jewelry. Jason, I can't accept this."

"Jewelry?" Mari gasped.

Jason's worry increased. "Um…yeah…It's an exact copy of the one you—"

"The only time a boy and a girl give each other jewelry is when they are very, very serious about each other," Kira said.

"What?" Jason's brief expression of terror almost caused Kira to laugh despite her upset. "No, that's not how it is on Earth. It's just a little thing. It doesn't mean— I wasn't trying to— I mean, it doesn't mean anything. No. That's wrong. Uh, friendship. It's just to supposed to…to symbolize friendship between our…worlds," he finished with a frantic note to his voice.

"We understand," Kira's mother said, her voice calm and reassuring. "Thank you for the thought. But it wouldn't be appropriate."

"Uh…but you have to…I have to…" Jason's expression changed. He looked down at the earring, his hands moving slightly before him. "Oh. Sure. Okay. I'm sorry. I wouldn't do anything to make…Kira… feel…anything."

"Welcome, Jason," Kira's father said. "We do not mean to intrude, and will leave you and Kira to talk."

"Me and Kira?" Jason got that panicked look again. "Senior Executive Vice President Talese Groveen asked me to…to let you know that she would like to talk to you again. In person. And…and if there's anything I can tell you to, uh, reassure you about our, um, intentions, to just, uh, ask."

"We're happy to offer you the hospitality of our home," Mari said. "I do admit that we were surprised to learn that your ship did not come from any government on Urth."

Jason shook his head. "No. It's private. That's happened before, back when Earth was being explored. A lot of expeditions weren't military or government, but run by private companies that were out for profit." He assumed the sudden expression of someone who realized he had said something that shouldn't have been said.

"What does your mother's company do?" Mari asked, sounding interested and encouraging.

"Um…" Jason waited, doubtless thinking before speaking this time. "Universal Life Systems has a lot of different subsidiaries, including spacecraft, communications, and some of the biggest defense manufacturers."

"Defense?" Alain asked.

"You know," Jason said. "Weapons. And defenses against weapons. Their primary business is still genetics, though. Mostly these days that means screening and combining the DNA of parents with gene pacs that offer benefits for health and, uh…appearance." He gave Kira a quick, apologetic look. "You know, so parents can make sure their kids fit in to physical fashion norms of the moment."

"Fashion norms?" Kira asked, trying not to sound revolted.

"It's not all that different from names being popular," Jason said, sounding defensive. "It's just that instead of one year getting a lot of girls named Emma, we get a lot of girls named Emma who have the same hair and the same nose and the same chin. We do have rules. Like…people. Maybe you can buy and sell gene packs for them before they're born, but it is absolutely illegal to buy or sell a person. You can mess with the parts, but the person as a whole has a lot of rights and protections. Parents can design their kids, within limits, but they can't sell their kids, and adults can't be sold or traded. Those are the strictest laws we've got."

"Within limits?" Mari asked. "What sort of limits?"

"Well," Jason said as he thought, "like when designing became possible, there were some parents who wanted to do things like make their kids mermaids, because they thought that would be really cool. Do you guys know what mermaids are? Okay. But mermaids aren't a viable life-form, at least not the way people wanted them to look. That kind of thing is illegal." He noticed that Kira, Mari, and Alain were staring at him and ducked his head to avoid their gaze. "Yeah, I know. 'O brave new world, that has such people in it.'"

Kira's gaze on Jason went from horrified to questioning. "You said that last line different. Is that a quote or something?"

"Yeah, from…" Jason sighed. "Shakespeare. Those Guilds kept that from you too, didn't they? He wrote plays and poems a long time ago. He's still the greatest ever. 'Time's glory is to calm contending kings, to unmask falsehood, and bring truth to light.' That's what you did," he said to Mari.

"Bring truth to light," Kira's mother repeated, gazing at Jason. "Yes. That is important. But it can demand a high price."

"You mean the war?" Jason asked. "That's something a lot of people on Earth know about. There have been vids and stuff about it. You know, movies. Visual re-creations."

"Of a war?" Mari said. "I can't imagine wanting to see that. My husband and I have seen too much of war already. You say your mother's company makes weapons, though?"

"Yeah, but we haven't had any wars for a while," Jason said, sounding oddly apologetic. "We've got great defensive technologies back in Sol Star System. For about the last century no one has been able to figure out how to build weapons that can get through the defenses. So we haven't had any major wars because nobody could successfully attack anyone else."

"What angers you?" Alain asked.

Jason gave him a startled look. "Uh, you could tell…? It's people back on Earth. There are a bunch who say we ought to have wars, that because we aren't we're all getting soft."

"Do you believe that?" Kira asked, appalled.

"No. It's really dumb. I think, from what history I know, it's because we haven't had a big war for a while. So these people don't really know what it would be like, and think it's all glory and excitement, like a game."

"It's not," Kira's mother said, her voice gone low but very hard.

Jason eyed her, curious and wary. "You fought in a war. You were a really big hero."

"I wasn't a hero," Mari said. "I did what needed to be done, and I fought because I had to. And I would do it again, if I had to in order to protect others. But war is ugly and terrible, and it eats lives. There's no glory in it."

Jason stared at the ground. "I didn't say that. Other people do."

"That is so," Kira's father said. "I hope you tell these others they are wrong."

"Nobody cares what I think," Jason grumbled so low that Kira barely heard it.

"We care," Mari said. "Please tell Talese of Groveen that we will speak with her again as she requests."

"It's, uh, Talese Groveen," Jason said hesitantly. "No *of*."

"What's it mean?" Kira asked. "Isn't Groveen where she's from?"

"No, it's her last name. It might have meant something else a long, long time ago, but now it just means she's part of the Groveen family." Jason grew more animated, looking around at them. "I was trying to figure out why you guys don't have last names, family names, and I think it's because when the crew decided to take over and rule everybody they didn't want people working together against them. If you had big families or clans those could have formed natural alliances among their members and challenged the crew, or the Mechanics I guess they became."

Mari raised her eyebrows at Jason. "That's an interesting theory. The Guild tried to instill in Mechanics the idea that it was our family, and did its best to break up any personal allegiances outside the Guild."

"And the Mage Guild sought to break all ties between acolytes and their former families. You could well be right," Alain told Jason.

Perplexed, Jason stared back at him. "Really?"

"Have you spoken with others on your ship about this idea?"

"Nobody listens to me." Jason abruptly closed down, scowling. "They think it's stupid."

"Why? You ask questions that are of value," Alain said. "All questions are of value."

Jason stared at them. "But…I'm just me. And, you know, that's not saying much."

"You sound like Kira," Mari said.

"Mother!"

Jason looked at Kira and then quickly away. "I'm…I'm nothing like her," he said, sounding depressed.

Mari nodded to Alain. "We should give you two some time alone to talk," she said.

Kira watched her parents enter the house, then turned a wary eye on Jason, who was once more focusing on the air in front of him as his fingers moved slightly before him.

"Okay. We can talk," Jason said. "I figured out that earring had a listening device in it and jammed that, too, already."

"With everything you must have on that ship," Kira asked, "why did they send as a gift an earring apparently identical to one I already had?"

"Probably so you wouldn't suspect there was anything different about it," Jason said, "and since they knew you liked one they probably thought you'd be sure to accept another like it." He gave her a rueful look. "This is all a set-up, isn't it?"

"What do you mean?" Kira asked.

"Wanting to talk to me again," Jason said. "You don't really like me that much."

"I…" Kira debated lying, then decided on truth. "No. But I don't *not* like you."

"You don't know me very well yet," Jason said, smiling slightly. "I'm sure there are a lot of guys you'd rather be with than me right now."

Kira shook her head. "Just, um, friends. I don't get to…see people too often. And I have to be careful with guys. Too many of them have tried to get with me so they can boast about making it with the daughter of the daughter."

"They're stupid if that's the only reason they're doing it."

"What?" Had Jason complimented her?

He got that panicked expression again. "Just remember what I told you. They're out to cheat you."

"Everyone on the ship? Is there anyone else on your ship that we could trust?" Kira asked.

"I don't know," Jason said. "Doc Sino, I guess."

"Dock of Sino?"

"No. Doc is short for doctor."

"Doctor?"

He gave her one of those astounded looks. "You don't have doctors? But who handles stuff when you get sick and need surgery and stuff?"

"Healers," Kira said. "We call those people healers."

"Huh. That makes sense." Jason got excited again. "You do that a lot, don't you? Instead of using some word based on some ancient concept, you just use a word that actually describes what something does. Far-talker. I thought that sounded silly, and then I thought, but that's what it does."

"You call far-talkers rah-di-ohs, right?"

"Radios. Or phones. Though I bet not many people on Earth could explain why they're called that without looking it up." He scowled. "They call you stupid. You're not."

Kira felt a thrill of anger run up her spine. "Who calls me stupid?"

"Not you. I mean, that's what most of the people on the ship call everyone on this planet." Jason waved around. "They sit there and use stuff that somebody else invented and somebody else built and somebody else programmed, and they feel all superior. But we're just jerks who happened to get lucky where and when we were born."

"Do you call us stupid?" Kira asked.

"No. I've been called stupid enough to know I don't want to call anyone else that."

Her opinion of him rose a bit. "Jason, we need to know more about whatever the other people on your ship want to do with anything they learn about Mages."

Jason frowned at her. "Why? Just don't tell them anything."

"Because we've received warnings," Kira explained. "A lot of Mages have had foresight warning that your ship was a danger to this world, but now they're also seeing warnings that it is a danger to Urth as well."

"Foresight? You believe in that?"

"It's real," Kira said. "Mechanics didn't used to believe in it either. But it's some way of visualizing or feeling future probabilities, and even though it's often hard to interpret, it does work."

"Probabilities? So…okay." Jason looked at her, puzzled. "How could anything we learn here be a danger to Earth?"

"We don't know."

"You really are worried about that," Jason said, looking at her as trying to see inside her head. "You don't know any of them, but you're worried about people on Earth being hurt. Your mother and father, why'd they talk to me like that?"

"Like what?" Kira asked.

"Like I was worth listening to, like they weren't better than me. They're the most important people on your whole planet!"

"Jason, they treat everybody that way."

Jason didn't look at her, didn't say anything for a long moment, then began speaking quickly. "There *is* something going on. I don't know what. I can tell they're excited. The techs and the engineers and the life-systems specialists on the ship. All I've heard is fragments like *if this works* and *if we can do this*. And one of the things I heard was *we could leave*, which would mean whatever this is would be more valuable than the genetic material from you and your mom. Maybe it has something to do with that Mage thing. I've been getting a real unpleasant vibe from hearing it."

"Vibe?"

"I guess that's like your foresight." Jason took a deep breath. "I'll find out what it is. And I'll let you know if it's something dangerous."

"You're scared," Kira said.

"Yeah, I'm scared. I'll have to run some risks to find out exactly what's going on," Jason said. "If I get caught, I'll really get hammered.

But if this thing is really dangerous…"" He finally looked at her again, his expression a mixture of upset and pleading for understanding. "I've never done anything. I've played games and learned things and watched ugly people do ugly things to other people. It's about time I did something, isn't it?"

"Jason," Kira said, "it's not a competition. Don't go looking for trouble because…because you don't like who you think you are."

"That's easy for you to say! You've got these incredible parents who've done incredible things!"

"You think that's easy?" Kira demanded. "Living with that?"

"Try living with my mom. I'm going to do this."

"Jason—"

"Huh?" he said, too loud and too abruptly. Jason's fingers danced in front of him for a moment while he shook his head at her.

The "app" must have failed again. Kira steadied her voice, trying to sound merely polite. "Thanks for coming," Kira said. "It was…fun."

"Fun?" He laughed and shook his head in disbelief, then looked at her again with that puzzled expression.

"Thanks." Jason backed away, stumbling into the side of his transport. The opening appeared in it and Jason got inside. He waved to her as the opening closed, and a moment later the transport rose into the air again.

Her mother and father came out as Kira stood looking up into the star-filled sky. "Anything else?" Mari asked.

"Not too much." Kira summarized their discussion, leaving out the parts about her personal life. "He seemed to take the warnings from foresight seriously after I explained it, and said the people on the ship have been excited about something. He promised to find out what it was."

"I hope he doesn't get into any trouble," her mother said. "He seems to have plenty of trouble in his life already."

"If he wasn't such a jerk sometimes I think he'd be fun to talk to." Kira shook her head, feeling anger rise. "I don't blame him for hating his mother. I've hardly met her and I hate her!"

"Do not hate," her father spoke firmly. "I have told you. Hate no one, hate nothing. Oppose those who do wrong, but do not hate."

"Why not?" Kira demanded hotly. "Doesn't she deserve to be hated?"

"I am not wise enough to know what anyone deserves. Kira, hate harms no one so much as the one who hates. Do not grant even the worst person such a victory over you."

"But if they're doing things that bad—"

"Then you work to stop them, without letting them harm who you are," Alain said. "Have you ever noticed, Kira, how easy it is to hate? It is like water running downhill. You just have to let it happen and it does. Is anything worthwhile ever so easy?"

Kira looked at him, her father in his Mage robes under the stars of the night sky, and at her mother beside him, emotions warring within her. "I know…that love is hard."

"Yes," Alain said. "Real love is hard. Forgetting yourself for another. Love is like fighting uphill against all of your worst instincts."

"And," her mother added, "Jason is the sort to bring out the worst instincts in someone. Thank you for making the effort to treat him well."

Kira couldn't help a brief laugh. "Yeah, that's my little version of holding the wall at Dorcastle. Being nice to a guy like Jason."

Her mother flinched. "*It's not a competition, Kira.*"

She was about to shoot back an angry response when she remembered that she had said the same thing to Jason. And she knew that her mother's heated tone was because in her reckless response Kira had flippantly mentioned Dorcastle. "I'm sorry," she muttered. "I shouldn't have brought up…that place."

Her mother had that look she got sometimes, as if she was gazing on the faces of everyone who had died in the siege of Dorcastle. "I know you didn't mean it, Kira. You brought it up, though. Why?"

"There's so much…you can't talk about."

"What do you want to know?" her mother asked, startling Kira. "I'll try to answer this time. Do you want to go inside while we talk?"

Aunt Bev must have spoken to her. Her mother was trying to reach out. Kira hesitated. "No. I like being out here. Can you tell me more about what she was like? Sergeant Kira. All you've ever told me is she was a great person."

Mari inhaled slowly and deeply before answering. "She was older than me, and taller, and she was the best shot in the Bakre Confederation. She had an older brother who was a sailor, and she hoped to find a man for herself someday and have a family. I knew her for four days before she died on the third wall. She…she took a crossbow bolt in the forehead and died instantly."

Kira shivered again, feeling cold. "Why did you name me after her?"

"I know I told you this, but it may have been a long time ago. I named you after her because I wanted you to be as brave and as strong as she was, and even though I couldn't save her I wanted her name to live on in you."

"Thank you. For finally telling me." Kira avoided looking at her mother, knowing how sad she probably was. "I know I'm difficult sometimes but I don't want to disappoint you. Ever."

"You have never disappointed me and you never will."

Her mother sounded as if she believed that. Kira wondered if she would ever be able to believe it herself.

After the tension of the night before, the next day proved to be a letdown. Nothing happened except for her parents having more meetings, and sending and receiving more messages. Instead of working on her studies, Kira spent a lot of time staring out her window, replaying in her mind what her mother had said last night. She also kept worrying about Jason, concerned that she had prodded him into doing something that would get him into trouble and make his life even more unhappy. His life wasn't her responsibility, but that didn't mean she had any right to mess it up even more than it already was.

Her parents were gone at dinner, at another meeting with Queen Sien, so Kira grabbed some leftovers and then as night fell gave up trying to work. She went to bed earlier than usual. hoping that the next day would feel less frustrating.

It felt like it was only a few hours later when Kira started awake, knowing from the silence of the world outside that it must be well after midnight. What had woken her?

A bump at her window. Kira sat up in bed, pulling her sheet around her.

It was Jason. He was standing outside her open second-floor window as if the empty air was supporting him. "Kira? I need you!" he said in a whisper.

She glared at him, barely remembering to keep her own voice down so her parents wouldn't hear anything. "Are you kidding me? You show up at my bedroom window in the middle of the night and announce that you *need* me? Just how desperate do you think I am?"

"Huh? What are you—?" Jason's panicked look appeared. "No! That's not what this is about!"

"Really? You visit girls' bedrooms at night for other reasons?"

"Yeah!" Jason looked around, his expression growing frantic. "Kira, please. I need help."

Either he had become an extremely good actor since the night before, or Jason really was scared. "Turn around." Kira ordered.

"What?"

"Turn. Around. I need to get dressed. And if I catch you looking I will break parts of you that will never heal right."

"Okay."

Kira, thinking that her rebellious habit of sleeping naked didn't feel particularly clever at the moment, waited until Jason had pivoted so his back was to her window. She kept the sheet around her as best she could as she struggled quickly into clothes. "All right. What is this about?" she demanded as she finished buttoning her shirt, leaving it hanging outside her jeans.

Jason turned to look at her again. She noticed he was sweating despite the coolness of the night, and was gripping a triangular object a bit larger than his palm tightly in one hand. "Can I come in?"

She almost said no, then thought about the security patrols around the house and the possibility that they might spot Jason at any moment. "Yes. As long as you stay right next to the window."

He climbed inside, gasping with relief. "Do you remember what I told you last night? About the thing I wanted to find out about? I planted some bugs."

Kira gave him another glare. "You planted insects?"

"No! Bugs! That's what we call really small things that allow us to listen in to people."

"You spied on them?" Kira said. "Using a far-listener device?"

"Yeah. Exactly," Jason said. "I was able to see and hear their conversations through most of the day. Do you remember your dad doing some Mage stuff for them?"

Kira had to think back to that first day when the ship had landed. "Yes. He said he had demonstrated a small spell."

"They scanned him while he was doing it. Not a surface scan or a shallow scan, a full deep scan. Which is hugely illegal to do without permission from the subject. Massive invasion of individual privacy. Anything derived from such a scan would have to be destroyed along with the scan itself." He held up the triangular object, dull black with rounded edges. "That's why they loaded it all directly onto this, and only on to this, so there would be no trace in the ship's systems of what they'd done. And they also ran all their analyses and calculations off this and stored them on it. This is the only copy of all that. There's no backup that might trigger a legal investigation when the ship returns to Earth."

She looked from the object back to Jason. "Why does what's on there scare you? Is it what the foresight warned about?"

"It must be. Because they saw enough of how your dad does things to figure out how to use something like the Mage stuff to create weapons that could penetrate any known defense system back at Earth."

Kira sat down on her bed, hard. "Why would they want to build weapons like that? It would break the stalemate that's kept peace on your world."

"Because if anybody makes weapons like that, everybody would have to buy them. Every government everywhere in Earth's solar system would have to buy a lot of those weapons. Because the only way to keep from being attacked would be to have the ability to hit back the same way." Jason shook his head in despair. "I heard them arguing. Some said maybe they shouldn't. Because it would shift us from all being safe behind our defenses to being constantly worried about being attacked, and if anybody misjudged a situation or miscalculated, millions of people could die. Maybe billions. I'm not exaggerating that number. I swear it. But they rationalized going ahead, because building those weapons would be worth incalculable amounts of money to ULS's defense industries and earn huge bonuses for them as individuals. Someone would invent something like this someday, they said. It might as well be them. And all ULS would be doing was manufacturing the weapons. It wouldn't be their fault if someone else misused them."

Kira studied Jason, appalled, hoping she would see falsehood in him, some sign that he was lying about any of this. But she saw nothing but desperate truth.

"It's all on this Invictus Drive," Jason said, his voice as grim as his expression. "Without this, they can't do anything."

"You're sure of that?" Kira demanded. "They can't remember enough to recreate their work without it?"

"No way," Jason said, shaking his head. "I took a look at it, and it's just like I heard some of them comment. This stuff is incredibly complex. Without the reference of the scan of your father's work, there's no way they could rebuild it."

"Then destroy that thing!"

"I can't. You can't. It's called an Invictus Drive for a reason." Jason turned a bit, waving toward the night outside. "Drop it in a volcano, and it wouldn't even notice. Drop it in the deepest water, and the pressure wouldn't hurt it. Fasten it to a bomb, and it wouldn't even be dented. If we could shoot it into a star, like your sun, the fusion explosions and intense radiation would do the job. But there's no way to do that."

"Why can't we hide it?" Kira asked, belatedly realizing that by saying "we" she had taken partial ownership of the situation.

"It's got a beacon tied to biometric detectors. A transmitter. If it isn't within ten meters of at least one member of the crew, the beacon automatically activates, and my mom's ship finds it within seconds."

Kira studied the object that Jason held. "I guess you're a member of the crew?"

"Yeah. By default. If they had taken time to look at the list of authorized holders they would have deleted me, but they were probably in a rush when they initialized it."

"You have to be within ten meters? That's about five lances." Not very far at all. "Can they call that thing? Make it tell them where it is?"

He smiled shakily at her. "I knew you'd be smart enough to ask about that. Normally, yes, they could broadcast a call and it would answer. Unless the Invictus Drive was set to quiet mode, which is what they did to make sure that inspectors back on Earth wouldn't discover it. They didn't think they'd ever have to look for it themselves."

Kira bit her lower lip as she thought. "What if your mother knew where you were, but you were being protected by people from this world? What would she do?"

"She wouldn't care about me," Jason said, "but the drive, that's another thing. There are so-called defensive weapons on the ship. Stuff way beyond what you guys have. She'd use those weapons to get me and the drive back, and justify it by saying you kidnapped me or something. She'd destroy whatever she had to. Trust me."

Once again he wasn't lying. "You must have some idea of what to do," Kira said. "You came here and said you needed me."

"There's only one thing that might work," Jason said, his voice growing desperate again. "I have to hide myself. I have to find a place on this world where I can hide and keep the drive hidden until the ship is forced to leave. They'll look for me. They'll use every tool they've got. They can find me using the same biometrics, if they get sensors close enough to me. That's why I need to find some place a long way from here to hide, where they wouldn't think to look. That's why I need you. I'll probably have a little trouble blending in. I need some quick tips on how to talk and act and…everything. Oh, and where to go. And how to get there."

She stared at him. "Quick tips? How long do we have?"

"Maybe a couple of hours."

"A couple of hours. Jason, if I had a couple of *years* I might be able to teach you enough for you to blend in here. What you're suggesting is impossible. You wouldn't last half a day. Everybody you interacted with would immediately know you were…very different."

"But I have to," Jason insisted, now despairing. "It's the only way to keep this information away from them. If I don't, ULS will build those weapons and sell lots of them, and those weapons *will* get used and… You were right, Kira. This stuff is a huge danger to Earth. Kira, please. You're so smart and…and…awesome. You must know a way I can make this work."

"You must have me confused with my mother," Kira said. "Jason, there isn't any way you can do it. You'd need—"

She suddenly realized that there was a way.

Kira gazed out the window into the darkness behind Jason, thinking.

Thinking about how she had spent most of her life feeling sorry for herself because she wouldn't have the chance to do anything important. About all of the people who might die back on Urth if the greedy, selfish crew of the ship brought back the secret for weapons that no one could stop. About her mother simply saying *I had a job to do.*

Her mother couldn't get involved in this. Lady Mari had to be neutral, the fair and disinterested person everyone could look to. Mari couldn't draw the world, any part of it, into a conflict with Urth. Especially not when she'd be trying to keep an object stolen from the Urth ship away from its legal owners.

And her father was the same. Master of Mages. Lady Mari's Mage. He had to avoid directly confronting the Urth people as well.

But if Kira told them they would feel obligated to try to help. Her parents, who had already given so much, would take on the burden of this as well, a burden that Kira would have handed to them because she wouldn't accept it for herself. And if either of them did get involved, if Queen Sien got drawn into it, too, and tried to keep that drive thing from Talese Groveen and her minions, the Urth ship had weapons which might kill many people here on Dematr. Innocent people, caught in the line of fire.

That left her. The only person that Jason could trust, and that had any chance of hiding Jason from everyone else. Because Jason was right. He and that drive would have to be hidden, and Kira was the only person who had a chance of making that happen. She felt her life balanced on a knife edge, knowing that every tomorrow would be changed by whatever happened now. She could not be afraid. Not when something this important had to be done.

"Kira?" Jason had no trace of sullenness or anger to him. Just fear, and hope she could tell was centered on her.

"Sorry," Kira said. "I was just thinking. How long would the ship look for you before it had to leave?"

"Before it *had* to leave? Maybe a couple of years if they stayed as long as possible and got food from the local environment."

Stars above. Why couldn't he have said a couple of months? Kira nerved herself and took a deep breath. "If we're going to have any chance of not being caught, we're going to have to leave right away."

He gave her a puzzled frown. "We?"

"You can't do this alone. It has to be done. So, it's my job, too."

"No." Kira hadn't thought about how Jason would react, but she was still surprised when he shook his head angrily. "No way. That wasn't why I came here. I can't expect you to do something like that."

"You didn't ask me to do it," Kira said. "But there isn't any alternative. You have to hide. You need someone with you, someone from this world, who knows it and can help you blend in. Do you know anybody else we could turn to?"

"No, but—"

"I don't want to do this. I don't like you that much, and I'm not looking forward to spending a long time in your company. But if I don't, you fail."

He looked angrier. "I know I'm not fun to be around, but I'm not useless."

"That's not what I meant," Kira said. "Do you think I can handle myself? What do you think my odds of blending in would be if I tried hiding on Urth?"

"Lousy." Jason made a helpless gesture. "Kira, your mom and dad are the most decent people I ever met. I don't want to repay them for that by stealing their daughter!"

"One, you're not stealing me," Kira said. "No one is. I am choosing to do this. Two, my parents have shown me that being decent means doing the right thing. Even if it hurts. They'll understand. I'm…I'm sure of that. Three, we're wasting time."

She grabbed her pack and began loading it. Not too much. They'd have to travel light. A spare shirt and jeans, spare socks, underwear, first aid pack, water bottle, the box of spare ammunition…

Kira noticed Jason's eyes widening as he watched her strap on her shoulder holster. "Do you really think we'll need that?" he asked. "It won't do any good against the personal defense screens anyone from the ship would have."

Kira shook her head at him, fighting down qualms at the idea of having to shoot at other people instead of targets. "Your mother isn't why we might need this. The downside of having me along is that some of my mother's enemies might recognize me, and if they do, they'll come after me."

"You mean…real gun fights and stuff?"

"Not if I can help it. The pistol is if I fail to avoid situations where I need it."

"Oh. Um…I'm going to need clothes they can't track."

"Yeah," Kira said, looking Jason over and for the first time noticing that both his belt buckle and chest insignia were missing. At least he'd had the sense to leave those behind. "You'd need something that looked like you belonged here, anyway. There aren't any clothes here that would fit you, though. Oh, wait." She dug in her closet, surfacing with an old Mage robe. "Father let me have this." Kira spun around, facing away from him. "Get all your clothes off and get those robes on! Hurry!"

It seemed to take a ridiculously long time before Jason spoke again. "How does it look?"

She turned to see, nodding. "Yes. Once we get among people, keep the hood up and your face hidden inside it. We'll have to find you common clothes because Mages attract too much attention some-times and some of the symbols on those robes identify them as my father's. Any other Mages will be certain to notice that. But this will do to get us started."

Kira scooped all of her Tiae Crown coins into her wallet, wishing that she had more. Her knife, a sailor's knife like her mother's, went into the sheath at her belt. Her good outdoor coat. Not fancy, but tough and warm. She spotted an old neck chain in her drawer, made of woven steel by a new workshop wanting to impress Kira's mother. "Can you put that drive thing on a necklace?"

"It's got a loop, yeah."

Kira passed him the necklace so he could thread the drive onto it, screw the clasp closed tight, then pull it over his head.

What else? "I need to tell my parents what's going on. They need to know. I'll leave a note."

"How?" Jason asked. "I thought you guys didn't have that stuff."

"What stuff?" She sat down at her desk, grabbing a pen, ink, and a sheet of paper. Jason gaped at her as she dipped the pen in the ink and rapidly wrote out a description of what he had told her and her own plans to help hide him. *I know you will understand why I had to do this*, Kira wrote at the end. *It's my job. I love you both.*

She centered the note on her desk, noticing that Jason was still watching her in amazement. "What is it?"

"You wrote a note on paper," Jason said, as if he had just witnessed something hard to comprehend. "For real."

"Seriously? That impresses you?" Kira paused to think, her eyes on the map of Dematr above her desk. "Your mother knows you've been here, so this will probably be the first place she comes looking for you. The farther away we can get before anyone knows you're gone, the better."

Jason pointed out through the window. "I've got the flier, and it will be at least another hour before the ship realizes it's gone. We can use it to go someplace not too far off, and then I can send it back to the ship with orders to wipe its route memory just before it gets there."

"We need to go north," Kira said, tapping the map, remembering her own trips and the stories her parents and their friends had told. "And we need to stay around lots of people so we can hide in crowds, at least at first. Your flier can take us over the security patrols around this house without raising an alarm right away. There's a town that's grown up where the road from Pacta Servanda meets the Royal Road, and a train station there for the new rail line heading into the Bakre Confederation. We'll take your flier to the outskirts of that town, get you some common clothes, get rid of the Mage robes, and head for Debran and then Julesport. From Julesport we can take a ship across the Sea of Bakre."

Kira paused, looking at the map. Many of her mother's enemies who had stayed in the west had gone to ground, blending in with everyone else. They could be anywhere, or so she had been warned more times than she could count. But there were two places that Kira knew she had to avoid.

"We need to stay away from the Empire, and this city called Ringhmon, but there are places in the northern parts of the Western Alliance and the areas north of Ihris where we ought to be able to hide, and if I need to contact Mother and Father I have relatives near Ihris who can get word to them. What do you think?"

Jason shook his head. "Why are you asking me? I've never done anything like this."

She frowned at him, trying not to sound angry. "I'm asking you because we're partners in this, and because you know everything about the Urth ship and what it can do."

"Yeah, but…" Jason shrugged, his expression shifting too rapidly for Kira to follow. "I don't know."

"Yes, you do! Stars above, Jason, you've got a good mind! Why are you afraid to use it?"

He stared at the floor, unhappy. "Maybe because all my life I've been told my mind is below average. Nobody listens to me."

"I'm listening!" Kira insisted. "I need your help on this!"

Jason looked at her, baffled. "Um…okay. Uh…they only have a few drones they can send out to look for me, and you're right about being in crowds being better for hiding my biometrics. Yeah, they'll send the drones out around the ship first, then out here. They can manufacture more drones with the printers on the ship, but that'll take time. And they can't make enough to cover everywhere. If you think up north there is best, we should do that."

"Good. Let's get going," Kira said, standing again and putting on her pack. She did her best to sound confident, trying to reassure Jason and deny the worries tightening her guts when she thought of everything that might go wrong.

But millions of lives. Maybe billions. She couldn't let that happen. Her mother had put herself between the Great Guilds and the world, her father had literally almost given his life to save her mother, and she would either do this or go down fighting.

Speaking of which… "Jason, just so we're clear, we may be partners for getting this done, but we are *not* partners in any other way. If you ever touch me without permission I will beat you bloody."

Jason shrugged. "Sure. I'm used to that from girls. Most of them are a little more diplomatic when they threaten me with bodily harm, but I understand."

She couldn't help smiling. "Then we shouldn't have any problems."

Her smile faded as Jason stepped out the window, where Kira now saw the Urth flier waiting, its big egg-shaped outer surface somehow changed to a dark shade that blended with the night.

A small platform extended out from the opening in the flier, giving Jason something to step onto before he entered the device. Inside, Kira could see a few seats and odd objects fastened to the floor and the walls.

Kira took a deep breath, thought again about whether this was the right thing to do, then with her heart pounding with anxiety followed Jason into the dark.

CHAPTER FOUR

"Alain!"

The morning had begun with no sign of immediate trouble, but the urgency in Mari's voice brought him to Kira's room as quickly as he could move.

The first thing he noticed was that Kira was not there. Mari was sitting at Kira's desk, holding a sheet of paper, her expression both resigned to fate and worried. "Now we know why that vision showed Kira being involved in the danger from Urth."

Alain took the letter and read rapidly. "The vision showed our future daughter standing with us against some danger from Urth. But Kira is facing part of this threat on her own."

"As you have often told me, foresight isn't exactly precise." Mari looked out the window as if it offered a view of their daughter somewhere in the distance. "There's no doubt this involves some serious danger. She says they were going to use that flier thing to get past the security patrols around this house and put some distance behind them, but Kira didn't say which way they were going."

"She believes that you and I must not be directly involved as targets for the ship from Urth."

"And she's right about that. This is the first place that Talese Groveen will come looking, and we couldn't have protected Jason and that device. Legally, we wouldn't have a leg to stand on trying to keep the device from her."

"Millions of lives?" Alain asked, looking back at the letter. "Billions? What do those numbers mean?" His training as a Mage had denied the meaning of such things as Mari's "math" and Alain still had trouble grasping it.

"Can you visualize a hundred people?" Mari asked. "That's about the size of a company of foot soldiers."

"Yes," Alain said.

"Can you see ten groups of a hundred? That would be a thousand. Now imagine that group of a thousand people, repeated a thousand times. That's a million. Imagine a million repeated a thousand times, and that's a billion."

He could not grasp such numbers, but he knew they were huge. "So many lives depend on this?"

"Kira would have been able to tell if Jason was lying about that, right?"

"Yes. She tells us that she saw truth in his words."

Mari stood up, looking around the room, distressed. "It seems like only yesterday that little Kira was toddling around. I hope we've prepared her for this. We did our best to give her the skills to handle any situation, but should we have told her earlier about the foresight?"

"If we had told Kira, she would have spent every day focused on that danger to come. It would have warped her life," Alain said. "But does she understand the danger? There are many who would like to harm her or capture her to use against you."

"Only if they know she's out there," Mari said. "We have to keep it quiet. And keep attention focused on us."

"Kira resembles you," Alain cautioned. "Many pictures of you have been made since the war."

"Fortunately, most of those pictures aren't very good," Mari said. "And they all have the Mage Mark showing in my hair," she added, touching the white streak over one temple. "Kira doesn't have that."

He could tell that Mari was trying to build up her confidence, but still felt he had to say one thing more. "She does have the boy from Urth with her."

Mari sighed heavily, rubbing her hand over her face. "Yeah. Jason. Not the most impressive boy we've ever seen. But he has to have something in him, Alain. He took the risk of warning us, and now he's risked himself by trying to hide that information."

"He takes risks," Alain said. "He knows nothing of our world."

She eyed him, then surprised him with a smile. "And he's a boy. That's what you're really worried about, isn't it?"

Alain shook his head, feeling misjudged. "I am concerned about how he may act."

"With our daughter." Mari stood up and embraced Alain, who was still feeling defensive. "The fate of two worlds hangs in the balance, and you're worried about our daughter being out there with a boy her age. Alain, talk to Bev. Kira knows how to handle herself. If Jason tries anything, Kira will tie him into a knot and kick him so high he'll hit the moon."

"I thought you would be more worried," Alain said.

"I am." She looked at him and he could see it in her eyes. "But not about Jason, because I trust my daughter. I'm terrified of what else might happen. Which means that you and I are going to do our best to help Kira in any way we can. If that turns out to mean trying to find her and help her directly, we'll do that. But for now let's try to keep the attention of the people from Urth and those from our own world focused on us, here."

She stepped back and looked toward Pacta Servanda. "Those things called drones that Jason told Kira about. Those must be what have been seen the last couple of days flying around Pacta. Alli saw one and said it looked like it was moving in some sort of search pattern. I wish I knew what they're looking for. We've never been able to answer some of the puzzles about that town."

"I wish that I had seen the device the Urth boy carried," Alain said.

"Jason said it couldn't be destroyed. Kira would have known if he was lying about that."

"He also told Kira that Mage skills might be able to get through the defenses used by the people of Urth," Alain said. "Is that also true of the thing that Jason stole?"

"Or would even trying to find out set off some alarm on the thing?" Mari asked in return. "Could we afford to risk that, knowing that if we failed, the Urth people would be able to regain it?"

"I do not know. As you say, Kira did what we would have done. Even waking us to explain might have cost too much time when they had to get as far from here as they could before the Urth ship realized what Jason had taken." Alain gazed around the room, at the many objects that his daughter had left here, remembering her so much smaller and younger, feeling another pang of fear for the girl who like all children had grown up seemingly overnight.

And as he looked around, an image appeared before him. He stared at it, trying to fix every detail in his memory before it quickly faded.

"What was it?" Mari asked. "I know that look. Your foresight showed you something."

"I saw Kira, running along the flank of a mountain, her Mechanic weapon in her hand," Alain said, still looking at the spot where the vision had briefly appeared. "Someone was with her. A young man. Jason, I think. I cannot be sure."

"She was being chased?" Mari stared at him. "There aren't any mountains nearby. Could you tell which range she was at?"

"No. It was not the rough areas in the inland of Altis," Alain said. "But the mountains could have been anywhere else except for those around Ringhmon."

"Kira isn't crazy enough to go anywhere near Ringhmon! How long do we have, Alain? Can you guess from the vision?"

"It did not feel far into the future," Alain said. "Months, I think. Not years. Kira had not aged that I could tell. It is odd…"

"What's odd?" Mari demanded.

"The boy with her…at first I thought he did not feel like the boy Jason, but then I think he did have the feel of that boy. If it was Jason, there was something different about him."

Mari nodded. "If he's with Kira, he'll either change for the better, or she'll kill him."

"You are joking," Alain said, not sure if that was so. "What will we tell the people from Urth when they come seeking Jason?"

Mari did not answer, turning her head to look out the window again. "Speak of the Dark One. Here they are. No time to come up with a cover story. We'll use our usual plan while we're talking to them."

"The plan where we make it up as we go along? It has served us well for twenty years." Alain nodded toward the outside. "The people from Urth do not fear us. They will try to overawe us."

"I've seen that, too," Mari said. "I've had experts try to overawe me, without much success on their part. As for fear, if anything happens to Kira because of them, they may find out just how much they *should* fear us." She picked up the note from Kira, folded it carefully, and placed it in an inside pocket of her jacket.

Preparing himself to cast spells if needed, Alain followed Mari outside to where the egg-shaped transport waited.

It had come to rest on the lawn before the house, the morning sun striking an iridescent sheen on its silvery surface just like that of the big ship from Urth. There was a smug sense of arrogance to the way it sat before the house, implicitly proclaiming the right to go anywhere it pleased.

Alain wondered if a Mage spell would affect that smooth material as it would anything else. He thought the people from Urth were very confident in their sense of superiority and their devices, but he had dealt with that before. The Mechanics on Dematr had been the same way. If necessary, these people from Urth would be surprised by Mage abilities just as those Mechanics had been.

Mari paused on the porch, waiting for a reaction, then walked toward the egg. As they approached, the egg opened one side to reveal a furious Talese Groveen. "Where is my son?" she demanded.

Mari gave the Urth woman a puzzled frown. "Why are you asking us?"

"My child attempted to wipe the transport's memory, but enough tracking data was recovered to show he came here."

"Of course he came here," Mari said. "The night before last. You knew of that."

"He was here last night as well!"

Mari shook her head. "He's not here."

"Have you checked your daughter's bed?" Talese Groveen snapped.

Mari's brow lowered in warning. "I don't care for your tone or your accusations. You are a guest on our world, so we have been willing to excuse your behavior, but I will not tolerate insults aimed at my family."

"Your world?" Groveen laughed scornfully. "You think because these barbarians worship you that you can ignore the laws of civilized societies. There is theft involved here and kidnapping and—"

"Theft?" Alain asked, using his blandest voice that didn't go all the way to emotionless Mage tones. "What was stolen?"

Talese Groveen hesitated. "Private property."

"Did you know that Mages can tell when someone speaks false-hoods to them?"

Talese Groveen glared at him. "I'm sure such assertions are not admissible in any court of law. My son has been kidnapped. A valuable item has been stolen. We expect full cooperation in recovering both my son and the item."

"We'll notify Queen Sien," Mari said.

"He came here! I demand that you immediately produce my son and the item stolen from our ship."

"As I already told you," Mari said, her voice growing colder, "he is not here. We don't know where he is. Nor do we have any item stolen from your ship."

"Where is your daughter?" Talese Groveen demanded, her eyes narrowing.

"That's none of your business," Mari replied, returning glare for glare. "If you have problems, you deal with me."

Alain saw Groveen's eyes focus on the air directly before her, her hands making those odd gestures before her. "I can't detect any human presence in that house or the surrounding structures. She's not here." The woman from Urth gave them a triumphant look. "My son is missing and so is your daughter, the same girl who asked to see him again! Do you think I don't know what's going on?"

"What is going on?" Alain asked, keeping his voice almost toneless, before Mari could reply.

"You convinced my young, idiotic son to steal an important item in the hopes of gaining favor with your daughter," Groveen said. "It's so obvious."

"And so wrong," Alain said. "Have you not overheard every word we have spoken to your son?"

"What—?" Thrown off balance by the realization that her opponents knew they had been spied on, Talese Groveen fumbled for a reply.

"We have every reason to be concerned about your son," Alain continued, still letting little feeling enter his voice, knowing that his speaking style would further discomfit the woman from Urth. "We will contact Queen Sien, and conduct a thorough search of Pacta Servanda."

"That would be a good starting point," Mari agreed, regaining her composure. "We should work together to—"

"I am not interested in delays that might imperil…my son!" Talese Groveen insisted. "He needs to be returned to me before he…" Alain saw suspicion appear on her face. "Just what has he told you?"

"About what?" Mari asked.

"He has nothing of value! Except what he might know," the woman from Urth said. "And even he may eventually figure that out. Time is of the essence."

"Yes," Mari agreed. "We will contact Queen Sien-"

"I intend crowd-sourcing this search," Talese Groveen informed them. "Far faster, and more efficient, and more likely to quickly locate my errant son and your daughter." She paused, eyes on that place before her nose, her hands moving rapidly before her.

Alain leaned to whisper in Mari's ear. "She lied about Jason having nothing of value. She is not certain that he knows the value of what he took, and I do not think she suspects he already told Kira or us the truth about it. But she fears that he will. Should we stop her?"

"We don't even know what she's doing! And how can we stop her without attacking her?" Mari mumbled in reply. "Not that I wouldn't like to at the moment."

Finishing whatever she was doing, Talese Groveen smiled triumphantly at them. "I have ordered my ship to send transmissions on the frequencies used by the primitive radios on this world, telling them that my son and your daughter are unaccounted for and must be found. I also offered a significant award for their-"

"*You did what?*" Mari shouted. "You told the entire world my daughter is out there? Do you have any idea how many people still want revenge on me?"

"If that concerned you, you should have-"

"You stupid, arrogant troll!"

Alain, accustomed to hearing Mari having to speak diplomatically as the daughter, felt a grim thrill at her letting loose on the woman from Urth.

"If anything happens to my daughter because of you," Mari continued with only slightly more control, "I swear that I will take you apart, piece by piece, and dump the pieces into the depths of the ocean so that any bottom-feeders desperate enough can choke on your venomous flesh!"

Alain, feeling the same anger as Mari, diverted it by using his Mage training. For the first time in a long while his face took on a full Mage aspect, so totally lacking in emotion that commons called such Mage expressions "dead."

Talese Groveen, seeming uncertain whether to act offended or angry, looked from Mari to Alain and physically recoiled at the sight of his face.

"You would be wise to leave here now," Alain said, his voice now completely devoid of feeling, and sounding all the more menacing as a result. "And take no other action without first gaining approval of the leaders of this world."

"Do not threaten me!" Talese Groveen cried, backing up another step.

"Oh," Mari snarled. "You thought that was a threat? It wasn't. It's a promise. Get out of here before I do something I might eventually regret!"

"We will do whatever we deem necessary to…to protect a citizen of Earth!" Talese Groveen insisted, but she backed away from them as she spoke, reaching behind her to fumble for the edge of the opening in her flier. "Tell your queens and emperors and other obsolete, barbaric rulers that they either deal with us on our terms or we will act as we wish!"

They watched the flier rise and vanish in the direction of where the ship from Urth still rested outside of Pacta Servanda.

Mari exhaled, then slapped her forehead. "Did I just start the war we were trying to avoid?"

"Not a war," Alain said. "I think Talese Groveen merely said openly the beliefs that the people from Urth have acted on since arriving. We are not, in their eyes, their brothers and sisters, or their equals. We are something to be…"

"Exploited," Mari finished, her expression growing determined. "Like a crop to be harvested. Why would Urth have sent someone like that?"

"Perhaps they have let those like the Senior Mechanics of the old Guild, or the elders of the former Mage Guild, gain too much power among them."

"The seed that gave us the Great Guilds must have sprouted from somewhere," Mari said. "I never thought of that before. All right. First thing, I get on the far-talker and start notifying people of what's happened, even though they'll all probably have heard that woman's announcement already. I need to try to get everyone to agree on how to deal with the Urth people now that things are out in the open. And do it in a way that doesn't sound awful when the Urth ship listens in. How do we keep any other Mage, including Dark Mages, from demonstrating their skills to the Urth people?"

An idea came to Alain. "According to Jason, the ship from Urth stole information about my powers. What if all Mages heard that what the Urth ship seeks is to steal their powers? That demonstrating even the smallest spell for them would give the Urth people the means to drain a Mage's power for all time so that it could be used by the ship from Urth?"

"Would Mages believe that?" Mari asked.

"Mages know that devices of Mechanics can do things that Mages cannot. They know that Healers can directly do things to the body of a person, which Mages cannot. They do not understand those things, but they know others can do them. Mages are not supposed to admit to fear, but one thing they all fear is the loss of their powers. That was one of the strongest tools the elders of the Mage Guild used to maintain their control, that deviating from the wisdom the elders proclaimed would cause Mages to lose their powers."

Mari nodded, her eyes distant with memory. "You told me that a long time ago, that you had feared losing your powers when you fell in love with me. You've never admitted how much that must have scared you."

He smiled at her. "My powers were nothing compared to what I felt for you. That has never changed."

She shook her head at him. "I got so lucky. All right. You can get those rumors going? Spread them as rapidly as possible so any Mage would hear them?"

"I can. But we must also think of Kira."

"Do you think I'm capable of forgetting about her for even a moment?"

"When the Empire hears that Kira is away from our protection, they will see a great opportunity," Alain said, trying to keep his own anger under control.

"Yeah. A lot of people will. Plans have changed, Alain. We need to find Kira."

"She will be doing her best to hide from everyone."

"I know. And with the Urth ship listening in to our far-talkers there's no way to tell her who to trust." Mari had been worn by her responsibilities as the daughter, by the challenges and dangers they had faced even since the end of the war with the Great Guilds, but now as she looked at him Alain saw once more the woman who had first saved him in the wastes outside of Ringhmon and stood with him in the face of a charging dragon. "Ready?"

"With you?" Alain said. "Always."

Jason complained.

The easiest part of the trip had been in the Urth flier, things that Jason called screens showing images of the outside world zipping past as if they were windows. Kira had sat in one of the seats, a strap fastened across her to hold her in place. As the flier's hatch had closed, glowing symbols and marks had appeared before Kira as if inviting her touch, but she kept her hands in her lap. An odd humming sound and a slight vibration were the only signs of whatever power the flier was using as it zipped through the sky.

"What do you think?" Jason asked as soon as the flier settled on its course.

"I prefer flying by Roc," Kira said.

"A Roc? You mean a giant, mythical bird?" Jason said with a brief laugh.

"Yes. I rode one up to Danalee once."

"Uh, yeah. I mean, for real."

"So do I," Kira said.

Jason had given her a troubled look, but afterwards stayed mostly silent with worry until he set the flier down just outside of Sima's Crossroads, the predawn darkness hiding them from sight. After Jason entered some new commands in the flier, it rose back into the air and darted off in a different direction.

Kira led them into the town, waiting impatiently until a store opened, then leaving Jason in an alley while she hastily bought some clothes, including spares and a pack for Jason to carry them in. After he changed again, she buried the old Mage robes in a refuse container. So far, everything had gone as she had hoped.

But Jason complained. About how uncomfortable his new clothes were. About how badly his new shoes fit. About how far they had already walked. About the food that Kira had purchased from a sidewalk stall for breakfast. About the way the water tasted. About the way the air smelled. Jason complained.

Kira, having spent the morning battling increasing worries and self-doubts, finally snapped. Just before they entered the train station, Kira shoved Jason into an alley, locked a fist on his shirt, and pinned him to the nearest wall. "Knock it off! I'm beginning to think that saving millions of lives may not be a worthwhile trade-off for having to spend another moment with you!"

Jason glowered sullenly at the ground. "Okay."

"And stop saying okay! Nobody says that here!"

"Okay!"

"Did you do that on purpose?"

To her surprise, Jason took a moment to answer, and began smiling as if he couldn't stop himself. "No. But it would have been funny if I had, wouldn't it?"

"No," Kira insisted, but found herself unable to stop from smiling as well. "You could try being funny more often," she added, releasing her grip on his shirt. "If you do, I think I might someday be able to tolerate you, if I don't kill you first."

Jason grinned. "That's the nicest thing any girl ever said to me."

"I can believe that." Kira stepped back. "You need to watch how much you talk where other people can hear. Keep your voice down. Your accent is unusual. Just stay beside me and be quiet while I buy us tickets to Julesport."

"Aren't you worried about being recognized?" Jason objected. "You look so much like your mom."

Kira hesitated. They were still pretty close to Pacta Servanda. The odds of running into someone who had seen Mari were uncomfortably high. "You're right. I'm going to coach you on how to say 'two tickets for Julesport' in a local accent. I'll be right there but pretend I'm looking somewhere else so my face isn't too visible."

Jason stared at her with that puzzled expression. "Wait. You're not going to argue with me?"

"Why would I argue? You're right. We're still too close to home."

He blinked at her, shrugged, then listened with what seemed to be an exaggerated amount of concentration as she led him through the phrase several times until Jason could say it with something like a local accent.

When the station agent, who once would have been a Mechanic Guild apprentice but since the fall of the Great Guilds was just a normal worker, gave Jason the price, Kira kept her face averted while she passed him the coins. As she led him to a bench to wait for the train, she noticed that Jason was grinning with delight. "What?"

"That was money!" Jason whispered. "Real money!"

"Um…yeah," Kira said. "You've never paid for anything before?"

"Sure I have! Lots of stuff! But I've never used money!"

"What do you use?" Kira asked.

"An auto-link to a payment app."

She nodded slowly at him. "So you don't use money on Urth?"

"Sure we do. We just don't use *money*."

Urth must be incredibly strange. "What do…I mean, you asked me once what we do for fun. What do you do?"

"Back home?" Jason slumped, looking at the wooden floor of the station moodily. "Play a lot of games, I guess. Do my classes."

"Don't you go out with friends?" Kira asked.

"Sometimes. I mean, just people I know. Nobody like…like you."

Not sure what that meant, Kira dismissed it with a shrug. "Yeah, sure. I'm exotic, you said."

He gave her a curious look. "Does that bother you?"

"Of course it bothers me. I don't like being judged by how I look, and I don't like other people judging how I look."

"But…it's good. Saying you look exotic is a good thing."

"Not. The. Point. No one else has a right to decide whether I look good or bad or exotic or whatever."

Jason frowned at his lap. "You wouldn't be happy on…where I come from. Everybody judges everybody else all the time. Usually on how they look."

Kira studied Jason, recalling some of the things he had said, and how the other members of the crew of the ship from Urth had looked oddly similar. "People got down on you for looking different?"

"Odd guy out," Jason said, trying to sound uncaring and failing.

"Didn't the people who knew you—"

"Everybody." He looked at her. "We're all linked. People you've never met feel free to comment on what you look like, what you said, what you did…"

Kira stared at him, trying to find words and failing, horrified at the idea of mobs of people criticizing others they didn't even know. Fortunately, at that moment a rumble and the hiss of steam announced the arrival of the early morning train.

She started to walk toward the passenger cars at the back of the train, but suddenly realized that Jason was standing still, gazing at the steam locomotive as if entranced. "What are you doing?"

"I'm…I'm…" Jason took a deep breath. "That is so great!"

"The locomotive? Yeah, it's a nice design. About ten years old with some improvements to make operation and maintenance easier. Let's—"

"Operation and maintenance?" Jason's stare shifted to her. "Can you do that?"

Kira shrugged, feeling strangely selfconscious. "Yeah. Some I learned at school, but Mother also took time to go over it with me."

"You can drive a steam locomotive? For real?"

"Yes," Kira said, wondering why a boy who had come to another world in a silvery ship would find that impressive. "Come on! We need to get good seats."

Jason followed, staring around like a kid from the Great Woods encountering his first Mechanic devices. Fortunately, there were still enough people like that on Dematr for his behavior to attract only a few amused glances from the others getting on and off the train.

Remembering some of the stories she had heard from her parents and their friends, Kira led Jason to seats at the back of the last car. She wasn't expecting trouble this early, but better safe than sorry.

Most of the car was still empty, the other passengers clustering near the front so that Kira felt safe speaking in a low voice. "We're lucky this new rail line is finished. While the Great Guilds were in power they didn't allow new rail lines. We would have had to ride or walk to Minut to find a Mechanics Guild train, but then by the time my mother and father came to Tiae the city of Minut had been controlled by warlords for years and the rail line abandoned."

"How come you don't have more going for you?" Jason asked, frowning out the small window beside their seats.

"Excuse me?" Kira said, thinking that she must have misheard.

"Why haven't you developed more? You ought to be a lot bigger in at least a couple of areas."

Kira stared at him, mingled rage and disbelief freezing words in her throat.

Jason glanced toward her and flinched away at her expression. "What?"

She finally managed to get a few words out. "*How…dare…you…*"

"I'm sorry! I just wondered why you guys hadn't developed your technology more in at least a couple of areas! I didn't realize you were so sensitive about that!"

"Our technology?" Kira looked away from him, inhaling and exhaling slowly. "What does the word develop have to do with technology?"

Jason looked at her as though he wasn't sure the question was serious. "You know, it means introducing new technology and making it widely available."

"Oh. Jason, during the centuries that the Great Guilds controlled this world, no one was allowed to introduce any new technology. We must have lost that use of the word *develop* during that time."

"Yeah," Jason said, nodding. "I can see how that could happen. What did you think I—"

"Never mind! Um…it takes time," Kira told him. "You can't just suddenly start making really advanced devices like I've seen in the tech manuals. It requires having the right tools and capabilities. We're in the position of having to build the tools that can build the tools that might be able to build the tools we need. We've had to build new foundries and new workshops and new mines. There are a lot more trains than there used to be, and new tracks being laid all over the place. More steam-powered ships, too. Far-talkers are much more common. And…and a lot more Mechanic weapons. Rifles and pistols and cannon."

"It figures people would make those first," Jason said, sounding sour.

"I'm sorry we disappointed you," Kira whispered angrily.

He glowered out the window. "I didn't mean it that way. To be honest, a lot of people thought we'd be a lot further along. Technology back at my home, that is. But we mostly seem to have hit another ground state."

"Ground state?" Kira asked. "Uncle Calu has told me about that. But that's about particles, isn't it?"

"Yeah!" He gave her a surprised look at her knowledge, which shaded to discomfort as Kira gave him a glare for being surprised that she knew it. "Uh, we also use that term now to talk about what can be done with an existing level of technology," Jason explained. "Sometimes you get big breakthroughs and the ground state jumps to another level and everybody pumps out all kinds of new stuff for a while. But other times you go a long period stuck at a certain level, pushing it as far as it can go, but not able to get past that until there are some more breakthroughs. We've made some real progress since the colony ships went out, but nothing like people once predicted. There are some people arguing that we've pushed technology as far as it can go, and the next step would have to be something totally different. Something like the Mage stuff you have here, but nobody has managed to crack that." He looked down at where the drive lay concealed under his shirt. "Not before now."

"You've got an entire society built on Mechanic arts," Kira said. "Mage arts require you to see the universe in a totally different way."

"I guess they figured out how to mimic it using tech," Jason said. "We can do that, but it's not as good as the real thing. Like, um, artificial intelligence? It's real good at doing a lot of tasks that a person could do, a lot better at some stuff, but it's not really intelligent or self-aware. It's still pretending to be that. I thought maybe someday I could-" He stopped talking, watching as the train began moving, the buildings of Sima's Crossroads quickly giving way to the open country of northern Tiae.

"You could what?" Kira asked.

He shrugged. "Work on that stuff. But it's really advanced."

"So?"

"So aside from being a jerk, I'm really not all that smart." Jason balled his fist. "It's okay. I'm okay at it."

"Don't say okay," Kira reminded him.

"Uh, yeah. I could make a guaranteed living at it. I don't love it. I can't imagine getting up every morning for who knows how many years and doing it. Not because there's anything wrong with it but just because I don't think I love it."

Kira let out an exasperated sigh. "Why don't you study something you do love?"

"I don't know what that is." Jason shook his head, looking like he was torn between laughing and crying. "Do you know what I'm doing right now? I'm going nuts, because I'm completely off-line. I had to leave everything behind because the ship could have tracked it. I can't listen to music or chat or trade vids with people on the other side of the planet or anything. That's what we do. We spend all of our time doing that stuff instead of talking to the people right next to us, the people who know us. I don't know them and they don't know me.

How can you find yourself when you're part of an infinite crowd and everybody is yelling?"

Kira tried to grasp what he was saying, but failed. "I don't understand."

"Of course not." Jason made an angry gesture. "You couldn't possibly understand."

"I could try," Kira said.

"Don't bother. It's too complicated. You're not—" He stopped speaking.

"I'm not what?" Kira asked, her own anger flaring again. "Not smart enough? Stupid?"

"I didn't say that!"

"Were you thinking it?"

He shot her a hostile look. "You're not my mother but you're sure sounding like her."

"How dare you mention her and me in the same sentence!" Kira whispered, furious. "You are such a jerk!"

"I know! People tell me that all the time!"

Quiet fell, both of them sitting in self-righteous silence. If the people in the front of the car had noticed the angry, whispered argument they didn't give any sign of it.

Kira watched the open fields go by, feeling guilty and seeing her father's face, knowing what he'd be advising her to do now. Finally she clenched her teeth and forced out the words. "I'm sorry."

"Huh?" Jason sounded genuinely surprised.

"I'm sorry," Kira repeated. "I shouldn't have called you a jerk."

"Um." He didn't seem to know how to handle her apology. "That's ok— I mean, all right."

"It's not all right," Kira said. "Illusions can have great power, and I have no right to force my negative illusions upon you."

Jason blinked at her as if shocked by her words and her attitude. "Really, it's all right. A lot of people think I'm a jerk."

"That's not all right. You mustn't believe it is."

"Why does that matter to you?"

Kira hesitated. "I don't know. But people can hurt other people or they can help other people, and I don't want to be someone who hurts." She looked down, avoiding his gaze. "You're not a jerk."

"Thanks."

"You're welcome."

Time and the landscape passed by for a while with little conversation. The train made occasional stops, a very few people getting off and a lot more getting on. Kira tried to stay awake but found herself drowsing off occasionally. Jason appeared to be lost in thought.

At the last stop in Tiae before the train reached the Glenca River that formed the border with the Bakre Confederation, some Mechanics boarded the train, sitting not far from Kira and Jason. The Mechanics Guild no longer required those trained in the Mechanic arts to wear dark jackets to mark their status, but like Kira's mother the great majority of those with the skills still did so as a matter of pride or familiarity, making them easy to spot.

Kira hunched over, pretending to be asleep just in case any of these Mechanics might have met her mother and could spot Kira's resemblance. But she had no trouble hearing the excited conversation among the nearby Mechanics.

"That reward the ship from Urth is offering might be something like the gadgets the librarians at Altis have, but in working condition!"

"How can you trust them?" another Mechanic argued. "How can we even know they'd pay up if we found that Urth kid and Mari's daughter?"

"We don't, but everybody is going to be looking for them."

"Yeah. Everybody. Including a lot of people who hate Mari."

A third Mechanic joined in, his voice a low growl. "For good reason. She knocked over a lot of things. Killed a lot of people. Ruined a lot of lives."

"If you're talking about Mechanics," the first speaker said, "take a look at the records discovered after the Guild collapsed. The Senior Mechanics killed plenty of Mechanics to suppress dissent."

"Supposedly," the third Mechanic scoffed.

"If you're so unhappy," the second Mechanic said, "why didn't you go to the Empire where the remnants of the Guild are?"

"Because I didn't want to be a slave to the Imperials." Kira, her head lowered, could barely see as the third Mechanic looked around the car, running his gaze across her and Jason without apparent pause. "I saw Mari once. I'll know if I see her daughter."

"Where'd you see Mari?" the second Mechanic asked.

"At Dorcastle. I had her in my sights, but my rifle jammed."

Silence fell for a moment.

"Well," the second Mechanic finally said, "if she and the boy from Urth try to take a train north they won't get far. I heard the customs agent at the station we left say soldiers were on the way. By the time we get to the stop on the other side of the river you can be sure that Confederation troops are going to be there and checking every car."

Kira tried to calm her racing heart. Had she already failed? Why would Jason's mother risk her son's life by telling the world he was out there, unprotected?

Because his mother didn't care what happened to him, as long as she got that Invictus Drive back.

The Glenca River wasn't far ahead, the stop not far on the other side. She had only minutes to think of a way out of this, or the foresight of the Mages would come true, and both Dematr and Urth would suffer.

CHAPTER FIVE

"What'll we do?" Jason whispered frantically. "Will any of them help us? That one said he was at Dorcastle where your mom—"

"Jason, he wasn't on my mother's side! He said he was aiming at her. There was a special group of Mechanics sent to Dorcastle. Guild assassins. They were supposed to kill my mother and make sure the city fell."

"But that was a long time ago—"

"They *hated* her, Jason! They wanted her dead not just because they'd been ordered to but because they wanted it. She escaped them at Altis and ever since then they've wanted to kill her. The survivors went from being the elite of the Guild to having to hide what they'd been. This one must have gone to ground, pretending to be just a regular Mechanic." Kira had kept her face down, but raised it slightly to try to steal another glance at the Mechanics a few seats ahead. Was it her imagination, or had the third Mechanic flicked another look back at her before settling down. She saw his right shoulder shift, as if he was feeling for something under his jacket.

Kira had seen a similar gesture by her mother and Aunt Alli and Aunt Bev countless times, when they were reaching for their pistols.

Maybe a pistol. Maybe a knife. He had something, and even if Kira took out the third Mechanic it would cause an immense commotion, focusing attention on her and Jason.

She took a deep breath, thinking. The windows were open for the breeze, the outside sounds and the wind and the rattling of the passenger car and the sound of the wheels adding to the background noise.

And the door at the back of the car was right behind her.

"Not a sound," Kira breathed to Jason. She got up as quietly as she could, sliding over to cautiously open the door, hoping the extra noise that let in wouldn't be noticed. She urged Jason through, then followed, closing the door softly behind her.

"Why'd we come out here?" Jason said just loudly enough for her to hear. The wind was whipping at them, the small platform on the end of the passenger car swaying as the train rolled over the tracks.

"We have to get off of the train!" Kira said. "Before it reaches the next stop."

"How?"

"We have to jump."

He stared at her, eyes wide, then over the side of the car where dirt and grass and rocks were rolling by at a disconcertingly fast rate. "For real? Not in a game? Jump off a real train, that's moving, onto real rocks?"

"No, of course not," Kira said.

Jason looked relieved.

"We'll wait until we're going over the river and then we'll jump."

Jason's relief vanished. "Nobody really does that!"

"I've been on this line, Jason. The trestle across the river is low so we'd only have to fall about three lances," Kira said. "That's about six of your meters."

"I am not going to jump and fall six meters!"

"My mother and father jumped off of trains all the time!" She didn't mention that as a result her father, normally unexcitable, still tended to get nervous on trains.

"Good for them!" Jason said. "But seeing as I have more sense than the people on this planet, I'm going to do something else. I'm going to wait until the train stops and then blend in with the crowd leaving and—"

Kira interrupted, seeing that the train had reached the bridge and was starting over the river, leaving them just seconds to act. "It won't work, Jason. Because of that!" She pointed dramatically forward and off to the side of the train.

"What?" Jason leaned out to look.

Kira shoved both hands into Jason's back as hard as she could, pitching him off the train. She took just enough time to get her feet positioned before leaping after him.

Jason hit the water with a mighty splash, arms and legs flailing, just before she entered the river feet first in a clean drop. That and the weight of her clothes and pack took her deep enough that Kira was very grateful when she struggled back to the surface through water that shocked her with its cold. Fortunately the seals on her pack kept the air inside so it could also provide a little buoyancy.

The first thing she saw as she blinked water from her eyes was the train, heading onward with no sign that their departure had been noticed. The second thing was Jason's furious face popping up near her. "How did you know if I could swim?" he demanded, shaking water from his face. "Shouldn't you have found out if I could swim before you threw me into a river?"

"Yeah," Kira said. "I should have done that. Let's—"

"You're insane! Rational people do not shove other people off of trains!"

Kira, seeing the riverbanks go by as the current carried them downstream, pointed at the north bank. "We need to—"

"No! I am not listening to you!"

"Jason, if you really think I'm crazy, and you know I have a weapon, wouldn't it be smart not to make me angry? We need to get out of the river. Come on."

They struggled through the water, being carried farther downstream before finally staggering ashore, soaked and out of breath. "We're lucky our delay in jumping off the train landed us close to the north side of the river," Kira gasped.

Jason managed to stop his raspy breathing long enough to glare at her. "You jumped. I got shoved."

"Fine." Kira stood up and looked around. "There should be a lot of trails and dirt roads through this country. We just have to find one that heads north and follow it."

"I thought you wanted to go west to the coast once we were this far."

"I did. But with everyone stirred up so quickly looking for us, that would be too risky. That former Mechanic assassin must not have noticed us leaving the car, but he'll realize we're gone when he reaches that next station, and if he has any friends nearby he'll tell them we're in the area. I think our best chance now is heading north to Danalee and then Dorcastle. That's the shortest, quickest route. From Dorcastle we should be able to get a ship or boat to the north side of the Sea of Bakre."

Jason sat up, his hair still dripping water on his face. "Who is coming up with this plan? Smart Kira or Crazy Kira?"

She grinned. "Smart Kira, though according to my mother in the last few years there may be a fine line dividing her from Crazy Kira." Sitting down, Kira began pulling off her boots and socks. "You should do this, too. We'll have to wait until they dry out before we can walk in them."

Jason looked at the grassy knolls rising to the north. "Barefoot? Through the countryside?"

"Barefoot will hurt a lot less than the huge blisters we'll get if we walk a long ways in wet shoes and boots," Kira said.

"Why not change into our spare outfits? Our bags stayed water-tight."

"Because then we'd have no way to dry out the wet clothes, and our boots would still be wet. Sorry."

Jason slumped over, his eyes closed. "Gotta save lives," he mumbled. "Gotta save people." Opening his eyes, he began working off his own boots.

Kira took the lead as they walked away from the river, their wet clothes dripping water onto the tall grass. She hadn't gone far before the discomfort of her wet trousers reminded her that her pants were clinging to her rear end.

And Jason had decided to walk behind her.

Kira, very tired after what had already been a long day, felt her temper flare. She spun about angrily, fully expecting to catch Jason with his eyes locked on her butt.

But his head was down, his eyes apparently fixed on his bare feet in the grass.

Almost bumping into her before realizing that Kira had stopped, Jason looked up at her. "What?"

"What were you looking at?" Kira demanded.

"Grass." Jason swung one bare foot through the stalks of vegetation.

She studied him, perplexed. "You like girls, right? Because that was my impression."

"Yeah, I like girls."

"This is going to sound like a weird question," Kira said. "Why weren't you staring at my butt?"

Jason shrugged. "I didn't think you wanted me staring at your butt."

"I don't."

"Then I don't know why we're having this conversation."

"Um…yeah." Kira turned and started walking again. She gradually realized that Jason had been acting very courteously by not taking advantage of the opportunity to stare even though she might never have known he was acting that way, and that he hadn't in any way called attention to the fact that he was doing that. "Jason?" she called without turning this time.

"I'm not looking at your butt!"

"I wanted to thank you. For treating me respectfully. Every once in a while I see a Jason who does something because it's right, who shows that he cares about other people. You usually keep him hidden."

There was a long pause as they walked down the side of a low rise on the land. Finally, Jason spoke again from behind her. "Ok— All right. So?"

"So I wish I'd see more of him. I kind of like that Jason."

"Really? Why?"

"He's not like a lot of the guys I've met," Kira said. "I mean, my butt is nothing special, but it has sometimes attracted far more attention from guys than I am comfortable with."

"Yeah," Jason said. "That happens back home, too. It makes my friends uncomfortable so I don't do it to them."

"You think I'm your friend?" Kira asked, surprised.

"Um, not really, I guess," Jason said, looking away and mumbling his response.

She smiled. "If we're going to spend a lot of time together, and you're going to treat me with respect, there's no reason we can't be friends someday."

Kira set off inland again, looking ahead for any sign of roads or paths, moving with the quick, steady stride she was accustomed to from her training. She had been moving like that for a while before it occurred to her that Jason might not be as well conditioned.

She looked back, seeing that Jason had lagged behind her. His face was strained with effort and he was clearly having a hard time keeping up, but he seemed determined not to stop or ask her to slow down. Kira slowed down a lot, moving to one side so Jason came up even with her.

He gave her a defiant look. "I was doing okay."

She nodded. "Yes, you were." Jason seemed braced for an argument or a put-down, and appeared puzzled when neither happened.

"Can I ask you something?" Jason said, breathing heavily. "Had you ever done that before? Jumped off of a moving train?"

"No," Kira admitted. "I've just heard my parents talk about it. Father always said if I was going to jump off of a train I should try to aim for water because hitting dirt hurts but not as much as landing on rocks."

"My father always said not to trust anybody else," Jason said. "Always look out for yourself."

She didn't know what to say to that, so Kira just walked, keeping her pace slow enough that Jason could gradually recover as he stayed beside her. Kira kept watching for any sign of pursuit, wondering if that trace of foresight her father said she had experienced would show up again to warn her of danger. But both her mother and father had always talked about how unreliable foresight was, and it certainly hadn't shown up on the train to warn of that former assassin. And she had to admit to herself that the idea of having foresight worried her. If her mother and father and their friends were all concerned about the impact of having both Mechanic skills and Mage skills might have on her, Kira had to respect that, even if she also shied away from the idea that it might cause serious problems.

The warmth of the sun was welcome as her clothes dried, but grew a bit hot as the afternoon waned. A light breeze rustled the tall grasses they were walking through, and birds swung by in dizzying acrobatics as they chased insects or each other.

Kira noticed Jason also looking around, his expression not concerned but pleased.

He spotted her watching and looked embarrassed. "What?"

"Nothing. You just seemed to be enjoying yourself."

He appeared startled by the idea, then shrugged. "It's kind of nice. I've never been any place so quiet."

There it was again, something that just sounded strange. "We're in the country. It's usually quiet here."

"I've always had music with me. Or chats or vids." Jason gazed around. "Always. This is…different. I recognize some of those bird species. Are there any native life forms here, or are all the plants and animals and fish and stuff from what the colony ship brought?"

Kira shrugged. "The librarians on Altis say the early descriptions they still have talk about the world being 'mostly barren,' but they don't know exactly what that meant. The founders of the Mechanics Guild destroyed any records that might have told us if any living things were here before the ship came."

"I'm sorry," Jason said.

"You didn't do it. Although," Kira couldn't help adding, "if the people on your ship helped us, we could identify anything that might not have come from Urth."

"They're looking for that sort of thing in their surveys," Jason said. "But they won't tell you whatever they find out. I know they're frustrated that they haven't seen any dragons here yet. I know your drag-ons are just sort of dinosaur knock-offs like some of the ones on Earth, but all anyone on Earth has seen so far of yours are low-res faxes of drawings."

Kira blinked, surprised. "You have dragons on Urth? I thought you didn't have any Mages."

"We don't," Jason said. "Some dragons we make with genetic manipulations. They're pretty limited though, because there's only so much you can do with living tissue even with some tech augments. I mean, powerful muscles and armored scales and strong forearms and flying ability and breathing fire and all the other stuff? Can't be done. But they've also made mech dragons with living cultures for skin. Those can do just about everything, but they work best on Mars because of the lower gravity."

She stared at him. "Then you make dragons for weapons, too."

"Weapons?" Jason laughed. "They're not weapons. They're just for fun. Toys."

"Toys?" Kira wondered if her voice sounded as bewildered as she actually was.

"Yeah. Just fun. Throw in some humanoid mechs to fight them and it's quite a pageant. Or dragon on dragon. They have tourna-ments to see whose dragon can win. The death matches can be pretty gory because of the living cultures." Jason noticed Kira's expression. "What's the matter?"

"Toys?" she repeated.

"Yeah. What about it?"

"You create living creatures for toys?"

"Uh . . ." Jason seemed taken aback by the question. "They're not really living."

"That what Mages say about dragons, and trolls. You said living cultures."

"Well, yeah, on the outside, but they don't even have a pain mech-anism. They just have a damage feedback cycle so when they get hurt they react defensively or with anger or whatever."

"When they get hurt? That sounds like pain."

"No!" Jason appeared bothered by her questions. "They're just toys. I… That does sound sick, doesn't it?" He looked ahead. "Is that a road?"

Kira looked as well, recognizing that Jason was trying to change the subject and granting him that. "Yes. Not a heavily traveled one, from the looks of it. The sun's near setting. We can't keep walking in the dark, and I don't want to bed down on that road." She pointed. "Let's go up that small hill and make camp on the top. When we lie down we'll be hidden by the grass, but if we look around we'll be able to spot anyone coming our way."

As she climbed the slope, she felt the weariness of the day's labor settling on her like a heavy cloak. Jason had to pause before finally joining her at the top, where both of them sank down gratefully.

Kira eventually sat up, bringing out her water bottle and drinking half before digging out a bag of the trail mix she had bought at Sima's Crossing.

Groaning, Jason sat up, too. "Kira, I need to, uh, do some business."

She frowned at him, then understood. "Oh. Use the south slope. We won't walk back down that way. There should be some paper sealed into a bag in your pack. Don't use too much."

"I'm too tired to be mad about you saying that," Jason said, stumbling down the slope in the gathering twilight.

She took advantage of his absence to pull off her clothes and spread them out to finish drying overnight, putting on the spare clothes from her pack. When Jason got back she sat looking away while he took what felt like forever to do the same.

By the time total darkness fell, Kira had scraped together some nests from the grass around them. They lay looking up at the stars. "Which one is Urth?"

Jason laughed. "You can't see Earth from here. Earth's sun is, uh, I think that star. It feels weird to be lying here looking at that little dot, knowing it's Sol."

"I've looked through a really big far-seer," Kira said. "One made since the war. I could see the twins chasing the moon, how they really are part of the great ship that brought people to this world."

"Yeah," Jason said. "You know, they're going to overtake your moon someday."

"How could that happen?"

"They're in a slightly closer orbit. They're traveling a little faster than your moon so they're gradually closing on it. Someday, if you guys don't go up there and do something, they'll pass your moon and it will be chasing the, uh, twins."

"Oh." Kira looked up, daunted by the immensity of the star-strewn sky. "The Mechanics Guild didn't let anyone look at the stars, so we don't have many records of things like that."

"They really messed with you guys, didn't they? Uh, Kira? Are you scared? About what we're doing?"

"Yeah. Why?"

"I just wanted to be sure it wasn't only me." Almost invisible in the dark, he sighed. "Why am I doing this?"

"Because you're a better person than you think you are." Kira, uncomfortable with both the topic and the grass under her, shifted her back. "It's a good thing I'm worn out. Otherwise I'd never get to sleep. Mother never talked about this kind of thing," Kira complained. "Of course, she hardly ever talks about anything important."

Jason shook his head. "You don't know how lucky you are. My parents talk about everything in front of me."

"How can that be bad?"

"They talk about their sex lives."

Kira stared toward him, horrified. "Their sex lives?" she whispered.

"Yeah," Jason said. "My mom and dad are always going on about what they did with who and what they claim the other one is doing with other people."

"Oh, that's…disgusting."

"So are we in agreement that you're lucky?"

"Yeah. In that respect, absolutely. You won that one, Jason."

Silence fell for a moment, only the sounds of insects disturbing the night. "You know what's weird?" Jason asked.

"I can think of a lot of things," Kira replied.

"I've spent my life dreaming about being on my own, away from my parents and having adventures and everything, and here I am on my own and with a…person like you…and having an adventure on a different planet. And what were we talking about? My parents."

Kira smiled even though she felt saddened. "We were talking about my parents, too. Even out here I can't get out from under their shadow, especially Mother's."

"Do they…hurt you?"

"Why would you ask me that?" Kira demanded, shocked at the question.

"When they come up, you sometimes sound like they're…I don't know."

Kira frowned up at the stars. "Jason, my parents are dragons. I realized that a long time ago. Not bad dragons. They're wonderful dragons. But when a dragon is there, that's all anyone sees. A dragon is big and impressive and dangerous, though my parents are only dangerous to people who want to hurt other people. And I'm this girl, in the shadows, in my *mother's* shadow, and all anyone sees is the dragon. It's an amazing dragon. I *love* that dragon. But because of her, no one ever sees me. No one ever will. They see her. And I'm not her and I never will be. No one can ever be like her." She stopped, appalled to realize how much she had just said of her inner feelings to this boy from Urth.

Jason took a little while to reply. "That's weird, too, because I'd call my mom a dragon. And not a wonderful, great dragon. The sort of dragon that chews up people and spits out the bones. My dad, too. I've been stuck in their shadows because they won't let me out. They want to keep me small, because they think that hurts the other. And I don't *want* to be like either one of them. But I'm afraid I might be like them. And there might not be anything I can do about it. I'll grow up and be awful and that's that, because that's who my parents made me."

"You don't have to be," Kira said. "Every once in a while, Jason, you slip up and let me see under that protective shell you've built around yourself. I think the Jason you're protecting in there is a lot better than your parents. I mean, look what you're doing. You're risking yourself to keep your mother's company from maybe causing the deaths of many, many people."

Jason's answer came after another pause. "My mom would say I'm doing this for another reason."

"Why?"

"It doesn't matter. Never mind."

"*Why?*" She might not be her mother, but Kira had learned from her how to demand an answer in a way that made people listen.

"She'd say it was because," Jason said reluctantly, "I just wanted adventure with…someone like you."

"Well…that's stupid," Kira said. "Why would you want to jump off a train into a river?"

"I didn't jump. You pushed me."

"You keep saying that like it's a bad thing, but it kept us from being caught, remember? Anyway, it's not like I'm always nice to you. I mean, I've got my mother's temper, and I know I've yelled at you."

"I deserved it when you did."

"It doesn't matter whether you deserved it or not! I shouldn't be doing it!"

"Why not?" Jason asked, sounding like he was mocking her. "If I deserve it, why shouldn't you yell at me?"

Her father's words came back to her. "Because it's not for me to decide what someone else *deserves*. I want to be better than that! It's not about you. It's about me, wanting to be…"

"Like your mother," Jason finished for her. "Because you're going to be a dragon, too. Just like them."

"*No.* When did you become this big expert on my mother and who I am and what I'm going to be?"

"I'm not," Jason said, sounding surly again.

"Good night," Kira said, giving the words finality.

"Yeah."

Kira lay there as the stars looked down on her, mocking her insignificance.

Queen Sien of Tiae had been through a lot in her life, surviving the anarchy of the once-broken kingdom to help reforge her country as the last remaining member of the former royal family. She was still in Pacta Servanda, trying to deal with the people from Urth, when Mari and Alain sought her out.

Mari couldn't help but feel reassured when she embraced Sien. "Things have gone seriously off the rails."

"I've heard the latest warning you sent out by far-talker," Sien said. "*Do not cooperate. Do not trust.* Most of what you said after that could not be heard."

"I think the ship from Urth was sending some kind of signal over the same frequencies I tried to use," Mari said. "I checked the tech manuals and there's something called 'jamming' that sounds like that. Deliberate interference, rather than signals accidentally interfering with each other."

Sien's residence in Pacta was the old town hall, where she had lived during the desperate years when the walled town was the last place in Tiae where the flag of the kingdom still flew and any measure of law existed. Mari looked around the room they were in, remembering her first meeting with Sien. The once-blank walls now boasted tapestries, joined by displays of artifacts and weapons from the time when Pacta was under siege. A large map of Dematr hung on one wall. Mari went to it, pointing. "Kira didn't tell us where she was trying to go, but I think we can make some good guesses."

Sien came up beside her. "Kira is surely wise enough not to have headed south or east from your home. There is much open country there, but fewer people and longer stretches of still-deserted land. She and that boy would too easily stand out."

Alain nodded. "She also knows that the area around Awanat is where the remnants of the warlord gangs still lurk."

"And Tiaesun," Mari said, pointing to the capital, "is both too obvious and would be far too hard to hide in. Alain and I have family and friends to the north and west, though."

"There are many places in the Confederation she could hide," Sien said. "But if Kira takes after her mother, as she does, she will not go for half-measures."

"Somewhere beyond the Confederation," Mari agreed. "We still might be able to find her before she gets that far, but I think right now we need to keep that ship from Urth looking for her here."

Sien made a most unroyal face of displeasure. "They have acted with total disregard for our authority, using their flying craft to block ships trying to leave the harbor while sending their smaller flying devices and some of their people to search every ship and boat in the harbor. I have given orders not to confront the Urth people directly, but their arrogance implies they do not fear us acting against them."

"Kira said Jason told her the Urth people have some kind of personal protection," Mari said. "Some sort of armor we can't see. He also said they can find him using something that can identify one person from a distance, even if he's hidden, if it gets close enough."

"How do we defeat such devices?" Sien asked. "Especially when the ship from Urth is blocking your use of far-talkers?"

Alain spoke, his eyes not on the map but gazing inward. "When Mari and I first met, we began to learn not only what the skills of the Mages and the devices of the Mechanics could do, but also what each could not do. What are the weaknesses of the Urth devices?"

Mari nodded at him. "That's my Mage. Let's see, they are trying to block my use of the far-talkers, but they have to leave far-talkers able to work otherwise so that if anyone finds Kira and Jason they can call the Urth ship."

"And call they will," Sien observed. "In the days of the broken kingdom, when what remained of the royal family were being hunted everywhere, there were a thousand false or mistaken reports of where such a person might be for every one that was true. For years after her death, my older sister was being 'seen' in many places."

Mari looked away, still unsure what to say even after all the years she had known Sien. "I'm sorry we brought up such memories."

"You know as well as I that the memories live inside even if we do not speak them," Sien said, her eyes dark. "False reports will mislead the search of the Urth ship." She gave Mari and Alain a grim smile. "Sometimes, in those days, I would make cause for such false reports to place me elsewhere, not trusting to chance. We can do that. Tiae's army has many young men and women. If those closest in appearance to Kira and the boy are chosen, the women dressed in the manner of Kira and the men looking somehow different from most people, and we send them out in pairs to travel through many places, calling attention to themselves…"

"The Urth ship will get a lot of false reports from people who wanted the promised reward," Mari agreed. "But there would be risks to those young men and women, Sien. My enemies might try to kill the women, while someone seeking foolish leverage against the Urth people might try to kidnap the men."

"Ah, yes, the reward." Sien gave a royal snort of derision. "You told me earlier that the boy said the Urth ship would give us only toys. The reward will be such a toy, I am sure."

"Something flashy and useless," Mari agreed. "And probably designed to stop working after the ship from Urth leaves here."

"As expected. Mari, I will ask for volunteers. No one will be ordered to serve as a decoy to mislead the people of Urth."

Alain shook his head. "Queen Sien, Mari is loved in your kingdom second only to yourself. If you ask a deed on her behalf, no one will turn away."

Sien gave him a severe look. "Would you have me do nothing, Sir Mage? These people from Urth have openly mocked me, treating me as if I were a powerless figurehead such as apparently still exist in some places on their world. They have disregarded the laws of this land and disrespected the officers who represent and protect the people. I have no desire for war, but I would have those of Urth know that the people of Tiae are not sheep, passively waiting to be sheered."

"The queen of Tiae is wise," Alain said.

"Not so wise that she does not need her decisions questioned. My thanks for doing so. What else can be done?"

"Alain has already sent messages that should reach every Mage, warning them that the ship from Urth seeks to steal their powers by asking them to demonstrate those powers. Sien, odds are that by now Kira is out of Tiae, but if you send out cavalry patrols it will help mislead the Urth people."

"And what is my cavalry to do if it finds Kira?" Sien asked.

"If Kira and the Urth boy are still inside Tiae, then something has gone wrong. Can your cavalry hide them?"

"Not for long," Sien said. "Too many people would talk. I can order that they immediately notify me and not inform anyone else, because of the importance of the matter. That will allow me to decide based on the exact circumstances. As you say, if Kira has not managed to leave Tiae by the time the orders go out for my cavalry to search, something must be wrong."

"The Urth people would overhear your cavalry informing you, would they not?" Alain asked.

"Sir Mage, if you have any better suggestion I would welcome it."

"Unless those Mages who send messages are available, I can think of none. The Bakre Confederation will send out cavalry as well," Alain said.

Mari studied the map. "The Confederation is probably already sending out cavalry to search for Kira, because they'll think they are doing me a favor. I sent out warnings not to cooperate with the people from Urth, but if the Confederation picks up Kira they'll be doing that without knowing it. There won't be any way to keep it quiet, and then the Urth people will fly in and demand what they have every right to: Jason."

"Even if the cavalry is ordered not to pick up Kira," Alain said, "she will not know who she can trust. She will do all she can to avoid being taken. That is wise, because not every official or individual soldier in the Confederation can be trusted to put our requests above their own desire for reward."

"The more we can tell people about the true motives of the people from Urth, the better," Mari said. "We need to send messengers out by horse, ship, and train. The Urth people seem to have odd blind spots. Kira left me a note with a lot of information in it, but that Talese Groveen just used what she called her sensors to look around and never seemed to think or ask about written messages."

"I have not seen any of them use paper," Sien said. "Always they move their hands before them as if taking notes in that manner."

"The hand and finger movements are some sort of interface to electronic records," Mari said. "The sort of thing mentioned in the most advanced technical manuals we have, but still beyond what we can make. If we send written messages, the Urth people might not try to stop them because they no longer think messages can come in that form."

"Those Mages who can send and receive messages," Alain said, "can also assist."

"Yes," Mari said. "But they can't grasp any technical terms or concepts, so anything like that would be garbled. We'll have to be careful how we phrase anything sent that way."

"What else do you intend?" Sien asked.

"First, visit with Camber and tell him that the Empire better not try anything with Kira."

Sien nodded. "Camber still has great influence with the Emperor, but the Emperor grows old, and numerous princes and princesses in the Imperial household grow ever more bold as they maneuver for power and status as successor. Some of them may attempt to take some action if they think Kira is within their reach. And for all the respect Camber holds for you and Alain, his loyalty is to the emperor and the empire."

"I know," Mari said. "The empire has been chafing at the restraints on its actions almost since the signing of the peace accords after the war with the Great Guilds. Until the ship from Urth arrived, my biggest worry was that the empire would push too far and finally trigger a large-scale conflict. For now I'll do what I can to prevent the Imperial household from trying anything relating to Kira. Second, Alain and I are certain that the people on the Urth ship are keeping track of where we are. One of those drone things always seems to be nearby. So sometime after midnight Alain and I are going to get some horses and sneak out of Pacta, riding south to Tiaesun."

The queen's eyebrows rose. "The unpleasant Talese Groveen will be certain that you are going there to aid and protect Kira and the boy."

"Thus keeping her attention focused on the south."

"Can you be certain that Kira went north?"

"It's what I would have done," Mari said. "There are more routes north and more places to hide among people. She and Jason can't afford to hide out by themselves until they're so far from here that two people alone in the countryside wouldn't immediately draw the attention of the ship from Urth. Alain, let's go talk to Camber. It's going to be a long night. I hope Kira gets a better night's sleep than we will."

The idea of waking up in the country to the singing of birds, the rising sun shining a glowing welcome to the day, had appealed to Kira when she was a little girl. The reality—waking up stiff and sore from the hard ground and yesterday's exertions, insects buzzing around so loudly that the birds could barely be heard, morning dew chilling her while the sun glared into her eyes and as yet provided little warmth—wasn't nearly as fun.

Especially when the person she woke up with was a tired, sore, grumbling-under-his-breath Jason.

"Your feet are swollen," Kira said as she helped him get his boots on.

"Yeah," Jason said, gritting his teeth.

Kira had never realized that one word could carry such depths of accusation. She felt sympathy but knew she couldn't afford to give in to it. "We have to keep moving."

Progress was slow, though. Jason was obviously doing his best, but even an easy pace was giving him trouble. Kira let him take brief breaks, but got him moving again each time before he could stiffen up. Despite some ugly looks, Jason always got back to his feet. At least the road, slightly rutted dirt that it was, offered an easier path than striking overland, and despite swings to either side to avoid natural obstacles, was clearly tending north.

They reached a place where the road met another going east to west, a low bluff defining one corner of the crossroads. As they paused to let Jason rest again, Kira heard something. "Jason, we need to get off the road."

"Why?" He didn't get up.

"Because there are horses approaching! Can't you hear them? And they're being ridden pretty hard. The riders are trying to get somewhere fast." Kira grabbed Jason's arm and tugged him to his feet. "Up on that high ground! Fast! We have to hide!"

Too shocked or scared to complain, Jason hastened along with her up one side of the bluff and into the thick grass on top. Kira pulled him down next to her and then tried to calm her breathing and her racing heart. Insects swung lazily down to land and crawl across her skin. "Don't move," she whispered to Jason. "No matter what." She could catch glimpses of the road through the grass, its hard dirt surface not showing obvious signs of their recent footsteps.

The riders came up out of a dip in the road to the west, moving at a canter in a cloud of dust and sweat. There were a half dozen of them, Kira saw, one with a Mechanic rifle, another with a Mechanics Guild revolver, and the rest with swords and crossbows. As they reached the crossroads, the leader slowed the group to a halt, the horses hanging their heads and blowing heavily.

The leader swung his arm toward the south, along the road that

Mari and Jason had just come up. "I'll take Ivor along the road. The rest of you string off and go overland, you two to the west of the road and you two to the east. Stay in sight but spread out."

"We ought to walk the horses a while," another suggested.

"Yeah. She can't have come this far yet, not dragging that whelp from Urth with her, so we can afford to go a little slower now. That Confederation cavalry looking for her is still off to the east near the rail tracks."

"What if we see her?" one of the others asked in a voice rendered hoarse by dust.

"Yell to alert the rest of us, then wait for us so we can rush her all at once. We want her alive, but if we can't do that I'll take her dead."

Kira heard Jason's breath catch and hoped he wouldn't betray them.

"Mari won't pay to get her back if she's dead," a fourth rider objected.

"We'll still get the reward promised for the boy. But, yeah, I want her alive. I want the joy of listening to her screams as we chop off her fingers one at a time and send them to her mother."

Kira felt her entire body go cold despite the growing heat of the sun. She looked toward Jason and saw him gaping at her, horrified.

But some of the other riders laughed. "You want her to die slow?" one asked.

"Die? Blazes, no! Mari will get her back alive, but that girl won't be in very good shape by then!" More laughter followed the statement.

Kira concentrated on breathing slowly and carefully, her eyes focused on the strands of the grasses just before her face. She knew what hate was, had heard of the things hate could cause people to do, but had never heard hate spoken so clearly, had never heard it directed at her.

Fear threatened to paralyze her, but Kira remembered her father's calm face, her mother's determination, and let some anger build in her to help her think. She was lying on her stomach, unable to reach her pistol without moving a lot, but if the riders saw them and started coming up the bluff she would have time to—

One of the riders glanced up toward the top of the bluff, seeming to look straight at Kira through the screen of grass stalks.

She stopped breathing, wishing she could still the rapid beating of her heart, which felt like it was loud enough to be heard down on the road. Her right hand quivered, ready to plunge inside her jacket where her pistol rested.

CHAPTER SIX

Let's go." The rider looking toward Kira finally glanced away as he and the others dismounted, the group spreading out on the road and to either side, the men and women leading their horses as they walked them south away from the crossroads.

Kira inhaled cautiously, feeling weak with relief. She waited until the group was at least a hundred lances away before daring to whisper to Jason. "We'll have to wait here until they get far enough way they won't see or hear us."

Jason shook his head. "You've got to go back."

"What?"

"Didn't you hear what they said?"

Kira had to take another deep breath to control her voice. "Yes, I heard. I told you my mother's enemies might come after me."

"You didn't say they'd torture you and maim you and…and who knows what else!" Jason insisted.

"I didn't know," Kira admitted.

"I never would've agreed to let you come along," Jason said. "I'll keep on north, keep trying to hide, maybe draw them off if they come back this way, but you head east. That cavalry they talked about will protect you, right?"

Kira lowered her forehead to the dirt, fighting off an urge to run, to give up now before something horrible happened. Her stomach had tightened into what felt like a permanent knot in her midsection. If only she were her mother, absolutely fearless. "If we do that, you'll be caught within the next day or two, and your mother gets that drive back, and millions of people probably die."

"You know what?" Jason said. "I don't care. Not right now. Not if it means there's a danger of something like that happening to you!"

"I'm not worth millions of lives, Jason."

"You are to me! And…and to your mom and dad!"

Kira raised her head up enough to turn it to look at him. "Jason, my mother always says that no one counts for more than anyone else, and my father says that every person is a reality, something special and unique that helps form the world we think we see around us. I can't believe I matter more than so many other people. I mean, I guess I could start to believe it if I let myself, but I can't afford to start believing it."

"This isn't philosophy class, Kira!"

"If I only believe something when it's easy, when it doesn't cost anything, then I don't believe it, do I?" Kira asked him. "I knew it was dangerous. I'm not giving up."

Jason looked back at her, angry and frustrated. "You *are* like your mother!"

"Give me a break."

"Try being like *my* mother for a little while! Long enough to be safe!"

"No." The riders were much farther away. Kira rose up enough to pull out her pistol and check the magazine, making certain the safety was set before she placed it back in its holster. Her Aunt Alli seemed to be speaking to her, repeating a familiar lesson. *Don't let having a gun make you confident, because confident people do stupid things, and if you need a gun you can't afford to be stupid.* Thinking that it wouldn't be too hard to stay scared in this situation, Kira tried to smile at Jason. "This is important. We'll get it done."

"Kira, please…"

"Jason." She didn't want to just shut him down, because she could tell he was scared not for himself but for her. "Listen. Even if we did what you said, there would still be a chance that I'd get caught by those guys or someone like them before I found that cavalry. And you'd certainly get caught pretty soon. If something really bad is going to happen, I want it to be while I'm trying to get something important done, not while I'm running. How about you?"

"You're asking me? You really want to know how I feel about it?"

"Yes."

Jason screwed up his face, hesitating as he thought. "I'd want to, uh, go down fighting."

"Then let's do that. They're far enough away and not looking back. Let's head north, but be careful until they're completely out of sight."

They eased cautiously down the bluff, keeping its bulk between them and the riders for as long as possible, heading north at a fast pace. Jason was obviously still having trouble walking, but he kept moving with a new determination.

As the riders finally vanished from sight behind them, Kira remembered something. "Jason? When we were arguing, I said I wasn't worth millions of lives, and you said something like I was as far as you were concerned. What did you mean by that?"

He kept his head down so Kira couldn't see Jason's expression as he paused before answering. "Um...you're my friend. I mean, someday you might be my friend. Maybe."

"Well, it's kind of ridiculous, Jason. Friends are important, but not that important."

"Yeah. I guess you're right."

There was obviously something else that Jason wasn't saying, but at the moment Kira was too busy listening and watching for any other danger to spend time worrying about whatever Jason had meant.

They kept moving north as the sun rose to their right. Jason didn't want to take any breaks, but Kira forced him to, growing more worried about his physical condition. They couldn't afford to take a long stop, but Jason was clearly pushing himself hard.

At one point, as they walked along a higher stretch of the road, she caught some glints of light far to the east and pointed them out to Jason. "There's some cavalry. That's sunlight reflecting off of their helms."

He squinted, his face drawn from effort, sweat drawing lines through the dust. "Why do they still wear armor that gives them away like that? It's not going to stop a bullet."

"It still stops other weapons," Kira said. "I don't know. Change is really hard when nothing changed for such a long time, I guess." She heard something and held up one hand to stop Jason's reply. He waited while she listened, his eyes wide with worry. "It's a wagon," Kira said. "Two horses pulling it."

Jason gave her a baffled look. "How can you tell that?"

"I can hear it!" A moment later the wagon came into view. Kira saw one man on the bench, and a brace of horses trudging steadily ahead. The wagon wasn't covered and had only low sides, so unless someone was lying down there was no one else on it. The driver didn't seem to have any weapons. "Let's wait for him."

Kira waved as the wagon drew near. "Can you give us a ride?"

The man, middle-aged and slightly stout, looking like someone who had spent a life working the fields, pulled back on the reins to bring the wagon to a stop. He eyed Kira and Jason with slow appraisal. "I'm going to Denkerk. Where are you headed?"

"Debran," Kira said, deliberately misstating her destination. "But we need to see someone in Denkerk on the way, so if you can take us there that would be great. We can pay."

"No need for money if we're going the same way. Wouldn't mind the company." The man jerked his thumb to indicate the bed of the wagon, where some bales and barrels were lashed in place. "There's enough space for one of you to ride back there and the other up here."

Despite Jason's obvious distrust of the wagon driver, Kira got Jason into the back where he could recline against one of the bales, then pulled herself up next to the driver. He flicked the reins, the horses ambled back into motion, and the wagon began rattling down the dirt road again. It was a rough ride, but far better than walking.

"Where you going in Debran?" the driver asked.

"Family," Kira said, thinking that since she was actually heading for Danalee Aunt Alli and Uncle Calu sort of qualified for that description, though she had no intention of contacting them even if they had gotten back from Pacta Servanda. She indicated Jason, making up a story as she talked. "He's my step-brother. We were down in Tiae seeing some people on his side."

"Oh. Down in Tiae? When I was a boy nobody went to Tiae for fun. No, sir. It was worth your life to go south of the Glenca. That was before the daughter fixed things. I guess you're too young to remember that."

"No," Kira said. "I was born after that."

"Did you see her when you were down in Tiae? The daughter? No? That's a shame. I've always wanted to." The driver gestured vaguely toward the west. "My sister now, she's older. She was in the daughter's army and saw her a lot. Still proud of it, too, I tell you. If the daughter called right now, my sister would come running, ready to fight for her again."

Kira nodded wordlessly, imagining the proud veterans of her mother's army facing whatever weapons the ship from Urth had.

"I don't know how many young folks would answer, though," the driver said. "If the daughter called, I mean. They don't know what it was like before."

"I'd answer," Kira said. She had never really thought about it before, but the moment the driver spoke of it Kira had known what she would do.

"Good for you." The driver gave her a sidelong look. "You got people looking for you?"

Kira hoped her expression hadn't frozen too obviously. This man didn't seem to be the sort who would have access to a far-talker. "Why would anyone be looking for us?"

"Don't know, but I passed some folks in a hurry a ways back who was looking for a boy and girl. That's not you?"

"None of our friends should be looking for us," Kira said.

The man nodded, his eyes on the road ahead. "One of them said there was a reward. Don't worry. I didn't much like that fella's attitude anyway. Like some Mechanic in the old days. Seeing as you're willing to fight for the daughter, I don't see any sense in helping someone like that, reward or not."

They crested another ridge. Kira looked back and saw that Jason was barely awake, nearly passed out from exhaustion. She hadn't realized that he had been pushing himself that hard.

"Cavalry over there," the driver said, gesturing to the east. "You can see them when they're moving on the high ground. Wonder what they're doing out? Maybe looking for them fellas I saw earlier. When I was your age, seeing the cavalry would have scared us. It would have meant some big trouble, maybe a warlord or bandits coming north out of Tiae. Not now. Folks don't realize it could change, though. It got worse once. It could again."

Kira swallowed. "The daughter wouldn't let that happen. She'd stop it."

"The daughter won't be around forever," the driver said. "I hope that girl of hers is up to it."

"Wh-what?"

"Her girl. The daughter has a daughter, right? Somebody to pick up the job when the daughter gets too old or we lose her, may that not happen for a long time."

Kira tried to swallow again but couldn't manage it, her throat suddenly tight. She stared at the hooves of the horses, coming up and going down in a steady rhythm. Her head was filled with a strange, tight, buzzing sensation.

"And her father is that master of mages," the driver continued, looking ahead and not noticing Kira's reaction. "Can you imagine? She's got to be something really special, she does."

Kira finally managed to swallow. "What...what if she's not?"

"Not what?"

"Not special. What if she's...just a regular person? Not...not able to do the sort of things her mother could do?"

The driver laughed and reached over to slap Kira's shoulder. "Oh, don't you get all worried about that! Let me tell you something. Folks never know what they can do until they really have to, and then like as not they discover there's a lot more in them than they ever thought."

"Y-yeah. I guess they do." The driver fell silent for a while and so did Kira. She stared ahead, not really seeing the road, terrified at the thought of having to fill her mother's shoes. How could people like this think she could do that? Because they didn't know her. But she had just discovered that they would be expecting her to take over, expecting Kira of Pacta Servanda to be able to match Lady Master Mechanic Mari of Dematr, dragon-slayer, pirate queen, leader of the army of the new day, the daughter of Jules.

Did her mother and father know? Had they kept from her that the world would be expecting Kira to inherit the role of the daughter? *No. No. No. I can't do it. Nobody can. Except her.*

If I wasn't already trying to hide I'd be doing that now. Hide somewhere where no one can find Jason or me.

They met a couple of other wagons as the day wore on, the drivers nodding or waving in greeting as they went by. The driver of the last wagon that approached them from Denkerk called out as they passed, though. "Main road is backed up a bit! The militia is checking everyone coming through!"

"That'll slow me down," the driver said. He glanced at the setting sun and then at Kira. "Is there any chance you and your step-brother would like to step down and walk from here? If you cut across those fields you'll come into Denkerk soon enough."

"Yes, thank you!" Kira said, leaning back to see that Jason had woken and was sitting up.

The driver brought the wagon to a halt as she and Jason climbed down. "You two stay out of trouble, hear?"

"We'll try," Kira said. "Tell your sister that the daughter will take time to see any veteran of her army who visits Pacta Servanda. She always makes time for that."

"Is that so? Who should I say told me?"

"A girl you gave a ride to heading north toward Denkerk," Kira said. She and Jason watched as the driver flicked the reins again and the wagon rolled slowly onward toward the main highway.

The rest had done wonders for Jason, who walked steadily and didn't complain as they crossed the fields, the sun setting behind their left shoulders. "Why did he help us?" Jason finally asked.

"I guess he could tell we were all right. Mother and Father always told me to treat people right," Kira replied. "They said if you do that then people will treat you right. Most people, anyway."

Jason grimaced, looking over at her. "You don't act like a princess, you know that?"

"Excuse me?"

"I thought when I met you, this girl is the daughter of the most powerful people on the planet. She's going to be so full of herself. But you aren't."

"How could living with my mother and father make me think *I* was a big deal?" Kira said with a laugh. "Did you hear what he said about Denkerk? They're already checking traffic."

"Should we go around Denkerk?"

"Walking is a very slow way to travel," Kira said. "And we need food. Trail mix isn't enough for the kind of travel we've been doing."

Jason felt his stomach. "I'm not going to argue that. Ok— All right. We've met a helpful non-player character and are entering a new area. I hope there aren't any monsters lurking in it."

"Denkerk? Why would you think Denkerk had monsters?"

"That's how games always go," Jason said, grinning to show it was some sort of joke.

Kira shook her head, pointing to where lights were coming on ahead in Denkerk as night fell.

By the time they reached the town it was dark enough to provide plenty of shadows for Kira to lead them through. She followed lights, noise, and the smell of food to the large inn and coach stop on the north side of town.

A dimly lit courtyard boasted a well with a small, hand-operated pump. A bored-looking child seated next to a pile of bottles looked up as they approached, pointed to a bottle and wagged two fingers. Kira brought out four Tiae brass pennies, then held up two fingers as she showed them to the child. A quick nod and the child filled a couple of the bottles with water from a bucket under the pump. Kira traded the coins for the bottles before leading Jason to where a large tree loomed. During the day the tree would shade the courtyard. At night, it offered welcome and deeper shadow to mask them from the sight of others.

Kira settled down next to the trunk as she and Jason drank and rested. "There should be a window selling food for the road," Kira whispered to Jason. "We'll—"

She broke off as three figures strode into the courtyard, confronting a woman who had been walking toward the pump.

"You're the mistress here?" one of the three demanded.

"What of it?" she replied. "Do you have a complaint?"

"We're looking for someone."

Kira shrank back into shadow, gesturing to Jason to stay silent.

"You and half the countryside, it seems," the woman answered.

"We'll share the reward with you if you can tell us anything. Have you seen them?"

"What reward would be worth betraying the daughter herself?"

Another of the three spoke with exaggerated kindliness. "We want to help her! We're on your side and the side of the daughter."

"Are you now? Doesn't matter," the woman answered. "Haven't seen her or the boy."

"Watch for them, and you'll be well rewarded."

"Sure. I'll do that."

Kira tried to hold herself immobile in the shadows as the three walked briskly out of the courtyard. She'd barely begun to breathe again when the woman turned and walked toward the tree where Kira and Jason sat.

The woman raised a hooded lantern in one hand and opened it just enough for weak light to illuminate Kira. After a moment, the light was hooded again. "Come on," the woman urged.

Kira scrambled to her feet, gesturing to Jason to follow as the woman wended through more shadows before stopping at a closed door in the back of the main building. The woman produced a key ring, selected one, and opened the door, ushering Kira and Jason inside before joining them and relocking the door behind her.

The woman sat the lantern on a shelf in the small room, opening it again slightly and staring at Kira in the dim light. "It's you, sure enough. I saw her, nigh on twenty years ago. I was already past my youth when the daughter stayed the night at Denkerk on her way to Dorcastle, and in the morning I was there alongside the road to see her ride on. She looked so tired, and I thought she looked scared, too, like she knew she'd die there, but she was riding to Dorcastle for us anyway."

The woman shook her head as she gazed at Kira. "You look just like her. I've never forgotten her face as she smiled at me and nodded, riding past. Like I was a friend of hers."

Kira smiled despite her nervousness. "Mother likes to talk about how nice Denkerk was. How nice all the people were."

"We're not all nice. And some who come to visit aren't so nice at all. Lucky for you I saw you come into the courtyard and you sat down quiet before those three came looking for me. Have you heard what those folks from Urth have been saying?"

"No," Kira said. "I'm sure they're lying."

"I haven't heard it first-hand myself, but the story is that you two have run off together and are in all kinds of danger because you're so young and foolish, so tell the Urth people on a far-talker if you see them and you'll get a reward such as no one on the world of Dematr has ever seen. I heard that and I thought, the daughter of the daughter of Jules might be young yet, but she can't be a fool. There's more here than the Urth people are saying. That girl is her mother's daughter, and if she's out with that boy then there is good reason, probably something the daughter needs done. And it must be something important to all of us or the daughter wouldn't have risked her girl."

"That's true," Kira said.

Jason spoke up in a low voice. "And that reward they're promising is just shiny trash, something that will look great but is worthless."

"I guessed as much." The woman bowed her head slightly toward Kira. "What does the daughter's girl need from me?"

"We were hoping to get on a coach heading north," Kira said.

"That's easy enough, but the militia is out and they're watching everyone on the roads," the woman cautioned. "They think they're doing the daughter a favor, you see, not thinking that if the daughter wanted that she'd ask it of us herself. If you're seeking to avoid them as well, you'll need some special arrangements."

"We do have to avoid them," Kira said. "We have to remain hidden from the people on the Urth ship. I can't tell you why, but it's not because we've done anything wrong, I swear. The people from Urth want to do something wrong. My mother knows why we're hiding, and it has nothing to do with being young and…"

"Being young is no crime," the woman said, smiling at her. "Your word is all I need. I'll set something up."

"We have money—"

"Not a word of that! Your money is no good here. So, you need a way north, quiet and unseen, and I'm guessing some food?"

Kira smiled again. "Yes. We haven't had a decent meal for a while."

The woman nodded, smiled in return, then left by an inner door.

"I'm glad she left the lantern," Jason said, looking around. "This place is a little creepy."

"It's a storeroom," Kira said. "Those are herbs hanging above us, and I think these are flour barrels we're sitting on." She heard a rustle of movement. "And there are mice, of course."

"Alien mice?" Jason jerked his feet up, then suddenly started laughing quietly.

"What's so funny?" Kira asked.

"Alien mice!"

"What does that—"

The woman returned, bearing a covered tray that she sat down on a crate. "Eat your fill, then wait. It'll be a little while, but we'll get you on a coach."

"Thank you," Kira said. "We need to—"

"Don't tell me! It's the daughter's work. That's all I need to know. That and who you are."

A platter under the cover held two small roasted chickens, a pile of potatoes and carrots, and two large mugs of watered wine. Kira thought she had never had a better meal.

Even Jason didn't complain about the food, wolfing down the chicken. "This planet has the best food I ever tasted," he said after draining his mug. "Hey, what that woman said reminded me of something I've been wondering. All of the accounts we've heard on Earth say that Mari, your mom, died at Dorcastle but your father brought her back somehow. Most people think that means her heart stopped or something and he revived her within a minute or two. Is that what happened?"

"I don't know," Kira said, sighing contentedly with a full stomach. "Mother always insists that she didn't die. The healers who were there say she did. She stopped breathing, her heart stopped, she had lost a lot of blood and had an awful wound in her chest. Then father took her hand and he…he healed her."

"How?" Jason asked, peering at Kira through the dim light.

"His Mage talents. Somehow he was able to give her body the means to heal its injuries almost instantly, and new blood and everything. Enough that Mother was able to survive. But it almost killed him. Aunt Asha told me that she was afraid that my father would die. Well, she wasn't *afraid*, because Aunt Asha is a Mage, but she was really worried."

"So that's not just a story?" Jason asked. "It's true?"

"It's true," Kira said. "Father almost gave his life to save my mother."

"Huh." Jason looked down, appearing depressed. "What's it like having parents like that? You must never have any fights or arguments."

"Sure we do," Kira said. "Mother and I…we don't agree on some things."

She was spared from elaborating on her family fights when the woman returned, carrying a bag. "Here's more food for your travels, and a canteen as well. Stay quiet and follow me."

Outside again, the woman led them to a quiet, dark spot where a large coach sat while a fresh set of horses were hitched on. She took them to the back, where the baggage compartment jutted out, and urged Kira and Jason to climb in next to the boxes and bags. "Stay quiet in here. Tom, he's the driver, will take you all the way to Danalee and not say a word. He's a good man."

Kira reached to grasp her hand before the woman could seal the compartment. "What's your name, so I can tell my mother who helped me?"

The woman smiled shyly. "Izbelle. Izbelle of Denkerk."

"Thank you, Izbelle."

The compartment cover came down and locked. Kira squirmed into a corner that wasn't too uncomfortable, feeling both cramped in the confined space and depressed.

Izbelle hadn't helped her because she was Kira. Izbelle had helped her because Kira's mother had freed the world from the Great Guilds. Once again, Kira was living on the gratitude of others for what her mother had done. Because people looked at her, and saw her mother.

Jason took that moment to say exactly the wrong thing. "They really do worship your mother on this planet, don't they?"

Kira's reply was as sharp as she could make a whisper. "No one worships her! She earned everything she gets, and I don't need that rubbed into my face all of the time!"

She later thought that Jason displayed an impressive amount of wisdom by not saying another word for the next few hours.

Alain kept his right hand shielded in front of his body as he gestured behind them, above and to one side. "Something there follows us." He did not know what it was, but he did not want whatever it was to see him pointing at it.

"It's in the air?" Mari turned in the saddle, apparently looking back down the road but raising her eyes just enough to sweep the area that Alain had indicated. "I can't see anything," she said, sitting forward again. "Are you sure?"

"My foresight has warned of it twice," Alain said. "Somewhat like the same feeling when someone is aiming a weapon at you."

"Oh. Great. Actually, that is great. It must be something from the Urth ship, keeping an eye on us. We still have their attention."

"There is a sense of danger," Alain emphasized.

"From the device itself? As if it were a weapon?" Mari paused in thought. "Or if it carried a weapon. Could you stop it with your heat spell?"

Alain shook his head. "I cannot tell exactly where it is, and I must see where to place the heat."

"Then we have to keep moving and keep acting as though we're sneaking our way to Tiaesun. We should walk the horses for a while." Mari winced as she dismounted. "I wish we could have taken the train, but that wouldn't have looked sneaky."

"Trains are not safe," Alain said, dismounting as well.

"Yes, they are. For most people." Mari bit her lip. "How long will they wait, Alain? Talese Groveen didn't strike me as a patient woman, and you said she was worried that Jason would realize what was on the thing he took and tell us about it."

"They were certain that their devices would find him and Kira, with the help of the 'crowd.' When it becomes apparent that is not happening, they will become frustrated and try something else."

"And *something else* is likely to involve open threats and weapons," Mari said. He saw her touch the place on her jacket under which her own weapon rested. "I hope diplomacy works, but I've got a bad feeling."

"Let us hope that Kira can remain hidden from them, and from any others who would harm her," Alain said.

Kira wasn't sure how long they had been in the baggage compartment. The coach jolted along the road, the air inside the compartment stuffy and hot, assorted bags and boxes making it impossible to stretch out or get comfortable. The coach had made several stops. Twice during those stops Mari had heard someone asking questions of the passengers in the coach, who they were and where they were going. But no one came back to the baggage except Tom the driver, who pretended not to see Kira and Jason as he took out some bags and put in new ones.

The coach lurched to a halt once more, she heard the passengers leaving, and then Tom coming back to open the baggage compartment again. For the first time the driver looked at her, jogging his head to indicate she should get out. "End of the line," he whispered.

Her entire body stiff, Kira managed to clamber down and stand without falling over. Jason was having the same trouble. Even though Kira wasn't thrilled at the contact, they had to hang onto each other for a while to be able to walk. Behind them, nobody at the large coach stop bustling with people during the mid-morning rush seemed to have noticed two extra passengers leaving the back of the coach.

"Public bathroom," Kira rasped. "Over that way."

After all of that time stuck in the baggage compartment, Jason didn't argue. Kira wasn't sure that she'd make it to the bathroom, but she did.

Jason was already waiting just outside when she was done. He was somehow managing to look exactly like someone who was trying not to be noticed. Kira led him away from the coach stop, her legs still protesting every movement. "How are you doing?" she asked.

"Everything hurts," Jason said.

"Yeah. We're in Danalee, but we can't stay. We need to head north, but if we get spotted leaving the city heading north, that would give away that we're going to Dorcastle, so we need to head west."

"We need to go north so we're going west?"

"Right."

"Sure," Jason said. "That makes sense." He looked up, as if searching for something.

"What are you looking for?" Kira asked, irritated by his last response and by the lingering aches in her body.

"Drones. The ship only has a few. I don't know how long it will take it to make more, and I don't know if they have everything they need to make very many. But they'll probably deploy what they've got to places like this, that people have to go through to get somewhere else."

She stopped walking and punched his shoulder, angry. "Why didn't you tell me about that before?"

"Because it's so obvious!"

"No, it's not! You can't assume that—" Kira suddenly realized that their argument had attracted the attention of a nearby police officer.

"Keep it down, young lovers," the officer advised in a voice that carried warning but not hostility.

"Yes, ma'am," Kira said, tugging Jason into motion again. "Stars above, that was stupid of me! She noticed us! We need to get out of this city now!" She took her bearings and turned at the next corner. "Young lovers! How embarrassing!"

"For you," Jason said. "It's a pretty big compliment to me."

"Don't even start," Kira warned him. "We need to get into the rail yard without being spotted so we can sneak aboard a freight train. Mother and Father did that to escape a city once."

"Another train?" Jason said, suddenly wary.

"Yes. We'll hide in a freight car until we get out of the city." Given Jason's attitude, Kira decided not to tell him anything else about her plans.

The streets of Danalee were full of people at this hour of the day, the sun shining down on crowds Kira couldn't help thinking were all watching for any sign of the missing boy and girl so they could collect the reward from Urth, or because they were worried about the daughter's girl. To make it worse, Jason kept staring at passing horse-drawn wagons and carriages as if they were an amazing sight.

An open market in a square offered food and drink at some of the stalls, reminding her of how long it had been since they'd finished the last of the food Izbelle had provided. Despite the need for haste and worry about being recognized, Kira swung by to get enough for Jason and her to make a walking lunch out of.

The crowds got thicker around the entrance to the rail yard. Kira tugged Jason to one side, working down a side street next to the rail yard with a lot fewer people. "If my father was here he'd just imagine a hole in that wall around the rail yard and we'd walk through," Kira told Jason. She hesitated, half-worried and half-hopeful, as she wondered if her Mage skills might someday allow her to do that. It didn't matter, though, because she certainly couldn't do it now.

"How about that door?" Jason said, pointing to a side entrance.

Kira walked up to it, seeing a large padlock on the door. "This is just what we need."

"We don't have a key," Jason said. "Are you going to shoot the lock off?"

"Shoot the lock off?" Kira asked. "I have no idea how hard that would be, but I do know it would make so much noise that we'd have half the city on us before we got the lock open." She dug in one pocket and pulled out a small leather case. "I'll pick the lock."

"You can pick locks?"

"Mother taught me how," Kira said. "Sort of a mother/daughter bonding experience, I guess," she added as she pulled out some picks and went to work.

"Mother/daughter bonding experience?" Jason asked. "Yeah, learning how to pick locks sounds like the sort of thing most mothers and daughters bond over."

"If you're done making bad jokes, I need you to stand so no one can see what I'm doing," Kira said.

He had to stand uncomfortably close to do that, but she couldn't complain, instead doing her best to focus on her work. The lock clicked, she pulled it open, and Jason stepped back as she put away her lock picks. "What's the matter?" Kira asked him. "Why so gloomy? We're doing all right at the moment."

Jason shrugged. "You can do anything. I can't do anything. I'm totally helpless here."

She rubbed her face in exasperation. "You should have figured out by now that I can't do everything. And you are doing things. You're helping."

"How?"

"You…kept people from seeing me pick that lock."

"Yeah," Jason said scornfully. "I make a good portable wall."

"If you don't like who you are, then change who you are!" Kira told him. "If we can keep from being caught you'll have a chance to learn how to do other things."

"You don't like who you are," Jason pointed out.

"You know what? This is not about me. Come on." The door, having apparently not been opened for a while, protested but eventually gave way to their combined tugging. Kira motioned Jason inside, then followed, trying to act as if they were doing something completely normal. As far as she could tell, none of the people on the street had reacted with suspicion to her and Jason's actions.

Inside the wall, this part of the rail yard was a bit isolated, spare rails and ties stacked so that they had almost blocked the door. Kira stood a moment, looking around, listening to the sounds of locomotives and hammering on metal and the other achingly familiar noises she associated with happy times with her mother and her friends.

Sighing, Kira opened her jacket and loosened her pistol in its holster, ready to draw.

"Why are you doing that?" Jason asked. He wasn't still moody, but looked like the kid from Urth again, someone who played strange games and was out of his depth in a place where real things were happening.

"Jason, there's a much bigger chance that anyone we meet in the rail yard will know my mother or have seen her," Kira explained. "Or maybe even have met me. I worked in this rail yard for a couple of weeks last summer."

"Why did you bring us here if people knew you?"

"Because this is the fastest and surest way out of this city and on our way!" Kira ran a hand through her hair, fighting down nerves. "If anyone notices us, we probably won't be able to talk our way out of it. So let's not get noticed."

She remembered enough about the layout of the yard to take a path toward the outgoing rail lines that minimized their chances of encountering anyone, approaching a line of coupled freight cars from the side opposite where people should be working on them. "There. That's a boxcar carrying general freight. We don't want one with livestock that would act up and give us away, and maybe hurt us, and we don't want an ice car. If these cars are ready to go, they'll have been inspected and locked, so I'll just have to pick another lock to get us inside."

She knelt down, examining the lock, Jason kneeling nearby to watch her anxiously.

"What are you doing there?" a sharp, authoritative voice demanded.

Kira hand moved the small distance necessary to reach under her jacket and grasp her pistol, her thumb releasing the safety as she spun about and leveled her weapon.

CHAPTER SEVEN

Kira's pistol lined up on a young man in the jacket of a Mechanic apprentice. She stared at him as he stared back, wordless.

"Gari," Kira said.

"Kira?" Gari stared at her pistol. "Why are you threatening me?"

"I need to know that you won't give us away," Kira said, the words almost sticking in her throat.

"You don't need to hold a pistol on me to know that," Gari said, offended.

"I guess not." Kira set the safety and put away her weapon.

"You know this guy?" Jason asked.

"Yeah. Gari is one of Aunt Alli and Uncle Calu's boys. He's sort of my big brother."

Gari shook his head at her. "Do you know what my mother would say if she knew you'd pointed your pistol at me? What are the rules, Kira? Don't point unless you're willing to shoot!"

"I was willing to shoot," Kira said in a low voice. Gari stared at her again, this time in shock. "I'm sorry. This is really, really important. We can't get caught, and we can't get stopped."

Gari's eyes shifted to Jason, appraising him with cold distrust. "We. That's the guy from the ship from Urth?"

"Yes. His name's Jason. What do you know about this, Gari?"

"What the Urth ship has broadcast several times. And my father got a far-talker message to us telling me and Andi not to help the Urth people."

"Which means you have to help me," Kira said.

"No, it doesn't. What are you doing out alone, sneaking around a rail yard, threatening people, with some *guy*—"

"I'm not *with* him," Kira said. "It's not like that at all. I have a job to do."

Jason spoke in that self-mocking way. "She doesn't even like me."

"Neither do I," Gari said. "Not if you've gotten her into some mess."

"Excuse me," Kira said. "I am perfectly capable of getting myself into a mess. Isn't that what the Senior Mechanics tried to say about my mother? That someone else was leading her astray? I'm in this mess because of *my* decisions." Somehow that didn't sound as good as she had thought it would. "There are lives riding on this, Gari. Millions of lives."

He paused, eyeing her. "Millions? How?"

"Jason has a device from the Urth ship that tells how to use Mage skills to create new weapons. The ship was going to take it back to Urth so they could make lots of those weapons. That's why Jason stole it, and that's why we have to stay hidden until the ship has to leave."

Gari frowned, rubbing the back of his neck. "Are you sure that's true?"

"I'm positive."

"I…guess I have to not interfere."

"Don't tell anyone you saw us," Kira added.

"Uh-uh. I'm going to tell my parents as soon as they get back to Danalee. Don't even try to convince me otherwise."

Kira shrugged. "Aunt Alli and Uncle Calu should understand. But my mother can't get involved. You know why."

"She might be getting involved anyway. I can't tell for sure with the Urth ship interfering with far-talkers. But I know what you mean. I'll leave it up to my mother and father when they get back."

"I can't ask for better than that," Kira said. "Gari…have you ever heard people talking about me? About me…" The idea was so absurd that Kira had trouble forcing the words out. "Inheriting my mother's responsibilities?"

He paused long enough before answering to make the reply obvious even before he spoke. "Sometimes."

"Sometimes?"

"Yeah, I mean, it's something that people talk about. Sometimes."

She gave him a disbelieving look. "Why didn't you tell me? Why didn't any of my friends tell me?"

"Kira, we thought you'd freak out if you heard it."

"That was really perceptive of you guys. Because I am freaking out!"

"Kira—"

"You know me! How could you possibly think I'd be able to equal *her?*"

"Not yet, maybe, but—"

"Stars above, am I the only sane person in the world? And everybody I know seems to think I'm crazy!" She gestured toward the freight cars. "This is heading west, right?"

"Yeah. Slow freight to Julesport. Due to leave in about half an hour. I'm supposed to be checking the locks on each car," Gari added.

"You already checked this one and it's fine," Kira told him.

He hesitated again. "All right."

"Thanks," Jason said.

Gari gave Jason a hard look. "Kira really is like a sister to me. I'd be really unhappy if she got hurt."

"So would I," Jason said. "I tried to talk her out of it. I…I promise that I will do anything necessary to protect her."

Kira split her displeasure between both boys. "I don't need to be protected."

"Yes, you do," Gari said. "That's why when you were here last year there were bodyguards watching you. And I know how you hated that, but there are people who'd do terrible things if they got at you, Kira."

She shuddered, remembering the words of the rider north of the Glenca. "I know. Thanks, big brother." Kira walked closer and gave him a hug, feeling the tension in Gari's body. "Trust me."

He hugged her back. "I do. Get the blazes out of here before I have an attack of common sense."

About an hour later, the morning sun having risen to near noon, Kira stood in the partially opened door of the freight car, fields of crops going past as the train left behind the outlying buildings of Danalee. "We have to jump now."

"Jump?" Jason shook his head, holding back. "You didn't say anything about jumping again."

"Because I didn't have time to convince you that we'd need to do this!"

"There's no river to jump into!"

"We're not going very fast yet!" But the train was slowly speeding up. Jumping would get more hazardous with every moment that Jason delayed them. "There's a nice soft spot right up ahead. It looks like sand."

"Sand?" Jason came up to the door, leaning to look out.

Kira grimaced and shoved, then followed Jason out the door and onto the dirt and grass lining the tracks.

She rolled to a stop right next to the first row of crops, breathing heavily, trying to figure out whether she had acquired any hurt worse than bruises. Kira waited until the rest of the train had passed before she stood up, cautiously testing for anything sprained.

Jason was lying still, unmoving. She walked over to him, fearing the worst, but his eyes were open, gazing upward.

"Are you all right?" Kira asked.

"You throw me off a train again, and then ask if I'm all right," Jason said, his voice flat. "Why do I doubt your sincerity?"

"I don't want you to be hurt, Jason, but we needed to get off that train."

"You really are crazy. I know you're not thrilled to be stuck with me, but at least *I'm* not homicidal!"

"Can you walk?" Kira asked.

"I don't know. I'm beginning to think I should let the bad guys find me. What are they going to do to me that you aren't?"

"Very funny. Get up." She offered him her hand to help.

He glared at her, ignoring the offer as he rolled to his side and then stood up, refusing to say anything else.

Kira shrugged and led them north through the fields.

Jason didn't speak again until the day was nearly over. It had been a long walk past the outer edges of Danalee, the banks of the Silver River beckoning ahead.

"I can't believe that I fell for that again."

"I'm sorry," Kira said.

"Are you? You're pretty good at shoving people off of moving trains."

"Jason, before I met you I had never shoved anyone off of a train."

"I guess that makes me special," Jason said. "And you must have a natural talent for it."

She smiled for the first time in hours. "It's nice to know I'm good at something. Do you forgive me?"

"I guess so. Kira, I've already tried several times staying mad at you and I can't do it." He looked ahead. "That river is flowing north, isn't it?"

"Yes. The Silver River. That's our road to Dorcastle." Just like her mother, nearly twenty years before. "There are always barges moving downriver. We'll hitch a ride on one."

"Is that safe?"

"If you pick the right barge. I was told to look for a family, young children, on a barge kept neat and tidy." The banks of the Silver River were low along here, just outside the city of Danalee, so it wasn't hard to approach the water. Kira stood looking upstream while Jason sat on the riverbank watching the water go by. She wondered how often he had ever done things like this, simply observing the world instead of being "linked" to lots of people yelling at each other.

The first barge that she saw going past had a group of young men visible topside and several kegs of whiskey tied on the top of the deck-house. Kira didn't need the raucous shouts directed her way when they saw her to know that getting on that barge would be a really dumb thing to do.

The next barge that came past had an old man at the tiller and no one else visible. Many barges on the river had been riding the waters for decades, but this barge looked its age. Kira nodded to the man as the barge went past but that was all.

A third barge followed not far behind. Also not new, but neatly kept. A string of laundry flapped in the breeze, including a few diapers. Kira could see the small shape of an older child onboard, playing alongside his mother as she sewed, and the man at the tiller had the tired, respectable look of a hard-working father. Kira waved and called. "On the barge! Can you give us passage to Dorcastle?"

The woman looked at her and stood up. "Two of you? What do you offer?"

"Two Tiae crowns!"

"Not enough! Make it six!"

The barge drew steadily closer, riding the river current, as Kira yelled her reply. "Three!"

"Five."

"I'll pay four." She would have paid more, but acting too eager would have aroused suspicions.

"Four it is! Gabe! Swing us in near them! Mind the shoal."

The man guided the boat close to the riverbank as Kira and Jason hastily pulled off their boots and socks. Kira waded out into the river as far as she could, wishing that she'd remembered to roll up the legs of her trousers. Jason came behind, looking around as if fearing sharks.

The deck of the barge was only about half a lance above the river's surface. The woman tossed down a line and Kira grabbed it, hand-over-handing up until she reached the deck, then turning to help Jason.

Kira counted out the crowns and gave four to the woman. The

woman looked them over, finally smiled, and pointed to the deck. "Have a seat."

They sat down, backs against the deckhouse. After the exertion of walking for more than half a day, Kira thought being able to sit, stretch out her legs, and watch the riverbanks slide by was delightful. But she had to shift position as the hard wooden deck made it clear that Kira had acquired more than one new bruise when jumping off the train.

Sunset wasn't far off when a faint smell of cooking came to Kira. The woman showed up soon after. "Blankets?"

"How much?" Kira asked.

"You can each have the use of one for another couple of crowns."

"How about we have one blanket each for one crown total?"

The woman studied Kira. "How about three crowns, and include the blankets *and* meals until we reach Dorcastle?"

"Deal."

After the woman left, Jason spoke softly. "Kira. Look."

She followed his pointing finger. The road next to the river had few travelers with night coming on, but in the distance toward Danalee Kira caught the glint of light off of burnished metal as the setting sun shot nearly level rays across the land. She watched the glints bob in a familiar, rhythmic way. Riders on horses, wearing helms. Coming this way from the city.

"What do we do?" Jason whispered.

"Sit here and hope," Kira said. "We can't move any faster by any other means. The cavalry should stop searching once full dark comes on."

"If they're after us—"

"Shhh! Look at the movement of the helms. The horses are trotting, not cantering or galloping. If they were in pursuit, they'd be moving faster."

"How can you—?" Jason shook his head at her in admiration. "Oh, yeah. You're an officer in that cavalry of the queen's."

"*Honorary* officer," Kira corrected. "And don't say that! We can't afford for anyone to overhear it."

The cavalry drew steadily closer as the sun sank, twilight coming on. The river narrowed, higher banks closing in either side, and the current flowed more swiftly, pushing the barge along faster. Kira had worried that the barge would stop for the night when dark fell, but the woman lit a lantern at the bow and they kept on.

She could barely see the oncoming cavalry in the dimness when the river swept around a bend and Kira lost sight of the riders. It bothered her that the cavalry had kept moving as dusk fell, but they would surely have to stop soon for the night. Unlike the barge, horses needed rest.

The woman brought Kira and Jason chunks of stale bread and two large bowls of stew, then went back to relieve her husband at the tiller. Kira found that the stew contained a few vegetables, some fish, and a lot of watery broth.

"I liked the food in Denkerk better," Jason grumbled.

"They get water and fish from the river," Kira said. "We'll probably have this every meal."

He stopped eating and stared at her. "You mean this fish and the water in this stew came out of the same river we're on right now?"

"Yeah," Kira said, wondering why Jason looked alarmed.

"Was everything processed and sterilized?"

"What?"

"There are, like, animals using that water! And people!"

"Yes," Kira said. "She boiled the stew. You can tell from the fish."

Jason lowered his head, anxiously studying his bowl of stew. "If she brings us sushi, I am not eating any."

"What's sushi?"

"Raw fish. A lot of people eat it back…where I come from. It's good."

"You eat raw fish?" Kira almost gagged at the thought. "And you're worried about stew that's been boiled?"

"It's good," Jason insisted. "Sashimi and stuff."

"You gut it first, right? You gut it and scale it before you eat the fish raw?"

"Of course we do!" Jason started laughing. "I figured some stuff that you guys ate might gross me out, but I never realized some stuff I ate would gross you out too. I guess it's all what you're used to."

Knowing that they really should stand watches during the night, Kira was too weary to care. She spread her blanket on the deck.

"Kira?" Jason asked. "Where are the bathrooms?"

She pointed over the side of the barge. "The river."

"The river?" Jason groaned. "I don't think I'm going to be able to eat any more stew."

"Suit yourself." Kira must have fallen asleep almost immediately, her dreams haunted by images of worlds ravaged by terrible weapons that struck down millions at a blow.

They had reached Tiaesun about noon after another day and night of travel. Mari was standing by a window, looking out over the reborn capital city of Tiae, when a guard led a Mage into the room. "A message, Lady."

"Thank you." Mari glanced at Alain, waiting until the guard had left. The Mage waited too, her expression impassive, not engaging in even the unspoken social interactions that normally occurred among people. "What is it?"

The Mage's voice was impassive as well, not the dead tones of old, but still heavily influenced by the former Mage Guild's rejection of any form of emotion. "Elder," she addressed Mari, using the Mage term of respect, "this message came to this one from a Mage in Danalee. Master Mechanic Alli and Mechanic Calu of Danalee speak of one Gari, and say that one met the one Kira in their city. The one Kira rode a creature of the Mechanics to the west where Julesport lies. That one Jason was with her. Both looked well. Master Mechanic Alli adds that the one Kira threatened that one Gari with her Mechanic weapon, and that one Alli asks to know what the elder Mari has been teaching the one Kira."

The Mage stopped reciting her message, turned, and left to wait outside.

"Thank you," Mari called after her. "Isn't it just like Alli to add a comment to her message even at a time like this?" she asked Alain. "Although I can imagine Alli was pretty upset at the idea that Kira might have shot Gari."

"Danalee," Alain said. "Kira did go north, as you guessed. Perhaps you understand her more than you thought." He was seated at the small table which held the remnants of their morning meal.

"I don't understand her nearly enough!" Mari winced as she sat down opposite him. "Have I mentioned how much I hate long, hard rides on horses?"

"Not since before the Mage brought the message."

"My funny Mage," Mari said. "I should have known you were trouble when you first started trying to make jokes. Kira is not going to Julesport."

She still liked being able to elicit a surprised reaction from Alain. "Why do you say that?"

"Because Kira is smart and sneaky."

Alain nodded. "She gets those things from you."

"She gets smart from both of us, but most of the sneaky from you," Mari said. "Which is why I know that if Kira was going to Julesport, she wouldn't have let Gari know she was heading that way."

"Dorcastle, then," Alain said.

"Do we go there?" Mari asked. "Kira might need us, but if we do go to Dorcastle that might draw the Urth people's search there as well."

"If others saw Kira and Jason in Danalee, reports of that may reach the people from Urth," Alain said.

"Good point." Mari stood up again. "I'm going to ask the long-range far-talker operators here to listen for anything from Danalee or near it, and ask that message Mage to send a reply asking for anything Alli or Calu might pick up. We're supposed to be looking for Kira, so if solid reports of her draw everyone else's attention that way it would look very odd for us not to go to Danalee."

"And if that happens, the Urth people will still search near Danalee, not elsewhere," Alain suggested. "They believe that we do not know they watch us."

"Have you noticed that we're getting reports of more of those drones being seen over cities and roads, but the one following us is remaining hidden? The Urth people must be deliberately letting most of their drones be seen."

"To overawe and worry the people of this world," Alain said.

"I am worried," Mari admitted. "But I'm a long ways from being overawed."

Morning on the river brought another bowl of stew and enforced inactivity. Kira sat next to Jason as he choked down his stew, thinking how strange it was that the opportunity to rest she had craved had so quickly become hard to endure as the barge made its slow, steady way down the Silver River.

"There isn't any faster way to Dorcastle, except on a Roc, and I didn't dare try to hire a Roc Mage in Danalee," Kira told Jason. The woman was back at the tiller, nursing the baby as she steered the barge, out of earshot if Kira and Jason spoke quietly. Her husband and the other child were asleep inside the deckhouse. "Too many Mages know what my mother looks like, and Father said other Mages might be able to sense who I am if they get right next to me."

"How could they do that?" Jason asked, shuddering as he put aside his empty bowl.

"I don't know. It's some skill that Mages have—" To detect the presence of Mages powers. No way should she be telling Jason about that.

Jason, not seeming to have noticed Kira's abrupt ending to her sentence, squinted toward the riverbank. "At least I haven't seen any drones, so my mom's search probably hasn't expanded this far north. Why isn't there a rail line along here, running between Danalee and Dorcastle? I don't even see any signs of one being built."

"Mother has been involved in that," Kira said, hugging her knees as she looked at the passing traffic on the road. "Trying to work out something. It's the people who work the barges, and have done so for a long time. They think if a rail line gets built it will take a lot of their work away, and Mother says they're right. A lot of the families on these barges wouldn't be able to make a living anymore."

"Yeah," Jason said, "but you can't just keep things the same."

"Jason, how do you tell someone whose family has worked barges on this river for generations that things have to change and they have to find some other work somewhere else?" Kira bit her lip hard. "Sometimes I can understand why some people are angry at Mother. She couldn't just change the things almost everyone wanted changed. She also had to make things change that people liked."

He nodded, giving her a somber look. "That's the way it's been back home. Always. Stuff changes."

"It's hard to imagine," Kira said. "But Father says if Mother had failed, the storm would have come."

"Storm?"

"That's what the Mages called it, the visions that they saw," Kira explained. "The common people sort of going crazy, rioting in mobs, destroying everything. It's hard to believe that could ever happen, but the Mages saw it."

"I can believe it," Jason said, surprising her. "That's happened sometimes back home. Not a whole world, but parts of cities, even entire cities and sometimes countries. Everybody stops believing it will get better, everybody loses hope, everything falls apart."

"So you think the Mages were right?"

"I thought you were the one who believed in foresight," Jason joked. "But yeah, centuries of being forced to serve someone else, your guilds preventing any change, I'm amazed it didn't all blow up earlier."

"Why does change have to be so hard, Jason?" Kira watched as they passed another barge, this one tied up alongside the river, a family working topside. "If change has to be, why does it have to be hard?"

"I don't know," Jason said, his eyes on the same barge. "It's like growing up, isn't it? That's change. Remember being a little kid and how amazing the world was? All of this new stuff to see and to learn, and new friends everywhere you looked. You didn't know enough to be scared of other people or of what was happening in other places or of what the future would be like. And even simple things were so much fun. Remember that?"

Kira smiled, remembering life before she had learned that her mother was the daughter. "Yeah. That really was a great time."

"Would you want to be like that forever?"

She bent her head, thinking. "We'd give up a lot, wouldn't we? We lose things when we grow, but we gain things, too. I already know how much I'd have missed if I had never gotten older than six. I can't imagine everything ahead."

"Change," Jason said. "It hurts, but it has to be, and it gives us new things."

Kira turned her smile on him. "Why do you say you're not smart? Jason, you have great ideas."

"Nah." He looked away, embarrassed. "I probably heard that some-place."

"No, you didn't. You came up with it yourself. Jason, stop listening to people who tell you that you're not smart."

He laughed. "Who am I supposed to listen to?"

"Me."

Jason's laughter stopped abruptly. "Why…why do you care?"

"Um…I don't know," Kira said, startled by the question. "Can't somebody care about somebody else?"

"Sure they can, but you…and I'm…I'm just a je—" He broke off. "I almost forgot I'm not allowed to call myself a jerk anymore."

"See," Kira teased, trying to lighten a mood that had shifted in ways she didn't understand, "you're listening to me already."

"Why are doing this, Kira?" Jason asked, his face averted from her.

"Doing what?"

"Making it seem like maybe it's possible that… Never mind!" He turned his body away, hunching over to close out the world.

"Jason? Are you all right?"

He didn't answer.

She looked over the water at the banks of the river going by, wondering why Jason was upset and why her stomach felt so tight.

The female Mage returned to Mari and Alain's room, speaking her new message in the same impassive tones. "Elder, this message came to this one from a Mage in Danalee. Master Mechanic Alli and Mechanic Calu of Danalee speak of several who say they have seen the one Kira in their city. Three have been overheard since the day before using the Mechanic message creatures to speak with the ship from Urth in search of reward. That one Alli speaks of Danalee buzzing with those who seek to find the one Kira. The Urth creatures called drones have been seen flying. That one Calu says he thinks the elder and the master of mages should come to Danalee."

Alain looked to Mari after the Mage had left. He knew she was torn between rushing to her daughter and trying to protect Kira by keeping attention focused elsewhere. "Two Roc Mages wait on us. We need only decide to go."

"Is one of them Mage Alera?" Mari asked.

"No. Mage Saburo and Mage Alber. I am told that Alera is north of the Sea of Bakre, seeking again to speak with her relatives."

Mari grimaced, looking down at the table. "We should be helping her with that. Even Mages a lot more outgoing than Alera have had trouble reconnecting with the families they lost when the Mage Guild took them for training."

"We have been busy, and you are not speaking of Danalee," Alain prodded gently.

"I am deliberately avoiding that, as I am sure you know," Mari told him. "We shouldn't rush it. If the Urth people aren't already focused on Danalee, you and I going there will bring their full attention to that city."

"Three have spoken to the Urth people, saying they have seen Kira there," Alain reminded her.

"But there have been other claims, in a lot of places," Mari said. "The long-distance far-talker in Tiaesun has picked up several of them. Sien's decoys are doing their job."

"Why do you seek to argue yourself out of going to Danalee?" Alain asked.

She didn't answer for a moment, hunched over the table, her eyes closed. "Because I want so badly to go. I want to be there. I want to be right beside Kira. I want to be between her and any danger!"

"You do not need to second-guess yourself. Calu believes that danger is already focusing on the area around Danalee," Alain said. "He would not urge you to come unless he knew that was so."

Mari opened her eyes and looked at him. "If we go there, that danger will focus on us."

"Yes."

"Then as Kira's mother and father we have to do that." She gave Alain a rueful look. "I have a lot more sympathy for my parents than I used to, even though they never actually got shot at because of me."

"You can remind Kira of how much you have sacrificed for her," Alain suggested, remembering a number of such arguments in the past.

"Oh, yeah. That always goes over well." Mari stood up. "Let's go. At least we're flying this time. Let's find out how well that Urth drone can follow Rocs."

By late afternoon, Jason had apparently gotten over his upset, though he refused to respond to a couple of careful questions from Kira about it. He was sitting a short distance from her when the boy on the boat ran around the corner of the deckhouse and tripped over Jason's outstretched legs.

Kira had only a moment to wonder if Jason would react by yelling at the boy in a way that might betray them.

Instead, Jason laughed and helped the boy stand. "Careful there, Munchkin. You might go overboard."

The boy gave Jason a puzzled look. "What's a munk-kin?"

"Little guys who live in a place called Oz," Jason said.

"Is that where you're from? Is that why you talk funny?" the boy asked.

"Yes," Kira interjected hastily. "Oz is a place way…to the south."

The woman appeared, shaking her head at the boy. "The math lesson isn't done. Come along. Excuse my son," she told Jason.

"You're teaching him math?" Jason asked.

The woman stared but didn't comment on his unusual accent. "Yes. He'll need it if he inherits the boat. And if the boats go away as some say they will, he'll need it elsewhere. But he doesn't like it."

"Math is important," Jason said to the boy, startling Kira. "How about you and me take a look at that lesson."

Kira watched, horrified, as Jason got up and walked around the deckhouse with the boy. Had he lost his mind? Drawing attention to himself and his strange accent and his unusual way of speaking?

She scrambled to her feet, peering over the edge of the deckhouse to see Jason sitting down next to the boy, holding a chalk tablet as he talked. As Kira watched, he began walking the boy through simple math exercises as if he had done the same thing a thousand times, though he had obvious problems with using the chalk.

She should intervene. She should stop this. But Kira only watched.

Eventually, Jason stood up. "Keep on that!" he advised the boy, who grinned and nodded.

"What was that?" Kira whispered to Jason when they were both seated again on the other side of the deckhouse. "Why did you do that?"

Jason's shrug felt defensive. "He needed some help."

"Do you do that? Back on…where you live?"

"Yeah. I tutor kids in math."

Kira stared at him. "You have a job? You never mentioned having a job."

"No," Jason said, as if uncomfortable having to explain. "I volunteer."

"Volunteer? Do you get paid?"

"No! They couldn't pay me even if they wanted to. I do the tutoring by links and use a fake persona." He looked toward the other side of the barge. "It was kind of neat to be tutoring face to face."

"Why do you use a fake persona?" Kira pressed.

He looked like he wouldn't answer, then shrugged again. "Because I'm not doing it so people will think I'm great. It needs to be done, I can do it, so I do, and I don't want people making a big deal out of it."

Kira realized that her mouth was hanging open and closed it. "You sound like my mother. And my father. Which I never expected to say to you."

Another shrug. "Is that a good thing or a bad thing?"

"In this case it's a good thing. Do your parents know? Maybe if you told them they'd think more of you."

His laugh was short and sharp. "They'd think less. My mom and my dad both think volunteering is for dummies. Give away your labor? Give away your skills? That's for suckers."

"Oh." Kira searched for what to say next. "You shouldn't have done that. Calling attention to yourself and everything. I'm glad that you did, but…we have to remember how many lives depend on us not getting caught."

"I know." He looked around in obvious search of a way to change the topic. "That's weird," Jason said, nodding toward a barge with a large family on it. "Four kids."

"Why is that weird?" Kira asked, willing to let the matter slide since she was still trying to get used to this new aspect of Jason.

"I guess maybe it's not here. Where I come from, families usually only have two kids or maybe just one, like your parents did."

Kira felt tension fill her like old pain. "My parents had two children."

"Huh? But—" Jason paused. "Was it something bad? The way you said that…"

"Yes." She took a deep breath to calm herself. "My little brother Danel died soon after being born. Something was wrong with his body that no one could heal."

"Oh. That— That—"

She looked over and saw Jason staring fixedly off the side of the barge. "It's all right. It was a long time ago."

"It doesn't sound like it's all right," Jason mumbled. "Why didn't— No, I shouldn't ask, should I?"

"Shouldn't ask what?"

"Did they decide not to try again?"

Kira closed her eyes, remembering her mother's face every time the topic had come up. "They couldn't. Something happened to Mother. I don't know if it was caused by Danel's birth or if it was something inside her that…that…also hurt Danel. We can't talk about it, so I don't know. She can't have any other children."

"Oh." Jason sounded dejected. "I'm really sorry. That doesn't happen back home any more. They can save every kid no matter what. They could probably fix what's wrong with your mom's body, too. I know life sucks, but that's…that's just awful."

She looked over at him again. "Father almost died, too," Kira said, not knowing why she was finally sharing something she had rarely been able to talk about. "He tried to heal Danel with his Mage skills. He kept trying, getting weaker and weaker, and Mother was the only one who could break his focus and save him. She had to rise from the birth bed and shake him out of it. They've never told me that. A couple of other people who were there did."

"He nearly killed himself trying to save his son?" To her surprise, Jason laughed, the sound full of pain. "Oh, man, my dad would've done a happy dance if I'd died at birth."

Kira stared at him in shock. "Jason, I know you've said he's awful, but that can't be true."

"It is." Jason sighed. "There's a guy named Tolstoy who wrote stories, and he said that all happy families are the same, but every unhappy family is unhappy in a different way. Something like that. I guess that's true. Look at you and me."

"My family isn't unhappy," Kira denied.

"You don't seem happy whenever you talk about them."

"I—" Kira frowned down at the river. "Really?"

"Yeah. Any idea why?"

"I don't know." She felt her frown deepening as she thought. "They're so happy together. I mean, sometimes they argue. Mother has…well, I inherited her temper. But they love each other so much." Kira paused, trying to find the right words. "Maybe it bothers me that…I know it sounds stupid and selfish, but how could I ever find someone like that, someone I would risk dying for and someone who would risk death to save me?"

"Why do you think that'd be hard for you?" Jason scoffed. "I'll never find that. But you… You're you."

"What is that supposed to mean?" Kira demanded, feeling defensive and upset even though she wasn't sure why.

"It means you'll find that person," Jason said, his voice growing brusque at her reaction.

"No, I won't."

"You will," Jason insisted.

"No!"

"Yes!"

"Not in a million years." Kira glanced at him again. "You can keep trying, but I'm going to get the last word on this."

To her surprise, his grumpiness shifted to a laugh. "How can you do that? I was all ready to sulk again for the rest of the day and you made me laugh."

"It's a gift, I guess," Kira said, finding herself smiling slightly.

"You'll find that guy, Kira."

"No, I won't."

"Yes, you will."

"No."

"Yes."

"Maybe."

He laughed again. Even though Jason didn't say anything else, he seemed cheerful.

But Kira looked at the water of the river going by on its journey to the sea that had always been and always would be, and wondered if Jason was right, if every time she talked about her family she sounded unhappy.

"We'll be at Dorcastle by evening," the woman said as she walked around the side of the deckhouse. "We owe your friend there for his teaching of our son. It's the first time I've seen him work hard at it." She fumbled out one of the crowns that Kira had paid. "Please. For the lesson."

Kira glanced at Jason. "He doesn't want to be paid. He does it because he likes to. Keep the money."

"If you insist," the woman said. "But we'll put you off anywhere you like at Dorcastle, even if we have to go beyond our dock."

"We'd like off at the first good landing," Kira said, thinking that it would be far too easy for anyone searching for her and Jason to check every barge coming downriver. On foot, they'd be able to take different paths through the city and hide more easily if necessary, plus the barge would be delayed by the time required to get through the locks along the river inside the city.

She wondered what was happening in Danalee, and whether the search had reached Dorcastle yet. Because Kira knew that getting through Dorcastle without being recognized would be the roughest test they had yet encountered.

CHAPTER EIGHT

The boy waved at Jason as they left. "I hope you get back to Oz soon!"

"Thanks!" Jason said.

Near midnight, this part of the city was very quiet. By the time they reached the areas near the harbor, where sailors frequented bars far into the night, it should be close enough to dawn that even the latest drinkers should be trying to sleep off the excesses of previous hours.

"Where is Oz?" Kira asked as they strode off the unlighted landing and onto a dark street leading down into the city and toward the sea.

"All I remember is that you can get there from Kansas," Jason said.

"Is that really your home on Earth?"

"I wished that more than once, but no." Jason's brow furrowed as he looked around. "This is going to be home, isn't it? I'll have to stay here when the ship leaves. This world, I mean. I guess I hadn't really thought about that."

"Is staying here so bad?" Kira said.

"No. It's not bad at all." He stole a quick glance at her, then away.

Elated to have finally reached Dorcastle, she decided to ignore the glance and whatever it might have meant. "There are a lot of places on Dematr that you haven't seen yet," Kira cautioned. "And you're not going to see much of Dorcastle. I cannot walk around this city in daylight. We need to get through the length of the city before dawn."

"It doesn't look like the movies they've made back on Earth," Jason commented as they walked through the outlying neighborhoods, heading downward toward the sea. "But then, your mom doesn't look some of the actors who played her. Some of them were good, but you'd probably see a lot of mistakes in what they did."

"How would I see mistakes?" Kira asked, hearing her voice grow cold.

"Uh…your mom…" Jason fumbled.

"My mother has rarely told me anything about the battle here," Kira said, trying to relax. "Aunt Bev says…she can't."

"Oh, yeah," Jason said. "Post-traumatic stress."

"What?"

"PTS. It afflicts a lot of people who've endured serious stress, like fighting a battle like the one here."

"How can you know that's what she has?" Kira demanded, feeling guilty. Had she been resenting her mother for some sort of trauma her mother was still suffering from?

"I don't know for certain," Jason admitted. "But it sounds like it. It's another form of injury in combat. It doesn't show, but it's sort of a wound. Not to the body, but to the person inside."

She didn't answer, gazing ahead to where the bulk of a massive wall rose against the dark of the night. The last wall defending Dorcastle. The sight tore at her, since that wall had long represented everything that she resented about her mother, loved about her mother, and did not understand about her. Had she finally learned at least a little more? And her mother had reached out earlier, telling Kira more about her namesake Sergeant Kira. "Do you want to see it?"

Jason looked at Kira and around him. "See what?"

"Mother's statue. It's up on the wall. That one."

"That's the last wall they were defending? Are you okay with show-ing me that?"

"Yes, I am. And don't say okay." Kira walked to the stairs leading upward, trying once again to imagine the soldiers racing up these steps almost twenty years ago. Soldiers already exhausted from a long struggle, fighting without hope to hold the last barrier standing between victory for the Imperials and the Great Guilds.

Kira and Jason reached the broad walkway at the top of the wall, its dimensions matching the width of the wall itself, the stone parapet facing toward the water marred by numerous chips and other scars from the impact of projectiles.

Just a few steps down, someone seemed to be standing sentry, only the absolute lack of motion revealing that it was not a real person. "There it is," Kira said, pointing. "They put the statue where Mother was when she rallied the defenders to throw back the last Imperial assault."

Jason walked toward the statue, but almost tripped over a large, flat metal plate set into the stone. "Why is that there?"

Kira sighed. "It protects the area where my mother's blood stained the stones after she was shot."

He stared at her, then at the plate. "Not really."

"Really. There's a belief in Dorcastle, and I guess in the whole Confederation, that as long as the daughter's blood stays in the stone, this wall can never fall."

"Wow." Apparently unable to think of any other comment, Jason peered at the life-sized statue set at the battlement so it faced toward the harbor.

Kira had never forgotten any detail of that statue. Her mother, only a few years older than Kira was now, wearing her Mechanics jacket, her pistol held in one hand that was pointing toward the sea, her other fist defiantly raised to the sky, the statue's cold gaze forever confronting the vanished legions that had been broken before her.

"Mother doesn't like it," Kira said, looking into the eyes of the statue. "She says it makes it look like she was the only one holding the wall, when really she was only one of many."

"But it was because of her that they held the wall, right?" Jason asked, looking out across the darkened city.

"Mother says no, that they would have done it even without her. But everyone else says that without her the wall would have fallen, and Mother's tired army, strung out along the road, would have been hit by the legions as the leading elements reached the city. General Flyn—he commanded my mother's army—told me they might have taken serious losses and have had to fall back to Danalee."

Kira reached out to the statue, her fingers resting on the cold, hard surface of the sculpted jacket. She had once touched the real jacket worn by her mother that day, years ago when visiting the librarians on Altis to whom it had been given for safekeeping. Because she was Mari's daughter, the librarians had brought it out for her, still caked with dried blood, still bearing the hole where the bullet had punched through. Kira had almost fainted just from staring at it, knowing how close her mother had come to dying from the injury she had suffered on this spot. *You never want to talk about it, Mother. Maybe you really can't and I've been blaming you unfairly for a wound that's never healed. But how did you do it? How did you stand up here and face the Imperial legions? How did you survive such an injury even with the help Father gave you? How did you do all of the things the daughter did?*

And people think I could someday step into your shoes?

I look like you, but how can I ever be anything like you?

"Does it feel weird to you?" Jason asked, unaware of Kira's thoughts. "Knowing that your mom almost died on this spot? That her blood was right there?"

"Yeah. At first it was just weird because it was a statue of my mother, and I was six and that felt pretty strange. But then I learned the history and…" Kira shook her head. "It's one more thing I never could have done, never could do."

"Why do you say that?" Jason looked from Kira to the statue. "She looked a lot like you do now."

"Yeah. Looks. That's not the same as what's inside."

He didn't answer for a moment. "Isn't what's inside you the daughter's blood?"

She flinched as the question poked at too-familiar feelings of inadequacy. "So what?"

"If it can make this wall so strong—"

"That's just superstition, Jason! You of all people should know better!" She turned away, telling herself that her anger was fully justified. "We need to get moving."

He followed, not saying anything. On the way down the stairs, Kira's anger cooled enough for her to feel remorse over her treatment of Jason. "Mother got the Confederation to add something besides her statue. I'll show you when we get down on the street again."

She hurried them through the large tunnel formed by the passage through the wall to the gate on the other side, which stood open and unguarded in this time of peace. Once outside again, in the cleared area in front of the fortification, Kira turned and gestured toward the wall. "See? All those names, going along the wall and up it? They're the men and women who died defending the city. It took years to chisel them all." Looking at those many names made her own concerns seem very small, but also reinforced her resolve to ensure the drive that Jason protected did not fall back into the hands of Jason's mother and the others in the ship from Urth.

Jason gently ran his fingertips across some of the lowest names engraved in the stones of the wall. "That's a lot. I've seen memorials like this in other places. There's a big one on Mars to mark the first colony collapse. This kind of thing really brings home the human cost."

Kira pointed to the right and up. "You can't see it when it's this dark, but one of those names is Sergeant Kira of Dorcastle. It's up there. I'm named for her."

"So you're kind of a memorial, too?"

"I guess. For a long time all I knew was that she had died in the siege fighting next to my mother. Mother couldn't talk about it. I just finally learned a little more about Sergeant Kira." Kira paused, thinking. "It's funny, I've spent most of my life knowing I could never measure up to my mother. But I also have Sergeant Kira to measure up to. And I don't mind that. I hope I do her name proud." Something occurred to her for the first time. "Who are you named after?"

She couldn't see Jason's expression clearly in the dark, but his voice grew sharp and heated. "Nobody. The court said my mom got to name me, so she picked the least popular boy's name that year to make my dad angry."

Kira stared at him in shock. "Are you sure she really did that? That it wasn't some lie she told to hurt you?"

"I looked it up," Jason said, his words as stiff as his body language. "It was the least popular boy's name the year I was born."

"Jason, I'm so—"

"Don't say you're sorry! I don't want anyone feeling sorry for me!"

She stepped back from him. "Everything good in my life is a dig at your life, isn't it? That's why the first time we met you said you should hate me."

"Yeah."

"Why don't you?"

He didn't answer, and at first she thought he wouldn't. But Jason spoke in a rough voice. "Hating you, hating anybody else, wouldn't make my life any better. My parents think tearing other people down, tearing me down, makes them bigger. But I know it doesn't. It makes them smaller. And I am not going to be like them."

"You're not like them."

"What have I ever done to make you think that?" he demanded.

"A lot of things! All right, you're not exactly perfect. But the guy I saw helping that little boy with his math is a good person. Jason, you can make your name something to be proud of. Or you can change your name. But I think the best revenge on your mother is for people to know that Jason did something important."

He made a small sound of derision, staring up at the star-filled sky. "Yeah. Sure." His voice carried all the sullenness of the teenager she had first met.

"We should get going," Kira said, deliberately ignoring Jason's tone of voice because she knew she had inadvertently dug into an old scar.

"We need to be on the waterfront at first light so we can get a ride out of Dorcastle without risking being seen by many people. You saw how closely I resemble that statue." She started along the deserted street as it ran through the open area before the wall, heading toward where more buildings began. Jason followed, saying nothing.

They were nearly among those buildings when Kira heard the tramp of feet and the sound of some metal objects clanking against each other. "Jason! Follow me!"

She ran into the shadow of the nearest building, crouching behind the stairs at the entry. Jason had just joined her when several men and women came into sight not much more than ten lances away. They all wore stout leather armor on their chests and shoulders, and all carried short swords as well as hardwood truncheons. One also carried a pistol in a holster at his hip.

"It's a night patrol of the city watch," Kira whispered to Jason.

The patrol paused to look around the open area for any signs of trouble. Kira, still watching, held her head absolutely still to avoid giving them any movement to spot.

The leader of the patrol gazed up at the wall and saluted, speaking in a normal voice that carried easily in the quiet of the night. "All's well, daughter."

Kira felt a momentary jolt of worry that her mother was here, then realized that the patrol officer had saluted the statue atop the wall.

"What would happen if we didn't salute her one night?" another officer joked.

"I don't know, and I don't want to know," the first replied. "And you don't want the captain finding out you didn't do it. He was on that wall with her when they broke the legions, remember? If he hears you didn't respect the daughter he'll rip your hide off."

"Do you think her daughter is coming here? With that Urth kid?" a third asked.

"No telling. If we see them, we take them in. Those are our orders."

"What if the girl doesn't want to be taken in and she really is anything like her mother?"

"Then," the leader of the patrol replied, "we will all earn our pay and hopefully none of us get hurt too badly. But we do our jobs. We take them in."

"The daughter's girl wouldn't hurt cops," another said.

"I hope not. But the Urth boy is another matter. We don't take any chances with him."

"Why's the daughter's girl running away with him? Something doesn't fit."

"Maybe he took her hostage. I don't know. Nobody else does, either. That's why we take her and him in if we see them. And if he makes any false moves, we take him down any way we need to before he can hurt us or the daughter's girl."

Kira gritted her teeth. It was easy to fight bad people trying to do bad things, but what about good people trying to do something bad because they thought it was good? How could she hurt any of those police if they confronted her and Jason? But if the police were poised to hurt Jason at the slightest sign of trouble, how could she prevent him from being hurt or killed?

The police moved on, and Kira edged closer to Jason. "Listen. If we get trapped by the police or any other authorities here, I will bluff them as long as I can while you run. Don't hesitate when that happens. Just go, as fast as you can, and keep trying to hide."

"I can't do that," Jason said. She couldn't see his expression well in the dark, but he still sounded sullen.

"Jason, if the police pick you up, people will be talking about that on far-talkers and your mother will find you."

"I'm just supposed to run away and leave you to face everything alone?"

Kira sighed. "Jason, you heard them, didn't you? They think you're a threat. They might—"

"I thought we needed to get to the harbor before dawn."

She stood up, recognizing that continuing to argue would be futile. "Do what I said."

He didn't answer, following silently as Kira moved quickly along side streets, listening for more police and trying to avoid encounters with the few other people out in these hours before dawn.

As they passed the third wall from the water, Kira looked upwards. Somewhere on that wall, Sergeant Kira had died. She wondered what the namesake she had never met would think of her.

Was it just a coincidence that a light breeze chose that moment to play with her hair?

She pushed the pace, Jason doggedly keeping up with her even though she heard occasional grumbles under his breath. But it was getting close to dawn by the time Kira poked her head cautiously around the corner of a building on the waterfront to examine one of the piers where outgoing ships sold passenger tickets. "Wait here," she whispered to Jason, before dashing across the street.

The big board where sailings and prices were posted was easy to find, but so was a large notice also posted on it. Made of oddly glossy paper, it showed a picture of Jason that must be a "photo" like the old ones the librarians had. Apparently, despite Jason's shock at the use of actual paper, the Urth ship was capable of printing those notices. She peered closely at the notice, trying to see how it had been printed. Whatever method had been used, nothing on it looked like it had been done by hand. Kira looked down the pier, seeing other copies of the notice posted at the booths where the tickets were actually sold.

She ran back to Jason and shook her head. "They have pictures of you posted. I was going to have you buy the tickets again, but they'd be certain to recognize you. And they'd be certain to recognize me."

"So we can't get tickets? The only way to get them is in person?"

"We couldn't exactly preorder tickets through an agent!" Kira rubbed her eyes, tired and trying not to become frantic. Dawn was getting nearer. Time was running out, and she didn't have a plan. "Let's go down and check the other piers. Maybe we can buy passage on a cargo ship. There are going to be workers starting to show up very soon and we have to avoid being seen clearly by them."

They darted from shadow to shadow, street to street, Kira trying to keep to places where the shadows loomed like solid pools of black. She strained her senses for signs of danger, hearing the skitterings of rats and once jumping in alarm when a wharf cat darted past. But someone must have spotted them despite Kira's precautions. They had just reached the warehouses fronting on the cargo piers when three figures emerged out of the night as if they had been Mage creatures summoned into existence. Kira froze in mid-step, staring at the old-model Mechanics Guild revolver in one of the men's hands. The other man and a woman held daggers. Even in the dimness Kira could see that the hard faces of the three held no trace of mercy.

The man with the revolver jerked the barrel toward the alley entrance the three had come out of. "In there."

Kira judged her chances and didn't like the odds. Her pistol was still in its holster, since anyone seeing her walking around the city with a weapon in hand would have notified the police for sure. In the time it would take her to reach into her jacket and draw the pistol, the man with the revolver could fire several shots.

If it looks like you don't have a chance, don't throw your life away. Wait until they make a mistake, Aunt Bev had advised Kira.

She hoped the three were only thieves. "You can have our money."

"We'll take the money, and a lot more besides," the man remarked with a derisive laugh. "What are you worth? We already know the boy can earn us a big reward. But how much will the daughter pay to get you back?"

"Maybe," Kira said, trying to keep her voice level, "you should be worrying about what the daughter will do to anyone who hurts her daughter."

"Ain't planning to hurt you, girl," the man said. "Not much, anyway." He grinned unpleasantly. "You ever had a real man before?"

"A real man wouldn't be asking that question," Kira said, not having to feign the contempt in her voice.

"You'll see otherwise!"

"Vac," the woman warned. "We can't waste time."

Jason finally spoke, his voice that of the sullen teen again but with a quavering undercurrent of fear. "You're...you're not going to hurt me, are you?"

Kira was surprised that her foremost emotion at that moment was disappointment.

"No, boy, not as long as you're good," the man said with a scornful laugh. "Both of you, in the alley."

Kira, with the revolver pointed at her, began moving slowly toward the alley, watching for any opportunity, her body tense, adrenaline urging action, any action, while her mind commanded patience.

Jason followed Kira, slouching along with a defeated posture. What had happened to him? Had everything good she had seen of Jason since they left her home been an act?

The man with the pistol kept close enough to Kira to threaten her but far enough off to stay out of her reach. None of the three appeared worried about Jason, who was acting and sounding thoroughly cowed.

Jason suddenly moved, throwing himself at the man with the revolver. They stumbled sideways, hitting the wall on one side of the alley. The revolver went off as the man's finger jerked on the trigger, the bullet slamming into a pile of trash nearby. Both Jason and the man fell, Jason wrestling with him for control of the weapon.

The second man was just turning to lunge at Jason with his dagger when Kira exploded into motion. Her body followed years of training in self-defense. She darted forward and planted a hard punch from the waist in his kidney, causing him to reel back, staggering with pain. Aware of the remaining threat, Kira pivoted as the woman rushed in, leg lashing out with a kick that narrowly avoided the woman's dagger slash. The kick caught the woman square in the gut, doubling her over. Kira stepped closer, slamming her stiffened palm against the side of the woman's head, which snapped to one side as the woman fell.

The man with the dagger had managed to straighten and was coming at her this time, moving awkwardly. Kira dodged to one side, twisting around to slam a kick against the man's back as he stumbled past. The kick drove him against the other wall of the alley hard enough to knock him out.

As the second man dropped unconscious, Kira spun toward the first man and Jason. The man, substantially out-weighing Jason and clearly stronger, had twisted around on top and was gradually forcing down Jason's arms. Jason had a grip on the revolver but was losing the battle to control it.

Kira stepped closer and lashed out with a furious kick that connected with the side of the man's head, knocking him off Jason. He tried to stagger to his feet, but Kira slammed another kick into his head that hurled him against one side of the alley, the revolver flying unheeded from his hand.

"Are you all right?" Kira gasped as she pulled Jason to his feet.

"Yeah," Jason said, breathing heavily and staring at the three unconscious bodies. "You're really dangerous. Do you know that?"

"It runs in the family. That was an act? Sounding frightened and all?"

"Yeah. I learned a long time ago that being underestimated is my best weapon." He seemed to be slightly in shock, staring at her. "They would have killed you."

"Probably not," Kira said. "But they would have hurt me. I owe you." She heard the rap of hardwood clubs against stone streets. "The police heard that shot. They'll be converging on this spot. We have to run."

Jason still seemed dazed so she tugged him into motion, straight across the street to the warehouses on the waterfront. "Where are we going?" Jason asked. "What's that noise?"

"We're going to hide in that warehouse," Kira said. "The noise is police using their clubs to rap out a simple code and exchange information with other police in the area."

"They communicate over distance by using wooden clubs?" Jason seemed impressed again.

"Yeah, guy who came from Urth in a big silver bubble ship." She knelt by the door into the warehouse. "Oh, sweet, this is an easy one."

"What do I do?"

"Try to look like a wall." Kira worked frantically, knowing that she had only seconds to pick the lock. The welcome click came and she pulled it open. "Inside."

She shoved him in first, sliding through after and closing the door. She caught a glimpse of a pair of patrol officers running down the street, but neither seemed to be looking toward the warehouse.

Closing the door, Kira beckoned to Jason and wove her way through the barrels and crates crowding the warehouse. She kept going until they reached the large doors giving access to the quay.

Someone was talking on the other side of the closed door leading to the water. "If they shut the street down we won't be able to get our workers in here. You'll have to wait."

A gruff woman's voice answered. "We have to make the tide or lose most of a day."

"We can't load you without workers! If the police seal off the street because of whatever caused that gunshot *The Son of Taris* will have to wait just like everybody else."

The Son of Taris must be a ship, Kira realized. One eager to sail. She ran from crate to crate, looking for any marked with that name.

There. Several crates, one of them more than a lance-length wide and about as deep. "Here, Jason. This crate is our ticket out of Dorcastle. The shipping label says it's a big metal casting so there should be a lot of packing in there. Help me get it open."

She grabbed one of the pry bars left leaning against another crate and passed a second one to Jason. The argument outside was continuing, more voices joining in, while sound from the street was growing in volume as more police arrived and excited crowds of workers gathered. Kira could only pray that whatever noise she and Jason made breaking into the crate would be masked.

Kira levered the pry bar, Jason helping with his, the top of the crate rising with a protesting squeal from the nails holding it shut. Kira waited, but the argument outside continued with no sign the noise had been noticed.

She looked inside. A large, heavy casting. Packing material filled up the volume left empty inside the crate. Despite her nerves screaming for her to act as quickly as possible, Kira took a moment to study the inside of the crate, then yanked out some of the packing material on one side. "Can you fit in there?"

Jason grimaced, but squeezed himself inside, half-curled around the casting. Kira shoved a bit of the packing back inside to cushion him, then yanked out more on the other side of the casting to fit her. She ran back into the warehouse a ways with an armful of the discarded packing material, tossing it into a dark spot between two stacks of crates, then retraced her steps.

And as she stared at the Kira-sized rat's nest she had made within the crate, she hesitated, unable to move. This was quite likely a life and decision. She hadn't thought things through because there was no time for that. Did she dare trust her instincts? She wasn't her mother. She was the person who looked like her mother.

Kira glanced over at Jason, who was looking back at her, waiting for their next move. He trusted her. Should she repay that trust by leaping into the dark?

What made you decide to save Father the first time you met him? Kira had asked her mother years before.

Her mother had spoken slowly, as if wanting to make certain that Kira remembered every word. *I had to make a decision, and not making a decision would've been a decision to leave him to his fate. I couldn't do that. So I decided to save him, and he followed me, I don't know why, and because we kept moving we managed to survive.*

Not making a decision was making a decision not to move. A decision to fail. Kira inhaled deeply, nerved herself, and wriggled into the nest in the crate, using one hand to pull the top of the crate back into place from the inside. When she got far enough inside, Jason was able to grab the top and help her.

They matched up the nails to the holes, then pulled as well as they could from the inside. "That's not tight," Jason whispered to her frantically.

"I know!" Kira whispered back. "Shhh!"

She heard the big door nearest the crate opening, and footsteps approaching.

"This is the cargo for those swabs on the *Taris*. Get it moved so we can get them off our backs."

"Hey, this one's damaged." Kira waited with a sinking heart as she heard the two workers running their hands over the top of the crate.

"It's just a little loose. Pound it tight and they'll never know."

Blows from a pry bar on the cover of the crate echoed painfully inside it, and soon thereafter the crate jerked as it was being moved out onto the pier to be loaded into *The Son of Taris*. Sunlight formed tiny threads of brightness along the seams between the planks making up the crate. Kira caught a clear whiff of the sea, grateful that the openings in the seams of the crate were large enough to admit a little air.

The dock workers walked into the warehouse to get more cargo. Kira heard the tiniest whisper from Jason. "Now what?"

"We wait," she breathed in reply.

"And then? What will happen once we're on that ship?"

What would her mother do? Her father had told her the answer to that. "We'll improvise."

"*Improvise?*"

"Do you have a better plan?"

The workers returned and fitted tackle to the crate. Kira felt it swinging upward and over, her stomach lurching at the motion. After hanging for a short time that felt much longer, the crate began lowering to the shouts of those outside. The light leaking in through the small gaps in the boards vanished as the crate entered the hold of *The Son of Taris*.

Kira lay in the crate, fighting fear of being in the dark, confined space, wondering if the air inside the crate was growing fouler without a breeze to drive fresh air inside, and wondering what would happen next. Had she just doomed herself and Jason?

CHAPTER NINE

Flying on a Roc should have been terrifying. Mari didn't know why it wasn't. After all, not only was she high in the air, so high that houses looked like small toys, but as a Mechanic she knew that it was physically impossible for something like Rocs to fly. The fact that the Mages insisted the Rocs weren't real birds, that they were imaginary, shouldn't have been any comfort. But then, Mages insisted that the entire world and everything in it was imaginary, illusions created by people. And there was something immensely comforting in the strength of the Roc beneath her. She lay along the upper back, the vast wings stretched out on either side, feeling the Roc's muscles moving beneath a cushion of feathers which were each large enough to overtop Mari's height if stood on end. Mage Saburo sat in front of Mari, just behind the Roc's neck. Hunter, Saburo called his Roc. Among the other changes since the fall of the Great Guilds, Mages who created Rocs were now allowed to name the creatures they created.

A flight without stops all the way from Tiaesun to Danalee was a lot to expect from Rocs, but both Mage Saburo and Mage Alber insisted that their birds could do it. Neither one would have admitted to basing their assessment on their pride in their birds, because pride was an emotion they would not admit to, but Alain had reassured Mari that if the Rocs faltered the Mages would admit to error and bring them to ground short of Danalee.

Looking over to the side, Mari saw the other Roc with Alain lying on its back. Alain looked back at her and raised one arm, waving in a pattern she recognized. The unseen drone of the Urth people was still following them, pacing the Rocs somewhere behind. Mari bit down a curse of disappointment. She had been hoping that the Rocs would be something the Urth people couldn't match, a means to counter the Urth ship without directly confronting them.

She lay there, suspended between the world below and the stars above, but her thoughts kept going to somewhere ahead of her, to wherever Kira was now. The daughter was the most powerful person in the world, but even the daughter could do nothing but hope that her own daughter was all right, was using every skill and trick taught her, and above all was trusting in herself enough to make the right decisions. It had been painful seeing how little Kira thought of herself, a problem that had gotten worse in recent years, but no matter what Mari and Alain tried Kira continued to measure herself against some impossible standard that she thought represented her mother's abilities.

And her mother, all too human and all too aware of her own failings, had found the words that might explain remained locked inside of her. Unable to do more, she could only hope that Kira would finally believe in her own competence and inner strength. If that inner strength really was there, if Kira didn't bear some internal flaw that would cause her to crack under pressure. .Mari believed in her daughter, but she knew that no one could be sure of the strength of their own inner self until tested. She had hoped that Kira would never have to face such a test, but fate had had other plans.

After an all-night flight, the morning was well along by the time Danalee came into view. The two Rocs winged their way over the city before beginning a spiraling descent toward an open square inside Danalee, not far from where Alli and Calu lived and worked

As Hunter came to a halt and settled down, Mari slid off the Roc, feeling gratitude that her feet were resting on solid ground again.

"Elder," Mage Saburo said, "this one has learned."

Mages volunteering information was unusual, even Mages as familiar to Mari as Saburo. "What is it?"

"Hunter tells me the thing followed. Hunter can feel the thing. Hunter wants to know if the thing is prey."

"The thing?" Mari looked to Alain as he walked up. "Is Hunter talking about the drone from the Urth ship?"

"The Roc must be speaking of that," Alain said. "How does Hunter feel the thing, Mage Saburo?"

"The wind," Saburo said. "The thing cannot be seen, but Hunter feels the thing move the wind and the wind move around it. Hunter does not…like the thing."

Mari nodded. "That's good to know. Mage Saburo, we might need to ask Hunter to strike the thing. It is well that you told this one. Hunter is a mighty Roc."

They saw Alli and Calu and began walking toward them. "You have learned how to speak to Mages in ways that mean the most to Mages," Alain commented to Mari.

"And for the Mages who create Rocs, that means saying nice things about their imaginary, giant birds," Mari replied. "Even though the first Roc I met tried to kill me."

"That was a long time ago."

"Not long enough," Mari said. "Hey, Alli. Anything new?"

She shook her head, uncharacteristically subdued. "Just more and more people coming out of the woodwork claiming to have seen those kids."

"Those kids? You mean Kira and Jason?"

"Yeah."

"Alli, what's the matter?" Mari asked, ignoring Calu making warning gestures behind Alli.

"What's the matter? I'll tell you what's the matter. The next time your daughter points a weapon at one of my sons I'm going to give her a lesson that even a kid of yours will remember!"

Mari, worn out from the long flight, fought down an urge to respond with equal heat. "I understand why you're unhappy, Alli—"

"*Unhappy?*"

"Angry. But you know Kira wouldn't have done it unless—"

"*Unless?* There is no excuse—!"

"Shut it, Alli!" Mari growled, day after day of frustrations and worries boiling over. "I am trying to save not one world this time but two! My daughter is out there where every enemy I've made can get at her, in the company of a boy whose bad attitude is the only characteristic that stood out, while people with weapons far beyond what we have become increasingly threatening! Can we please put off this discussion until I am only dealing with one world's worth of potential warfare?"

Alli was about to fire back, her expression furious, when Calu stepped between them. "Alli, Mari, please. You two have been best friends for almost all your lives. Our kids are best friends. And I am really scared to be standing between you two right now but I'm going to stay here until you both cool down."

"You are an idiot," Alli grumbled.

"I love you, too, dear."

"All right. Truce, Mari."

"Truce," Mari agreed. "I'm sorry, Alli. Kira must have been scared, but that's no excuse."

"She could have done worse," Alli conceded. "Gari noticed that when she laid down on him she kept her finger straight along the guard instead of on the trigger. At least she had the sense to do that so she wouldn't accidentally fire without even knowing who she was aiming at!"

"She had a good teacher," Mari said.

"Oh, so it's my fault!" Alli pushed Calu aside and embraced Mari. "I'm sorry, too, your daughterness. I know you're under a lot of pressure and scared for Kira."

The term "daughterness" usually aggravated Mari, but this time she took it only as a sign of affection. "Thanks. Is anything going on besides the people reporting sightings?"

"Several of those drone things wandering around," Calu said.

"Here, along the rail line to the east, and over Julesport. Gari didn't tell anyone besides us about seeing Kira and the boy sneak onto that freight, but the picked lock and the open door on one of the freight cars attracted a lot of attention, especially since other people saw them entering the rail yard. How did Kira learn to pick locks?"

"I did not teach her," Alain said.

"It's a family tradition," Mari said. "Passed on from mother to daughter for two generations now."

"Why aren't you worried about that, Mari?" Calu said. "The Urth people are searching Julesport, and while the great majority of Confederation citizens are refusing to act against your daughter, enough are joining in for the promised reward or because they hate you to make things ugly. Plus the government feels obligated to send out search teams to keep the Urth people from blaming them, and because they're worried about Kira, so there are also ground soldiers and cavalry scouring the areas east of here."

Alli shook her head in admiration as she looked at Mari. "You're not worried because Kira didn't go toward Julesport, did she?"

"I don't think so," Mari said. "She left too many clues that she was going there. She has had very good teachers."

"Kira went north? She's going to have an awful time getting through Dorcastle without being recognized," Calu said. "Your twin on the wall there means everyone in Dorcastle knows exactly what you look like."

"My twin on the wall looks even more like Kira than I do, since the twin never ages," Mari said.

"I still think we should call the twin Mara," Alli remarked.

"Not funny."

"Neither is this." Calu offered a sheet of paper.

Mari took it, frowning at the lifelike image of the Urth boy. "The Urth people remembered what paper is. That's Jason. And the text repeats the offer of a reward for finding him. Did you read this? The reward is for 'return of the boy.' Not 'safe return' or 'unharmed.' How could the Urth people have been so careless in their wording?"

"Maybe they weren't careless," Calu said. "Maybe they want the boy back more than they want him safe."

"You remember the Senior Mechanics we had to deal with," Alli said. "They managed to rationalize doing just about anything, because so many of them never questioned their own motives."

"How many of these notices are there?" Mari asked.

"The Urth drone dropped hundreds over this city. They're probably doing the same elsewhere."

"Hopefully not in Dorcastle yet. Excuse me. Here come the city leaders. I need to—"

"Lady!" called out one the city officials hurrying toward them. "The ship from Urth! It has come to rest in a field just outside of Danalee!"

"Our plan is working," Alain said. "The attention of the Urth people remains on us."

"Great. I hope it's helping Kira."

By the time Mari reached the field where the Urth ship had come to rest, troops were pouring in to control a large crowd that was getting larger by the minute. As she walked past the crowd, Mari heard the same old cries of relief, the same cheers, the same confidence that the daughter would handle this problem. And she felt the same old determination to do her best, tied to the same old feelings that these people should not have so much faith in such a fallible person as her.

She and Alain were still walking up to the ship when the opening appeared in its side and Talese Groveen descended the ramp to confront them. To Mari's surprise, the woman from Urth was smiling in welcome, her attitude that of someone greeting a friend. "I'm glad that you're here, Lady Mari."

Mari smiled in return despite the tingling of her nerves as she wondered what Talese Groveen was up to. "Welcome. What brings you to Danalee?"

"We should be able to help your search. I know how concerned you are about the fate of your daughter and deeply regret any hasty actions that might have contributed to her facing such serious danger."

"Thank you," Mari said.

Groveen looked toward the city. "You came here by an interesting means of transport. Would it be possible for one of the Mages who, uh, create such things to demonstrate for us?"

Mari kept her smile in place. So Talese Groveen wanted an opportunity to "scan" more Mages doing their spells, probably in the hope of being able to duplicate the data on the drive that Jason had taken. "I'm sorry, but those Mages who brought us here on their Rocs are exhausted. It will be some time before they are recovered."

"Oh. Unfortunate. Perhaps later." Groveen's expression shifted to earnest sympathy. "We have monitored some transmissions indicating how serious the danger to your daughter is. There is a way we can assist in the search for her far more efficiently and effectively, and it requires only the tiniest assistance from yourself."

"What is that?" Mari asked.

"If you agreed to provide us with a genetic sample, we could use that to help spot your daughter's location. Our drones could be provided with the necessary biometric data. I know you are worried about her safety and would want to do everything possible to help locate her. It would be terrible if something awful happened to your little girl because we were unable to locate her in time."

Tired and worried, Mari hesitated. She knew this was a transparent attempt to gain the genetic material from her that the people from Urth wanted, but as far as she knew it would also help in the search.

She didn't trust Talese Groveen at all, but the woman's self-interest lay in finding Kira because that would mean finding her son and the device he had taken.

Millions of lives. But those were abstract, a possibility in the future, in a place very far from here. One life was in real peril here, the life of her only surviving child. Mari knew how much she had given to this world, how much she had risked and lost. Was it too much for a mother to want in return the safety of her girl?

Alain was beside her, leaning close, his voice a bare murmur. "What would Kira want? She is our daughter. What would you want her to do if your roles were reversed?"

Mari looked down, breathing slowly. "My Mage, you know I'm only human. Not the perfect, wonderful daughter of Jules that everyone else wants to see. And you know what I would want in Kira's place, because I have made decisions like that, no matter how much they hurt. Do you think Kira would forgive me if the worst happens and we someday meet again in the dream beyond this that you speak of?"

"Kira is our daughter. She would forgive and understand. Mari, we want her to believe in herself. That means we must also believe in her, and show that by our actions as well as our words. And lest you doubt," Alain added, enough pain entering his voice that Mari could hear it clearly, "I do not wish to make this decision. I do not want Kira harmed. But we must believe in her, or doom her to the insignificance she already fears is her fate."

Mari nodded, knowing that if something happened to Kira her next words would forever echo with inner guilt. She looked at the woman from Urth again. "I am sorry, but that is not possible."

"Not possible?" Talese Groveen sounded puzzled.

"I am aware of why you want my genetic material. Using the danger to my daughter as leverage to pry that from me is cruel."

"How could you…?" The Urth woman's eyes narrowed, her outward appearance of sympathy and friendship vanishing. "My son told you something? Whatever he told you, he lied."

"As I have told you," Alain said, "Mages can see when someone speaks the truth, as your son did. And when someone does not speak the truth."

"You're clearly withholding information," Talese Groveen said, ignoring the clear implication of Alain's last statement. "Where is my son?"

"We're looking for him," Mari said. "Surely you've seen the extent of the search activity underway."

"The *appearance* of search activity, perhaps. Why haven't you broadcast an order to your daughter to turn in herself and my son to the nearest authorities?"

"Your ship has been interfering with my attempts to use far-talkers," Mari replied. "I'm also still trying to understand why my daughter would have left with your son," she added.

"Are you really that naïve?" Talese Groveen asked.

"Not at all," Mari said, trying not to lose her temper again. "Because I know and trust my daughter. She's not the problem, in any event. We wouldn't be facing this if you hadn't lost your son to begin with. Why is your son trying to hide from you?"

Groveen waved a dismissive hand. "Adolescent rebellion. Mindless, unthinking, hormonally driven attempts to circumvent adult authority."

"Do you often refer to your son as mindless and unthinking?" Alain asked.

"When it fits! I believe in holding people accountable for their actions and for their failures. You would do well to remember that, especially since my patience is rapidly running out."

"Calling someone mindless does not hold them accountable," Alain said in impassive tones. "It excuses their failures by assuming they can do no better if given responsibility and advice. If your son is as incapable as you suggest, even the best efforts of our daughter could not have kept them from being found before now."

"Blaming your failures on my son's efforts? Pitiful. I understand he was on a train but somehow no one intercepted him at the train's stop!"

"He and Kira were not aboard when the train arrived," Mari said. "They must have jumped from the train while it was moving."

"You do think I'm a fool! My son? Jump from a moving train? Something that requires skill and bravery? He couldn't do anything like that, not even with your daughter goading him on, doubtless feeding his hopes of physical reward—"

"Did you actually just say that?" Mari's voice was sharp enough to halt Talese Groveen's words. "Is Urth really such a backward place that they believe girls exist solely to use their bodies to tempt boys?"

"Of course not!" Groveen insisted. "But in this case—"

"If you knew as much as you think you do, then you'd know that I was accused of doing the same thing to Alain when we had first met! I am not sympathetic to charges that my daughter is trying to seduce your son!" Mari took a moment to calm herself. "I repeat that we are trying to ensure the safety of my daughter and your son, and that any actions you take are likely to further imperil both of them. I request that you refrain from further interference in the affairs of this world."

The Urth woman's eyes went to the space before her face, her hands moving before her. "I have been very patient. There are laws governing these situations. If you have not produced my son by this time tomorrow, I will be forced to initiate active measures in defense of his life and the security of the other citizens with me."

Active measures. That sounded bad, the sort of phrase used to cloak actions that no one wanted to openly talk about. "I ask again," Mari said, "that you refrain from actions that might worsen the situation and further increase the risk to your son."

"You have until this time tomorrow," Talese Groveen repeated. She turned and walked imperiously back into the ship from Urth. The opening vanished, leaving Mari and the others facing a solid surface, their distorted reflections visible amid the silvery sheen.

Mari turned away from it. All around, people were looking at her. Waiting for her to lead them. She felt incredibly tired.

Calu stepped close. "A message Mage just passed word to us. Things have been happening in Dorcastle."

"What things?" Mari said. "Is Kira all right?"

"We don't know."

Kira thought the air inside the crate was getting worse, but couldn't be sure. She did know that if there wasn't enough air getting in, she would get confused and then pass out.

There had been more noise around them as the rest of the cargo was loaded, then vague noises elsewhere, shouts hard to make out clearly, and the lurch of the ship leaving the quay. The ship had shifted about as it wended its way through the harbor, then Kira felt the ship's motion change to a long, twisting roll endlessly repeated and knew that they were in the open sea.

"Kira?" Jason whispered. "What are we going to do?"

"I'm still working on that."

"How did you do what you did back in the alley? Take down those three bam bam bam?"

"Muscle memory," Kira said. "I've been taking self-defense lessons since I was five years old, and my teachers really pushed me."

"Do you think you could show me some moves?"

"Sure. When we get a chance."

Jason fell silent again. The hold was quiet except for the sounds of the sea against the ship's hull, the tromping of feet on the deck above, and the occasional skitter of what Kira was pretty certain were rats. She held out, knowing that the further they were at sea if discovered the less chance that the ship would waste time returning to port to get rid of her and Kira. Was there any way to avoid being discovered?

Kira heard someone enter the hold and walk past the crate she was in, pausing at intervals. She guessed that the cargo was being checked to be sure it wasn't shifting due to the rolls of the ship. She realized that her breathing was fast and shallow. She either needed to act now or perhaps die in this crate.

Kira rapped her fist against the inside of the crate twice, then twice again.

The footsteps stopped, then came close to her crate.

A pry bar appeared at one place near the top of the crate. Kira reached for her pistol, then stopped. *Think before you use it.* What happens if I do? I'm on a ship away from land. Am I ready to kill every person in the crew of this ship? Am I ready to kill even one of them?

She let her hand fall outside of her jacket and waited as the top of the crate was levered open by the pry bar.

A stout woman with a hard expression and the weathered skin of someone who had spent many years at sea glared at Kira and Jason. "Get out. Both of you."

Kira recognized the voice. This was the woman who had been arguing with the dock workers.

She pulled herself out of the crate, then helped Jason out. Jason gave her a questioning look and she shook her head. "Not this time," she said.

The woman looked them over, then pointed to Kira. "Your knife."

Kira pulled the knife from its sheaf and handed it over, then deliberately opened her jacket to show the pistol in its holster.

That earned her an even harder look. "You have that? Why didn't you use it?"

"Because I'm not a fool," Kira said. "I'm also not a killer."

"Hand it over."

Kira removed her shoulder holster, ensuring that the pistol was strapped into the holster, and gave it to the woman.

The woman looked Jason over again. "She's carrying all that and you have no weapons at all?"

Jason replied with a sullen shake of the head.

The first mate went through their packs quickly, then jerked a thumb to indicate which way they should go. "All right. Up on deck. We'll see what the captain wants to do with you."

Determined not to look frightened, Kira went up a steep ladder onto the deck, blinking against the bright sunlight after being in the dark for so long. *The Son of Taris* turned out to be of only moderate size and square-rigged, sails visible overhead on two masts. Steam-powered ships were becoming more common, but sailing ships similar to this still carried the great majority of seagoing trade. *The Son of Taris* could have been built at any time in the centuries that made up the history of Dematr.

Kira caught glimpses of men and women in the crew watching with curiosity as she and Jason were marched aft to where a man in a long greatcoat stood watching them grimly. "What have we here, First Mate?" he asked the woman.

"Stowaways, Captain. They were inside one of the crates we loaded at Dorcastle."

The captain gave Kira and Jason a look that measured them and did not appear to be impressed. "Was there any damage to the cargo?"

"No," Kira said. "The casting was not damaged."

"Oh? So you're a master mechanic, then, girl? Quiet until I ask a question of you!" The captain turned to the first mate.

The first mate shook her head. "They pulled out packing, but the contents of the crate were not damaged."

"Lucky for them," the captain said. "Your names?"

Kira almost sagged with relief as she realized that these sailors, making only a brief stop in Dorcastle, did not recognize her and had not seen the posted pictures of Jason. Since this ship was highly unlikely to have a far-talker aboard, the crew might have little knowledge of recent events. "I'm Kara. Kara of Minut. This is J'son of…Cape Henri."

"Cape Henri?" the captain questioned. "I've met few who even know where that is, and never anyone from near there."

"Well…I am," Jason said with a glance at Kira and a surly nod.

"Are you now? You speak oddly enough."

"The girl was carrying this," the first mate told the captain, offering the pistol in its holster.

The captain looked it over like someone examining trade goods for value. "This isn't a cheap copy out of Ringhmon. It's fine work out of Danalee, with the mark of Master Mechanic Alli herself on it. And this holster is well crafted, too, out of Tiae from the finish on the leather. Yes, there's the royal maker's mark. Where did you get both?"

"My mother gave them to me," Kira said.

"And is your mother Master Mechanic Alli?" the captain asked sarcastically. "Or perhaps the Queen of Tiae?"

"No, sir. Neither one," Kira said. She wondered what the captain would have said if she had claimed both Aunt Alli and Queen Sien as friends.

"You were wearing this when the first mate found you? Why didn't you threaten her with it?"

"She asked me the same," Kira said. "I'll give you the same answer. Because I'm not a murderer and I'm not a fool."

The captain gave her a sidelong look. "Why carry a weapon you say you'd never use, girl?"

"I didn't say I'd never use it. If she had come at me with knife or sword, I would have done what I had to. But if I had threatened her and she had called my bluff, I couldn't have killed someone for trying to protect herself."

"Bold words." The captain removed the pistol from its holster, examined it again, then suddenly tossed it to Kira. She caught it in a proper grip without thinking. "It's loaded, is it not? Make it safe."

Kira released the magazine, caught it, pulled back the slide to ensure the chamber was empty, then set the safety. "It's safe."

"Now ready it again."

She had never been one to show off, but sensing a need to impress these sailors Kira twisted the magazine in her free hand, ramming it home in the pistol, her thumb releasing the safety so that the slide could rock forward again and load a bullet. The process took only a couple of seconds, after which Kira paused, the weapon pointed up at the sky, her forefinger straight alongside the trigger guard.

She heard murmuring from the watching crew behind her.

"Safe it again." The captain held out his hand, palm up.

Kira removed the magazine, emptied the chamber, and set the safety again, then returned both clip and pistol to the captain.

"You just passed two tests, girl," the captain said. "You showed that you truly know how to use that weapon, and you showed that you know when not to use it. Anything else?" the captain asked the first mate.

"Her knife," the first mate said, handing it to the captain.

The captain looked it over, a stern frown forming on his stony face. "Where did you get this?"

"Also a gift from my mother," Kira said.

"Your mother is a very generous soul, it seems. A sailor's knife. With the mark of the fellowship on it. Where does this mother of yours sail, girl?"

"She hasn't sailed for a long time," Kira said, realizing the reason for the captain's suspicion. The fellowship was the name pirates called themselves, a very loose and very ill defined grouping that nonetheless had certain shared traditions. One of those traditions honored Jules, revered by all sailors and the most famous pirate in the history of the world, as well as being an ancestor of Kira's mother, and Kira herself. "When she did, it was in the Umbari."

"The Umbari? Does she hail from Syndar?"

"No!"

The vehemence of Kira's reply produced a brief, grim smile from the captain, one that quickly vanished as he looked at her. "And what of you? You sneak aboard my ship and we find a knife on you with the mark. Is it fellowship business you're on?"

"No," Kira said. "I have no ties to the fellowship. My mother gave me that knife. That's as far as it goes. And she only preyed on ships of the Empire, Syndar, and the Great Guilds."

"The Great Guilds? So it was twenty years ago that your mother sailed in the Umbari?" the first mate demanded.

"Yes," Kira said. "With the daughter's ships."

"What ship did she sail on?" the captain asked.

"The *Pride*. With Captain Banda." Which was true enough, though in fact Captain Banda had served under Mari's command.

The captain nodded, his expression staying stern. "You have a good story, and if your mother sailed with Banda on the *Pride* you have reason for pride yourself. But if I get any hint that you're pursuing the work of the fellowship, you'll be over the side and greeting the fishes no matter how far we are from land. *The Son of Taris* is an honest ship."

"I understand," Kira said. "We've broken no laws, and intend breaking no laws."

"You've broken a law by stowing away on my ship, girl! Your mother should have told you that when she was handing out such grand toys to you!" The captain's frown shifted to Jason, who Kira unhappily realized when confronted with an authority figure had shifted back into sullenness. "And what of you?"

"I'm with her," Jason mumbled.

The captain shook his head as he looked at Jason. "I am a merciful man, so you two won't be going over the side to take your chances with the sea. Nor will you be locked below and handed over to the authorities at the next port where we make call. I will give you two the chance to earn your passage with honest labor. Do that, and you'll be free to leave at the next port. Oh, one thing more." The captain gave Kira and Jason another stern look. "Whatever else you two are up to, you're both clearly below legal age. While you're on this ship you'll keep your hands and your bodies off each other."

Kira felt her face heating up. "We're not like that."

"See you prove it. First Mate! Take these two in hand and see what you can do with them."

"I'll make sailors of these two," the first mate said, her smile and the tone of her voice nearly making Kira shiver with worry.

"Them?" the captain questioned. "Five crowns you can't."

"Done. Five crowns I can." The first mate smiled at Mari and Jason again. "Shall we begin?"

The first mate walked back and forth a few times, studying Kira and Jason. "You'll need something suitable for work." She pointed forward. "Go."

To Kira's relief, Jason didn't balk but went along without protest, inside an open hatch and down a short ladder to a compartment near the bow lined with bunks. The first mate went to a chest, opened it and began pulling out shirts and trousers similar to those worn by the crew. She tossed one outfit to Kira and another to Jason. "Out of those land clothes and into working gear. Now."

Kira stared at the first mate and pointed at Jason. "Not in front of him."

The first mate raised her eyebrows. "Aren't you the bashful one? We live in close quarters. Get used to it."

Jason didn't say anything, but turned his back to Kira as he began undressing. She turned away from him, grateful that he hadn't taken advantage of the situation.

Kira changed quickly, the heavy, coarse material harsh against her skin. The first mate looked her and Jason over, and held out her hands. "Put all of your belongings into your packs and give them over. The captain will keep them safe until we put you off."

Kira saw no sign of deception in the first mate, so she did as ordered.

The first mate pointed to Jason and the drive from the ship he still had. "All of your belongings," she repeated. "What's that around your neck?"

CHAPTER TEN

Jason maintained a sullen silence, but to Kira's eyes also looked uncertain. They hadn't made up a ready lie to explain why Jason had to wear the drive around his neck, and they certainly couldn't tell the truth about it.

"Now," the first mate insisted, growing angry.

"It contains his father's ashes," Kira suddenly said, making up her explanation as she spoke. "He's oath-bound to keep them with him until he reaches his father's home for proper burial."

"Why didn't you just say that, boy?" the first mate demanded.

"I don't like to talk about my father," Jason mumbled.

"Neither do I about mine, but I'm smart enough to answer questions. I'll not separate you from it, then. The captain told you true. He is an honest man and this is an honest ship. If either one of you steal anything while you're onboard, from ship or shipmate, it'll go very hard on you. Now get back on deck."

Once on deck again, Kira stood, trying not to look nervous. She was acutely aware that Jason was still acting very much the surly teenager. Kira didn't know what was about to happen, but the smiles of anticipation she could see on the gathered crew didn't reassure her in the slightest. There were less than twenty in the crew, ranging from men and women who looked to be barely eighteen to grizzled old sailors who must have already been sailing long before Kira's mother changed the world.

The first mate looked them over again, shaking her head. "All right, then, girl, let's see what you and this boy have in you." She pointed up. "To the mast. See if you can reach the topsail."

Kira followed the gesture with a sinking sensation in her stomach. Maybe it wasn't actually that tall, but faced with climbing it Kira thought the mast seemed incredibly high, the highest sail a small patch against the sky. Someone shoved her toward ropes interwoven into squares, one end of the ropes fastened to the ship's railing and the other end to a small platform high on the mast. "Feet on the ratlines and up the shrouds, girl!"

Kira set her jaw and walked to the ropes, grateful that at least this test didn't involve personal humiliation. She made a clumsy effort of getting up on the rail and onto the ropes while the crew howled with amusement. On the other side of the ship, she saw Jason being shoved toward the identical shrouds and ratlines leading up on that side. Jason, his face set in surly lines, was taking considerably more punishment from the crew's rough-housing than Kira had.

The rope was rough, with sharp fibers sticking out randomly enough that they couldn't be avoided. Kira started up the shrouds cautiously, wincing at the pain in her hands as they gripped the horizontal ratlines. "Move it, girl!" the first mate roared, and two sailors sprang onto the ratlines behind her, racing up and past Kira in a flash, each one dealing a blow to her back as they passed. Kira tamped down her anger and moved faster, trying not to look at the deck and how far below it already was. After what seemed a long climb, she reached the platform, only to find her tormentors grinning and pointing at the smaller set of shrouds leading up the tiny platform serving the topsail.

Kira shot them an ugly look and grabbed the ropes again, pulling herself up and praying she wouldn't look down and freeze with fear. She heard shouts of derision and without thinking looked that way, seeing Jason still only halfway up the first set of ratlines and getting more blows to encourage him. Without realizing what she was doing, Kira let her eyes slide down from there to the deck.

It looked terrifyingly far away and ridiculously small against the sea. Kira felt her hands lock on the ropes as she shuddered with fear. Then a hand punched her shoulder and she looked over at one of the crew. "You're almost there, girl. Why quit now?" he asked in a rough but encouraging voice. "You afraid? Too weak for it? Too young?"

"I'll show you who's weak," Kira growled, her temper driving fear from her for the moment. She went the rest of the way up as fast as she could, reaching the top and hanging there, breathing heavily.

She heard the first mate yelling up at her. "So you made it, girl! Now come on down!"

Kira resisted the urge to yell something insulting back and instead started down, finding the process difficult in its own way. She saw Jason had made it to the first level, looking even angrier than Kira felt. But he started up the next set of ratlines as Kira went back down, already feeling tired by the time she staggered back onto the wooden planks of the deck..

The first mate smiled. "You're ready to race, girl. As soon as you win, you can rest."

"Race?" Kira asked. A sailor stood at the base of the shrouds, one foot on a ratline, grinning. "I have to beat her to the top?"

"Her or anyone else. Go."

The next hour was an agony as Kira got more and more tired, her muscles quivering with exhaustion, while the sailors swapped out often enough to stay fresh. Even though Kira got better at climbing and coming down, she couldn't beat the sailors and finally collapsed on the deck, unable even to stand. A bucket of seawater splashed over her and Kira managed to get to her feet, glaring at the first mate, who offered her another bucket with a brush in it. "Enough fun. The deck needs scrubbing. Get to it."

Grabbing the bucket and then almost collapsing under the weight, Kira stumbled past the laughing members of the crew and went to her knees. She pulled out the brush and started scrubbing, wondering how long it would take the ship to reach port and whether she would manage to avoid the temptation to murder the first mate before then. At some point she saw Jason also scrubbing, and coming in for even more abuse because of his attitude.

Kira lost all track of time, knowing nothing but the ache in her body and the pain in her hands and knees. At some point someone shoved her against the gunwale and pushed a cup into her hand. Kira drank the water automatically, and when some hard biscuit was given her chewed slowly, her stomach threatening to revolt at any time. Either the day was drawing to a close or her vision was darkening. Kira couldn't seem to focus on anything well enough to tell. "That's enough," she heard someone say. "We don't want to kill them. Get them below."

Kira was half-carried forward and down the hatch back to the crew's living area. Some hammocks had been slung and Kira was dumped into one. She passed out almost immediately.

When Kira woke she was aware of the sounds of other people sleeping in the compartment, which was now pitch-dark without even a weak lantern to provide light. Her hammock was swaying with the motion of the ship, something that would have been soothing under other circumstances. She heard shallow, pained breathing close by and cautiously extended one hand to feel another hammock. "Jason?" she whispered.

The labored breathing paused. "Yeah."

"Don't fight it. Don't act stupid. Do your best and work."

"They're crazy," Jason muttered.

"We can't beat them. We have to prove we're good enough."

He took a moment to answer. "I'm not good enough."

"Yes, you are! Jason, you can do this. Just keep trying."

"I can't."

"Yes. You. Can. I *know* you can." She was lying, actually filled with fear that Jason would collapse under the pressure, but learning from her father how to spot truth in others had also shown her how to lie in a very convincing way. It wasn't a skill she was proud of, but sometimes it came in handy. And in this case it might save Jason.

Jason took much longer to answer this time. "I'll try," he finally said.

Kira dreaded the dawn, but discovered to her relief that the ordeal of the day before had been part training and part hazing of a new recruit. Having endured and survived, she was still subject to rough treatment but wasn't run to exhaustion. Jason made an obvious attempt to act better, putting his best effort into his tasks, and after a short spasm of additional maltreatment was also permitted to work alongside the rest of the crew. They learned by doing, members of the crew usually showing them how to do something once and expecting them to pick it up immediately. Kira, who had sailed on ships before, gained a new appreciation for the work that went into the ship, from frequent trimming of sails to working the bilge pump. The height of the mast gradually grew familiar, so that she could climb all the way to the top without balking.

Kira had worked hard at times in her life, but never this hard.

Late on the second day, a passing sailor gave her backside a lingering pat. Kira's leg flashed out as the sailor walked away, planting the flat of her foot on his butt and knocking him down. The sailor came up with a snarl and rushed her, Kira ducking under his charge and then flipping him so that his back hit the deck with a wham. As the sailor got to his feet again, one hand reaching for the knife at his belt, the first mate intervened. "Enough of that. You know ship's rules, Ori. No pawing at anyone who doesn't want it. I'll remind you that this girl is underage besides, and no one better be giving cause for port police to come aboard this ship looking for those who messed with a kid."

Ori nodded. "Sorry."

"Shake on it and be done."

Kira and the sailor shook hands, he eyeing her with respect. "How'd you do that, girl? Dump me on the deck? Can you show me?"

"I can show you," Kira said.

The winds at this time of year weren't favorable for sailing east, so the sails needed trimming frequently as *The Son of Taris* beat her way east-northeast, tacking back and forth to make slow progress.

Dinner was salt pork boiled with potatoes and onions. After the physical exertions of the day, Kira wolfed it down. The rest of the crew did the same, barely pausing in their eating until bowls were empty. They ate on deck for the clean air and the room it offered. The fifteen men and women who normally made up the crew in addition to the first mate and the captain filled the crew quarters. With Kira and Jason added those crew quarters were cramped.

"Do you know any stories?" one of the sailors asked Kira as everyone relaxed. "Anything new?"

"Yeah," another said. "You've been to Tiae? Did you ever meet the daughter or hear any new stories about her?"

"No," Kira denied, worried about telling these sailors things that would reveal who she was. "I'm not much for stories."

"What about you?" the first sailor demanded of Jason, clearly not expecting much.

Jason looked back at the sailor, then around at the rest of the crew. "You mean, like, some epic or something?"

"Whatever you got, if it's new. We've all heard each other's stories until we can tell 'em all by memory."

Jason glanced at Kira, who nodded to him, curious to know what he would do.

"All right," Jason said. "Have you guys ever heard of a sailor named Odysseus?"

"Funny name. Where from?"

"Uh, Ithaca. It was an island, in a sea a lot like the Sea of Bakre. This is a story they tell where I come from, a really old story, about a place like this only different. Odysseus had brought ships and soldiers to fight in a war that took ten years…"

Kira listened with growing admiration as Jason spun a story about strange islands with strange creatures, a bag that held the winds, and a sailor trying to get home. As he spoke, he grew more energetic, making gestures and acting out the story of galleys with white wings sailing the wine-dark sea. The crew listened raptly, not interrupting until Jason finally stopped after Odysseus reached home and killed all the men who had been trying to steal his home and his wife.

The applause that followed made Jason blink with disbelief.

"Where did you hear the like of that?" a sailor asked admiringly. "Did you make it up yourself?"

"No," Jason denied. "A guy named Homer did, a long time ago."

"Do you know more?" another of the crew asked eagerly.

"Yeah. There are a lot more."

"Tomorrow night, then," the first mate said. No one had noticed her stopping to listen along with the others. "It's time to trim the sails, and then you'd all best rest because you'll be doing it again at least twice before dawn."

Everyone groaned as they got up and headed for the shrouds.

"I don't get it," Jason whispered to Kira as they climbed. "They… they seem to like me."

"You're a good storyteller," Kira told him in a low voice. "And you told them a great story. They respect that."

"But they hated me before."

"No, they didn't respect you," Kira said. "Carry your weight, and you'll be accepted as one of them. Go beyond that, prove they can count on you, and they'll respect you. Keep working hard, keeping showing them the Jason they listened to tonight, and you'll be fine. Why didn't you ever tell me that you're a storyteller?"

"I'm not," Jason protested. "All I did was tell them a story that someone else came up with."

"But you did it really well. They wouldn't have listened if you had done a bad job of it."

They got the sails trimmed and went below to the dark crew quarters. Kira fell asleep almost instantly, but awoke when the first mate called for everyone about midnight.

She was worn out. But she felt good. None of them knew who her mother was, but she was working well enough to fit in.

Her mother. Kira wondered what was happening back on land.

Dorcastle.

Mari had been back to the city every year since the great siege. The only anniversary she had missed had been soon after the death of her son Danel, whose namesake had fallen at Dorcastle. Every other time she had held herself together through the commemorations, speaking with the surviving veterans of the battle, paying respects to the dead. Every time she had been a wreck afterwards, her sleep haunted by visions of fire and dead comrades.

The siege had ended nearly twenty years ago. It still raged inside her. She wasn't alone in that. Even lighthearted Alli would get moody around the anniversary of the battle at Pacta Servanda where she had helped smash the Syndari attack, and Calu never wanted to visit the spot where Mari had fallen at Dorcastle.

If only there were a way to explain it to Kira.

So many times had Kira confronted her after the anniversaries, tears running down her face. "Why do you go, Mother?"

The only words Mari had ever been able to come up with were never enough. "I go for the living, and I go for the dead."

"But it tears you apart!"

"Kira, if I didn't go, it would hurt far more."

Her daughter didn't understand. How could Kira comprehend that it was possible to be able to live and find joy and embrace the world while also carrying memories that sometimes were very, very hard to cope with? Especially when Mari herself found the words locked within her?

As the Rocs brought her and Alain to the city after another flight through most of the night, Mari looked down on the walls she had once helped defend and had never been able to leave.

"Where are they?" Mari asked. Any city she visited generated crowds, but Dorcastle brought out the biggest ones. They gathered to watch and to cheer, and she smiled and waved.

Captain Hagen, who had stood with Mari on the last wall and

was now Dorcastle's senior police official, indicated a barge that was moored apart from the others. She walked to it, Alain beside her, seeing a family on deck gazing at them as they approached. Mari didn't like seeing the fear on the faces of the two adults. "Good morning," she said.

The woman looked about to collapse as she stared at Mari. "It *was* her. I swear, daughter of Jules, we didn't know!"

Mari reached to hold her hands, speaking soothingly. "You are not accused of anything. You have done no wrong. I'm not angry with you."

"My wife dealt with them," the man said.

"But you stand with her," Alain commented, as if no other course of action was possible.

"Y-yes, Sir Mage. Of course I do."

"We put them off on the first landing," the woman said. "They never gave their names. They talked to each other a lot. They were in good health when they left us, Lady, I swear it!"

The young boy standing next to his father startled Mari by speaking loudly. "He was nice! He taught me math!"

Mari stared at him, kneeling to be at his level. "The boy? He taught you?"

"Because I didn't like it, but he showed me how to do it," the boy said. "He's from Oz."

"Oz?" Mari rose, looking a question at the mother.

"He did, Lady. The boy. I didn't ask it of him. He wouldn't take any payment." She held out several crowns. "This is what they paid for passage and for food and blankets. That's all of it, I swear it."

Mari folded the woman's hands over the coins. "Then you earned it fairly. You have my thanks for bringing them safely to this city. I will tell the city to release your barge and let you continue your trade. Thank you," she repeated. Mari looked back at the young boy. "He was nice?"

"Yes, Lady," the boy said.

She, Alain, and Captain Hagen talked as the barge was released to return to the docks where its cargo would be sold. "There's no reason to doubt her story," Hagen said.

"She spoke truth," Alain confirmed.

"About dawn of the day after they say they dropped off your daughter and the boy, there was a gunshot on the waterfront. When the local patrols got there they found three known criminals unconscious in an alley. The shot had come from a revolver that was lying with them."

"They shot someone?" Mari asked, suddenly frightened.

"Shot at, perhaps. There was no trace of blood in the alley or on the street outside. My people were on the scene very quickly. There would have been no time to clean up blood."

"But nothing since?" Alain asked.

"No, Sir Mage."

"You know I am but Alain to you, comrade of the wall."

Hagen smiled. "Even after so long it still feels odd to call you so, Alain."

"They didn't try to board any ships?" Mari asked.

"Not that we know of. But an even dozen ships left the harbor in the early morning before we realized they might have snuck aboard one of them. Our one steam cutter pursued, but only managed to run down a single ship, and the two were not aboard."

"Where were the others headed?"

"All over the Sea of Bakre, Mari."

"Blazes." She looked up. "Trouble is likely to follow us to Dorcastle, Captain."

"The ship from Urth?"

"Yes. They've warned us they will soon use 'active measures' if the boy isn't found."

"I had heard that the commander of the ship is the boy's mother. Would she risk harming him by hasty actions?"

"She cares less for her son than for that which her son took," Alain said.

"That sort? And the boy's the same?"

"No," Mari said. "He can be a little difficult to tolerate, but he has a sense of responsibility for others, is trying to do what is right, and risked revealing himself in order to help a little boy understand math. If you find him and my daughter—and I think you're right that both have sailed from here, but if you do—I request that you listen to both of them and do as they ask."

"A request from you is as good as an order," Hagen said. "Will you visit elsewhere in the city or must you move on?"

"At the moment, we don't know where else to move on to. We will visit Sergeant Kira's relatives as usual."

"Could you stop by the last wall?" Hagen asked. "One of those who stood with us died recently. His family will be there this afternoon for a memorial service."

"I will be there," Mari said. She smiled and reached to take Hagen's hand. "Even after so many years, we all still stand together."

As they walked past the crowds, Alain spoke to her. "You seem more relaxed than you have ever been here."

"I am. Isn't that odd? Kira fought her own little battle here, didn't she?"

"Three to one and she left them unconscious. Bev will be pleased."

"Maybe Jason helped," Mari said. "I know that sounds ridiculous but…he helped that little boy."

"He has also put our daughter in great peril," Alain reminded her.

"That was our daughter's decision. You know it was." Mari looked at the nearest wall, still pocked with the scars of war. Her hand went to the place on her upper body where a bullet had once entered. "She's picking up the banner we didn't even ask her to bear, Alain. Maybe that's what I needed to find more peace. To know that the world we worked for, fought for, will be in good hands. Kira will make her own decisions. But if what has happened so far is any indication, they'll be good decisions, as we always hoped. I know that now."

The next day the ship from Urth arrived at Dorcastle, settling on the cliffs that ringed the city on two sides. The great silvery ship looked down on Dorcastle like a looming fortress magically raised in an instant. The citizens of Dorcastle, the city that had never fallen to attack, looked up at the ship from Urth with mingled defiance and resolve.

"Are you certain that we should do this?" Alain asked as he and Mari prepared to go meet with the people from Urth. "Confronting them again holds danger. That woman looked upon you when she spoke of 'active measures.'"

"We have to talk to them," Mari said. Her expression grew wry and self-mocking. "Haven't you heard the talk on the streets? The daughter is in Dorcastle! Nothing can threaten this city while she is here!"

"If you ever started to believe that of yourself," Alain said, "I would be even more worried."

"I have to act as if I believe it," Mari said. "Not arrogant, but sure of victory. They need to see that. And since the Master of Mages is beside me, we should be able to handle anything that happens. Remember, if you have to take action, do it quickly. As fast as possible. If we catch them off guard, they won't be prepared to 'scan' you when you do a spell."

"We cannot be certain of that," Alain cautioned.

"You've seen them. They don't think any of us are a threat. Including you."

"I have seen this, and heard it," Alain admitted. "What is magic?"

"Something the Urth people believe can't hurt them, even though they think they can use something about your talents to hurt other people," Mari said. "How much heat did you create above your hand that time you demonstrated for them before we realized we shouldn't?"

Alain shook his head. "I barely warmed the air."

"And they probably think that's the best you can do. Alain, other Mechanics and I have tried to use our devices to detect the power that Mages draw on for their spells. We've never succeeded. Maybe the Urth people can't spot it, either. How much could you do if you couldn't access the power the world holds?"

"You know this," Alain said. "Only the tiniest of spells. No Mage can do more with only their own strength. You are saying that if the Urth people do not believe that other power exists, they would assume that is all I could do?"

"They should know better," Mari said. "They've seen the Rocs. But that would mean admitting we know something that they don't." She squared her shoulders. "Give me a kiss, my Mage. And then let's go see if we can keep this situation from getting any worse."

They walked to the waterfront. Alain, certain that there would be trouble this time, prepared himself to quickly cast spells. Areas near the water did not have the strongest concentrations of power, but there should be enough for whatever Alain needed to do.

One of the smaller flying craft left the large one, making a long, slow pass over the city before angling down toward one of the open areas on the waterfront. It came to rest, waiting for Mari, Alain, and their escort to arrive.

Alain wondered if the people from Urth realized that they had set down near the same spot where the Great Guilds and the Imperials had demanded the surrender of Dorcastle. As omens went, it was not a good one.

Captain Hagen had joined them with a squad of his best, looking ceremonial in their dress uniforms but with weapons at their belts that were ready to use. Whether a few Mechanic pistols, a score of swords, and an equal number of hardwood clubs would accomplish much if needed, Alain did not know.

He saw soldiers taking up position on the wall that looked down on this portion of the waterfront. Those soldiers, though decked out in their finest scarlet uniforms and standing like an honor guard, had the Mechanic weapons known as rifles. The Bakre Confederation still bought most of its weapons from the workshops of Master Mechanic Alli of Danalee, so Alain knew those would be the best rifles the world of Dematr had to offer. What he could not know was whether they would be of any use against the protection the boy Jason had said that the Urth people wore.

An opening appeared in the side of the smaller flying craft and Talese Groveen stepped out, this time followed by two other people, both holding objects that did not look like Mechanic weapons to Alain but had a disturbing sense of being weapons nonetheless. The two were relaxed, casual, looking around with indulgent smiles at the city and people of Dorcastle.

"Your day is more than up," Talese Groveen said, standing in nearly the same place where Imperial Prince Maxim had once stood.

"We're looking," Mari said, her dark Mechanics jacket an odd complement to the black pantsuit worn by Talese Groveen. The two women looked at each other, neither of them backing off in the least. "We are trying to ensure that your son is found without risking harm to him," Mari emphasized.

"You are stalling. You are withholding property that was stolen. Trying to learn secrets, perhaps. Or hoping to get us to offer greater rewards for the return of the object stolen from my ship. And for my son," Talese Groveen added quickly. She began speaking in a formal cadence. "In accordance with the laws of the many states of Earth, Mars, and all other governments within the Solar System, I hereby invoke the right to self-defense and protection of individuals."

"Do not do anything that we will all regret," Mari said. "Watching us are representatives of the librarians of Altis. They will send a report of whatever you do back to Urth using our Feynman unit. We have means to transmit that report to Altis so it can be sent even before your ship could reach the island and attempt to prevent it."

"You have no idea what my ship is capable of," Talese Groveen said. "Your barbaric technology cannot even conceive of its power. But I have no intention of taking any action that would create legal problems back on Earth. I will act only in accordance with our rights to employ force majeure. In this case, that means taking involuntary custody of you, interrogating you under scan to find out the truth, and extracting sufficient genetic samples from you to meet our needs in programming our drones to be able to spot your daughter as well as my son."

Mari shook her head, her expression hard. "You've picked a very poor place to threaten me."

"As I believe you once said to me, that was not a threat," Talese Groveen said. She gestured to the two Urth people standing just behind her.

Captain Hagen barked orders and his squad ran forward to stand between Mari and the people from Urth, not drawing weapons but linking arms to form a solid barrier. Alain saw the honor guard on the wall bringing their rifles up, canted forward, not yet aimed but ready.

But he saw no sign that any of these measures had bothered the Urth people in the least. The two continued walking forward as if they had no care in the world, the same slight, superior smiles on their faces.

One raised the object in her hand. Light flashed. The line of police officers guarding Mari jolted as if struck and fell limply to the ground.

Captain Hagen jumped in front of Mari and fired. Alain saw the Mechanic bullet stop in mid-air a hand's breadth from the woman, as if it had run into an unbreakable barrier, then drop at the feet of the Urth woman.

Hagen was firing again when the woman, smiling wider, pointed her device at him and he also fell.

The second of the Urth people raised his hand, pointing at Mari, who was watching him with the same determined expression but had not moved.

Alain, wishing not for the first time that he had married a woman with less stubbornness and more caution, had his spell ready. Whatever self-protection the Urth people used stopped anything from going through it. But his heat spells did not travel from place to place. He created them above his hand, then sent them to appear wherever he could see. They were in one place, and then another.

He focused on the hand of the man pointing his device at Mari. He could not directly harm that hand, but he could put his heat on the device.

The air above Alain's hand suddenly glowed with heat. An instant later the same intense heat was around the device pointed at Mari.

The Urth man shouted in pain. His device was glowing hot, parts of it melting, sparks and smoke flying from it. He went to his knees, trying to free the object from his badly scorched hand.

The woman turned a startled look on Alain, but he had already prepared a second spell. She staggered back with a scream, her device and her hand also burnt and useless.

It had taken only a few of what Mari called 'seconds.' Alain, trying to mask the weariness caused by using two such spells within a very short time, relaxed his Mage powers completely, making no preparations for another spell.

Talese Groveen stared at the other Urth people, then at Alain. Shaking herself out of her surprise, she focused on Alain. Her fingers moved before her, but whatever she belatedly sought to do instead provoked a grimace of frustration.

Alain heard commands called from the wall. The rifles there were now pointed at the three people from Urth.

Mari finally moved, but only to cross her arms as she gave Talese Groveen a warning look. "That's only a sample of what we can do to defend ourselves. If these men and women were harmed," Mari said, nodding toward the police before her, "I will be very upset. If any are dead, you will be guilty of ordering murder and will be held accountable."

"They were only rendered unconscious," Talese Groveen said, trembling with anger. "But you…you have attacked and seriously injured two of my crew!"

"Self-defense," Mari said. "Protection of individuals. We are willing to overlook your unprovoked aggression as long as these men and women were not harmed and such actions are not repeated." She pointed to Alain, who was keeping his expression Mage-blank and Mage-menacing. "Anything he can see can be dealt with." Mari looked toward the smaller flier, then up at the large ship on the cliffs above. "Anything."

"You would not dare. An attack on our ship—"

"Will only happen if we are forced to defend ourselves again," Mari said. "In case you are wondering, or planning to use some long-distance weapon, Master of Mages Alain is not the only Mage capable of such spells. There are others. They are spread out, and they are watching your ship. No matter where you go, they will be watching. Mages do not have to wear robes. Many do not. You will not know who they are until they act. I would advise you once again not to force us to take action in self-defense."

Alain watched Talese Groveen glare at Mari, but while her anger remained, it was joined by calculation and caution. Whatever else she was, the woman from Urth was not a fool.

"I have underestimated you," Talese Groveen said. "Apparently the stories were not as exaggerated as many believed. My…apologies for…overreacting. I assume you are aware that hostilities between us are not in the interests of anyone."

"I am aware of that."

"I have a right to have my son and the object he took returned to me."

"I understand. There are many searching for them." Mari left it at that, and if the Urth woman noticed that she did not promise to return either boy or object she was smart enough not to make an issue of it.

"Is my ship allowed to continue its research?" Talese Groveen asked.

"Yes. However," Mari continued, "such activities must be open and visible. We will not permit further spying on us. Alain."

Alain turned and called. "Mage Saburo. Tell Hunter that the thing is prey."

The Roc hove into sight, swooping down in a swift strike, its huge claws closing on seemingly empty air over the harbor. Hunter flexed its claws, shrieked, and acted as if hurling something invisible.

An object appeared and fell toward the harbor, its outer shell rent and dented. It hit the water with an eruption of steam as energy suddenly vented.

"You have badly damaged valuable property," Talese Groveen said, eyeing the Roc.

"Feel free to recover it and repair it. But if it flies again, Hunter will seek it out. Rocs do not like sharing the air with things they cannot see."

"I understand. We will not leave until we have what is ours."

"I understand," Mari said.

The other two of the people from Urth had already staggered back to their flier. Talese Groveen turned and walked back to join them. The opening closed and the flier rose into the air before heading directly back to the large ship perched on the cliffs.

Mari finally relaxed, walking to Alain. "That was hard."

"You should have dodged their attack," he said.

"Alain, I told you that I had to stand firm against those people. Our people needed to see that."

"Perhaps they will build another statue of you on this spot," Alain said, still put out at Mari risking herself that way.

"Ouch. You must be really upset. I'm sorry," Mari said. "It's the daughter thing."

"There are times I like the daughter thing even less than Kira does," Alain said.

"I'm sorry," Mari repeated.

Healers had come running to examine Captain Hagen and his police. "It's like they're asleep," one told Mari. "They don't seem to have been hurt, though."

"Let me know the moment they awaken," she said. Mari turned away from the Urth ship, eyeing Alain. "It looked like that woman wasn't able to scan you."

"She revealed only frustration."

"We'll soon know if we're right. If they were able to scan your Mage work, and they're worried about what we might do to their ship next time, that ship might leave without Jason. But if they still need the information on the drive Jason took, they'll hang around despite any other worries."

"But they will act more cautiously," Alain said.

"I think so." She looked toward the large ship looming on the cliff.

"Do you remember the first time we talked to Urth? Right after the Great Guilds fell? We thought it was so wonderful."

"It was wonderful," Alain said. "It still is."

"I guess so. We'll keep trying to make things work. There'll be other ships someday." Mari smiled at him. "You saved me again."

"We are not keeping score," he reminded her.

Hunter had settled onto the breakwater protecting the harbor, preening and looking immensely pleased with itself. "Hunter is a mighty Roc," Alain said to Mage Saburo.

"Hunter is…happy," Saburo said. "He did not like the thing that followed us. Hunter wonders if the larger flying objects we can see are prey."

"Not yet," Alain said.

"Hopefully never," Mari said. "Talese Groveen is not a stupid person. I don't think she's going to do anything else that would seriously risk losing her chance at getting back what she wants. Get your rest, Sir Mage," she told Saburo. "We're going to need you, Mage Alber, and your Rocs the moment we hear something else about Kira and Jason."

Seven days after leaving Dorcastle, the first mate sought out Kira.

"The captain believes that you've earned your passage," the first mate told Kira. "You and J'son will be allowed to leave when we reach Caer Lyn tomorrow."

"Caer Lyn." Kira looked across the water, her stomach suddenly tightening. "May I make a request?"

"What is it?"

"Can J'son and I work our way to your next port of call?"

The first mate crossed her arms and eyed Kira. "That would be Kelsi."

"Kelsi? That would be great!"

"Is there something about Caer Lyn you wish to avoid," the first mate asked, "or something at Kelsi that draws you?"

"Both," Kira said.

"You told us you'd broken no laws. If there's a warrant out for you—"

"No," Kira said. "There's no warrant. But…there are a lot of Imperials at Caer Lyn. And we do need to reach the Free Cities. We will work just as hard as we have so far. We'll work harder, if that's what's needed."

"Girl, the first rule of bargaining is not to let the other know how badly you want something." The first mate studied Kira again. "I'll ask the captain."

Jason came by while Kira was waiting for the first mate to return. "What's up?"

"I asked them to let us stay on the ship longer."

He stared at her. "Us? Shouldn't you have asked me first?"

"I'm sorry. I didn't have time. Jason, it is important that I not be ashore at Caer Lyn. If we do end up there, we'll need to get out again as fast as possible. But it would be very risky."

"Why is it riskier there?" Jason asked.

"The Imperials. They have a lot of influence in the Sharr Isles. And they want me."

His gaze grew puzzled. "Why?"

"Because…" She gritted her teeth, embarrassed to have to talk about it, and looked around to ensure no one else could hear them. "They want me to marry one of their princes. And even though I'm underage, the emperor could make an exception to that law in a heartbeat."

"But if you don't want to marry one of them—"

"They'd drug me, Jason, or threaten Mother, or something. The Imperial court is a vicious place where the princes and princesses are in constant competition, which means everything from spreading nasty rumors about each other to assassination attempts."

"Wow." Jason nodded to her. "I'll do anything I have to so that won't happen."

"Thank you. You'd have every right to complain."

"Somebody warned me that if I kept complaining she'd hurt me," Jason said, grinning.

Kira laughed. "Sometimes I'm not very subtle." She turned as the first mate returned, straightening to attention as she saw the captain was there as well.

The captain frowned at her and at Jason. "You wish to remain aboard as crew until Kelsi?"

"Yes, sir," Kira said.

"There's a problem. I could in good conscience work you without pay on the way to Caer Lyn, because you were stowaways. But from Caer Lyn to Kelsi you would be crew, and deserving of crew pay. We already have a full crew, so it would be a stretch for the ship to afford that."

"That's all right," Kira said. "We would work for passage again."

"All right with you, perhaps," the captain said. "But I have ever insisted on paying an honest wage for honest work. It would not sit well with me to not pay you the wages you have earned. Nor would the crew be happy, worrying that perhaps I was planning to short them on pay if I could find the likes of you willing to do the same work for little or nothing."

Kira glanced at Jason, who shrugged helplessly. What would her mother do if faced with this kind of thing? Try to find some way of satisfying the captain's worries. Queen Sien had talked about the need to balance the ledgers, so she could understand the need to— "Oh. Sir? You know I brought money aboard."

"Aye," the captain said. "It'll be returned when you leave."

"What if we pay for our passage? What if we pay you the same amount that you'd pay us as crew? It would be a fair exchange of money. That way we get where we need to go, make sure the ship is not shorted, and ensure that our labor is justly compensated."

"'Justly compensated,' she says," the first mate commented.

The captain gazed steadily at Kira for a long moment, then nodded slowly. "Aye. That could be done. If you regard it as a fair deal."

"I would," Kira said, looking at Jason.

"Me, too," Jason added.

The captain exhaled heavily. "Done, then. You'll be crew as far as Kelsi. But still you've cost me five crowns. Serves me right for betting against the mate."

The first mate held out her hand, grinning, as the captain gave her a coin. "I told you I could make sailors of them."

The Son of Taris worked her way into the harbor of Caer Lyn the next morning. Kira took quick glances around as she helped with the sails, remembering that her mother had once lived here, had spent her years as a Mechanics Guild Apprentice here, and had married her father here. Her grandparents had lived here before choosing to move to Altis so they could avoid Imperial pressure on the parents of the daughter. Kira wondered if she would ever have a chance to actually visit and see the places where her mother had grown up.

The ship was brought in to a pier to offload cargo. As soon as the lines were sent over to the bollards on the pier and tightened, the crew went to work shifting cargo, bringing crates and barrels up from the hold and moving them to shore. It was backbreaking work, but Kira told herself that the quicker it was done the quicker the ship could leave.

The only pause in their work came about noon, when they were eating a quick lunch. "Look at that!" another one of the crew called out.

Kira looked along with the others, seeing a sleek shape entering the harbor of Caer Lyn, coal smoke belching from a large funnel amidships.

"It's all metal," someone said. "Like that old Mechanics Guild ship, the one the daughter sank."

Kira watched the Imperial ship cruise majestically to another pier, trying to make out the flags flying from a single mast. 'There's an Imperial prince aboard. I can't see the flag well enough to tell which one."

"If there's an Imperial prince here," the first mate said, spitting over the side, "then the sooner we're clear of this port the better. Back to work! We won't be able to get done in time to catch the evening tide, but we can sail first thing in the morning."

As Kira and Jason manhandled a crate, he nodded toward the Imperial ship. "Coal. This planet may have been mostly barren when the colony ship arrived, but it must have had a lot of vegetation once."

"How do you know that?" Kira said, wincing as she struggled with the weight of the crate.

"That's where coal comes from, ancient vegetable matter that's been buried underground and compressed." Jason looked around the harbor. "Something must have happened. Maybe a really bad solar flare or a really big meteor impact that nearly wiped out life. And then long after that, but before the planet could recover, humans came with a new ecology."

"What does that mean?" Kira asked.

"It means we're all part of a story that's been going on for millions of years," Jason said. "Cool, huh?"

"And a little scary," she said.

"Yeah. That, too."

Then they were among the rest of the crew again and worked together silently for the rest of the day, until the sun had sunk below the horizon in the west and the last of the cargo had been off-loaded, on-loaded, shifted about, and secured to the satisfaction of the first mate.

Kira and Jason were sitting at the table in the crew's quarters when the first mate entered with a lit lantern and an expression even sterner than usual. "You and you," she said, pointing to Kira and Jason, followed by a crooked finger demanding they come with her.

Worried, Kira followed the first mate down a ladder and into the small forward lower cargo hold. "Move that crate over here," the first mate ordered her and Jason. "Fast!"

As soon as that portion of the deck was clear, the first mate knelt, knife in hand, and began prying at one of the planks in the deck. It came up, along with two others fastened to it, revealing a hidden space beneath whose dimensions were too much like that of a coffin for Kira's peace of mind.

"Even honest ships sometimes must hide things," the first mate said in a low voice. "Imperials are coming down the pier, searching ships. The captain and I have a good idea who they're looking for. Get in," she ordered, pointing to the hidden compartment.

CHAPTER ELEVEN

Kira stared at the small compartment. "There's hardly enough room in there for one person. How are we both going to fit?"

The first mate rolled her eyes. "A boy and a girl and you wonder how you'll fit. I know you're underage but I didn't think they still raised them that innocent. You!" she told Jason. "Get in, on your back."

Jason did as he was told, lying down in the cramped space and looking up with an apprehensive expression.

"Now, you," the first mate said. "On top, facing him."

"What?" Kira demanded hotly. "I am not—"

"Get in there or say hello to the Imperials."

Kira climbed down, clenching her teeth, and lay on top of Jason, facing him. No sooner was she down than the first mate lowered the top in place and pulled the crate back over part of it to hold it down.

"Not a word," the first mate ordered, her voice muffled by the deck boards. "No sounds until I open that again."

Kira, trying to breathe shallowly, heard the sound of the first mate's footsteps departing. The boards were pressing down on her back, forcing her body against Jason's. Her chin rested near one of Jason's shoulders. "Don't. Get. Any. Ideas," she warned Jason in the lowest and most threatening voice she could manage.

"Can't move anyway," he whispered back.

She could have tried turning her head to look at him, but she didn't want to. Kira lay in the darkness on top of Jason, her body rigid, feeling humiliated and angry, until the clomp of several pairs of feet sounded nearby and added fear to the mix. "Are we done?" the captain asked, his tone cold and correct.

"Yes," someone replied. Kira recognized an accent from the area around the Imperial city of Emdin. Her Aunt Bev still retained traces of that accent. "If you see them, there is a substantial reward in it for you as well as the favor of the Emperor."

"We'll keep that in mind," the captain said.

The feet thudded away, leaving Kira and Jason alone again in the confined, dark space. Kira had been trying to breathe lightly so that her chest didn't rub against Jason, but she had to take deeper breaths as the air inside the confined space grew fouler. The stink of the bilges coming up from below only added to her misery. She began worrying about passing out. Jason was pinned beneath her, and even though he hadn't moved his hands at all he probably could move them a little. What would he do if—?

One set of footsteps came quickly into the compartment. The crate scraped over the deck as it was moved, then the first mate was prying open the hidden compartment.

Kira took deep breaths as the first mate helped her up, then pulled Jason out as well. "Put that back," the first mate told Jason, pointing to the raised deck planks. "Then stay here. You," she told Kira, "come with me."

Kira walked after the first mate, trying to steady herself. To her surprise, they didn't go on deck, but continued aft belowdecks to the small safe hold near the stern.

Inside the sturdy room, usually kept locked, a lantern hung from a hook overhead. The captain sat on a chest, before him a keg of rum resting on one flat end. On top of the keg was a sheet of paper with a color picture of Jason's face, like one of those that they had seen in Dorcastle.

The first mate closed the door, going to stand by the captain as both regarded Kira with stern expressions. The captain indicated the picture. "Tell us, then."

She didn't try to lie. "Yes. Jason, that's his real name, is from the ship from Urth."

"Why is he here, hiding?"

"To save lives. The people on the ship from Urth are here to cheat us and to take from us. Jason warned us. And when he found out that the other Urth people were planning to do something that would result in terrible wars with many, many people dying, he took part of their ship that would prevent them from doing that."

The first mate nodded to the captain. "That three-sided thing. I didn't think it looked like anything I'd ever seen before."

The captain eyed Kira. "Why hasn't he tossed it overboard?"

"Because it has a little thing like a Mechanic far-talker inside. If Jason isn't near it, it will call the Urth ship on its own."

"You believe that?"

"Yes."

"So it's to save lives he's doing this?"

"Yes. A lot of lives."

"That's where his stories come from?" the first mate asked. "From that Urth place?"

"Yes," Kira said. "He never claimed he made them up himself."

"True enough, though he told them well."

A few moments of silence passed while the captain thought. "And what is your role in this, girl? When we first saw you two we thought it was the old story of young love, but it's been clear enough the two of you are but friends."

Kira nodded. "Jason needed someone to help him hide. Urth is very different from our world. I was the only one who could help him."

"And who are you?" The captain looked Kira up and down again. "The Imperials pretended to mention you in passing. *Oh, yes, and there's also a girl. We'd like her, too.* But I've been in trade long enough to know when someone wants something very much, and the Imperials want you something fierce. Quite a reward was offered for you. Why?"

How could she answer that without telling them everything? Without confessing to being Lady Mari's daughter, and the desire of the Imperials to force her into a marriage if they could get their hands on her? "You wouldn't believe me if I told you, sir."

"Try, and let's see."

"It concerns the Imperial household," Kira said, trying to avoid the entire truth. "They want to take me there."

She had expected looks of derision, but instead both the first mate and the captain nodded as if she had confirmed their suspicions.

"You've tried to hide it," the captain said, "and you're in no way the stuck-up type, but it's been clear that you have the manners of someone comfortable in high circles. You came aboard with that pistol, not the kind of trinket most can afford, and had training in its use. You can fight better than most twice your age. One time you forgot yourself and gave me the quality of salute I've only seen from the sort of soldiers who form honor guards. And today the first mate tells me you knew what the flags on that Imperial ship meant and could have identified which prince was aboard if you'd seen the banner clearer. That's not a common talent. What do we have, then? A runaway Imperial princess?"

Kira, standing there in her worn sailor clothing and knowing how badly she needed a bath, couldn't stop a brief laugh at the idea. "I'm no princess."

"But a lady, perhaps?" the captain said. "Or a hostage, raised at the Imperial court to keep that pirate mother of yours from preying on Imperial shipping again after the war? No, we don't need details. With your work you have earned the right to your secrets. Just affirm that you have committed no crime for which the Imperials would have legitimate right to pursue you."

"I swear I have not," Kira said.

The first mate and the captain exchanged glances. The captain tapped the top of the barrel of rum again. "Nigh on twenty years ago, when I was a young officer on this ship serving under another captain, *The Son of Taris* was swept up in the Imperial net and forced to help carry provisions for the attack on Dorcastle. I have never forgotten one single incident of the times when the Imperials disrespected our captain, myself, and the others aboard. Their arrogance earned no love from us. This ship left the harbor of Dorcastle a day before the Imperials collapsed in the face of the daughter's wrath. We returned to the Empire with a deck covered with the wounded and our holds full of the bodies of the dead being brought back to their families."

The captain looked at Kira. "I'll never forget that, either. The empty faces of the dead and the stench and the terrible waste of it all. You say that you and the boy seek to save lives from those who would take them in war. You say the Imperials have no just cause to seek you. That's enough for me. Keep your head down, continue to work hard, and I will take you both on to Kelsi as agreed. For tonight, stay below deck and sleep in the forward hold with the door blocked, in case someone sneaks aboard in search of you during the night. The first mate will call you up in the morning when we're clear of the harbor."

Kira blinked away tears of relief. "Thank you, sir." Overcome, she forgot herself and offered the captain the best salute that could be given by an honorary lieutenant in the Queen's Own Lancers of Tiae.

"Get on with you," the captain ordered, touching his brow in response. "You're not getting anything that you haven't earned."

Kira went back toward the forward hold where Jason waited, elated by the news but also feeling reluctant. Once there, she discovered that she couldn't look at Jason, instead gazing to one side at the planks of the hull. "We're all right. The captain and the first mate know who you are. I told them the truth, that this is about saving lives, and they agreed to keep quiet and take us on to Kelsi."

"Really?" Jason sounded incredulous.

Was there also a note of glee in his voice? He was probably grinning at her, remembering their forced physical contact. "Yeah, really," Kira said, refusing to look his way.

"How did you manage that?"

"I just told the truth," Kira repeated, gazing fixedly at the crate to one side of her. There was a pause while Kira wondered what she should do or say next.

Jason broke the increasingly painful silence. "Kira? I wanted to tell you I'm sorry."

"For what?"

"For what happened. It must have been really uncomfortable and unpleasant for you when we were in there. I'm sorry."

Startled, Kira finally looked at Jason and saw him gazing back not with a knowing grin but with an unhappy expression. "You're apologizing for that? I thought you'd enjoyed yourself."

"I would have, if it had been something you *wanted* to do," Jason said. "But you didn't want to. You had to. And that was not something I wanted, or something I could like. All I could think of was how miserable you must be."

"Really?" He wasn't lying. She could see that. "It wasn't your fault. Like you said, we had to."

"Yeah, but I could feel how tense you were to be jammed in there with me, and heard how angry you sounded, and felt awful the whole time because you were forced into it. I don't want that," Jason said. "Not with anyone, but especially not with you."

She brushed some hair back from her eyes, gazing at Jason in surprise. "Thank you. I'd been starting to like you some at times, and if you had enjoyed that I couldn't have liked you anymore."

"Huh?" Jason seemed shocked by the news, then relieved. "Guess I dodged that rock."

"You really weren't thinking of that?"

"No, I just felt bad about what you'd been through," Jason said.

He was telling the truth again. "Yeah," Kira decided. "I do like you. Don't tell anyone."

"Ok— All right. I don't believe you, but all right." Jason shook his head. "They're not turning us in? Despite the reward? My mom and dad are so wrong. People can be really decent."

"The captain and the first mate are doing what they are for their own reasons, Jason. So am I. None of us are perfect."

"You're not selfish, greedy monsters, either," Jason said.

"No. And you're pretty decent as well. Um…we're supposed to sleep in here tonight, and block the door. Help me move some things." They got a couple of crates across the door, then Kira sighed. "I'm kind of worn out."

"Yeah, me, too. Long day moving cargo and then this. Emotional strain, I guess," Jason said. "I'll go over there and sleep."

Kira found a spot on the other side of the hold, bringing the lantern with her. "Are you ready?" She put out the light, causing total darkness to fall.

Getting comfortable on the hard wood and jumble of crates proved to be not just difficult but also impossible. Kira finally gave up, staring into the darkness and realizing that if Jason hadn't apologized for the time they were jammed close together, if he had shown any delight at the experience, she wouldn't have felt at ease sleeping alone in here with him. Which caused her to realize that she had never asked him about his own feelings. "Jason? How hard was it on you? Were you uncomfortable in there, too?"

"Yeah," he replied in a low voice from the other side of the hold. "I mean, dark, confined space, and what felt like a Kira-shaped statue lying on me."

"I was that tense?"

"Yeah, like solid rock. And then, we were in that little space and so close together, and, well, I know neither one of us has had any chance to take a bath or a shower for a while—"

"Jason, don't go there."

"Um…right. Anyway, between the physical discomfort and knowing how unhappy you were, it wasn't any fun."

Kira looked into the dark, where her imagination created swirling shapes. "Are all boys from Urth like that? Do they all respect girls' bodies and choices?"

"No," Jason said again. "I mean, lots of guys do care about that, but there are also some who like forcing things. A friend of mine got assaulted once. I'll never forget how miserable she was."

"That's awful."

"Yeah. I never want to be the reason somebody feels like that."

"Good for you," Kira said. "She was a friend? Have you had girlfriends? On Urth?"

"No. Not really," Jason said. "I mean, friends who are girls. But not real girlfriends. Uh," Jason continued, trying to sound casual despite the tension that Kira heard in his voice, "what about you? Boyfriends?"

"Not really," Kira replied, deliberately echoing him. "A couple of guys I thought maybe could be someone but weren't, and…" She sighed. "One guy I liked a lot. A couple years older than me. I thought he really liked me."

"What happened?"

"Well, my father is…you know. The guy had been pressuring me about going to one of Mother's public appearances, all of us together, and even though I was crushing on him I didn't want to because I've always felt uncomfortable at those kinds of things. Father took the guy aside and asked some direct questions, and he could tell when truth or lies were being spoken, and even when something wasn't being said, and it turned out the guy didn't care about me. Didn't actually even like me. He just wanted to be close to my mother so he'd get some reflected glory." She smiled sadly into the dark. "I was really mad at Father at first, but then I forgave him because he'd saved me from someone who didn't care about me. That's when Father got really serious about teaching me Mage skills for knowing when people are lying or telling the truth."

Jason didn't say anything for a little while. "You can tell when people are lying?"

"And when they're telling the truth, yeah. Usually. I'm not as good as Father, but I'm pretty good at it."

"Oh."

The worry in Jason's voice was so obvious that Kira couldn't help laughing. "You're fine. You haven't lied to me."

"I haven't?"

"No."

"But I'm always— Not even once?"

"Not yet."

This time the silence lasted a lot longer. "Kira? Thanks."

"For what?"

"Being somebody I never lied to. I didn't think I could do that."

"You're welcome," Kira said. "There are probably a lot of things you could do, things you could be, that you don't think you could."

"That's true of you, too, you know."

"Not the same thing, but thank you. Rest well, Jason."

Two days out of Caer Lyn, two or three more left to reach Kelsi.

Kira and Jason sat on the platform high up on the mainmast, looking at the unusually calm waters of the Sea of Bakre. A light breeze drove the ship at a steady but slow pace through the inky sea. The stars still shone amid the darkness but a brightening to the east showed where the sun would soon be rising and the new day beginning. But for now the high platform offered a place to be alone and not be overheard. They didn't talk for a while, though, just sitting beside each other. The platform wasn't very big, so they had to sit right next to each other, but that didn't bother Kira any more. "It's beautiful up here right now, isn't it?" she finally said.

"Uh, yeah," Jason said, as if startled out of deep thoughts.

"What were you thinking?"

"Me? Uh…I was thinking…why is this ship square-rigged?"

Kira laughed. She could tell that Jason wasn't being entirely truthful about his thoughts, but he had the right to some privacy for those. "That's a funny question. You mean why are the masts and sails like this? Because that's the way it's usually done."

"But a lateen rig or a fore-and-aft rig is a lot more efficient."

Kira gave Jason a skeptical look. "When did you become an expert on sailing ships?"

He shook his head. "I'm not an expert in terms of actually sailing. But I've played sims with sailing ships in them, and the way the sails were rigged mattered. It was one of the options when designing a ship, so I had to learn a little bit about them. I'm just wondering why your world ended up with an older, less efficient design. I mean, it looks really great. But—"

"It looks great." Kira sighed. "One time when I talked with a librarian— You have librarians on Urth, right? The protectors and distributors of knowledge? We were talking about how our world is, and the librarian said it seemed like when the crew members from the great ship founded the Mechanics Guild they sometimes chose things for the world just because they liked that thing. They liked it and they were deciding what would be in the world, so they put it in."

Jason's jaw dropped as he looked at her. "No way. They treated it like they were designing a game. Putting in stuff they thought was cool. But they were playing with real people."

Kira stared downward, feeling angry at old injuries done to her world. "Jason, I wish Urth had sent another ship to find out what happened when communications stopped. Another ship could have done something about what the crew did here."

"Not necessarily," Jason said. "The crew could have fabricated some pretty nasty weapons, and the colony ship would have had beta field generators, which are still about as nasty as it gets."

"What's a beta field generator? A bomb?"

"No. Bombs leave stuff behind. Beta field generators were created to dispose of stuff like asteroids that were threatening human-occupied moons and planets or something like a colony ship. They just… make anything inside the field go away."

Kira frowned at Jason. "Are they still on the remains of the great ship above us?"

"No. We scanned that. Your ship was completely stripped of useful equipment." Jason scratched his head. "The crew must have brought them down, maybe so they'd be sure of having access to them if another ship did come. I wonder what they did with them?"

"Once the Urth ship leaves," Kira said, "we need to get you to the librarians' tower on Altis so you can see if those beta things are there. The librarians say they have no weapons, but maybe they wouldn't recognize them. Anyway, Urth didn't know the crew had deliberately broken off communications. Why didn't they send a ship?"

He blinked in surprise. "They haven't told you? I mean, over the ERIS transmissions?"

"Just generalities. My mother says they kind of talk around it."

"I guess they consider it controversial." Jason leaned back against the mast, his expression unhappy. "I'm going to talk money first, even though that wasn't the main reason. They would have had to build a ship. It wouldn't have been as expensive as a colony ship, but it would've been a lot of money. On top of that, when the transmissions from here stopped, they had to wait until the light from your star reached Earth so we could tell if there had been some solar disaster that wiped you out. That took a long time. Years. The sense of urgency was a lot lower by the time Earth saw that nothing had happened that could be spotted from so far off."

"All right," Kira said. "Expensive, and you had to wait. Those weren't the biggest reasons?"

"No." Jason looked at her. "They didn't have the Asaro-Ashmead drive that the ship I came on uses, so the trip here to find out what had happened to you, if there were any survivors, would have taken more than a century. The crew that started out would die along the way, and their children and children's children would be the ones who arrived here, just like on the colony ship. All Earth knew was that whatever had happened to you had hit so suddenly and so completely that none of the status reports had mentioned any problems before they cut off. Whatever had caused that was probably still here. So when the second ship finally got here, they might fall prey to the same thing. The ethics of sending a crew on what seemed to be a one-way suicide mission was bad enough, but sending the unborn children of a crew on a mission like that? Knowing the crew would have to have those kids and raise them knowing that they'd probably be killed by whatever had happened to you guys? How do you decide doing that is okay?"

"Don't say okay," Kira reminded him. She frowned, feeling depressed. "It wouldn't have been. Not if there was every reason to believe they'd die when they got here. Didn't anyone consider the possibility that the crew had deliberately stopped communicating? That they were disobeying their orders and their responsibilities to the passengers?"

"No," Jason said. "It didn't happen anywhere else. Some of that second- and third-generation crew on the ship that came here must have been major sociopaths with mad political skills, but how could anyone tell that from brief status updates? Even now—" He stopped speaking abruptly.

Kira recognized Jason's reaction when he had said too much. "What?"

He shrugged. "There are people descended from families that the crew came from. And they've been arguing ever since you reestablished contact that you guys are making things up, that there was some other disaster caused by the passengers and that you guys are blaming the crew to hide your own responsibility. I never believed that," Jason added hastily. "Not many people do. But some listen. Imagine how those families would have reacted to pure speculation that it was all the crew's fault."

"Nobody would've wanted to believe it," Kira said. "Would they? So they would have assumed a natural disaster of some kind, or a disease."

"Yeah. Something."

"Or the storm the Mages foresaw, that was going to destroy so much on our world if my mother didn't stop it from coming." Kira stared at the distant line where sky and sea merged, the light growing where the sun would soon rise, old feelings of misery rising as well in her. "And she did it. The daughter of Jules, come at last. She's not just brave, she's fearless. And she had me. I'm all she and Father have. How can people expect me to take over the daughter's job?"

Jason frowned. "What did that guy say, Kira? The one who gave us a ride to Denkerk? Didn't he say that he *hoped* the daughter's girl would be up to the job?"

"I can't…yeah, I think he did."

"He did," Jason said. "I don't think everyone on this world *expects* you to take over your mom's job. I think they're *hoping* you'll be able to do it."

She felt an unseen burden lifting off of her. "Do you think so? That would be rational, wouldn't it? And it means the pressure's off! No one who actually knows me is going to think…" Her momentary elation shifted to puzzlement. "Why didn't Gari tell me that? Why didn't he say, 'Don't worry, Kira, everybody who knows you knows that you couldn't ever do that.'"

"You'd want people to say that to you?" Jason asked.

"Um…maybe not, but it's the truth, so they ought to. Right?" He didn't answer, the only sounds the ship's wood creaking, the ripple of water alongside, and the wind sighing through the rigging. "Isn't that right, Jason?"

"Do you want the truth?" he said in a low voice. "Or do you want what you think you want to hear?"

"What does that mean?" Kira demanded.

He looked at her. "It means that you want me to tell you that the people who know you don't think you could do the sort of stuff your mother did. But the truth is, they think you're a whole lot more than you think you are."

She stared at him, unable to sort out the feelings clashing inside her. "Why would you say something like that?" Kira finally got out.

"Because you asked me what I thought the truth was."

Anger and frustration finally came to rest amid the other emotions pummeling her. "Then I guess I'd better not ever ask you something like that again! If you won't be honest with me—"

"I am being honest with you!"

"How could—" Kira stopped speaking, puzzled, as a black cloud suddenly appeared where the sun was just beginning to rise in a blaze of red splendor. "What's that?"

"What's what?" Jason asked, looking in the same direction.

"That black cloud. It's right where the sun is rising. It's getting darker! And there are, like, purple swirls in it…and…and dark lightning! How can there be dark lightning?"

"Kira, I don't see any black cloud." His gaze on her grew worried. "Are you all right?"

"I'm fine! I…it just went away. Disappeared." She felt a shiver run down her back. "Foresight. Father has told me foresight shows up that way sometimes."

"Foresight?" Jason stared at her. "You have foresight?"

"Ummm…"

"How can you have foresight? That's a Mage thing, isn't it?"

Kira fixed her eyes on him. "Don't tell anyone. The important thing right now is that there's danger coming. Serious danger."

"All hands up!" the first mate hailed from the deck. "The glass is dropping fast! We've got a big storm on the way!"

The moment she heard those words, Kira realized that was what her foresight had warned of. Not just a big storm. A very dangerous storm.

The crew spent the entire morning tying down every loose object on deck and below deck, lashing everything with double and triple lengths of rope and multiple knots. The first mate and the captain examined their work, often shaking their heads and ordering another line, pulled tighter, with more knots. All the time they were working the wind grew in strength, veering around to the east so that *The Son of Taris* was taking it square on the starboard quarter aft, and the swells on the surface of the sea built in size. Clouds had streamed in, first a high, thin layer, then heavy thunderheads that hung menacingly low in the sky and blocked so much sunlight that by midday it seemed night was coming on.

"Are you frightened, girl?" the first mate asked Kira during a momentary pause in preparations.

"No," Kira said. "Actually, yes."

"Good. You should be. I am. If you've never felt the sea's wrath, girl, you've never learned your place in the world. For all our pride we're nothing measured against an angry sea." She fixed Kira with a look. "But if you let the fear rule you, it will kill you. Remember that."

Kira stared at the increasingly rough waters, wishing that she was without fear, like her mother.

The first mate ordered them aloft, bringing in all sails but the mainsail and topsail. They'd scarcely come back down the rigging before they were sent aloft again, this time with orders to reef the mainsail, fastening part of it to the spar so that the sail area was reduced by half. By now the wind had risen into a gale, occasional more powerful gusts setting the taut rigging to singing as if the entire ship were a musical instrument about to be played by clumsy giants.

Despite the sea legs she had acquired in her time at sea, Kira staggered as the deck tilted up then twisted as the ship corkscrewed down into a trough. The seas had risen even more while they had been aloft, the swells looming higher and higher while the troughs gaped deeper and deeper. When the ship rose stern-first to meet a swell, the motion was as abrupt and sickening as an impossible fall upward. But each rise was followed by another twist and fall as the ship slid down the back end of the swell into the trough.

Kira hung onto the mainmast, staring at the swells which were now rising higher than the deck. The sheer force of the water was awesome. She understood now what the first mate had meant. Against the immeasurable power of the sea, Kira's own strength seemed of no value at all. The ship itself was already dwarfed by the forces of nature which kept rising to higher levels of fury. Around her, Kira could see fear on the faces of the rest of the crew.

The first mate came running back from the quarterdeck to address the crew gathered near the mainmast. "The captain's lashing himself to the wheel along with Fasi and Dax," she shouted over the increasing ferocity of the storm. "It'll take all three of them to keep the ship under control. If we don't keep her stern to these seas we'll be swamped in short order. All of you lash yourselves to a mast with a stout lifeline."

Kira stared for a moment, then seeing everyone else grabbing rope and tying one end to the mast and the other end around their waists started doing the same. She lost track of Jason for a moment, then saw him at the foremast, tying himself to another line. He looked her way, his eyes unusually large in a face drawn with apprehension.

A moment later the rain hit, not in a gentle buildup of raindrops but as if the heavens were emptying an endless series of buckets on the ship. Kira wavered on her feet, pummeled by the battering sheets of rain, as she hastily finishing knotting the rope about her waist.

The ship rose again with a sickening lurch, the bowsprit seeming to aim for the sky, then fell as if the bottom had dropped out of the sea beneath them. The bow buried itself in a welter of water and foam that burst out to either side and along the deck, washing over Kira's feet. She clung to the mast, staring at the roaring seas towering about them, blinking away the rain sheeting across her face and flinching under the lash of the wind which had grown steadily colder.

Another wave, surging across the deck and tugging at Kira's ankles. *I can handle this,* she kept repeating to herself, wondering if it were true, as the fury of the storm battered at her inner illusions just as it tore at her on the outside. *It's scary. I've never felt so tiny. But I can face this, I have to face this, just like my mother faced the Imperial legions. This can't be as bad as that was. I want you to be proud of me, Mother, even though I'm not you and could never be you. That's all I've ever really wanted. Please don't let me do anything that would make my mother ashamed.*

Yells and pointing arms alerted her to something on the starboard quarter where the seas were coming at the ship. Kira looked aft, then froze, unable to move for a moment.

A wave stood there, coming higher and higher over the rail, rising above it like the hand of a giant, dark water tipped with white foam. It rushed down upon the ship with a thunderous blow that shook the vessel, breaking in solid water across the deck. Kira had only a moment to gape at the monstrous shape sweeping down on her, then it struck with tremendous force, driving the breath from her. Her grip on the mast failed instantly under the titanic force of the wave and Kira tumbled through the water, helpless, until she reached the end of the rope around her waist. It jerked her to a painful stop, then with a snap that sounded over the roar of the storm it broke where unseen rot had weakened it and Kira found herself borne by the onrushing water forward and toward the other side of the ship, grabbing frantically for anything she saw. A halyard dangled from above, whipping wildly in the wind, and Kira made a desperate lunge for it, getting only a partial grip on it, hanging on for a few seconds until the wet line slipped from her grasp.

Out of the corner of her eye she caught a glimpse of Jason. He was engulfed in the wave as well, but staring at her, a knife in his hand slashing at the rope holding him to the foremast. Then she lost sight of him as the rushing wave twisted her about. She caught at the gunwale, pitting human strength against the force of an angry sea, but felt her grip loosening as the irresistible weight of the water pushed her to the rail and over.

CHAPTER TWELVE

Kira saw the gunwale falling away from her as she was pushed toward the hungry waves below. Everything seemed to move so slowly: her arm raised toward the rail now just out of her grasp and forever beyond her reach, the rage of the storm and her own futile efforts almost frozen in what Kira knew must be the last seconds of her life.

As if in a dream someone's arm shot into view over the rail, then Jason appeared, riding the wave, one hand locking onto the top of the gunwale, the other reaching for her, Jason himself over the side but holding on, arms fully extended, his free hand closing on her arm just below the wrist and clamping tight with a grip so hard it hurt.

Kira's fall halted with a jolt, the last rush of the wave past, her dangling over the waves, Jason holding her arm and clinging to the rail, his face twisted with effort. "Let go of me!" Kira shouted. "You'll fall, too!"

"No!" Jason yelled, straining to pull her up.

The ship jerked upward as she rolled toward the next trough, bringing them hard against the hull. Kira used the motion to boost herself against the side of the ship, managed to get one hand onto the rail, then she and Jason twisted over the top of the gunwale and fell to the deck inside.

Kira barely had time to blink in disbelief that she was still alive when over the roar of the sea and the storm she faintly heard shouts of warning. "Here comes another!"

A second monstrous wave rose on the starboard quarter, already sweeping toward them. Huddled against the inside of the gunwale, Kira ran her arm through a tiedown next to her, wrapped the other arm firmly around Jason, then curled up to take the force of the wave.

It hit in a welter of solid water and foam that slammed her against the gunwale, seeming to take forever to subside. Kira gasped for breath as the water finally eased, looking over at Jason, trying to understand what had just happened, what he had just done. But there was no time for anything except trying to survive the next wave. Kira got her arm loose and helped Jason stand against the force of the wind, the rain, and the pitching deck, both of them staggering toward the mainmast.

The first mate yelled something as she freed her own lifeline. Kira and Jason scrambled that way as the deck tilted wildly and the wind howled with renewed fury. "—take in the sail!" Kira heard the first mate saying. A piece of rigging snapped, the rope swinging through the air with a wooden tackle block attached. The first mate had barely an instant to realize the heavy wooden block was coming at her before it hit, striking a glancing blow to her head and tossing her to fall in a heap, her lifeline loose beside her.

The rest of the crew stared at her as another monster wave rose off the stern of the ship. As one, they began backing away in the direction of the nearest hatch belowdecks, their hands on the knots of their lifelines, while Kira watched, appalled.

She leaped forward recklessly and seized the first mate's limp body, grabbing a firm hold on the mast with her other hand, then screamed at the other sailors, her voice somehow rising above the storm. "Get back here *now!*" They stared at her but they came, responding to her command. "Help me hold her!"

Other hands came, and when the wave washed brutally past they barely managed to hold onto the first mate. "Tie her to the mast!" Kira ordered, fumbling for rope. Once again the crew did as she said, propping up the unconscious first mate and running a rope under her arms to fasten her in a standing position against the mast.

Only then did Kira look around, just in time to see another wave coming and crouch to take the blow on her back, the force pinning her to the mast. Staggering up again, Kira stared at one of the crew as water ran from her face and body, whipping away under the force of savage gusts of wind. "What was she saying?"

The sailor pointed up, his face contorted by fear. "We have to take in the mainsail. Even reefed it's drawing too much in this wind. We'll lose the mast."

Lose the mast. Kira had no trouble imagining what would happen to this ship if the mast broke. As if to emphasize the sailor's words, the mast emitted a tortured groan as a renewed gust of wind hurled itself into the sails.

But no one was moving. They were huddled there, faces stark with fear, trying to keep from being swept away. Kira looked over at Jason and saw him staring at her, his face a mask of dread in the gloom.

She knew what had to be done. She looked up, seeing the mast and spars swinging dizzyingly against the storm-tossed sky, knowing what it must be like up there. Kira glanced down again, seeing the sailors starting to stare at the hatch belowdecks once more. With the first mate unconscious, and the captain tied to the helm, unable to see what had happened through the murk of the storm, they lacked a voice to tell them what to do, to focus them on something other than their fear. If something wasn't done, they'd panic and flee, and the sail would stay taut and the mast would break and they'd all be at the mercy of a sea which had no mercy this day.

I had a job to do, her mother had said.

"Listen!" Kira screamed again. "We need to go up there and bring in the mainsail!"

"It's death to go up there in this!" a sailor roared back.

"It's death not to go!" Kira yelled. There was no helping it, she knew, even as fear froze her insides. "I'm going up!" Rain pummeled her face, momentarily clouding her vision. When it cleared, she could see everyone watching her. "I'm going up!" she repeated. "Come on, all of you! Follow me! We're bringing in the mainsail!"

She never knew where she found the strength to let go of the mast and throw herself at the shrouds leading upward. Her hands grasped the rough rope and Kira swung herself up onto the ratlines, trying not to look around or think about what she was doing. Another wave swept across the deck, snatching hungrily at her lower body as it passed, then Kira began pulling herself up, step by step on the ratlines, her eyes locked on the sections of rope just before her eyes.

The ship heeled far over and her feet slipped, leaving Kira dangling over the water with only her grip on the rigging between her and the voracious sea. Then the ship swung back and Kira was thrown against the shrouds and ratlines with painful force.

She kept moving, trying not to think, just focusing on the next handhold and then the next after that.

Kira realized that Jason was climbing beside her, then spotted other figures in the shrouds on the other side of the mast. They were following her up.

She reached the spar, needing another burst of effort to release her grip on the rigging so she could slowly move out along the spar, her arms gripping it for dear life and her bare feet finding a perilous hold on the rigging set below the spar for that purpose. The vibration of the mainsail, thrumming under the force of the winds, could be felt even through the fury of the storm. The mast groaned again and another massive wave hit with a mighty crash, almost paralyzing Kira for a moment with fear that the ship had begun coming apart beneath them. Focusing again on the area just before her as Jason and the rest of the crew joined her on the spar, she began bringing in the rough, soaked canvas. The sail bucked under the wind's blows, its coarse fabric tearing at the skin of Kira's hands as she punched and wrestled one-handed to help get it furled and tied down. Red blood swirled across the wet canvas, then vanished under the driving rain, but Kira felt only mild stings on her numbed hands.

At some point Kira realized that she was tightening the rope that tied the sail to the spar, quivering with reaction and praying the ordeal was almost over. The ship pitched and bucked, jerking the mast through the sky and threatening to hurl everyone in the rigging down to the angry water or, just as bad, to the solid deck to be broken before being swept over the side.

Someone else was yelling, but the voice wasn't clear enough for Kira to make out. She looked to the sailor next over on the spar, whose face reflected the same terror and exhaustion Kira felt. The sailor stared at Kira. "The captain says the mast's still under too much strain!" he yelled, his voice barely able to be heard over the storm. "We need to reef the topsail."

"The topsail?" Kira braced herself and looked upward. At the end of the pendulum formed by the mast, the spars of the topsail seemed impossibly higher and even more dangerous than where the crew now clung. Kira looked down again, gasping with fear. She gazed to one side along the spar and then the other, looking for the person who would lead them up to the topsail.

But everyone else was looking at her.

The wind and rain tore at her. The spar bucked beneath her like a living thing determined to throw her off. Kira gritted her teeth, feeling a stubborn resolve rising from somewhere, battling against the fear that threatened to paralyze her. *This is what you wanted, right? For everybody to see you, to look at you and not at your mother. What are you going to do about it?* "All right," she whispered to herself. Then she raised her head and yelled. "Let's go! Reef the topsail! Everyone up there now with me!"

The slow progress back along the spar was a nightmare, then Kira had to grasp the shrouds leading higher up even as the pitching of the ship tried to throw her into space. The rigging was slick with water and blood from the torn hands of the crew, but everyone went, feeling the motion getting worse the higher they climbed.

Kira knew her hands were trembling with fatigue and fear, but she kept moving. Her mother had told her that. Sometimes the worst thing you could do was stop, because then you'd never get moving again. And her mother should certainly know. The part of Kira that had envied her mother's adventures looked out upon the raging seas, blinked away the wind-driven sheets of rain, and realized that her mother had spoken the truth when she'd denied enjoying them. *Sometimes I've been so scared I couldn't breathe.* Knowing the things her mother had done, Kira had never believed her mother could truly have been afraid, but now Kira watched herself climbing higher while the storm tore at her, while icy claws of fear dug into her guts, and realized just how frightened her mother must have been at such times.

Along the spar again, Kira's temper rose at the blind fury of the storm, somehow warming her and giving her the strength to keep working to help reef the topsail, reducing its area enough to bring down the strain on the mast to bearable levels.

Done. The mast swung in a wild arc, almost pitching her off again. Kira clung to her holds and yelled once more. "Everyone back down! Get on deck! Be careful!"

The absurdity of her last comment was lost in a surging wave of terror as the mast whipped around again. Kira tried to move her hands and couldn't. They were locked onto their holds and refused to release. She clung there, frozen with fear, wondering how long it would be before the strength in her hands failed and she was hurled out into the sky.

Someone was tugging at her. Kira turned her head and saw Jason there, one hand pulling at her arm. He was shouting, looking at her with a puzzled expression. "Come on, Kira!"

How could he think she could do this?

But Jason wasn't going to move until she did.

Kira made a tremendous effort and one of her hands came free to reach for the next hand hold. Jason backed along the spar with her until they reached the shrouds, then they started down the ratlines, the water thrown into their faces beginning to taste of salt again as wind-driven spray from the sea mixed with the rain.

Kira made it down far enough to fall to the deck safely and stumbled to the mast, gripping it as another wave roared past and tugged eagerly at her. Her arms shaking with exhaustion, Kira felt like throwing up, but her stomach couldn't manage the effort. Still feeling half-stunned, Kira looked to make sure that Jason had made it to the mast.

Something felt wrong, Kira realized. The ship felt more sluggish. Had they taken in too much sail? She looked at the nearest one of the crew. "Why does the ship feel like this?" she shouted to be heard over the storm.

The sailor pointed downward. "We've taken on a lot of water!" she yelled back.

Taken on water. All of those waves across the deck, the pummeling of the seas, driving water between the planks of the hull. "The bilge pumps. We need to work the bilge pumps." Kira turned to the other sailors. "Get below and start working the pumps!" She looked back at the quarterdeck, where the shape of the captain and the other two sailors lashed to the helm could barely be made out through the murk of the storm. "Someone has to tell the captain."

"I'll do it," Jason volunteered, then lunged away before she could object. Kira watched Jason stagger across the deck as it pitched and rolled, breathing a gasp of relief as he reached the base of the quarterdeck before another wave washed across the deck. She felt a sense of amazement that the boy from Urth had agreed to run that risk. What had become of the sullen Jason who had alternated complaints with a superior attitude?

Jason came back, moving frantically as another wave rose, reaching the safety of the mast just before another deluge swept across them. "The captain says we need to keep those pumps going! No letup!"

She thought of the labor involved in driving the pumps, feeling the ache of weariness already filling her. "Let's get going."

The other crew members were already below. Kira and Jason rushed to the hatch and tumbled through together, pulling it closed after them. She had a moment of realization how much she and Jason were touching each other and how little it bothered her, how much in fact that contact was reassuring.

Belowdecks offered less a refuge than a different kind of terror as they stumbled through the darkness of the hold to the dim lanterns illuminating the sailors working the pumps. Inside, with the waves crashing against the hull, the ship groaning and planks cracking under the strain, everything tossing and jerking around, and the howl of the wind still easy to hear, it felt as though the entire world was coming to an end and about to collapse about them. When Kira reached the pumps, two sailors were working them slowly while staring around the badly lit hold, the rest of the crew huddled nearby.

Kira's temper went off again, giving her strength she hadn't imagined she still had. "Don't you want to live? Get working! I want two lines, one for each pump. Work it as hard as you can for the count of twenty, then let the next in line take over and go to the end of the line. Move it!"

They jumped in response to her words, doing exactly as she said.

"I told you so," Jason gasped as he stood next to her, holding on to a fitting as the ship lurched wildly.

She had no idea what he was talking about and no time or energy to pursue it. Kira kept the crew going, alternately encouraging, berating, and threatening them, finding herself using a lot of the words she had heard the sailors use, words that she would get in a whole lot of trouble for if she was ever foolish enough to use them in the hearing of her parents.

The pumps were all of the agony she had expected. When it was her turn she forced the pump handle through twenty up and down yanks, then reeled back so the next sailor could take over, staggering to the end of the line, her arms feeling like useless weights as the motion of the ship threw her against objects to either side. The water inside the ship sloshed below them and more came trickling down from above or along the planks of the hull. But they kept pumping, trying by hand to overcome the efforts of the sea to sink the ship by slow measures if it couldn't destroy it quickly with the fury of wind and wave.

This, surely, was the eternal punishment some people spoke of, Kira thought. The darkness would never end, the world would never stop pitching and heeling, and the work would go on and on while her muscles burned in the cold, wet place of her torment. But she kept going, and if anyone faltered she got them going again. Because that was what needed to be done, and she would do it if no one else could.

The endless dark night finally gave way to a dreary day. Kira sat, more exhausted than she ever would've believed possible, her back to the gunwale, looking up at the gray clouds scudding by low overhead. The wind was chill on her soaking-wet clothing, but she was only vaguely aware of it. Her body hurt with one big, dull ache and her hands felt numb and swollen. The sea salt that coated almost everything stung the rips and cuts in her hands. Occasionally a rent would appear in the clouds, showing blue sky beyond like a promise of deliverance. The wind, still strong but no longer dangerous, propelled *The Son of Taris* through seas which had subsided to merely rolling and choppy. Whitecaps sprinkled the water like an endless field of dark horses with bright manes and tails.

Jason slumped beside Kira, looking stunned with tiredness, or perhaps surprised that they were still alive. They were sitting so close their hips touched, but that was all right, that was comforting.

The clomp of heavy boots along the deck announced the approach of the captain. He stopped in front of Kira and Jason, looking down at them, his clothing thoroughly soaked like that of everyone else on board, his face haggard behind the stubble of an unshaven beard, white salt crystals shining amid the dark stubble. The captain eyed the two for a moment, then spat over the side before speaking. "Don't get up, you two. You've earned some rest. I'll not deny when they first brought you both out of the hold that I thought you no better than unneeded ballast," he said, his voice hoarse with weariness. "Useless weight, I thought. But I'll admit I was wrong." He nodded to Jason. "You've toughened up well, lad, and yesterday you showed your courage when it counted. You did a man's work and you did it well. As for you, girl," he shifted his gaze to Kira, "you don't belong in the crew."

Kira looked up at him, bewildered. "I…I don't?"

"No. You're a ship's officer, you are." He inclined his head toward the forward part of the ship. "The first mate owes her life to you, and we all owe our lives to you for getting the crew up that mast. Many a seasoned sailor would've run below to hide while those sails tore this ship apart rather than face climbing the rigging in that weather, but you led them up and you got the job done. Then you got them on the pumps and kept them going through the night. Very well done, I say. You're brave and smart, girl, and more to the point a leader to be counted on when it's needed most. I'm happy indeed to have you on my ship. I give you my hand on it." He leaned forward and solemnly shook Kira's hand while she gazed up at the captain, astonished. "You'll be rated second mate on the ship from the day we left Caer Lyn and draw the pay a ship's officer merits. If you stick with the sea you'll be captain of your own ship before you're twenty, or I'm no judge of sailors. Now, if the pair of you want to stay on after Kelsi, you're more than welcome in my crew. Or if you want to move to another ship I'll be pleased to provide you references."

With a gruff nod, the captain moved on.

Kira just stared after him, unable to find words.

She heard Jason laugh softly and briefly. "I can't believe he offered me a job. Because of what I did. I earned it."

"You did," she said, remembering Jason following her up into the rigging.

"So did you. You're a ship's officer now."

"Yeah. Right." Kira leaned back, sighing, too tired to think clearly. "He's just saying that because of my mother. It doesn't really mean anything. People are always saying nice things to me because of her, because they think I must be like her."

"Kira, he has no idea who your mother is."

It took a moment to sink in, then Kira fixed a shocked look on

Jason. "He doesn't. He doesn't know who my mother is."

Jason nodded. "And he thinks you did a good job. A real good job."

"Jason, this is the first time in my *entire* life that I know someone is saying something nice to me because of me and not because of who my mother is." She felt tears starting and blinked furiously, wiping her eyes with one soggy sleeve, flinching as the salt on the cloth stung her eyes.

"Why are you crying?" Jason asked, worried.

"Never mind. I'm fine." She breathed deeply several times and took control of herself. Jason was right. She had gone up that mast, and those other sailors hadn't followed because she was Lady Mari's daughter. They'd seen something in her, Kira, that made them listen to her, made them follow her. Something Kira had never believed she possessed. And she had been scared, more scared than she had ever been, but somehow she had done what was needed. It seemed impossible, but there were the captain's words, and the ship still floated. What did it mean? If she wasn't who she had always thought, a small figure lost in the shadow of the daughter, who was she?

She looked over at Jason, who was haggard with tiredness but gazing into the distance again. Who was he? Not the guy she had thought when they first met. He was smart. He'd shown himself to be kind. He respected her. And yesterday he had proven his bravery. Kira had a flashback of herself going over the side of the ship, helpless against the force of the wave, Jason appearing over the gunwale, his hand reaching to grasp hers in a grip of iron that did not relax until he had pulled her back aboard to safety.

And he had said nothing today about that, about risking his own life to save hers. Had not asked for thanks or praise. Had not expected any reward.

Kira reached out to grasp Jason's chin and turn his face toward her. He was still looking at her in surprise when she kissed him, tasting the sea salt on his lips mingling with that on her own.

When she pulled back, the expression on Jason's face made her laugh. "What? Didn't you like it?" Kira teased, feeling breathless.

"Yeah," Jason finally managed to say, "I liked it. I liked it a lot."

"Good. So did I."

Jason rubbed his face as if trying to convince himself that he was awake. "What does it mean, Kira?"

She shook her head. "I don't know. I'm not sure of anything right now. Is that all right? But I might kiss you again sometime. If that's all right."

"Any time you want to kiss me is fine with me!"

Kira's laughter was interrupted by the arrival of the first mate, a large bruise visible on one side of her forehead.

"That's enough cuddling, you lovebirds. I hope you're not expecting easy treatment for saving my life," she added with a sharp look at Kira.

"Not from you," Kira said, smiling. "You don't do easy."

"Maybe you are as smart as the captain says. You might make a decent second mate," the first mate said. "Supervise the foremast. I'll take the main." She raised her voice to yell to the rest of the crew. "Everyone on your feet! The wind is slackening! Make sail! And give a hand for the ship's new second mate!"

Kira and the first mate leaned on the railing as *The Son of Taris* approached the harbor of Kelsi. The sun shone brightly on the waves, sparking golden glints from the water, while the breeze played with their hair and filled the sails of the ship. It was as if the angry sea they had fought a few days before had never been, and for a few moments, there was no call for work. "Are you sure you wish to leave us?" the first mate asked her. "The captain would be pleased to have you stay on with the crew. The boy, too. You'd likely be safer from whatever it is you're running from."

"Thank you," Kira said, smiling at the passing water. "But having us aboard wouldn't make you safer. Every time we pulled into port you'd face danger on our account. No, we have to land at Kelsi. There's something we must do."

"To safeguard that thing from the Urth ship?" The first mate gave her a speculative look. "You seem happier around him than when you came aboard."

"He's been showing me a lot of good character, don't you think?"

"Oh, aye. I myself have always been partial to those that save my life. Would your parents approve of all this, Kara? His and yours?"

"Yes," Kira said. "I am certain that my parents approve of what I'm doing. His parents…don't have a say in the matter."

"Well enough. Your mother served the daughter during the war, you said. What about your father?"

"Yes. He served the daughter as well."

"Were either of them at Dorcastle? On the last wall?"

No matter what other differences between people existed, Kira had always been aware of the most basic one her world knew. There were those who had helped hold the last wall, and there was everyone else.

Kira inhaled deeply as she thought of how to answer that. Not wanting to lie to the first mate, she finally told the truth. "Both of them."

"Both?" The first mate stared at Kira. "That's a proud heritage they gave you. Why didn't you tell anyone aboard before this?"

"My parents did some great things," Kira said. "But that doesn't say anything about me."

The first mate laughed. "I'd say they also raised their girl right if you already know that."

"Sometimes I wonder. Did you argue with your mother?"

"Oh, did I! The hills rang with it." The first mate's smile took on the slightly sad cast of someone recalling the lost past. "She was a farmer, and she loved the land. She wanted me to follow in that, but the sea called me. The day I finally left for the sea was a hard one, but I knew I had to go. No one should have to live the dreams of another. We have to find our own course."

"How do we find it?" Kira asked.

"We go looking. How else?" The first mate gazed toward the land to the north. "If I'd had a son or a daughter, and they had told me they wanted to work the land, I would have wished them the best. That's a mother's job, isn't it? To love them and try to raise them right, hope it all sticks, and when the time comes kick them out of the nest and let them be who they will. Don't forget where you came from, girl. Honor it. But you're neither your father nor your mother. Find the place where your heart lies and hold to it."

"What if…what if a lot of people expect you to do something? Hope that you'll do something? And it's important, but you don't think it's a job you could ever do?"

The first mate scratched her head as she thought. "That'd be a tough one. But if the job is all that important, it makes it all the more important that your heart be in it. And only you can answer that, girl."

Kira smiled at the first mate. "I think my mother would like you. If you ever meet her, you have to tell her that I said that."

"Oh?" the first mate asked skeptically. "And how would I know her?"

"I look a lot like her." It took a moment for Kira to realize that, for the first time she could remember, she had said that without any bitterness or sense of inadequacy.

The Son of Taris came to anchor in the harbor, putting the longboat over the side to transfer a small amount of cargo ashore and pick up some more.

"We'll send you ashore in the boat," the captain told Kira. "Here are your packs. Change back into your own things and make it quick."

She collected Jason and they raced belowdecks to the crew compartment, otherwise deserted right now as the rest of the crew worked moving cargo into the boat. Once again turning away from each other, they quickly shed the coarse sailor clothing and donned the tough land clothing that felt absurdly fine by comparison.

Kira was dressed and hurriedly strapping on her shoulder holster when Jason spoke.

"This is the first time we've been alone for a while. What was that foresight stuff just before the storm hit?"

She paused before turning to look at him, trying to think of a way to avoid discussing it. Jason was mostly dressed, tugging on his boots as he gazed back at her. "Can we just pretend nothing was ever said about that?" Kira asked.

"But…if you have foresight…that's a Mage thing, right?"

Kira sighed. "Yes, it's a Mage thing, and yes, I have a little of it, I guess."

Jason stood up, eyeing her curiously as he pulled on his coat. "But everything your world has told Earth about Mages has said that any Mage talents are incompatible with being able to do technical work."

"If by technical work you mean Mechanic work, that's true," Kira said. "There's something about the way the mind has been trained to view everything. My father has been with my mother for about twenty years, and he's seen her use her pistol I don't know how many times, and he is *smart*, but he still can't use it. Oh, if you gave it to him he might accidentally pull the trigger, but he couldn't load it or operate it. I've talked to my father a lot about it, and I think what's going on is that Mages see a pistol, or any other device, and they see a single object. They don't see all of the parts, so asking them to, oh, push a button on something makes no sense to them any more than my telling you to push a button on a rock would make sense to you."

"But you can use your pistol," Jason said.

"Yes."

"Which means people can have both sets of viewpoints-"

"Jason, I'm the only one," Kira interrupted. "The only person my parents know of who can do it." She thought she saw it in his eyes then, and her voice grew angrier. "Don't look at me like that! I'm not a freak!"

He took a step back from her wrath. "I don't think you're a freak. You're unique, maybe—"

"That's another word for freak, Jason! Isn't it enough that I'm *her* daughter? That my mother died years before I was born?"

Jason shook his head. "That's just wrong. Even if your mother's metabolic functions ceased for a short while, she was revived in time, and she was obviously alive when you were born."

"Tell that to the people of this world, Jason! The ones who stare at me when I go out with my mother or with bodyguards surrounding me and they whisper to each other about…about…"

He took a step closer to her. "You don't really know what they're whispering, do you?"

"Jason," Kira said, "you really don't want to go there."

He hesitated, then pressed on despite her warning. "You said the Imperials want you to marry into their family. Why would they do that if they thought you were…different?"

"You don't think they consider me different?" Kira asked. "Sure, the emperor and the royal family would love the political gain from having the daughter's girl in their hip pocket, but even they would have people watching me all the time. Do you know who Mara is? The Dark One?"

"That's the vampire legend on this world, right?" Jason asked, puzzled by the question.

"Mara was the consort of the first emperor, Maran, and he supposedly fell under her spell so much that he made a deal with the Mages to keep her young and beautiful forever. But in order for her to stay young-looking and beautiful, Mara has to drink the blood of young men she seduces."

"Yeah," Jason said. "A vampire."

"It is a common belief among the citizens of the Empire that my mother is actually Mara."

He looked at her, obviously unable to think of what to say.

"So when a lot of Imperials see me *without* my mother they assume I *am* my mother, staying young thanks to the young men I'm hauling into bed and sucking the blood out of!"

"Kira, they can't really believe—"

"A couple of years ago I was at Altis at the same time as a delegation of Imperial scholars, and the librarians held a party for them one night and invited me, too, and I have to attend formal functions sometimes but I never get to go to just plain old parties because it's too dangerous and I don't get to spend very much time with other boys and girls my age so I really was thrilled at going to this one and you know what, Jason? All the Imperial women showed up, and all of the older Imperial men showed up, but every one of the young men and even middle-aged men just couldn't make it that night and I stood around wondering why no one would talk to me!" She felt tears starting as the old wound flared to life. "I just want to be like everyone else, Jason. But I can't. And I can't be like my mother, either. So what am I?"

"The most amazing girl I ever met," Jason said.

She stared at him. "What makes you think anyone else would agree with that?"

"The captain does. So does the first mate."

"Maybe...maybe he's starting to guess who I am."

Jason surprised her with a smile as he shook his head. "Kira, he already knows who you are. Maybe he's starting to guess who your mother is, but he already knows who you are. The girl who saved this ship and the lives of everyone on it. The girl who got both of us this far even though I've been a dead weight most of the trip. The girl who I'm trusting with my life and the lives of millions of people back on Earth."

She looked at him, trying to grasp such an image of herself. Part of her tried to reject it out of hand, but... "I guess the captain doesn't know who my mother is, but he knows who I am. Jason, I never thought about it that way." Kira felt a sudden urge to hug Jason. Instead, she wrapped her arms tightly about herself, looking at him. "Thank you."

"Your one flaw is that you haven't seen who you really are," Jason said, looking embarrassed.

"You think that's my one flaw? Oh, are you in for some difficult surprises," Kira said. "Listen, we have to get back on deck. We can't talk about this stuff until we're alone again. Just remember that I'm fine as far as me physically, and as far as the Mage-powers thing goes, it's known to only a very few people so please don't discuss it with anyone else."

"What about the Mara thing?" Jason asked, grinning.

"Don't ever joke about that, don't ever talk about that, don't ever *think* about that, and especially don't do those things when my mother is around or you will learn the hard way just how hot my mother's and my tempers can burn."

"Got it," Jason said, looking to Kira's eyes properly worried by her warning.

On deck, the captain waited by the rope ladder leading to the boat. He solemnly shook Jason's and Kira's hands before they left. "Best of luck. May fair winds follow you."

The first mate ordered them into the center of the boat, then cast off from the ship, other sailors pulling at the oars to drive the longboat to one of the piers that thrust into Kelsi's harbor. The city hugged the coast, walls standing firm against storm and Imperial aggression, mountains rising behind to the north and east, a stretch of open land to the west rising to meet the mountain pass that led toward the high plains and the city if Ihris.

Kira sat huddled in the boat next to Jason, who was watching the oars being worked. She stayed quiet, trying to understand why she kept telling Jason things that she had rarely or ever shared with anyone else. What was it about him? She shook her thoughts, recentering them on the city ahead. They couldn't linger in Kelsi. It was far too likely that people were figuring out that she and Jason had sailed from Dorcastle, which meant every other port would be the focus of searches for them. How quickly could they leave? It was already afternoon, and some cities still sealed their gates at night. Kelsi, worried about smuggling and Imperial plots, was surely one of them.

The boat came alongside the pier, Kira and Jason jumping out to help tie up. The first mate nodded to them. "Get out of here, you two, before the customs officials starting wondering who you are."

"Thanks," Kira said. "I'll miss you, too." She waved to the other sailors, who grinned and waved their farewells, then walked rapidly down the pier with Jason beside her.

"What's the plan?" Jason asked.

"There isn't a train out of Kelsi—" Kira began.

"Thank you!" Jason said.

She glared at him. "As I was saying, the rail line to Ihris is still being built. We'll need to find another way to get there."

"Why are we going to Ihris?"

"That area has enough people to hide among, enough open space to make sure no one sees enough of you to know how different you are, and some relatives of mine who can help us if we need that. But our first priority is getting out of Kelsi before the gates shut for the night. I don't want to spend any longer here than we have to."

Jason looked around. "I don't see any drones. The search must not have expanded out this far yet."

"I don't see any of those pictures of you, either, but for all we know they could show up tomorrow." Kira pointed inland. "We can stop for something to eat, and some trail food, but we need to get through the city before sunset."

As they went through the city, getting only the occasional and apparently casual glance from others, Kira watched the lowering sun anxiously, trying to time their departure close to sunset but not too close. She veered into a market square, looking for food stalls, and got them quick meals. "These are really good," Kira told Jason, offering him some of the pastries stuffed with meat and gravy. "They have them in Alexdria, too."

"That's north of here?"

"Yes." Kira pointed into the mountains. "In a high mountain valley. It's really beautiful. Maybe we can go there sometime."

"Huh?" Jason eyed her. "You mean, you and me? On a trip? For fun?"

"Yeah, why not?" Kira smiled at him. "We are friends, right?"

"Right," Jason said, concentrating on his food.

After picking up some packages of trail food and some bottles of wine and water, Kira headed once more for the north gate. If anyone saw her leaving, she wanted them to think she was heading for Alexdria, one of the few places in the world where her father was even more popular than her mother. "It's a long story," Kira explained. "He risked his life to save a lot of Alexdrians when Mages never did that."

"Is there anybody in your family who's not a hero?" Jason asked.

"Uh, yeah. Me. Duh."

"Kira—!"

"Don't even," she warned him. "I did a job. That doesn't make me a hero."

The gate loomed ahead, sunset near, the evening rush underway, crowds of people, wagons, and riders streaming through in both directions under the bored gaze of the city sentries.

But Kira pulled Jason aside, studying the crowd, wondering what didn't feel right. "Do you see anything odd?"

He looked toward the gate, shaking his head. "Not that I can tell. That doesn't mean much."

There were men and women lounging near the gate, watching those leaving. That wasn't unusual. The gates were common meeting places, well-known spots where people could arrange to see each other. But some of these men and women looked too hard, too alert.

Kira inhaled slowly. "I don't know if I'm spooked or if there really is a problem. Maybe it's just my nerves."

Jason shook his head. "Kira, you've been right pretty much all the time."

"There are two Mages there," Kira said, startled as she realized she could sense them. "I don't know which ones. They're not wearing robes."

"How can you tell they're Mages?"

"I just can. Jason, most Mages still wear robes. But Dark Mages don't."

"Dark Mages are bad guys, right? Like Dark Riders or Dark Clerics?"

She stared at him. "Yes. Whatever a dark cleric is. Dark Mages always used their powers for personal gain, whereas Mages like my father were supposed to pursue wisdom."

"Got it," Jason said. "They're bad guys. Let's leave."

Kira turned to go, hearing sudden shouts from the direction of the gate. She looked, seeing several of the men and women who had waiting there now pushing their way through the crowds toward her and Jason. "Let's run."

CHAPTER THIRTEEN

B
ut before she could move Jason jerked and fell against a nearby wall, just as if he had been struck. "Hey, what the—" Jason staggered against the wall again, covering his head.

Kira looked about for whoever was attacking Jason, seeing nothing. But suddenly a column of light was visible to her, moving toward Jason.

She ran forward and planted a kick in the center of the column, hoping that she wasn't jabbing at empty air.

Her boot contacted something that felt like a person.

A Mage appeared, bent over, clutching at his side. Jason was gaping in surprise but Kira didn't hesitate. She pivoted on one foot, bringing her leg up again and whipping a kick at the Mage's jaw. It connected, sending him sprawling in the street among people who were staring and backing away.

Beyond, the people pushing through the crowd were getting closer.

Kira grabbed Jason's hand to help him stand. "Can you run? Because we have to run."

"I can run."

Kira dodged along the streets, ignoring the cries of people and shouts that sounded like they could be police. Threading her way between groups and dodging down alleys, she finally reached the edge of a crowded square and came up against the wall of a building just outside of it, breathing heavily from the run.

Jason stood next to her, also gasping for breath.

"Are you all right?" Kira asked.

"Got a headache," Jason got out between breaths. "You can really run, you know that? What happened back there?"

"There was a trap at the gate. You were right that I was right. There was a Mage close to us who was hiding, and he attacked you."

"Why couldn't I see him?"

"He was bending light around himself. Creating the illusion he was doing that. Nobody can see a Mage who's using that spell."

Jason spread his hands at her. "How did you know where he was?"

"I…" Kira covered her face with her hand. "I could sense it."

He lowered his voice. "That's another Mage thing, right?"

"Yes. Jason, I've never been able to do things like that."

"You're under a lot of stress. That can trigger latent conditions," Jason said.

It was her turn to stare. "Latent conditions?"

"Um, yeah. I think that's the medical term."

"Medical term? Like I'm sick?"

"No, not like that," Jason protested. "And not like the…the freak thing. There must be a genetic component. You got that from your dad. If it's a dominant gene. It's possible the gene is recessive, which would mean your mom carries it, too, and you got it from them both. Wow, that would mean a lot of people on this world might be carrying a recessive Mage gene. Unless it doesn't breed true. That happens sometimes and—"

"Stop talking like that!" Kira demanded.

"What?" Jason seemed stunned by her reaction. "Why?"

"I'm not some farm animal! You called me a 'hybrid' the first day we met. How dare you talk about me 'breeding'!"

Jason looked at her uncomprehending. "It's…it's genetics."

"So? Does that word make it all right to talk about people as if we're just animals?"

"But when it comes to different forms of genes and expression and evolution and reproduction, we are," Jason said. "We're just a different form of life. Me, too."

"Is that how they think of it on Urth?" Kira asked.

"Sure it is. That's just science."

"That genetics stuff is science, Jason. How people think about it, how people think about other people, is something else."

"I never…" Jason looked away, his expression tight with thought. "We're not special, Kira. People aren't special. We're just another life form."

"Every person is special," Kira insisted. "Every person deserves dignity and respect, and being thought of as something that matters. Maybe some person will be an awful person who I need to kick in the jaw, but even he is not an animal. Even animals deserve respect! They are not toys like those dragon things on Mars you talked about."

He gazed at her, for some reason sad. "We change them all the time. Fur, body, immune functions… To make them look like we want them to or be like we want them to. And then we started doing it to people, too. To fix things. To improve things. And to make them taller and thinner and whatever we thought was better-looking. Because it's just genetics, and we're just another life form."

"We're not," Kira said. "I'm not. You're not."

"You're right. Again. You do that a lot."

"Oh, stop it. I've just had good people in my life telling me things that I couldn't have figured out on my own. You think that more Mage talents are emerging in me because of the danger we're facing? Father said that. He said foresight could emerge in times of danger. So I guess it's all right." Jason didn't look entirely convinced, but Kira didn't want to pursue the subject any further. She looked around. She couldn't hear any traces of uproar from the direction of the north gate, so things must have died down. But the sun was setting, shadow stealing across the square before them to merge with twilight and darken the city. "Jason, they were waiting for us. Maybe someone recognized us when we got off the longboat. Maybe one of the Mages had foresight that we'd be in Kelsi and try to leave by that gate."

"That can happen?"

"Yes." Kira ran one hand through her hair, thinking. "They'll keep the gates under watch. And if some of them know we're here, others will find out. Kelsi is going to become very dangerous for us very quickly. But there is one way out they might not be watching. The harbor."

"How can we get to the harbor? Didn't we come in through a gate on the waterfront?"

"There will be sally ports," Kira said. "Do you know what a sally port is?"

"Um…a small door in the wall that defenders can use to sneak out and surprise attackers. Right?"

"Right! There won't be any sentries on them in peacetime. Just locks."

"Locks?" Jason smiled with relief. "Do you think you can open them?"

"There's a pretty good chance of it," Kira said, smiling back at him. "Let's head that way. It'll be full dark by the time we get back to the sea-facing wall."

They walked, trying not to look in a hurry or worried, Kira watching and listening for any sign of trouble. But no one seemed to be taking any particular interest in them at the moment.

She wasn't sure how late it was when they reached the wall facing the sea. Night had fallen, street lights had been lit, the world relaxing after the labors of the day. The gate was sealed tight for the night, a few sentries maintaining watch.

Kira strolled casually down the street inside the wall, searching for a sally port in the wall and finally spotting one. "There are still plenty of people out," she told Jason. "We have to look like we're not doing anything wrong. Do you see any police or militia?"

"No," Jason said, looking around. "You guys don't have any night-vision stuff?"

"What's night-vision stuff?"

"Infrared, cats-eye contact lenses, stuff like that."

Kira shook her head. "I heard that somebody tried to train cats to serve as sentries once, but that didn't go well."

"On Earth, they tried to make compliant cats," Jason said.

"That genetic thing? How did that work?"

"They got something that was compliant. It wasn't a cat anymore, though. I mean, it looked like a cat, but it wasn't a cat. It seriously freaked out people."

"Good," Kira said. The street traffic seemed momentarily light. "Let's stroll across the street to that sally port."

They made it without incident, Kira crouching to examine the lock as she pulled out her lock picks. "Nice lock. I can do this. Jason—"

"I know. Look like a wall."

Kira worked patiently. Kelsi had invested in some good locks. She was almost done when Jason hissed a warning.

"Stand up! Face me!"

Kira straightened, putting her back to the wall. Jason faced her, close, his arms on either side of her.

"Can you giggle?" he asked.

"I don't giggle, Jason. I can…chuckle."

"Do it!"

Kira managed a light laugh just as she saw two police officers walking past. They were close enough for Kira to see every detail of their faces in the light of the nearest street lamp, but she was shadowed from their sight by Jason's body, and all they could see of Jason was his back.

One of the officers cast a knowing glance their way as the police walked on without pausing.

Jason sighed with relief. "They thought we were, you know…"

"Making out," Kira said. "How did you think of that?"

"I saw it in a vid."

"It worked. Good thinking." Kira bent down again, working the lock. A final metallic snick announced success. "Here we go."

But as she swung the sally port open toward her, just inside it solid stone suddenly appeared, blocking the tunnel through the wall leading to the outer sally port.

Kira stared. If a Mage could create the illusion of an opening in a wall that didn't have one, why couldn't a Mage create the illusion of no opening where one had been?

She turned at the same time as she drew her pistol, flipping off the safety and readying it.

A number of people strolled the sidewalk opposite them. Others leaned against buildings, some talking to each other.

Kira saw people running toward her and Jason from both sides along the street. Their retreat was cut off and at least a dozen people were rushing them. Where was the Mage who had created the illusion of rock filling the tunnel? Whoever it was, the Mage had to have a clear view of the sally port. She could almost feel where the Mage was. Somewhere. Somewhere. Kira strained at something that she didn't really understand, trying to get it to work.

There. That woman leaning against the building opposite. To Kira's eyes, the woman's body glowed with the power being put into the spell.

Kira raised her arm toward the woman, then stopped, staring at her hand and the object in it. What was she supposed to do? How?

Jason grabbed her other arm. "Kira! What's going on?"

Kira shook her head, feeling as if the world had jerked around her. She blinked her eyes to clear them, looking back at the woman. She was still there, but Kira could no longer see the glow of the spell-work even though the female Mage was obviously still concentrating. Kira's arm was already up, the pistol in her hand pointed toward the Mage. She hastily aimed and fired, the shot tugging at one of the woman's sleeves.

The female Mage dodged away, losing her sight of the sally port as well as her concentration on the spell.

The sound of Kira's shot echoed down the street. Anyone not already aware that something was happening began running.

She backed toward the sally port, turning to see that the nearest attackers were almost on Jason, too close for him to run. Daggers gleamed in their hands, but Jason was between Kira and them so she couldn't get a clear shot. If only there had been time on the ship to teach him more than basic self-defense moves.

At the last moment, Jason leaped toward the two, throwing off their own attacks. The man went one way, the woman another, and Jason stumbled to a halt in the center before dashing back toward Kira.

As the man rose to slash at Jason, Kira lined up her shot and fired, the impact of her bullet knocking him back. The woman hesitated as Jason joined Kira, giving Kira time to shove him inside the tunnel, then back in fast herself, pulling the armored door closed behind her, holstering her weapon to use both hands.

Lightning rippled down the street, lashing at the door. Kira got thrown backwards, dazed. She was trying to get up when Jason ran to the door and yanked it the rest of the way closed. Total darkness engulfed them. "M-make sure the lock clicks shut," Kira gasped to Jason.

"It did." He knelt by her, his hands trying to find Kira. "How's your heart?"

"My heart?"

Jason grabbed her wrist and turned Kira's hand up, his thumb pressed on her inner wrist. "Your pulse is okay. The shock must have thrown you clear before it did too much damage. Did you get any burns?"

"I don't think so," Kira said as Jason helped her stand up.

"You weren't grounded. You got lucky." She couldn't see him, but could hear the anguish in his voice. "You could have been killed."

"I think that was the idea," Kira said, trying to make light of it. She paused, emboldened by the dark, then quickly hugged Jason. "Thanks."

"Sure." Jason still sounded shaky, but better, and she was recovering. "How long will that hold?" Jason asked.

"It's supposed to hold off an invading army for a little while. They'll need to get some soldiers to get the keys, because the police won't be carrying them. And it's possible the people chasing us can pick that lock, too. We don't have forever." Kira went down the tunnel as fast as she dared, feeling her way.

She found the door on the outer wall by running into it, then Jason ran into her. As soon as they untangled themselves, Kira felt for the lock, pulled out her picks, and went to work by feel and sound.

"What if they're waiting for us out there?" Jason asked, his voice echoing oddly in the tunnel.

"Then you and I are going to go through them like a stampede through a weak fence," Kira said.

"What happened to the Kira who didn't think she could do anything much?"

"Kira doesn't have the luxury of self-doubt at the moment. Hush. I need to listen to the lock."

He fell silent for a few moments, until Kira gave a gasp of satisfaction. "That's it. All we have to do is lift these bars reinforcing the door and pull the door open."

"Before we go out and stampede through whatever is waiting," Jason said, "how was it that lightning just happened to hit that other door? And why did the lightning look like it was traveling along the ground instead of coming down?"

Kira rubbed her face, trying to think how to explain quickly. "That was a Mage. My father is one of the rare Mages who can create the illusion of great heat. There are other rare Mages who can create the illusion of lightning radiating from them, directing it toward a target. The one who just tried to fry us could be the same one who attacked my parents a couple of times twenty years ago. He doesn't like my family. All right?"

"That lightning was an illusion?" Jason asked skeptically.

"Yes! So is this door and so is this stone and so is this floor! Really powerful illusions that feel absolutely real! That is how Mages see the universe, and it works for them! They believe in their illusions enough for their illusions to kill you! Now, can we finish escaping?"

"Uh, yeah."

"Fine! Thank you!" She knew it was ridiculous to be bothered by

Jason's questions when there were an unknown number of people trying to kill both of them. But something was tearing at her inside. She kept seeing the face of the man she had shot as he lunged at Jason. *There's no time for this. Later.* She and Jason lifted off the reinforcing bars. Kira drew her weapon again, taking deep breaths. "Now."

They pulled together, the heavy, armored door swinging inward.

Kira waited, watching, listening.

She heard a noise behind them, the sound of the inner door being opened. "No more time. Run, Jason. We're going to go out along a pier and get a boat."

They ran through the night, the high wall looming behind them, the waters of the harbor not far ahead.

Lightning flared again, this time from above. Had an actual storm moved in?

The lightning flayed the ground nearby as Kira and Jason dodged. She looked up, squinting against the brightness of the bolts, seeing they were originating at the top of the wall. The Lightning Mage was there, still trying to get them.

It was a long shot with her pistol. Kira stopped, planting her feet, holding her pistol with both hands as she raised it and aimed at the shadowy figure at the top of the wall, afterimages of the lightning dancing in her eyes. She exhaled slowly, squeezing the trigger, knowing that the Mage would require a few moments before being able to hurl lightning again.

She fired, lined up her sights for a second time and fired once more.

The shadowy figure disappeared.

"Did you hit him?" Jason asked as they began running again.

"I don't know. Maybe. Maybe I just scared the blazes out of him. Whatever, as long as he doesn't try to fry us another time."

People were running from the sally port behind them, others along the base of the wall. Kira holstered her pistol to try to blend in with everyone else in the darkness. "That pier we came in on had boats tied up. Which one was it?"

"This way," Jason said.

The sound of fighting broke out somewhere behind them. Jason tried to look that way and stumbled. "Don't look back," Kira said. "Whoever is fighting whoever, we need to get away from them."

The pier Jason led them down felt deserted, their feet on the wooden planks sounding far too loud as they ran to the end. Some larger vessels tied up on either side were dark and silent. Out in the harbor, ships swung at anchor, lanterns marking their locations.

They paused, Kira trying to catch her breath as she looked around. The sound of the fighting behind them had subsided. "It's quiet."

"Too quiet," Jason said, then laughed. "That's an ancient joke on Earth."

"The more I hear about Urth the stranger it gets." Kira pointed. "Look. A large dinghy. It's got a small mast with a sail, and oars. That'll get us out of here." She looked back, scanning the waterfront. Dark shapes flitted through the shadows. "They're coming. We can't be picky."

Before dropping down into the dinghy, Kira reloaded her pistol, topping off the magazine. "Mother and Aunt Alli always said reload whenever you can."

"Your mother has good advice," Jason said, looking toward the waterfront. "They're getting closer."

Kira lowered herself and dropped into the dinghy, the boat rocking under her. She grabbed a supporting pillar next to the boat to steady it as Jason followed.

"Are we stealing this?" Jason asked.

"We're borrowing it. I'm not happy about it, but it beats being captured or killed by the people who are after us."

"Good point," Jason agreed as he checked the single sail furled on its boom. "Good thing we've got experience with handling sails, huh?"

"What do you think you're doing?" A pile of blankets in the bow proved to be the bed of an enraged man. Just awoken from sleep, he glowered at them, brandishing a large knife. "Get out!"

"You're taking us for a ride," Kira informed him. "We're renting your boat. Cast off."

"Wrong, girl! The harbor master doesn't allow passengers in full dark. Now get off before I—"

The man's voice broke off as Kira pulled out her pistol and aimed it at him. She kept her finger alongside the trigger guard because she didn't want to risk accidentally shooting the man and didn't think he would notice in the dark. "You're taking us. Or you're getting off and we'll take the boat without you. Your choice." A part of Kira marveled at how calm and steely her voice sounded. "You have to the count of three to decide."

Speechless, the man nodded and helped Jason free the last lines holding the boat to the pier. Jason and the man shoved the boat away from the pier while Kira stood next to the mast, holding on to it to steady herself as she watched for approaching enemies. "I think they're coming down the pier. Get us away from here."

Jason hauled the small sail up, swinging the short boom so it caught the night breeze. The sail filled and the boat swung away from the pier.

Kira moved around the mast to avoid the boom and keep her eyes on the pier. "They're still coming. Blast. They've started running. They must have seen this boat moving away."

Reluctant to fire again and draw more attention, Kira stood as tall as she could in the dinghy, extending her arm holding the pistol as if aiming to fire.

As she had hoped, their pursuers dove for cover.

The boat swung on around, pulling away from the pier. "Where are we going?" Jason asked.

"Outside the city walls," Kira ordered. "Tell him to take us to a point outside the walls where we won't be spotted."

She heard a soft *thunk* from the direction of the pier, then something whistled past. Another *thunk*, then a louder sound of something striking wood. Kira saw a bolt sticking in the mast uncomfortably close to her.

"What is that?" Jason demanded.

"A crossbow bolt," Kira said. "A small one. They must be using small hand crossbows. We'll be out of range of them soon. Don't worry."

A flash of light and the boom of a shot was followed by the crack of a bullet whipping past. "That was a pistol," Kira called to Jason.

"Should I worry this time?" he called back.

"Maybe a little." She aimed at the spot where the flash of the shot had come from, cursing as the swaying and pitching of the small boat kept throwing off her sights. Another flash of light, another crash of sound, and another bullet tore by. Kira braced her back against the short mast and fired four times, pausing briefly between each to center her weapon as well as she could on the place where the shots had come from. "That should keep their heads down!"

Cries sounded across the water as sailors keeping watch on ships called out warnings that something was happening ashore. At least one of those ships would be part of the Free Cities navy, and she had no desire to get too close to them.

She glanced at the inside of the dinghy and saw the owner was huddled on the bottom with his head buried in his hands. Jason had taken the tiller and was steering the boat away from the pier. "Good job, sailor."

Jason grinned, his smile slightly frantic. "They make you a second mate and you're drunk with power, aren't you? Is there any chance our ship is still here?"

Kira shook her head. "They would have sailed well before sunset." She crouched down to where the owner was huddled on the deck. "Listen up. The sooner we're gone the sooner you'll be safe. Tell us where to go so we can land safely outside the city walls. We don't want to go out into the harbor. I promise we will pay you and not hurt you if you drop us off safely." The man didn't respond. Her temper flared. "Give us a course to steer, you—" adding a string of curses which had been the favorites of the first mate on *The Son of Taris*.

Hearing a sixteen-year-old girl swear like a sailor got the man's attention, shocking him out of his fear. He sat up slowly, looking around, then pointed a shaking hand. "That way."

"Two points to starboard," Kira ordered Jason.

"Aye," he responded, once again seemingly amused by something.

"What's so funny?"

"I was just imagining you talking like that in front of your parents."

Kira shivered at the thought. "That's not going to happen."

"They've probably heard worse."

"Not from me!" There weren't any more shots chasing them, and no other boats had left the pier in pursuit of them. She wondered why. A lot of lights on other piers warned that the harbor police might be getting ready to investigate the shooting, but as of yet there were no lights low on the water that would have shown police craft underway. Many more lanterns were visible on the anchored ships out in the harbor as awakened crews watched for trouble, but those were far enough off not to be a problem.

It seemed too easy, but for the moment the chase seemed to have let up. Kira straightened, holding to the mast again to steady herself as she searched the water for signs of trouble. "If my parents heard me talking like that they'd probably ship me off to be completely reeducated on proper behavior."

Jason grinned. "You've got better behavior than most adults I know."

"You must have low standards. You know, my parents were pirates at one time, so they must have heard worse language than that. That never really occurred to me before."

"They don't swear around the house, huh?"

"No. It's funny how much you don't realize about the people you've spent your whole life with, isn't it?" Kira reloaded again, trusting that Jason could handle the boat's owner if he tried anything, then holstered the weapon. She leaned forward to address the owner. "How far do we have to go?" The man shrugged. "I'm going to ask you again, and if I don't get an answer I'm going to get angry."

She had apparently impressed the man enough already for that threat to work. He stared into the night, thinking. "It's not far, but there are rocks along that shore. My boat could get badly banged up."

"Is there a better place along the water in this direction?"

"No. Not unless you want to climb a short cliff."

"Then steer us to the best place," Kira directed. "If you mess up, it's your boat that will suffer."

The man got up and grudgingly took the tiller from Jason. Kira and Jason moved forward a bit where they could talk privately. "I was just thinking something," Jason murmured. "If I was chasing some people and knew they'd taken a boat, I'd send someone to the best place to land nearby."

Kira grimaced. "How did you think of that?"

"It's what would happen in a game."

"A game?" But it made sense. It made way too much sense.

"Whoever they are," Jason added, "they seem to have a lot of people." He glanced back at the boat's owner. "I don't trust that guy. I think he'd do or say whatever it took to get us off his boat as soon as possible."

"We did hijack his boat," Kira pointed out.

"I thought we borrowed it."

"That was before we hijacked it." Kira glanced at the boat owner, who had the look of someone who was nervous for the wrong reasons. "Take it a point to port," she ordered the owner.

The owner glared back at her. "I know this harbor."

"Take the boat a point to port and hold it there." The man didn't move. "Do it now or you're going over the side."

He nudged the tiller as directed, his fear obvious. Jason was standing as far forward as he could get, peering into the darkness. He looked back at her briefly. "Why didn't they steal some boats, too?"

"I don't know. They didn't—" *Because they're watching this boat on the water and they've got people waiting just like Jason guessed and we're heading for the ambush.*

She rounded on the boat's owner. "Two more points to port." He hesitated. Kira whipped out her pistol and pointed it at him. "*Now.*"

The boat had barely begun to turn when Jason cried an alarm from the bow. "Hey, there's a beach real close."

"Get back here, Jason!" She didn't need foresight to know what was about to happen.

He'd just started to move when lights flashed on the shore, so close that Kira realized they would've run up on the land by now if she hadn't made the boat turn. The roar of the shots merged into one sound as splinters flew around the owner at the tiller. The owner, having apparently had all that he could take, leaped overboard without a word.

"Take the helm!" Kira ordered Jason, crouching and looking for targets. The rifles fired again, old-style Mechanics Guild repeaters by the sound of them. The same weapons which had once almost killed her mother. Fortunately, many of the surviving models were old and not very accurate. The muzzle flashes illuminated perhaps ten figures rushing into the water and splashing toward them as the bullets tore more splinters from the hull of the small boat. "Get us away from here!"

CHAPTER FOURTEEN

Jason dove to the tiller, grabbing it and swinging it hard to port. The sail fluttered as the boat swung, losing speed in the turn. It caught again, the boat moving away from the shore.

Then most of the boom disappeared, leaving the sail fluttering uselessly.

Kira searched for the Mage responsible, but couldn't see anything in the dark. She wasn't sure why, but she felt reluctant to strain too much to spot the Mage's spell as she had at the entrance to the sally port.

More shots thundered from the shore, ripping holes in the side of the boat. Two hands grasped the edge of the boat and a man reared up, a dagger clutched in his teeth. Kira kept her balance as the boat rocked, aiming a kick at his face that knocked the man back into the water. Another hand grasped at the stern sheet. Jason picked up the owner's dropped knife and jabbed at the hand, drawing a howl of pain. The hand fell away.

"Jason! Have you ever rowed a boat?"

"Uh, no. Not for real. But I watched them rowing earlier today, and I was a galley slave a few times in the Roma Imperia historical immersive massive group simulation so I think I remember how it's supposed to be done."

"What? Never mind! We're slowing down. Just get the oars in place and start rowing! If we don't get out of here they'll swamp us." On the heels of her words a woman rolled up over the side of the boat, coming to a crouch on the deck just in time to catch Kira's boot on her jaw. Kira followed up with a punch that hurled the woman out of the boat. "Move it, Jason!"

"I'm moving! I'm moving!"

She caught glimpses of Jason fumbling with the oars as he set them into the oarlocks, then Kira spun and fired at another hand grasping the bow. Splinters flew near it and the hand dropped away.

The boom finally reappeared, but the bottom of the sail was no longer attached and continued to flap uselessly.

A man heaved himself up near Jason, who was trying to set the second oar in place. Jason twisted, swinging one end of the oar to slam into the man's chest and knock him back overboard. A pair of hands was gripping the bow again, but Jason kept the oar swinging, bringing its broad end down on the hands. There was a howl of pain and they dropped away.

Another volley came from the shore, the bullets tearing past with cracking sounds that almost froze Kira's heartbeat. She faced the shore and yelled as loudly as she could. "I'm not worth anything to you dead!"

She knew that wasn't true, but she also knew that the Imperials would only pay for her alive, and plenty of her parents' enemies would want her alive for their own reasons, like those of the rider way back north of the Glenca. As she had hoped, her words made the shooters hesitate.

Jason had finally mastered the oarlocks and was rowing, grunting with the effort as the wooden oars bit into the water, the boat very slowly gathering speed again.

Two men grabbed on, one on each side, pulling themselves aboard too fast for Kira to stop. "Keep rowing no matter what!" she yelled at Jason while she planted a boot in one man's stomach and propelled him back overboard.

The second man grabbed her from behind before she could turn.

Kira struggled to break free, but he was bigger and stronger and she couldn't find any point of leverage with his body bearing down against her. He had one hand gripping her pistol arm so she couldn't bring it around. As the man's other arm across her neck started to choke her, Kira took a moment to identify where the man's groin was, behind and just to her left side. Stiffening her arm, she rammed her elbow into it as hard as she could.

The man emitted a squeal of pain. Kira gave him another elbow in the groin and his grip loosened. Breaking free, she pivoted and stiff-armed the man over the side.

Breathing heavily, Kira saw another hand reaching for the boat and drove the heel of her boot into the face that came up beside it. Part of her was horrified to be doing such things, but the rest of Kira knew she didn't have any choice at the moment.

They were definitely moving now, pulling away from the shore and the attackers struggling in the water. Kira couldn't see anyone else close enough to climb aboard. Jason was red-faced with effort as he pulled at the oars. Holstering her weapon, Kira dropped onto the bench beside Jason, shoving him to one side, and grabbed one of the oars, trying to pull in rhythm with Jason. Belatedly, more shots began sounding from the shore as it became apparent the quarry was escaping.

They kept pulling until they could neither hear nor see their attackers, then slumped with exhaustion over the oars, the boat drifting on the dark surface of the water. The lights of Kelsi glittered off to the east. The ships at anchor looked like they were on holiday, so many lanterns had been lit. Kira squinted, seeing other lights moving low on the water. "The harbor police are out. Maybe some of the Free Cities navy, too. Can you row some more?"

"The engines cannae take no more, Captain," Jason muttered in an accent stranger than his usual one, then turned a grin on her. "That's another ancient joke."

She returned an exasperated look. "What's it supposed to mean?"

"I don't know. It's just something you say when you're tired."

"Is every Urth joke really strange?"

"Not all of them. There's one about a Euro, a Martian, and an Ionion who walk into a bar and—"

"I don't want to hear it." Kira breathed deeply, staring toward the lights on the water. "I can't believe we survived that."

"I can't believe how you can fight."

"I was scared to death. I hardly knew what I was doing."

Jason shook his head. "I'd hate to fight you when you did know what you were doing."

Kira grinned. "You did good, Jason. What a fighter! Where did you get the idea to use the oar that way?"

"Robin Hood. Quarterstaffs, you know."

"Quarterstaffs? Is that what you call oars on Urth?"

Jason smiled and shook his head. "No, we call them oars. Quarterstaffs are big sticks that you beat other people with. They were used as weapons a long time ago."

"Maybe you can teach *me* some fighting tricks." Kira grabbed his hand for a moment. "We make a good team."

"Yeah. We do, don't we?" Jason hesitated, looking at her. "Um…I guess we should row again."

Kira looked away from the city and the boats on the water behind them, spotting off to the northwest an irregular line of white that came and went but stayed in roughly the same place. "That must be waves breaking on a beach. It's way to the west of where we got attacked. Let's head there."

By the time they reached the beach, where swells from the harbor rolled onto a long patch of gravel, Kira's back and arms ached. She looked up at the stars, seeing that most of the night had gone. Some distance to the east, but still too close for comfort, they could see lights on the shore and hear occasional gunshots, probably the city militia and police investigating the site of the ambush and running down the people Kira and Jason had narrowly escaped.

They grounded the boat on the gravel, both Kira and Jason leaning on the bow as they caught their breath again. She dug out some money and tossed it into the boat, hoping it would be enough to cover the cost of the damage.

"We're still paying him?" Jason asked.

"It is his boat. But, yeah, if he hadn't tried to run his boat aground we might not have run into that ambush. Ready for a hike?"

"No."

"Neither am I," Kira said. "Let's see how far we can get before we both collapse."

"Most people sleep at night, you know," Jason grumbled as they scrambled up a line of cliffs about two lances high that fronted on the gravel.

"Are you complaining again?" Kira gasped, painfully pulling herself over the top of the last vertical stretch. She helped Jason up as well, then dropped to her knees, breathing heavily, while he lay nearby. "We have to keep moving," she finally got out.

Jason groaned, but rolled to his front and got up, staggering a little.

It was still full dark, but the looming shape of the mountains to the west were easy to spot. "That way," Kira said. "There's a long stretch of open land west of Kelsi that slopes up to meet the pass leading to Ihris." She made a major effort and managed to get her feet moving.

Jason trod beside her, slumping as he walked. "Slopes up," he repeated. "We have to go uphill."

"Yeah. All the way to the pass."

"I can't believe it, but I'm wishing for a train."

They fell silent, struggling through the coastal grasses, high enough to reach their waists in places, the stalks and leaves tough. Pushing through that made the walk up the slope even harder. "This entire planet is trying to make me miserable," Jason said. "Demeter hates me."

"It's Dematr," Kira said.

"No, it's Demeter."

"It's my world, not yours. Dematr."

"Okay."

"Don't say okay."

She heard him laughing under his breath and wondered what could possibly be funny.

Neither one talked again for a while, concentrating on staying on their feet. Kira did her best to think of nothing except walking, but recent memories and emotions began to rise to the surface, things she had felt but hadn't dealt with yet.

Kira found herself stumbling, her eyes fixed ahead but not focusing. She suddenly stopped, breathing heavily.

Jason stopped walking as well, staring back at her with concern. "You never fall behind me. Kira? Are you shaking?"

She was, Kira realized. She was trembling.

"What's the matter?" Jason asked, frantic.

"Jason, I…I…shot that man. And a guy…trying to get in the boat. I might…I might have shot other people. I…I…I…might have… killed one of them."

Aunt Alli had warned her. So had her mother. It seemed so easy, shooting at targets. But a real person, that was very different.

"Kira," Jason said, sounding sad and helpless. "You didn't want to do that, did you? You had to. They attacked us. Attacked you."

"I know. I know. It's still…"

"I stuck a knife in a guy's hand," Jason said. "That was nothing like one of the games where you stab some opponent with a sword and you know it's all fake no matter how real it looks. I…I know how you feel. A little."

Kira's legs finally gave out. She dropped down into the high grass, Jason sitting beside her. The weight of the pistol under her coat reminded her of what she had done, of what she might have to do again. "I guess sometimes the way Urth sees things might be a lot easier. Just another form of life."

He shook his head. "It shouldn't be easier, should it?"

"No. It shouldn't." Kira covered her face with her hands. "I'll be all right, Jason. It's just really hard to talk about."

It's just really hard to talk about. How many times had her mother said something like that? And how many times had Kira pressed her anyway, demanding to know why her mother wouldn't share import-ant things with her? If those things hurt, wouldn't talking make it better? And why couldn't Mari talk to her own daughter about them? *I made it about me. Mother was hurting so bad inside and couldn't tell me why and I made it about me.*

I have to survive this. I have to see her again. So I can tell her how sorry I am.

She inhaled deeply again. "We need to keep moving."

"Kira, if we try to get up, both of us are going to turn into jelly."

She made an attempt to rise and realized that Jason was right. "We'll rest a little while. Then we'll move again."

Kira didn't remember falling asleep. When she awoke, the sun was high in the sky. Jason lay beside her, still dead to the world.

She struggled up, worried about how much time must have passed.

There were riders visible down the slope toward the city. They were riding this way, spread out in a search line.

And beyond them, gliding in over the sea from the south, were some of the flying things that Jason called drones.

Lady Mage Asha was one of Alain's closest friends, and close to Mari as well. She had been like an aunt to Kira since Kira was a baby. Fore-sight often required an emotional connection to another, so it was not surprising when Alain and Mari received a message from Asha saying that she had seen a vision of them going aboard a ship in the harbor of Marida. The name of the ship hadn't been fully visible, but ended with the word "Taris."

And the vision had held a sense of urgency.

"Get up!" Kira shook Jason. "They're looking for us!"

Jason stumbled to his feet, looking around, still dizzy from sleep.

"Who's looking for us?"

"Everybody!"

The road to the pass should still lie north of them, and even though they would be more likely to see and be seen by other people on the road, anyone heading toward the pass but avoiding the road would attract a lot more attention. Walking overland was also harder than using the road, and neither she nor Jason could afford to keep pushing themselves more than they absolutely had to.

Her throat felt dry as dust as they walked. They still had their packs but somewhere in the night the bag with the water bottles had disappeared. Fortunately they came across a creek meandering through the grass on its way to the sea and drank their fill. Jason seemed to have lost his worries about "unprocessed" water. As they got to their feet again, Kira looked Jason over, dismayed. "You look like you spent all last night fighting and rowing and running and then slept in the open in the grass."

"So do you," Jason said. "I'm sure it looks a lot better on you than it does on me."

"We have to hope nobody notices when we reach the road. Try to look a little nicer, though. As if we haven't done anything unusual and got dressed this morning in clean clothes."

"You're kidding, right?"

"I guess. Mother told me to take care of this coat and look at it!"

He grinned despite the fatigue and dust on his face. "I think it still looks real good. On you."

"Stop it." Kira headed up the slope again, angling west as well as north. The line of riders was still a good way off, but gaining on them, and the drones were moving in a pattern over the city and slowly expanding their search outward. "Jason, we have to move faster."

He didn't answer, but kept pace as Kira forced herself to walk more quickly. She could see people and wagons on the road ahead, some moving east toward Kelsi and some toiling up the slope westward to the pass for Ihris and the high plains around that city.

They finally reached the road, Kira's legs shaking with tiredness again. Jason appeared ready to fall over. Kira looked east, seeing the riders getting uncomfortably close and the drones nearly even with the riders now. They searchers had reached the point where the rail line being built west from Kelsi had so far been completed, the new twin rails gleaming beside the old, old road.

Jason shook his head. "Kira, I don't think we can stay ahead of them."

"We can't." Where could they hide? The grass wouldn't offer concealment up close, especially not from the drones overhead.

As Kira despairingly considered the few, bad options left to her and Jason, she felt something. A presence. One familiar to her. She stared in that direction, seeing someone sitting alone a bit north of the road. "Jason, this way!"

"Huh?" But he followed as Kira walked with renewed energy and hope toward the lone figure, seeing that the person wore Mage robes. She was right! It must be her! "Mage Alera? Lady Mage Alera?"

Mage Alera, one of her parents' oldest friends, stood up and turned to face Kira as she and Jason stumbled to a halt. Older than Kira's parents, Alera had been trained by the old Mage Guild using the brutal methods of the elders, then treated with disdain by those elders because of her special skill.

Her face was almost impassive as she looked at Kira, and Alera didn't say anything as they approached. Mages weren't much for social niceties.

"This one asks a great favor," Kira said as she tried to catch her breath again. "A great favor from Lady Mage Alera."

A trace of a smile flitted across Alera's face. "This one sees that one Kira. You ask...*help?*"

"Yes. Really big help. For this one, and that one," Kira said, pointing to Jason.

"That one needs Swift?"

"This one needs Swift. There is no mightier Roc than Swift."

"Where?" Alera asked.

"Somewhere near Ihris. Or at least over the pass. We have to get out of here as fast as possible. I don't know why you're here—"

"This one sought…family."

"Oh!" Kira said. "I hope it went better this time."

"This one thinks it did." Mage Alera looked dispassionately at Kira, then at Jason. "Both of you over the pass? Swift can do this."

Kira caught the trace of pride in Alera's voice. "Yes. This one has missed Swift."

"Swift has been resting. This one will call Swift."

"Thank you, Mage Alera!" Kira turned an exultant smile on Jason. "We're all right! Mage Alera will take us over the pass!"

Jason stared at Kira, then at Alera as the Mage walked a short distance away. "How? Is she going to carry us?"

"No, Swift is going to carry us."

"Who is Swift?"

A huge bird, somewhat like a hawk but immensely larger, suddenly appeared standing near Mage Alera.

"That's Swift," Kira said.

Jason gaped at the Roc. "Where did it come from?"

"Mage Alera made it. Mages who can create Rocs always make the same one, and the Rocs somehow remember. Even though they go away each time the spell is exhausted, the Rocs remember their Mage and things that have happened."

"It's a giant bird," Jason said, still looking stunned.

"Not really," Kira said. "It's the illusion of a giant bird."

"So it's a machine of some kind that looks like a bird?" Jason asked.

"No, it's not a machine or device," Kira said. "It's a bird."

"But not a real bird. How does it fly if it's an illusion?"

"It doesn't," Kira said. "The illusion of a bird creates the illusion of flight."

"It's not real," Jason said, "and it doesn't really fly."

"Right."

"So it can't take it us away from here."

"Of course it can," Kira said.

Jason gave her a baffled look. "How does the illusion of a bird creating the illusion of flight allow us to go from one spot to another on the actual surface of a world?"

"Because," Kira explained patiently, "the world isn't real, either. It's just illusions interacting with other illusions. And people. We're all real, but the world isn't."

Jason looked at her, looked at the bird, then back at Kira. "I'm sorry. I'm really having trouble understanding this."

"Mother is the same way," Kira said. "No matter how Father and I try to explain it, her eyes always glaze over."

"That's surprising," Jason said, "since it's such a simple concept."

"I know! Right? Wait. Are you making fun of me?"

"No."

"Yes, you are!" Kira said. "I could tell that you lied when you said no!"

Jason scratched his head. "Oh, yeah. I guess having a friend who's a girl who can tell every time I lie can be a little complicated."

"No," Kira insisted, "that's simple, too. This is the first time you've lied to me. Don't ever lie to me again. Now, the search line of riders and those drone things are heading this way. Are we going to wait here for them or are we going to ride this bird?"

"Ride the bird," Jason said immediately. "Do we just imagine that we're on it?"

"How could that work?" Kira asked. "We climb up."

"But if it's an illusion—"

"It's a strong illusion, Jason! Didn't we just go over this last night?"

Jason seemed oddly concerned about approaching Swift, who eyed him calmly as the boy from Urth got closer. "That's a really, really big beak."

"Yeah," Kira said. "Isn't it cool?"

"Not exactly the word I was thinking of."

Swift lowered and slightly extended one wing so that Jason and Kira could climb up onto Swift's back, Jason staring at the huge feathers under his hands. "How can this bird fly? It's impossible."

"Jason, I told you. It's not going to fly. It's going to create the illusion of flying."

"Oh, that's all right, then."

Kira helped Jason lie flat and fasten himself to the leather straps on Swift's back, pausing to stroke the feathers before she strapped herself in next to him. "Hi, Swift! I love you! Mage Alera is so proud of you and so am I!"

This time Jason stared at her. "It's a huge raptor. Why are you talking like it's a pet?"

"Swift is Mage Alera's Roc!" Why did some people have trouble figuring that out?

Alera took her place seated just behind Swift's neck.

"Is there a preflight safety briefing?" Jason asked nervously.

"A what?" Kira asked.

Swift ran a short distance, vaulting into the air, the immense wings on either side pumping to lift the Roc and its riders higher and higher. Kira felt the wind rush past, felt the movement of Swift's muscles under her, saw the land falling away beneath her, and laughed for the sheer joy of it.

She looked over at Jason to share the moment. He was lying stiffly, looking terrified.

"Isn't this great?" Kira called to Jason. She lifted up enough to look down and back. The searchers, both human and drone, were rapidly dwindling in size as the Roc flew higher and angled west toward the pass. "We made it!"

"Yeah," Jason said, his voice quivering. "Great."

Kira laughed again. You would think Jason had never flown before.

All the rest of the day Swift bore them westward, gliding among the peaks of southernmost reaches of the Northern Ramparts, the great mountain chain that lay across the land north of the Sea of Bakre. Wind currents battered them as they swooped past immense mountains, steep slopes of living rock sweeping by just beyond Swift's wingtips. They caught sight of occasional high mountain valleys and glades forming unexpected patches of green below them, then a mountain lake surrounded by peaks like a vast jewel in the most majestic setting imaginable.

Jason got over his initial fright, gazing around as the air grew cold and thinner, snow resting on the peaks that Swift flew past. Kira clutched her coat tighter about her and felt happy. It surprised her to realize that part of that came from having Jason nearby, being part of the experience. Had it only been a few weeks ago when she could barely tolerate his presence? But he wasn't the same person he had been then.

They cleared the last of the mountains as the sun settled toward the western horizon. As the final outliers of the mighty Ramparts fell away, ahead and to the north and south stretched the expanse of the high plains.

Swift angled down, coming to a landing just before the sun set. The plains here were dotted with bushes and only a few trees.

Kira helped Jason get his straps off and helped him down. "Thank you, Swift," she called, petting the feathers before sliding off as well.

Mage Alera stood near Swift's head as Jason and Kira tore apart some dead bushes for firewood. Kira got a fire going with her fire-starter, clicking flint against steel until the sparks caught in the wood. After offering Alera part of their food, Kira and Jason settled down to eat as darkness settled on the land and the stars came out in countless numbers above. Neither the moon nor the twins were up, but Kira was glad for that. The twins, remnants of the ship that had brought people to this world, would have been an unwelcome reminder of the Urth people.

Jason sighed as he finished eating his portion of the trail food. "I was never big on camping, but this is nice."

"Much nicer than last night," Kira agreed. "So how did you like riding on Swift?"

"Nobody back home would believe it." He looked outside the ring of the fire. "Where is Mage Alera?"

"She's with Swift. They can communicate without words. Since Mage Alera has so much trouble socializing with people, because of what the Mage Guild elders did when they were training her, her relationship with Swift means a lot to her."

"Yeah," Jason said. "Relationships are important." He frowned, looking at the fire instead of at Kira.

"You had a good time today, right?" Kira asked. "Wasn't it amazing?"

"Yeah," Jason repeated. "But anything with you is amazing."

A slowly growing suspicion crystallized inside Kira. "Jason, are you in love with me?"

He didn't answer.

"Jason, please tell me."

"Yes," he said reluctantly, "I think I am."

"Oh, that's just great," Kira said, exasperated. Her sense of contentment vanished. "Here I've been starting to believe some of the nice things that you've been saying about me, but now I can't believe any of it."

"Why not?" Jason demanded, finally looking back at her.

"Because love makes people delusional, Jason! You aren't seeing me anymore. Your delusions are causing you to see some illusion of me that is far, far better than I could ever actually be."

"I don't think I'm delusional."

"Of course you don't *think* you're delusional," Kira explained. "That's because you *are* delusional."

"How do you know?" Jason said. "Have you ever been in love?"

"Me? No. Just a crush. But Mother told me about it, and Father confirmed it. My father is the smartest, most rational man you will ever meet. He truly is wise. But when it comes to my mother, he's hopeless. He thinks my mother is better looking than Aunt Asha. I asked him. He actually said that. And no woman could possibly be better looking than my Aunt Asha."

Jason frowned at her. "Your Aunt Asha is really good looking?"

"Yes. You probably saw her the day your ship landed. She was the Mage with long blonde hair."

"That one? Yeah, she was pretty hot," Jason admitted. "But she's not better looking than you."

"Oh, blazes, you are in love with me!" Kira threw up her hands in frustration. "Stop it!"

"Kira, what if you have things backwards?" Jason asked. "You think I fell in love with you because I'm delusional."

"Because that's obviously what happened."

"But what if I didn't become delusional until after I fell in love? What if the real you is what made me delusional?"

Kira eyed Jason dubiously. "You're saying that you became delusional because you got to know me."

"Yes! Exactly! I got to spend enough time with you to get to know the real you!"

"Jason, I know that you mean that well, but basically you're saying that spending time with me drove you insane. I'm sure my mother wouldn't be surprised to hear that someone forced to spend a while with me went crazy as a result, but it's really not a compliment."

"I think it is," Jason said.

"It's not. You really need to work on the whole giving compliments thing. Trust me."

"I do. I trust everything you—"

"Stop it!"

She was apparently stuck with Jason being in love. At least he was being good about it, acting fairly normally. Fairly normally for Jason, anyway. Not like the way Gari had moped around like a sick duck a few years ago when he had a crush on what's-her-name.

If she had to choose between the complaining Jason with a bad attitude that she had started out with or an in-love- with her Jason who was acting pretty nice, that shouldn't be too hard a choice to make.

So why was she feeling conflicting emotions racing through her?

"Jason," Kira began, "I'm going to be honest with you. I owe you that. I mean, you saved my life in the storm and—"

"I didn't do that to put an obligation on you," Jason said. "Go ahead and tell me to get over it."

"I can't tell you that," Kira said. "I don't how I feel about what you've just told me. I'm…confused. I suppose you couldn't help falling in love with me." She winced and covered her face with her hands. "Stars above, that sounds awful. What I meant was, I don't think you tried to fall in love with me. It just happened."

"Yeah," Jason said, staring at the grass near his feet. "I actually tried not to fall in love with you, because I…I thought you'd be upset."

"I'm not angry," Kira said. "Just confused. About my own feelings. But I do know this. We have a very important job to do. Millions of lives depend on us. We can't forget that, and we can't let personal things get in the way of our job. That has to stay our first priority, and that has to be what we think about."

"Sure. You're right. Are you sorry you kissed me on the ship?"

"No," Kira said. "I'm not sorry at all."

"Thank you. Seriously. I never thought someone would say that to me." Jason got up. "I need to, uh, do some business," he said, waving into the darkness.

While he was gone, Mage Alera came and sat on the opposite side of the fire from Kira, but farther away from the fire than Kira. For a Mage, it was a pretty bold bit of socializing. Kira inclined her head respectfully toward her. "Mage Alera, this one has questions."

Alera inclined her head toward Kira in return. "This one listens."

"Do you know anything about love?"

The female Mage took a while to reply. "I know what I feel toward Swift. And I know what Swift feels toward me."

Kira sighed. "I wish all love was that simple and uncomplicated."

"When the elders ruled the Mage Guild," Alera said, "they taught that love was an illusion."

"I tried the illusion argument with Jason already. I don't think it worked."

Jason came back into the firelight, remaining standing and looking at the grass again. "Kira?"

"Are we going to talk about the same thing we just talked about? Because I don't think—"

"No." Jason grimaced. "This is about the job. Kira, one time when you were telling me about Mages, you said they could make things disappear, like making part of a wall disappear so they could walk through. That's what happened on the boat last night, right, when the boom disappeared for a while?"

"Not exactly," Kira said. "What the Mage does is overlay an illusion of an opening on the illusion of a wall. The part of the wall that goes away for the duration of the spell doesn't disappear. It never was. Until the spell is over, and then it is again. But only as part of a larger illusion."

Jason looked at her, frowning. "I'm not even going to try to understand that. Can Mage Alera do it?"

Alera shook her head. "This one's only talent is creating Swift."

"What about you, Kira?"

Kira almost said "no," then thought about it. "I never have, and I don't know if I can, but it's possible. Father told me a lot about how it's done. I've just never tried and I don't know if I have the ability. Why are you asking about this?"

Jason reached into the top of his shirt and pulled out the object he had taken from the ship, looking down at it as he spoke. "I know a little bit about Invictus Drives because I did a report on them. What's inside this case is sort of a big crystal, like a diamond, but artificial and a lot harder. When data is downloaded into it, parts of a matrix inside the crystal reforms and fixes in place. When the drive is full, or set to read-only, the entire matrix inside the crystal is fixed. That's really simplified, but—"

"All I could understand?" Kira asked sharply.

"No! That's about all anyone can understand. There are maybe a hundred people among the billions on Earth who get this. I only get the really simplified version myself." Jason stopped and licked his lips nervously. "To destroy the data, the crystal has to be broken. That's why the data is almost impossible to destroy, because breaking that crystal takes tremendous amounts of energy. But if the crystal is broken, the matrix inside is, uh, it's sort of like yanking the foundation out from under a building. Even if it's a really strong building, all the pieces fall and break apart."

Kira gazed at Jason. "You think that if a Mage could overlay the illusion that part of that drive isn't there, the crystal would act as if it had been broken?"

"I think there's a real good chance of that, yeah." Jason shrugged. "I can't be certain, though. And the act of doing something to the drive might set off an alarm. I'll know if that happens because a light will blink here on the drive, and then I could try resetting it and silencing it. But it wouldn't take very long for the ship to spot that alarm and get a pretty good fix on where it was. It's risky."

"If we'd taken that drive to my father when you showed up at my home, he could have tried that."

"At that time I didn't know Mages could do that," Jason said.

"And we don't for certain if it would work, but it might well set off an alarm that would bring the ship quickly," Kira said. "So trying it at my home would have been very dangerous. Your ship could have been there before we could get away."

"That's right," Jason said. "Even if I had known Mages could do that, I don't think it would have been smart to try it then."

"Yeah, but now we're a lot farther from your ship, and if your idea works, those weapons couldn't be built, right?" Kira bit her lip. "I know to try this I need a place I can concentrate, without any distractions. That means a room or something. And if that alarm goes off, we need to be able to lose ourselves quickly, which means being in a city where there are a lot of places to hide and a lot of people to hide among. We'll have to try it in Ihris."

Jason nodded, looking at the grass again. "Sure."

What was bothering him? Kira had felt a surge of hope at Jason's idea. If it worked—

If it worked.

She stared at Jason. "If we destroy the data on that drive, you don't have a reason to hide anymore."

"Neither do you," Jason said. "You can go back where you're safe."

"But your mother will find you. You'll have to go back with her and…and you and I won't be together any more." Kira inhaled suddenly. "We'd probably never see each other again. Jason, you just told me that you loved me. Why did you then tell me about a way to destroy that data that would probably separate us forever?"

He scuffed at the grass with one boot. "I didn't want to tell you. But you've been in danger ever since we left your home. People have been hunting you, and things got pretty hot in Kelsi, and before that there were the three at Dorcastle, and… Kira, I don't know a lot about being in love. I don't know what I'm supposed to do. But not telling you—letting you think you have to stay away from home and in constant danger and all, just so I could stay with you—would be really selfish. And I don't think that's what love is supposed to be about. Even if I am delusional."

Kira got to her feet. "You know what's important about love, Jason. My father always said that false love is an attempt to force another person to be subjugated to your own illusion, to make that person nothing but a part of you that you can direct and control. But real love means the other person's illusion is more important than yours. You put them first. Like you put me first."

She walked the short distance to him and kissed Jason, holding it a while before stepping back.

"You didn't have to do that," Jason said, smiling at her.

"I know. But I realized that if we try your idea, there might not be another chance. To kiss you, I mean." Kira shook her head at him, feeling miserable. "I guess if I was selfish I'd say we shouldn't try. But if we can destroy that data, we have to."

Jason tried to maintain his smile. "My dad would say we're both being idiots, giving up something for other people."

"Your father is an idiot. Is it okay if I say that?"

He stared at her. "You said okay."

"No, I didn't."

"Yes, you—"

"Stop trying to change the subject. Let's get some rest. It's probably going to be a very long day tomorrow."

She left him standing there, going off into the dark nearby to lie down with her pack for a pillow and stare miserably at the stars. *I have a job to do. All right, Mother. I understand. Sometimes the jobs really, really suck. But we have to do them anyway. Because people are counting on us.*

Mage Alera appeared out of the dark. "Mage Kira, this one must talk."

"What is it?" Kira asked, sitting up and wondering why Alera was calling her that.

"Your Mage presence is much stronger. It can now be felt by other Mages, even those who have not met you. This one can begin teaching you some of the ways to block your presence from other Mages. But we will only have a short time to work on it. When you enter Ihris it will be important that you focus on blocking your presence from other Mages."

Other Mages. Which Kira realized meant she felt like a Mage to Mages. Kira could just imagine how her mother and father would take that.

But if any Mage they got close enough to in Ihris could tell she was a Mage, or worse, know exactly who she was, it could be disastrous. As if she didn't have enough to worry about with the drive and Jason and…

"Why does everything have to be so complicated?" Kira complained.

"Everything is simple," Alera said. "Doing it is complicated. We must work. It is only two more days to Ihris. You must be ready."

CHAPTER FIFTEEN

The next morning, Jason tried to act as if nothing had changed. Kira, despite being tired from staying up late working with Mage Alera, did her best to act the same.

They got back on Swift, rising up into the clear sky, the sun appearing over the Northern Ramparts to the east as the Roc climbed.

The scenery wasn't nearly as interesting today: long vistas of long vistas, occasional herds of cattle visible down below. Kira, worn out, slept as much as she could, which also had the side benefit of eliminating the need for awkward conversation with Jason.

In the afternoon she was jerked awake when Swift suddenly banked and began spiraling downward. Kira looked over to the side and saw below them a herd of horses. "What's going on?" Kira yelled to Mage Alera.

Alera called back. "This one senses the presence of one who can *help*."

"Why does she say help like that?" Jason asked, nervous again.

"Because Mages were once forced to forget what help meant, and were forbidden from actually helping anyone," Kira explained as Swift dropped lower. "A lot of those Mages who have relearned what help means are proud of it and want others to know they understand such a special word."

Swift's wings flared as the Roc braked to a landing. Mage Alera stayed sitting but gestured for Kira and Jason to dismount. Kira unbuckled her harness and slid off the massive feathers, steadying Jason as he came down beside her.

A rider was coming toward them. Beyond, Kira could see other riders moving around the herd, which was milling about nervously at the presence of the giant raptor capable of snatching up a horse the way an eagle could pluck a rabbit from a meadow. They were near Ihris. A herd of horses. Could this be…? Kira squinted to see better. "Petr. Jason, it's my Uncle Petr."

"Another honorary uncle?" Jason asked, looking toward the herd.

"He's the closest thing I have to a real uncle. My father's cousin. He's actually a few years older than Father, but he's like a big kid in some ways."

Kira ran to meet the rider, who had dismounted when his horse balked at getting closer to Swift. "Uncle Petr!"

"Kira!" Petr ran up to her and wrapped in her a big hug that smelled of horse and grain and dust. "You're all right!"

"Petr, do you know anything about why I'm here?" Kira asked as she stepped back.

"I know that your mother and father sent a Mage to give us a message that if any of the family saw you we should do anything we could to help you," Petr said.

"My mother said that?" Kira asked, startled. "We need to get to Ihris. Without being noticed. Oh, Jason, this is my Uncle Petr. I told you that, didn't I?"

"Yeah, you did," Jason said, nodding to Petr. "It's nice to meet you."

"How does Mage Alera know you, Petr?"

"That's Mage Alera?" Petr waved, grinning. "Thank you, Lady Mage! I will help Kira from here on! Please honor my family with another visit!"

Alera waved shyly from her mount, then Swift vaulted into the air, climbing rapidly.

"Alain brought her to see us," Petr explained. "I had asked him if I could ever ride a Roc. Mage Alera let us ride Swift. She is very nice. We let her know she is always welcome."

"Petr, that is so great of you!" Kira said. She turned and waved a farewell to Alera as well even though Swift was already little but a dot in the sky. "What are you doing?"

"Taking our herd to market," Petr said. "At Ihris. You ride with us. When we show up, you'll look like just a couple more dusty ranchers visiting the city."

They began walking to join the others, who had gotten the herd back into motion now that Swift was gone. Petr introduced his two daughters and son, who were helping to herd the horses, and then his wife Signy, who was driving the wagon carrying supplies. Two more horses were saddled up as Kira talked to Petr and his family.

"Kira?" Jason whispered. "I've never ridden a horse. Not for real."

"You haven't? Petr! Jason hasn't ridden. Do you have a docile mount?"

"We've got old Reni. She's steady. How come you've never ridden, Jason?"

"He's from another world," Kira explained.

"All right, but they have horses, don't they?"

They managed to get Jason into the saddle of a mare who appeared content to let him pretend to tell her where to go. Kira mounted up, finding her mare considerably more frisky. "Petr, I don't think she likes me."

Petr laughed. "Your mother says the same thing about all horses."

"But she's right. Mother loves horses, but they don't love her. And this one doesn't love me."

"She likes you fine," Petr assured Kira.

"Then why is she trying to reach her mouth back far enough to bite my leg?" Kira jerked on a rein to bring the mare's head facing front again.

"A cavalry soldier like you shouldn't have any trouble, eh?"

They moved on, Kira's mount alert in that way that meant the mare was looking for a chance to bolt, so Kira kept a tight rein. "We'll stop soon for the night," Petr told her. "Tomorrow we get an early start so that we'll reach Ihris by mid-morning. We'll direct the herd to the corrals outside the city. There'll be enough people moving around there that it'll be easy for you and Jason to dismount and walk off without being noticed. The nearest city gate won't be far."

"Petr, I don't know how to thank you," Kira said.

"You're family," Petr replied as if that explained everything.

"Speaking of family, give my thanks to Great Aunt Bara as well." Kira hesitated. "How about my father's grandmother?"

"How about her?" Petr shrugged unhappily. "Nothing changed. She would rather hold to her anger than find any joy in Alain, or in you."

"What?" Jason asked, trying to bring his horse closer. "Your great-grandmother doesn't like you?"

"It's about Alain," Petr explained. "He was taken by the Mage Guild when he was very little. Some years later, raiders from the north hit his parents' ranch and killed his mother and father. My aunt and uncle-in-law. Alain was locked in a Mage Guild Hall, and still only about ten years old, but Grandmother blamed him. She still does."

"What could he have done when he was only ten?" Jason asked.

"Nothing. Nothing except maybe die with his parents. Maybe that's what Grandmother wishes had happened. I know! It's an ill thing to say. But she won't let it go. Alain is a Mage to her, a Mage as they once all were, without feeling or humanity, who treated other people like we were nothing. We tell her what a great man he is, all the good things he has done, and his wife, Mari, everyone knows the good the daughter has given all of us. And there is you, Kira. Who couldn't love you, eh? But Grandmother will not open her heart. I'm sorry."

"It's not your fault," Kira said. "You're a very good person, too. It means so much to Father that you and Great Aunt Bara accepted him, even before the rest of the world understood who he was."

Petr shrugged, embarrassed by the praise. "It's not so bad being the cousin of the daughter and the Master of Mages. Your mother knows that if she ever calls, I'll come, right?"

"Yes, she does," Kira said. "Petr was in mother's army, too," she told Jason.

"What does that mean?" Jason asked. "If your mother calls?"

Petr answered. "Lady Mari, the daughter, doesn't have an army you can see. She doesn't have a lot of soldiers standing around. But she has the biggest army in the world. After the war, the men and women who fought alongside her went home, but they all vowed that if she ever called again, they would come. Mechanics and Mages and us regular people. The daughter didn't ask that of us. We did it because we wanted to. And because we trusted her to call only if there was injustice that must be fought. Since then, others have sworn to answer the call as well if it ever comes. Every president and minister and even the great big emperor there to the east knows that if they do great enough wrong, the daughter can call her army to her and no one will be able to stand against it." He winked at Jason. "So they listen to her, eh? The daughter has no power, but she is the most powerful one in this world. Her word can make the mighty tremble, and give hope to the smallest. She is a great person, Jason, though Kira doesn't like to talk about that."

Kira gave Petr a cross look. "My mother is a great person. She's also my mother. I love my mother. It's just that sometimes I can't stand her."

"That's hard, eh? My daughters say that of my wife Signy, who is a gentle lamb!"

One of Petr's daughters called out as she rode by. "No, she isn't!"

"I guess being a daughter is hard," Petr said.

"So is being a son," Jason said.

"What does your father do?"

"He cheats people," Jason told Petr. "That's what he says he does. He's proud of it. He thinks that makes him the smartest guy around."

Petr gave Jason a long look. "How smart are you?"

"Smart enough to know I never want to do that with my life," Jason said. "If the daughter called, could anybody come? Even somebody from somewhere else?"

Kira stared at him. "Jason? Are you serious?"

"He is," Petr said. "You'd be welcome. The daughter can always use another good man, eh? But you'll have to learn to ride better than that."

"A horse has a mind of its own, doesn't it?" Jason said. "Horses don't just do what you tell them to do."

"Yeah, like people. But in a horse way. You have to think like a horse. Speaking of which, I'm hungry. Good thing we'll be stopping for the night soon."

When they stopped the herd for the night, Petr had to help settle the horses. Kira turned to Jason. "Why did you say that? About my mother's army?"

He shrugged, keeping his eyes on the horses. "Because I meant it."

"But if you leave this world, go back to Urth—"

"Maybe I won't. Maybe somehow…" He made a face, unhappy. "I've done real things here, Kira. Face to face. I know I can do real things now. I really don't want to go home."

"Because of me."

"Not just because of you! A lot about you, but not just because of you. There is nothing about Earth that I would miss. But there is so much about here that I would miss. . ." He shrugged again. "I guess it would be easier for you if I left, though."

"Maybe I don't want it to be easier," Kira said.

"What do you want?" he asked, his voice so low she could barely hear.

"I wish I knew."

After a dinner that proved to be a lot of fun as Petr's family teased each other and Kira, they all settled for the night. Kira offered to help ride herd part of the night to ensure the horses didn't spook, but her offer was politely declined in a way that didn't outright say Kira probably didn't know enough about the task to do it right.

Petr's family had spread some blankets for Kira and Jason a little ways off from the rest, a respect for their privacy that Kira found both welcome and uncomfortable. She looked over at where Jason lay nearby, wishing that the easy conversations they had become accustomed to hadn't become hard to reclaim. "Jason, I need to work on some, um, drills that Mage Alera taught me last night, so I shouldn't talk much."

"Sure. I understand."

Did he? Kira looked up at the stars, then stared. There was a star up there that she didn't recognize, and it was moving much faster than even the twins. "Jason? Do you know what that is? That light that's moving so fast."

He followed her pointing arm. "It's a satellite. The ship deployed some. They were supposed to do a lot of general surveys, but they've probably been reprogrammed to look for me. Don't worry. That one's way too high to spot me when I'm around other people and all these horses."

"How high is it?"

"Probably a couple of hundred kilometers."

Kira stared at the fast moving star. "A kilometer is a thousand of your meters, right? So two hundred thousand meters, which would be about one hundred thousand lances. How can you get something that high?"

He looked at her. "Kira, it's just technology. Someday, you guys will get to the same place and be able to enter space again. Even if Earth never helps you at all, even if they quarantine you like some interstellar theme park to 'protect' you, you'll get there. Someday, you guys will send a ship back to Earth. And when you get there, do you know what you'll say?"

"What will we say?" Kira asked, smiling.

"You'll tell Earth that you don't need any of their technology. But you have something that Earth needs. Because Earth has forgotten things, things about people, that you guys still remember."

"Do you really believe that?" Kira asked, her voice soft.

"Yes. They're not better people on Earth, Kira. I know you guys aren't perfect, but you're as good as they are. Better in some ways. They don't have anything on Earth you need to envy."

Kira looked at the stars, thinking. "You told me that on Urth they could have saved my brother's life. And helped my mother have other children."

He paused. "Yeah. I'm sorry. The medical thing is big. I didn't mean to sound like that wasn't important. I guess I take it for granted."

"That's all right. There are things we all take for granted. Until we need them and don't have them. Jason, I'm sorry."

"For what?"

"For not being able to say 'I love you' back to you. I might, someday. I don't know."

"Only a jerk would demand that you make up your mind now," Jason said, "and I'm told that I'm not a jerk."

"I do remember somebody saying that," Kira said. "Rest well."

She lay on her back, gazing upwards, trying to concentrate on the lessons that would help her hide her presence from Mages. Other Mages. When had that happened? And how? Her parents were worried about it. Everybody who knew was worried about it, even Jason who didn't know enough to know he should be worried about it.

There was nothing she could do, though, except hope that her Mage skills would be enough to do what Jason thought could solve their problem.

One of their problems, anyway.

The flight across the Sea of Bakre was long and hard, angling the long way over the waters, the Rocs pushed to their limits. But Mage Saburo and Mage Alber brought them safely to from Dorcastle to Marida.

People arriving on Rocs tended to get a lot of attention. When they proved to be the daughter and her husband, the only Master of Mages, the attention multiplied fast. Before Alain and Mari could reach the waterfront they had a police escort, and by the time they saw the harbor before them a military escort had arrived as well. "Taris," Alain said. "The name of the ship includes the word Taris."

"We know the one," a port official announced. "This way, Sir Mage."

The Son of Taris was tied up at a pier, but plainly preparing to get underway soon. Those preparations halted when a score of Marida's soldiers rushed up the gangplank as the crew were getting ready to haul it in. Alain and Mari followed, he studying the ship as they went aboard. A common enough merchant ship, neither large nor small, with nothing to distinguish it but the fact that it had appeared in Asha's vision.

The crew was lined up along one side of the main deck, looking as nervous as anyone could look. At the stern, before the raised quarter-deck, a tall man in a greatcoat and a stout woman stood waiting. The officials and soldiers of Marida stayed near the gangplank in deference to the daughter.

Alain saw the ripple of recognition that ran through the two ship's officers as they looked on Mari. "You have seen our daughter," he said.

The captain nodded, his expression grim. "I am not fool enough to try lying to a Mage. And I cannot believe that the daughter of Jules means harm to her. The girl called herself Kara. She was with the boy Jason, though he called himself J'son."

"What do you know of the boy?" Alain asked.

"We know he was sought by the Imperials. Kara told us that he had taken something from the ship from Urth in order to save many lives. I believed her."

"She spoke the truth," Alain said. "Her real name is Kira."

"Is she all right?" Mari asked. "Where is she now?"

The first mate answered. "She was fine when we set her ashore at Kelsi, Lady. Our last port before this. They had all with them when they left that they had when they came aboard. Kelsi was where she and the boy wished to leave the ship. What a dolt I am! She told me both of her parents were on the last wall at Dorcastle! Who else could that be but the daughter and her Mage? And then she said—" The first mate's eyes widened suddenly.

"Speak of it," Alain said.

"We…were discussing things," the first mate said with reluctance. "She asked me to pass a message to her mother if ever I should meet her."

"What message was that?" Mari asked.

"She said I should tell you that she thought you would like me," the first mate said as if the words were being pulled from her one by one.

Mari laughed with relief. "You must be the easiest first mate on the Sea of Bakre."

"Begging your pardon, Lady, but no," the first mate said stiffly, her pride affronted. "I am not easy. Ask any of the crew."

"Where did you get that mark on your head?"

"During the storm before we reached Kelsi. I was knocked out. That's when your daughter saved my life."

"Kira saved you?" Mari asked.

"She saved the entire ship," the captain said. "With the first mate down and myself lashed to the wheel, your girl led the crew up the mast in the worst storm I have ever encountered, got them to furl the mainsail and reef the topsail. Then she kept them working the pumps all night. If not for her, the mast would have gone, and the ship followed soon after."

"Kira did that." Mari looked at Alain and he saw the pride in her. He nodded to show that the captain and first mate had spoken true. "How did she get aboard this ship?"

"She and the boy stowed away in Dorcastle," the first mate said.

"I made them work their passage, as was my right," the captain added. "Part of the crew. They were worked hard, but treated fairly. Ask any man or woman aboard, Sir Mage."

"Why did she tell you who Jason was?" Alain asked.

"It was in Caer Lyn. We were tied up for the night, and the Imperials came down the pier, searching ships. Lady, every year the Imperials act more and more like they own the Sharr Isles once again."

"I know. I'm trying to resolve that short of war. It hasn't been easy," Mari said. "They were looking for Jason?"

"And your daughter, Lady, though they did not identify her as such. Offered great reward. But we had hidden the two of them so they were not found, and kept them safe until our ship left harbor the next morning."

"You knew there were rewards for both, but you protected them?" Mari asked.

"Aye, Lady. That was my decision."

"And you didn't know Kira was my daughter?"

"No, Lady. I knew she was a good sailor, and she had earned my trust. Nor do I care for the Imperials." The captain squinted as if suddenly realizing something. "Your daughter. And we protected her and the boy, and agreed to let them sail on with us to Kelsi, so they were aboard when the storm hit. The boy saved her, and then she saved all of us. I do not know what led to you offering us your favor, daughter of Jules, but without your daughter this ship and all aboard would have been lost."

"You saved yourselves by your actions," Alain said, having once again seen the truth in the captain's words. "You said the boy saved her?"

"Aye. Her line snapped. She was going over the side. The boy set free his own line and went after her. The wave nearly took both, but he managed to hold her and bring her back aboard."

Mari stared at the captain, then at Alain, then back at the captain. "Jason? The boy Jason did that?"

"Aye, Lady. I admit he did not impress when I first saw him, but he saved your daughter's life. There's not a doubt of it."

Mari looked at him and Alain nodded. She faced the two ship's officers again. "You brought my daughter and the boy with her across the Sea of Bakre, treating them fairly, safeguarding their possessions and seeing them safely ashore. You knew that substantial rewards were offered for both, and you still kept them safe. My husband and I owe you a great deal." Mari turned and beckoned to the officials from Marida. "This ship has done a great service for me. I ask that word to be passed through the Free Cities and other lands that I would like *The Son of Taris* to be given preference for official cargoes and mail. And I authorize this ship to fly the banner of the daughter from this day on, to show that the ship and the crew sail with my favor and under my protection."

"As the daughter wishes, it will be done," the most senior official said.

"Lady?" the captain said, sounding as if he doubted his own ears. "You honor us with such measures? They will guarantee the prosperity of this ship and her crew, and your favor might save us when all other means fail."

"You have earned it," Mari said, extending her hand. "Take my hand, both of you, and with it my thanks." The captain and first mate both shook her hand, the captain smiling broadly and the first mate looking like she was about to pass out.

"Luck from the daughter herself," the first mate said, shaking her head in disbelief.

"My daughter did say I would like you," Mari reminded her.

"If I see your daughter again I will have some words with her, Lady! Tasking me to deliver such a message to *you*. But she is a fine sailor, and a fine girl."

"Thank you."

Alain let Mari lead the way off the ship, passing the line of sailors who chattered among themselves in amazement. He stopped and waited as Mari paused, then went to the sailors of *The Son of Taris* and also shook the hand of each one. He knew how little Mari liked the superstition of sailors that her touch brought them luck, but Mari knew how much it meant to the sailors, and so she went through the ritual. Because that was how Mari was, and that was how she had been when first they met, and if he did not like that Alain knew he had no one but himself to blame for falling in love with her.

In truth, her concern for others had been what had first impressed him. And saved his life.

On the pier, Mari stopped again to speak to Alain, officials from Marida close by this time. "She left the ship in Kelsi just a few days ago."

"Kelsi?" a police commander asked. "A few days ago?"

"Yes. What is it?"

"We've just been hearing of a big fight in Kelsi a few days past.

Dark Mages and other scum. There was a fight in the streets at night, with gunshots, and more gun battles along the sea-facing wall, on the waters of the harbor, and the nearby coast."

Alain felt fear. "What else is known?"

"The criminals who were rounded up wouldn't talk, but with the help of a Mage the interrogators were fairly certain the incident did involve your daughter. I just this morning received the report from my counterpart in Kelsi."

"But what of our daughter and the boy Jason?"

The official shook his head. "No trace of them. Except that a boat owner claimed he was hijacked by a boy and a girl that night, and his boat was later found farther down the coast, abandoned."

Mari stared to the west. "We haven't heard any far-talker messages from anyone claiming to have the boy or my daughter. Have you?"

"No, Lady," another official said. "You know that the reward sheets dropped by the Urth ship are…vague on whether or not the boy and your daughter need to be found alive."

"Yes," Mari said, her voice almost as emotionless as that of a Mage. "We have noticed that."

"But still no one has tried to claim the reward," the official added hastily.

"Meaning they are not dead," Alain said.

"That is my assumption."

The police official spoke again. "Kelsi has been turned upside down since the fight. If the boy and your daughter were being held there, it seems unlikely that no one would have found them. And if your daughter had been found by any of your friends in Kelsi—and you have many, many friends in Kelsi as you do in all the Free Cities—the word would have come to me by quiet means so that I could inform you if I met you."

"Thank you," Mari said. "That is reassuring. Alain? Where would they have gone from Kelsi? Kira knows we have friends in Alexdria. General Flyn among them."

"Kira also knows that Alexdria can be reached only through a few mountain passes," Alain said. "They would be easily trapped there. You said the boat was found abandoned along the coast? In which direction from the city?"

"West, Sir Mage. A search was made there and inland as far as the entrance to the pass toward Ihris. On foot, they couldn't have outpaced the searchers."

"I am beginning to suspect," Alain said, "that it is a serious mistake to underestimate our daughter."

"But, Sir Mage, unless they flew…" The officials exchanged glances.

"Yes. Unless. Mari, I think we should go to Ihris."

"We'll need new Rocs. Mage Saburo and Mage Alber are worn out."

"I am certain some Mages who create Rocs are available for hire at the former Mage Guild Hall," another official offered.

Mari sighed. "Another night sleeping among the clouds. That's not nearly as restful as it sounds," she told the others. "Alain, are we sure we should draw attention to Ihris?"

He tried to put into words what he was feeling. "I have a sense that we will be needed there. Soon."

"Then we're going to get there, as quickly as we can."

As Petr had predicted, it was fairly easy to slip unnoticed through the bustle of the livestock market. Between the herds of cattle and horses and mules, and the buyers and sellers and herders moving and arguing, two more figures weren't noticed making their way to the edge of the market to join the intermittent stream of people between there and the city.

Kira didn't see any of the papers with Jason's face on them, so she had him lead the way through the city gates, keeping him between her and the guards. The guards, though, didn't seem particularly alert, relaxing and talking to each other. Nor did there seem to be anyone lounging about watching for them as there had been at the gate in Kelsi.

Any comfort that brought vanished as Kira was alarmed to "feel" a Mage somewhere. If she could feel one, another might feel her. Her Mage skills seemed to be changing and growing in erratic spurts. That wasn't how her father had described his own skills growing slowly and steadily with time and practice.

Kira did her best to focus on the drills that Alera had taught her, trying to ensure that no other Mage could feel her presence. Such a Mage might be friendly, or might be one of those still enraged by the fall of the Mage Guild and the loss of the impunity with which Mages once treated other people as less than nothing.

By the time they made it inside the city, it was late morning and the streets were fairly crowded. Horse- and mule-drawn wagons filled the streets, along with riders. Ihris, like much of Dematr, had prospered in the years since the overthrow of the Great Guilds. The Peace of the Daughter had kept conflicts to a minimum, so trade had flourished. And the freeing of technology had given new vigor to every city, even though not many changes had worked their way into everyday life yet.

"Where exactly are we going?" Jason asked, keeping his voice low so that passersby couldn't hear his accent.

"We're looking for a good hotel so we can get a room," Kira said.

To her surprise, Jason laughed. "Do you know how long I have dreamed about a beautiful girl saying that to me?"

"I really don't want to hear about those kinds of dreams, that is not why we are getting a room, and I'm not beautiful."

"It's my illusion and I'm sticking to it," Jason said. "Do you have any idea which way we should go?"

"I think I once heard Mother and Father say the district with the best hotels in Ihris is to the south. Let's head that way."

They moved along the streets, Kira trying to keep her head buried in her coat, trying to keep Jason between her and most people, and trying to maintain her concentration on the Mage-presence blocking drills.

As she and Jason went down a sidewalk, Kira noticed a pair of police officers sauntering down the street. Before she could slip around to the other side of Jason, one of them looked at her, looked away, then looked back, surprised. Without realizing it, Kira's concentration dropped, recentering on the police.

"Hey," the officer said, still looking at Kira.

But Kira felt something else, a sudden surge of power, and turned to look across the street where it was coming from. A man stood there, staring at her with abrupt yet clear recognition. And his eyes...

"If you ever meet a Mage who creates dragons," her mother had told Kira, *"you'll know it. There's something about their eyes. Something... fierce and brutal. I can't describe it better than that, but you'll know it when you see it."*

Kira realized she was staring back at a Dragon Mage.

Dragon Mages hated her mother and her father.

The police officers were walking toward her. Before Kira could react to that, a dragon appeared in the street.

The spell must have been a hasty one. The dragon was only about a lance and a half tall, about three of Jason's meters, but to Kira's eyes the claws on the dragon's forearms and the teeth in its gaping maw were huge.

And the dragon's eyes were fixed on her. She was its target.

The two police had begun turning, drawing their hardwood clubs, their faces reflecting shock, when the dragon backhanded both of them. They flew across the street toward Kira, tumbling to the pavement, one of their clubs clattering to land at her feet.

Without realizing she had done so, Kira had her pistol drawn. She flipped off the safety, chambered a round, then without knowing why crouched down to grab the hardwood club with her free hand.

Jason was running toward the dragon as it charged her, but another backhand swipe tossed him aside. Kira was vaguely aware of screams and shouts echoing around her as the other people on the street saw the monster, of the panicked snorts of horses reacting to the appearance of the dragon, but all she could see was the beast charging her.

It was on Kira in a flash. She raised both hands, arms extended close together, pistol in one and club in the other. The dragon's mouth gaped wide as it lunged down at her, engulfing both of her arms.

She never afterwards knew whether it was chance or her unconscious design that twisted the club as the dragon came at her, wedging the club between the top and bottom of the monster's mouth and holding it there so the jaws couldn't snap closed. The snout of the creature rammed into Kira's chest, knocking her against the wall behind her, the front teeth gleaming before her face, her arms stuck more than halfway into the dragon's maw as it fought to close despite the club jammed between its lower and upper jaws. The monster flailed at her, its foreclaws digging into and through her coat, as Kira, terrified, pulled her trigger as fast as possible, emptying her pistol into the dragon's mouth, some portion of her still capable of thinking well enough to try to aim the shots upward toward the creature's brain. The beast's armored scales and its thick skull, which would have kept the bullets from penetrating from the outside, instead kept them from exiting, so that they ricocheted wildly, doing even more damage.

The dragon jolted with the impacts, a high-pitched scream driving foul breath and the exhaust from her pistol shots across Kira. Then it abruptly broke away, falling backwards. Kira let the club go, hanging onto her pistol through instinct rather than design. She stayed leaning against the wall, shaking so badly with reaction that she wasn't sure she could stand.

The dragon lurched back and forth on the street, wobbling on its feet. It fell, limbs flailing and its tail sweeping wildly, the motions growing slower until they abruptly ceased.

Kira realized that she was staring at her hands, trying to reassure herself that they were still there and not inside the monster. She saw punctures in the shoulders of her coat where the dragon's teeth had penetrated but not been able to close enough to bite. The arms of the coat had been slashed where the teeth had caught when the creature was falling away. The front was torn to shreds, her chest and stomach stinging in places.

"You killed it."

She tore her eyes from herself to see one of the police officers staring at her.

"She killed it!" someone else yelled.

A lot of people were staring at her.

There was no sign of the Dragon Mage.

Kira jerked away from the wall as Jason staggered up to her. "Are you all right?" she asked. "Run."

People who had been fleeing had begun turning to run back and see the fallen dragon. Kira and Jason plowed into the gathering crowd, ignoring cries of "Hey!" and "Wait!" They broke through as people milled about on the edges of the crowd, running down the nearest alley. Kira shoved her pistol back into its holster, then pulled off her badly damaged coat as she ran, tossing it into a trash bin as they passed it.

"You're bleeding!" Jason cried as he yanked off his coat and passed it to Kira.

"I'm fine." She pulled on the coat to hide the blood and the damage to her shirt. They bolted out of the alley and down the next street as several police came running toward them. "Where is it?" one yelled at her.

She pointed, knowing that her breathless answer would sound like someone who had run in terror. "That way."

The police ran past, and Kira yanked Jason down a side street. She felt an overwhelming urge to stop and throw up but somehow managed to keep running. She led Jason across several more streets until she spotted a large building. "A hotel. Looks like a nice one. That's what we need."

She stopped outside of the hotel, trying to control her breathing. "Jason, you go in by yourself. Ask for a room for just you. A room for one. There's no way they would rent a room to both of us at our ages. I'll wait until everyone is paying attention to you and then I'll walk in like I already have a room and go up to the second floor to wait for you."

He shook his head. "They're going to ask for my multi-ID."

"Your what? You've got money! That's all they'll care about. Hurry! But don't let them think you're hurrying!"

Jason nodded, turned, and walked into the hotel.

While she was waiting, a man came running across the street and into the hotel.

Kira took another breath, and setting her face into the calmest lines she could manage followed the man.

Jason was at the desk, but most of the attention was on the man who had just run inside.

"—dragon! In the city!" he was saying excitedly. "You should have seen it!"

Unnoticed, Kira kept walking and went up to the second floor, waiting with jangling nerves and hoping no one from the hotel would come by and ask what she was doing.

She heard footsteps on the stairs.

Jason came up, grinning with relief. "The room's on this floor."

"Where?" Kira tugged him to the door. Jason fumbled with the key as if he had never used one before, so she grabbed it, yanked open the door, and dashed to the bathroom. She barely made it to the toilet before finally throwing up.

Gasping, Kira got to her feet. She washed out her mouth and splashed more water on her face, then looked at herself in the mirror, wondering who the wild-eyed girl looking back at her was. Opening the coat she was wearing, Kira flinched at the sight of the vertical slits torn in the lower part and top edges of her shirt by the tips of the dragon's claws and the red bloodstains along some of those slits where her skin had been sliced open. It looked horrible, but it didn't hurt much, and the bleeding didn't seem to be too bad since the fabric of the shirt was sticking to the cuts and serving as bandages. A cautious look inside one of the rips showed only a shallow cut.

She closed the coat again and walked out of the bathroom to find Jason waiting with an anxious and awed expression.

"Kira, that was a dragon, wasn't it? I tried to distract it."

"You were very brave to try, but no one can distract a dragon that has its eyes on its target," Kira said. "Jason—"

"You fought a dragon! You were bleeding. Are you okay?"

"I know I fought a dragon. It's just shallow cuts. Don't say okay. I'm fine."

"You threw up—"

"A dragon just tried to eat me! I'm a little queasy! Now listen, Jason. We stirred up a huge ruckus out there. People are going to hear, and a lot of people were looking at me, so someone may have recognized me. Getting out of Ihris may not be an option. There's no telling how much time we have left." She paused to control her breathing again. "I need to somehow calm myself and focus enough to try that spell soon."

Jason nodded, his eyes on her. "What do you need me to do?"

"Jason, that was the perfect thing to say." She looked around the room, lit well enough by the sunlight streaming in from a couple of windows. "That chair. Put it in the corner facing that little table. Get the junk off the table and lay the drive on it. I'm going to need you to stand a little bit behind me, and not say anything, and not make any noise."

He was already moving the chair. Jason brought the chain holding the drive over his head, looking down at it, then laid it on the table.

Kira sat down as Jason retreated to a spot behind her. With the chair facing a corner, all she could see was the little table with the drive on it. She didn't touch the drive, only looked at it, breathing slowly and carefully, remembering how her father had described creating spells like the one she had to manage.

Her father and other Mages had taught her a lot about meditation. Kira used that now, trying to block out the world, seeking the calm, strong center within her where her spirit rested. Even though a thousand things sought to distract her, she closed her eyes and methodically blocked out thoughts and feelings, narrowing her world to that center within her. She had no idea how much time was passing, and blocked any worries about that as well.

When Kira slowly opened her eyes, the only thing in the world was that table and the drive on it. No. The illusion of a drive, resting on the illusion of a table. Neither really existed. They were illusions created by the minds of people to give order to the universe. This building, this world, were nothing.

Nothing. Illusion.

Something shifted within her. Kira wasn't sure what, and didn't want the distraction of trying to figure out. Her eyes stayed on the oddly shaped rock on the table. The illusion of a rock. Kira felt power within her, and power outside, power that came from the world itself. Her mind took hold of that power as she focused on the rock. She would change that illusion, lay upon it a smaller illusion that part of the rock was not there. Never had been there. The rock was not that odd shape. One side wasn't there.

She felt the power flow through her and fix upon the illusion of a rock, and suddenly part of it was gone.

Someone gasped behind her, but Kira kept her attention focused only on the rock.

CHAPTER SIXTEEN

Alain had directed Mage Tania to land her Roc in a square inside Ihris. The Roc carrying Mari landed beside them. He felt an inexplicable urgency that canceled out his and Mari's concerns to remain little noticed until they knew what was happening in Ihris.

The nearest police officers came running up, saluting as they saw who had stepped down from the Rocs. "We're at your service, Lady Mari."

"Let your superiors know we're in the city. My husband and I need to move quickly, so let us pass."

"Did you come because of the dragon?"

"A dragon?" Alain asked.

"One appeared in the southeastern district a very short time ago, Sir Mage. But the latest report said it had been slain." The officers exchanged glances. "By you, Lady."

"I just got here," Mari said, then her eyes widened as she stared at Alain. "Someone who looked like me. Kira. She slew a dragon?"

"In hand-to-hand combat, Lady," the officer said as it not expecting to be believed.

"We need to go. Thank you."

The police stood aside as Alain strode rapidly down a street, Mari keeping up. "Where are we going, Alain? Do you think Kira is all right?"

"I have a sense I must go this way," he said, trying to keep his emotions under control. His daughter, facing a dragon. "Hand-to-hand."

"That can't be right," Mari said. "Kira would never be that crazy, and how could anyone survive…how could anyone…"

Alain stopped walking so abruptly that Mari had to come back two steps. "I feel something. A spell."

"Whoever made the dragon?" Mari said in a voice that promised vengeance.

"No." Alain realized that surprise must have shown on his face. "Kira."

"Kira is all right? Wait. Kira is casting a spell?" Mari demanded. "Since when can Kira cast spells?"

He shook his head, turning to find the direction of the spell. "She has never been able to do so. Only some great need or peril could have brought that ability to life within her."

"She's in trouble. She's in danger right now, maybe badly hurt. Where is she?"

"This way." Alain took off at a run, Mari beside him.

The rock contained some strange gemlike substance. It remained within the rock, but as Kira watched it began to flow and glitter like water dancing in sunlight. On one edge of the rock, a light began blinking like a guttering candle. She stared, wondering why rocks or gems would behave that way, but maintained her focus on the spell, feeling her own strength draining despite the flow of power from outside.

The glittering movement inside the rock ceased.

"Kira! You did it, Kira! You can stop!"

Kira let her focus relax. The rock was back as it had been, oddly regular. She slumped in the chair, exhausted.

Jason came into view, picking up the rock and tapping at it. Why was he doing that?

"It did set off an alarm. I've got it shut off, but it was on for maybe fifteen seconds. Since my mom's ship put up satellites, they'll know we're in this city, maybe even what part of the city."

"What are you talking about?" Kira asked, not understanding a word that Jason had said..

"The drive."

"The what?" That was an odd name for a rock.

The universe lurched.

Kira shook her head, feeling dizzy. What had happened? She had been… "The drive. Did we destroy the data?"

"Yeah." Jason was giving her a funny look. "For a minute there you didn't seem to have any idea what I was saying."

"It was probably because the spell was so taxing," Kira said. "I was just a little disoriented, I guess." She stood up carefully. "What do we need to do now?"

Jason followed as she walked slowly to the center of the room. "I have to reset the drive to read-only. Externally, it's going to look perfect, as if all the data is still intact. But the matrix inside isn't going to have any data. It's going to be locked into meaningless patterns."

The door slammed open.

Kira spun about, drawing her pistol as she did so, and ended up facing her mother, who was pointing her own pistol at Kira.

"Well, this is awkward," Mari said. She holstered her weapon as Kira did the same. "Your father detected a spell. From you. It ceased, but by then we were close enough for him to sense your Mage presence. We thought you were in danger."

"We are," Kira said, putting away her own weapon. "The Urth ship knows that we're near here. Mother, that device from the Urth ship! We broke it. No, we fixed it. Actually, we broke it so we could fix it."

Her mother shook her head. "You sound more like your father every day. The data on that drive that posed a danger has been destroyed?"

"That's what I said!"

Before Kira could say anything else, her mother grabbed her and wrapped her in a fervent hug. "All that matters is that you're all right,"

Mari whispered to her. "I was so worried."

Kira returned the hug, feeling better than she had in a long time, tears welling in her eyes. "Me, too."

Mari drew back a bit, looking at where Kira's coat sagged open a bit. "Is that blood?"

"Just a little. All right, more than a little. But the cuts were all shallow and they've stopped bleeding, I think. The dragon was trying to kill me!" Kira said.

"The dragon." Mari looked at Alain. "The police told us about a dragon being slain in the city by a woman who looked like me who killed it fighting hand-to-hand. We thought that was a wild exaggeration fed by rumors, or that you'd been badly hurt."

Kira shrugged, then winced because the gesture tugged at the cuts. "I wasn't hurt much. I guess fighting hand-to-hand was what it was. More like hand-to-claw, though."

Her mother shook her head at Kira. "You're not badly hurt?"

"No. Didn't I say that?"

"You fought a dragon hand-to-hand and killed it." Kira's mother surprised her with a smile full of pride. "I never did that, you know."

"You never—?" Kira stared at Mari. "I did something that my mother has never done?"

"That's right." Mari's smile broadened. "Of course, I still have you on numbers, five to one."

"Right now, maybe!" Kira said, laughing. "I have time to catch up!"

Her mother's smile stayed, but took on a wistful tinge. "I never told you, but your namesake was also a dragon slayer. Sergeant Kira killed one the day before she died."

"She did?" Kira wiped away sudden tears. "I hope she's proud of me."

"I'm sure she is, Kira."

Her father interrupted. "Kira, your presence has grown."

"I know. Mage Alera told me. That's how the Dragon Mage spotted me. I'm sorry," Kira said, feeling guilty. "Oh, Jason knows about the Mage-powers thing. I accidentally told him. Anyway,

Jason figured out that if I could make part of the drive go away, the crystal inside that protects the data would destroy it just as if the crystal had been broken. So I got us this room so I wouldn't have any distractions and I concentrated real hard and I remembered everything you told me about it and I was able to do it." She looked from her father to her mother and back again. "That's all right, isn't it?"

"I hope it is all right," Alain said. "Creating such a spell did not cause any problems for you?"

"Nothing that I noticed," Kira said.

"You were disoriented for a little bit," Jason said, extremely anxious as he eyed Kira's mother and father.

"I was exhausted for a moment," Kira said.

Her father nodded, then surprised her with a rare smile. "Managing such a spell on your own, under such conditions, is very remarkable. Your Aunt Asha will be impressed."

Jason had been working with the drive, and now held it out. "It's done. The drive looks great from the outside, but there's nothing in it. If my mom links it in and checks, she'd see that, but I don't think she'll do that because there isn't any known way to damage the data in the drive without destroying it. After losing the drive to me for a while, she won't take any risks. She'll take it and lock it away in her safe until she's back on Earth. And then they'll find out it's empty."

Mari gave Jason an appraising look. "Being around Kira seems to have done you some good. You said that your ship detected something and knows where you are?"

"Yeah. I mean, yes. Yes, Lady."

Kira's mother went to the nearest window and looked out. "I see one of those drones. There's another a bit farther off. They got here pretty quickly. I guess we don't have to worry about that any more, though. Jason doesn't need to hide any longer. He can return to the ship."

"Mother," Kira said with a sinking feeling inside, "about that. I…uh…you see…um…"

"Kira, we don't know how much time we have. Please spell it out short and simple."

"Jason's in love with me and I don't know how I feel about that but I'm not unhappy about it but I am unhappy about the idea of him leaving."

"Oh," Mari said. "That does complicate things."

"I know what you're thinking," Kira said, defending Jason. "You, too, Father! You're trying to hide it with your Mage skills but I can still see it! Nothing happened! Well, a little bit happened. I kissed Jason. Twice. But each time *I* kissed him. Jason is not the boy you met earlier. That was an illusion that Jason maintained to hide his real self. That Jason standing there is the real Jason, and he is smart, and he is nice to people, and…"

"And he saved your life in a storm at risk of his own," her mother added.

"Yes! He did that, too! And he didn't even mention it afterwards."

Mari studied Jason again. "So, you fixed him, Kira?"

"No!" Kira said. "He did it. I provided encouragement and, uh, recommendations, but Jason did all of the changing."

"I don't doubt it," her mother replied. "Remember me telling you that no one can bring out anything in another person that isn't already inside somewhere? Jason had to have that better person inside. But don't play down how important the motivation you provided was in making that happen." She looked Jason over once more. "The big question is, what do you want, Jason?"

"What?" Jason asked. "I mean, excuse me?"

"What do you want?" Mari repeated.

"You're really asking me?"

"Is that so unusual?"

"Yes," Jason said, his face working with emotion. "No one in charge ever asks me what I want. I just get told."

Kira's mother lowered her head and rubbed her forehead, then looked back up at him. "I'm sorry. But we will not do that. Alain and I want to know what you want."

Jason smiled at Kira. "I want, more than anything, to stay on this planet. Not to go back to Earth, but to stay here."

"Because of Kira?" Mari asked. "She doesn't know how she feels, Jason. Sometimes that means those feelings will deepen, but it might also mean she might decide you make a good friend and nothing more, or even less. That's how hearts are."

"I know," Jason said, dejected. "But even if that happens, this world is where I want to be. It's the first place I ever felt happy. It's the first place I ever got to be something, the first place I ever thought I could be something."

Mari sighed. "Are the laws on Urth the same as here? That until you are eighteen years old you are under the control of your parents?"

Jason sagged again. "Yes. Unless you get a court order of emancipation and the only source of that is a very, very long way from here. I tried getting one a couple of years ago, but Mom and Dad's lawyers killed it. They don't want me, but they don't want me free of them, either."

Tense with worry, Kira saw her mother and father exchange a glance. Her father nodded.

Mari faced Jason again. "Jason, even if our daughter didn't have as-of-yet unspecified feelings for you, we'd still owe you a debt. You warned us of the attempts to cheat us and harm this world, and you risked yourself to discover a serious danger to both this world and Urth, and then to prevent that danger. I promise you that my husband and I will do everything that we can to help you stay on this world. Unfortunately, I can't promise that we'll succeed. Your mother's ship has immense power."

"I don't want anyone hurt because of me," Jason said. "Especially not Kira's parents. Kira is the greatest person I've ever met. I know she's too good for me, but—"

"Did Kira tell you that she was too good for you?" Mari asked before Kira could say anything.

"No. She'd never do that."

"She'd never *think* that," Kira said. "Even when I didn't like you, I didn't think I was better than you. I may have been driving my parents crazy for the last several years, but I do listen to them."

"And I will not let you forget that you admitted to that," her mother said. Mari ran one hand through her hair, frowning in thought. "Alain? Any ideas?"

"We can return the item and continue to hide Jason," Alain said. "If he means as little to the Talese woman as he says, she may take the device and leave rather than continue to search."

"I don't think that will work," Jason said, shaking his head. "My mom may not care about me, but she never wants to lose. If I'm the trophy in a game, she wants the trophy, even if she'll toss it in the closet once she has it. Besides, those drones are close. I can't avoid being detected by them if we leave here, and even if we stay they'll find me soon."

"Mother," Kira said. "Please. I know what life has been for you. Everyone needing something important to them, and hoping you can help. I won't blame you if you can't help Jason. But there must be something we can do."

"Maybe," Mari said. She looked at Kira's father. "Alain, if we use the right illusion, we might be able to pull this off. We need to talk." Kira's mother pulled out her far-talker. "Let's call the Urth ship and announce that we've found Jason and the item he took. If we seem to be meekly surrendering, it might help put them off guard."

Jason spoke nervously. "They've got weapons. They might just—"

"We have shown them that using their weapons is not wise," Alain said.

"You did?" Jason shook his head in amazement. "Lady Mari, Sir Mage, thank you for not being mad at me about Kira. I'll never forget a single moment I spent with her. Even if there's not another day, I still–"

"Don't say that," Kira insisted. "As long as we're together, hope remains."

Her mother stared at her. "I wish you hadn't put it that way, dearest. I'll explain later."

★

The far-talker call made, they exited the hotel, finding a large force of police holding back crowds as well as a full troop of cavalry. "That's her!" someone yelled.

Kira looked, expecting as usual to see people pointing at her mother. But they were pointing at her. The police officer and his partner who had been the first to be attacked by the dragon were among them. Others chimed in, insisting that Kira was the one.

A colonel in cavalry uniform, his cuirass and helm gleaming, stepped forward and saluted Mari and Alain. "The city of Ihris is honored by your visit, Lady Mari, and yours, Sir Master of Mages. I have to inquire if you have any knowledge of a recent event in this city. There is a dead dragon a few streets away from here, and the witnesses claim that it was slain by a young woman resembling you, Lady Mari. Slain in a hand-to-hand struggle."

"Hand-to-claw," Kira said, embarrassed by all the attention.

"We have her coat, found in an alley," one of the police said, holding up the badly ripped garment.

"Oh, yeah," Kira said. "Mother, I ruined my coat. I forgot to mention that."

The colonel blinked at her. "It's true?"

Mari smiled. "Kira, open the coat you now wear."

The last thing Kira wanted to do was display the damage the dragon had done, but she reluctantly pulled open the coat, revealing the bloodstained vertical slashes in her shirt.

The silence that fell over the crowd unnerved Kira. Then cheers sounded, causing Kira to look around, confused.

The colonel nodded and saluted her, smiling. "Forgive me for doubting, Lady Kira. If anyone could slay a dragon fighting hand-to-hand, or hand-to-claw, it would surely be the daughter of the daughter herself. You have the thanks of our city for your fearless action. If not for you swiftly slaying the monster, it might have killed and injured many before being subdued."

"I'm just Kira," she insisted. "Not Lady Kira. And I wasn't fearless. I was actually pretty scared."

"All the more credit to you for fighting despite that fear, Lady Kira," the colonel said with another smile. "I see that in addition to her other gifts, you have inherited your mother's modesty."

It struck her like a blow, then. They were looking at her. Everyone was looking at her. Lady Mari and Master of Mages Alain were standing not much more than a lance length away from her, but everyone was looking at *her* and calling her Lady Kira. Not because of who her mother was, but because of what she had done.

Her father said the world everyone saw was an illusion, one that could be changed by those with the skills to do so. As she recently had in a minor way. But the changes Mages made to the world illusion were temporary, fading away as if they had never been when the power that fed them died.

But Kira's world had just changed, she realized, and would not return to where it had been. The shadow that had dimmed her life had lifted. Maybe it had never really been there. Maybe she had seen only the illusion of that shadow and let it dim her life. But it was gone.

She blinked in the sunlight, staring at the world about her.

"Colonel," Mari said, "may I ask the loan of four mounts? We need to meet the ship from Urth in an area south of the city."

"Certainly, Lady. We would be honored to assist you. And further honored if you would allow this troop of cavalry to escort you to your meeting."

"The honor would be ours to have such soldiers acting as our escort," Mari said with a smile.

As they were waiting for the four horses to be brought to them, Kira turned to her father. "Petr is here. At the market outside the walls."

"We will have to visit once our other tasks are done," Alain said. "Petr helped you reach the city?"

"Of course he did. He's a really great person." Kira paused. "Do you remember when I complained that Mother wouldn't let me be my own person?"

"I recall hearing that many times," Alain said, looking at her with a trace of a smile.

"I guess I did complain a bit. It wasn't the same thing, Jason," she added to him. "Anyway, Father, you and Mother would always ask me who I wanted to be, and I didn't know. But now I think I do."

"Then I am happy for you. As is your mother, who never tried to make you be anything," Kira's father added.

"I had to realize that for myself," Kira said. "Oh, Mother. I'm sorry."

"For what?" Mari asked.

"A lot of things."

"Me, too. New day?"

Kira grinned, recognizing the reference to her mother's campaign to overthrow the Great Guilds, to allow change in a world where change had once been forbidden, to bring a new day to the world of Dematr. "Yes. New day. For us."

It was well they had the cavalry escort, since the crowds lining the streets to cheer the daughter, the Master of Mages, and to Kira's continuing amazement the dragon-slaying daughter of the daughter, would have otherwise blocked their progress completely.

Finally through the gate of the city, they rode out toward the wide plain to the south, Mari and Alain side-by-side in the lead, Jason and Kira riding together behind them, the cavalry led by their colonel following. Several of the Urth drones flew at a distance to either side and behind, keeping watch on their progress. Kira could see her parents talking to each other intently as they rode, keeping their conversation shielded from the drones.

"What do you think they're saying?" Jason asked nervously.

"They're planning," Kira said, trying to sound confident.

"Do you really think they can do anything to help?"

"Jason, I've been told by many people that the only thing more dangerous than my parents when they're caught by surprise is my mother and father when they've had time to plan." She reached out toward him. "Will you promise me something? If the worst happens, if you must return to Urth, please don't go back to being the boy I met the first time. Try to remain the guy you are now, no matter what they do to try to change you back."

He reached out as well, touching her hand with his. "I'll do my best. I promise."

"And do not forget me," Kira added. "Not ever."

"No one could possibly forget you," Jason said, smiling through his worries.

A bright spot appeared in the sky, swiftly growing to become the silver shape of the ship from Urth. Kira watched it glide across the sky until it reached a spot a few hundred lances ahead of them, then settle onto the pasture.

Mari turned in her saddle. "You and your troop wait here, Colonel. Could you have someone hold our mounts? Thank you. Dismount, family. That includes you, Jason."

Handing off her reins to a soldier, Kira followed with Jason as her mother and father walked toward the ship from Urth. When they were less than ten lances distant from the ship, Kira's mother halted them.

"Alain, stand over there," Mari directed. "Kira, beside your father. Jason, right here between Kira and me." Four people facing the menacing bulk of the ship from Urth. It felt unnaturally quiet. The wind sweeping across the field held a cold edge brought down from the north that tempered the heat of the noon sun.

Talese Groveen came out, walking like a conqueror. She stopped in front of them, extending an imperious hand. "I am happy to see that you have seen reason and the futility of your opposition to me."

Mari reached out to Jason, who gave her the Invictus Drive. She then tossed it lightly to Talese, who caught it.

Talese examined the drive, tapping the surface and studying the results, before turning a thin-lipped look of triumph on Jason. "Your brainless, ill-considered actions have once again resulted in nothing but failure for you and embarrassment for me."

Jason gave her a level look in reply instead of a sullen frown. "I guess so," he said in a neutral voice.

She frowned at him, thrown off by his reaction to her disdain. "Get in the ship. We're leaving."

"Mom, I want to stay here," Jason said, not moving.

"Don't be ridiculous."

"Mom, please let me stay. I'm happy here. Happier than I've ever been."

"I'm sure, now that you've found yourself a plaything desperate enough to—"

"Don't talk about Kira like that!"

Mari spoke before Talese Groveen, startled by Jason's defiance, could say anything else. "My husband and I are willing to accept responsibility for Jason. We would ensure that he is well treated, protected, educated, and set on a path for a successful adult life. We ask that you grant us guardianship of him."

Talese Groveen laughed. "You think I'd actually consider that? For even one moment? Jason is *my* child. I will not give him away, no matter how much he or anyone else begs for it. Now, get in the ship!" she ordered Jason, turning away from Mari.

"*Wait*," Kira's mother said, using the sort of voice that even emperors and presidents paid attention to. "There's something that you've wanted ever since the first day you arrived. If you get that, will you reconsider?"

Talese Groveen paused, turning back to study Mari through narrowed eyes. "What exactly are you speaking of?"

"A sample of my genetic material, along with my approval for you to use it as you see fit."

"Mother!" Kira gasped. "You can't give that up!"

"Lady Mari!" Jason said, shaking his head frantically. "No!"

Mari held up a hand, palm out, to quiet them. "Well, Talese Groveen? If I agree to those things, can Jason stay here?"

"Agreeing to total control of your genetic material by Universal Life Systems?" Talese Groveen asked. "In accordance with the provisions in the ULS waiver we have already prepared?"

"Yes. If we get this over with before I change my mind."

"I have no desire to linger here," Talese Groveen informed her, smiling. "We have a deal." One of her fingers moved before her. "Doctor Sino! Come out here and bring your med bag!"

"Lady Mari," Jason begged. "Don't. I'm not worth this."

"Yes, you are, Jason," Mari said, giving him a glance. "Even if you weren't Kira's friend, you'd be worth it. The freedom of any person would be worth it."

"But she's not going to keep the deal! As soon as she has your stuff she'll try to haul me off anyway!"

Mari smiled at him. "Jason, sometimes you have to trust in people."

Kira saw the derisive look in Talese Groveen's eyes, but said nothing. She had seen that sort of smile from her mother before. It meant that somebody was about to learn what happened when they underestimated Lady Mari.

Only a few more moments elapsed before a woman strode out of the opening in the side of the ship, a bag slung over one shoulder. "What's the deal?" she asked Talese Groveen, displaying what Kira thought was just enough disdain for Jason's mother to get away with.

"Get a sample from her and a statement of unconditional release," Talese Groveen ordered, pointing at Mari.

But before the woman could approach Mari, Alain spoke. "As the partner of Lady Mari, I have a say in this. It is important that we are clear on the bargain being agreed to. You, Talese Groveen, will grant us custody of this boy Jason?"

"Yes! If there's nothing else, we need to get moving."

"This will be done in exchange for Mari giving you a sample and her agreement that you can use it?"

"Yes!"

"This sample is valuable, we have been told," Alain observed, his voice Mage-calm. "To restate, you have agreed to sell your son to us in exchange for the value represented by the sample from Lady Mari."

For a long moment, the only sound was once again that of the wind sighing through the grass.

"Is that not correct?" Alain said. "Is that not what this transaction represents?"

Kira, noticing that Talese Groveen appeared torn between fear and anger, finally understood. "Urth has laws against selling people. Jason told us that! And you were about to sell your son to us! You had agreed to sell him to us!"

Jason grinned. "I can't wait to get back to Earth and tell the authorities about it. They'll scan me while I testify and they'll know I'm telling the truth. What's the mandatory minimum jail sentence for human trafficking? Is it a life sentence?"

Talese Groveen finally found her voice. "What do you want?" she asked Alain as if every word was being dragged out of her.

"Let your son decide whether or not to stay here," Alain said.

"In exchange for?"

"It would be improper, as well as illegal by the laws of Urth, to put a price on your son," Alain said.

"I can't testify against you back on Earth if I'm here," Jason said. "Just let me stay. If I go back, I will testify. About that, and about a lot of other things."

"We will take good care of him," Mari repeated.

"You haven't won!" Talese Groveen snapped at her. "You can have him! He's never been anything but a useless burden. And you can keep your genes! I have something far more valuable." She held up the Invictus Drive, then spun on one heel, pausing to look at the other woman who had come out of the ship. "Give him a clearance physical and sign him out!" Talese Groveen paused again. "Take your time and do it right. Make sure there's a clean statement of a desire to stay here. Be sure to repeat it for him."

Having issued those orders, Talese Groveen stomped back to the ship and disappeared inside.

"Sure," the woman called to Talese Groveen's back. She walked up to Jason. "Hmmm. That's strange."

"What's strange?" Jason asked. He had been grinning in amazement, but the smile faded as he looked at the doctor.

"Physically you seem to be Jason Groveen, but you don't look like him. Are you really Jason?" Doctor Sino said, standing before him and looking at the space just in front of her face.

"You know I am, Doctor," he replied, sounding nervous.

"You can't be. The Jason I know never smiles, and I've seen you smile quite a bit recently."

Jason's grin returned. "I've got reasons to smile now."

"Uh-huh." The woman glanced at Kira. "I think I know what one of those reasons is. I'm Doctor Sino," she introduced herself to the others.

"Doctor of Sino?" Mari asked. "That is your home?"

"Uh…no. My name's Peggy Sino. I was born and raised on Horizons One Orbital Habitat, if that's what you're asking."

"*Doctor* is what people on Earth call healers," Jason explained to Kira's parents. "Doc Sino is, well, the closest thing to a friend I had on the ship. She's cool."

"I'm cool? Thanks. And you're in pretty good shape," Sino commented, her eyes still on that something before her. "Physically, really good. Much better than the last time I saw you. You've been exercising. What's this recent skin trauma?"

"That's probably from when the dragon hit me," Jason said.

"I see. I'll list it as an encounter with local wildlife. You need to eat more vegetables. Make sure you pay attention to that. Otherwise, you're good to go, Jason. Or good to stay, that is. You do want to stay here? That's for the official record."

"Yes, Doctor, I want to stay here."

Sino sighed, looking around. "I can see why. I'll miss you. Good luck."

"Doctor? Before you go, could I ask you a couple of things?" Jason said, nervous again. "Um, since I'm going to be here for I guess the rest of my life, I might, you know, someday want to, sort of, a family—"

"Yes," Sino said, smiling. "Your gene pacs are fully compatible with natural methods of reproduction. Your gene pacs are also still under license, but I seriously doubt that anybody from ULS is going to come here demanding sublicensing fees if you pass on some of those genes to offspring."

"The other thing was…" Jason leaned close and whispered to Sino.

The doctor looked at Mari. "Is it okay if I do a scan? Nothing physically invasive, no permanent record. Just a look."

Mari glanced at Jason. "It's all right this time?"

"From Doc Sino, yes."

"Go ahead," Kira's mother told the doctor.

"Oh." Sino nodded to herself. "I see. Yes, that's correctable. If you know what you're doing, and I'm guessing the surgeons here don't, know since it hasn't been fixed?"

"What are you talking about?" Mari asked.

Sino pointed toward Mari's abdomen. "The problems in there that interfere with a safe pregnancy. Jason, I could guide the local surgeons in fixing this. They understand antisepsis here, right? The only problem is that I can't stay to do it. Talese Groveen has made it clear that as soon as we're done here our ship is heading home."

"You can't stay a little longer?" Jason pleaded.

"I want to stay here long enough to handle this, Jason, but—"

Kira gasped as she saw the opening in the side of the Earth ship vanish. The ship jumped skyward.

Doctor Sino turned to look, startled. Her fingers moved rapidly. "My link is dead. No one's answering me." She paused, her expression worried. "Jason, what was the last thing I said before they took off?"

"You said…you wanted to stay here, but—"

"Oh." Sino exhaled heavily. "I should have realized that TG would seize on any opportunity to maroon me here."

"What happened?" Kira asked, guessing that TG was short for Talese Groveen but otherwise confused.

"What happened is that I said, while being monitored, *I want to stay here*. By using just that clip, TG can claim I decided to stay along with Jason. Oh, yeah. That's why she told me to repeat whatever Jason said about staying. I didn't, but I gave her what she wanted later."

"Why?" Mari looked dazed as she tried to take in everything the doctor had told her. "Why would she want to leave you?"

"Because," Sino said, pointing at Alain, "I was also out here when your husband tricked TG into admitting that she was to all intents and purposes selling her son. That made me another witness who could have testified against her on Earth. Now all I could do is rat her out using your Feynman Unit, but transmissions like that are not legally admissible evidence."

"I'm sorry," Jason said. "This is my fault."

"And ours," Alain said.

"Not entirely," Sino said, looking around. Her expression, angry at her abandonment by the ship, slowly shifted as she looked at the world around her, settling into a slight smile. "I left TG an opening for her to knife me, and she did. I'm not all torn up about not spending another two months cooped up with her inside that ship, and there isn't anybody left back on Earth that I'm particularly close to. That's why I accepted the mission assignment even though I was going to be gone for twenty years. And there are a lot worse places to be marooned. Hey, you're called Lady Mari, right? And you're in charge of this planet? Since I'm staying, do you think there's any chance I could have a pony? I've always wanted one."

"I'm not exactly in charge of the planet," Mari said. "I can promise you that if you come back to Tiae with us, Queen Sien will be only too happy to let you choose a horse from the royal herd. But, to be honest, every place on Dematr is going to want you and your knowledge. They'll all offer you whatever you want."

Doctor Sino looked at Jason. "I think to start off with I'll put my trust in the people who were smart enough to outfox TG, and who gave this guy reasons to smile. I like Jason, and it means a lot to me that you put yourselves on the line for him. Besides, I have to go where you do so we can get that surgery done. It's a good thing I've got my bag."

"You will help Mari?" Alain asked as he moved to stand beside her. Kira was surprised to hear how clear the hope sounded in her father's voice.

"I am a doctor. That's what we do. And she's already sort of my patient."

Kira watched in shock as her mother sagged, having to be supported by her father. "Are you all right?"

Mari got her feet under her again, giving Kira a smile. "I'm fine. I just never thought there'd be a chance that you could have another brother or a sister."

"A brother or a sister?" It finally hit Kira. "After the doctor works on you, you'll be able to have another child! But…"

"But what?" her mother asked.

"Aren't you a little old for that?"

Mari stared at her. "I am going to make you pay for that, young lady. You'll never know where or when. Oh, uh, Doc-tor? Kira was hurt. Can you do anything for her?"

"Hurt?" Sino frowned as Kira took off her coat. "If there are modesty issues here, everybody else turn while I take care of this." Kira opened her shirt, wincing as parts of the fabric stuck to the cuts pulled free, while Alain and Jason quickly faced in other directions. Sino whistled softly. "What did this?"

"A dragon," Kira said, uncomfortable.

"A dragon. What a cool planet." Kira felt a chilly sensation on the cuts as Sino sprayed something, the stinging and itching disappearing. "Was this the same one that hit Jason? What happened to the dragon? Did you slay it?"

"Yes," Kira said.

"Wicked! You had a nasty bruise developing on your chest as well, but the spray will also help bring that down quickly. There. You'll be fine. Next time you want to fight a dragon, wear some armor or something."

As Kira buttoned up her shirt, Sino pointed to the cavalry waiting not far away. "Do we get to go back with them?"

"Yes, we do," Mari said. "You can ride with us."

"Cool. Oh, you might not know that the crew collected some skin flakes so they'd have a head start on genetic material from you guys." Sino grinned, patting her bag. "Which were all stored here. When TG took off, she left those, too."

"I knew I could count on you, Doc." Jason started laughing. "I finally get it! Lady Mari, you told me that I needed to trust in people. You didn't mean my mom! You meant I should trust in you, and in people like Doc Sino."

"That's right," Mari told him. "Alain and I figured that Talese Groveen would be eager enough, greedy enough, and in a rush enough not to think through what she was agreeing to. She did flinch when you threatened to testify about other things. That may have been what caused her to give in."

Jason laughed again. "I made that up. I figured my mom must have a lot of bodies buried somewhere…uh, that's a metaphor for lots of stuff that she doesn't want anybody to find out about, because I don't think she's actually in person murdered anybody…and her guilty conscience made her worry that I'd found out about some of it."

Kira's mother grinned. "I'm beginning to understand more why Kira likes you now, Jason. That reminds me. What do we call you? Do you want to hold on to the name Groveen, or—?"

"No! Can I be, uh, Jason of Pacta Servanda?"

Mari shook her head. "You're not from Pacta. Isn't there any place on Urth you called home?"

It was Jason's turn to shake his head. "No. I never really had a place. Just, Earth, I guess."

"Jason of Urth? That can work."

They rejoined the cavalry, one of the troopers dismounting and double-riding with a companion so that a delighted Doctor Sino could take her horse.

"How are we going to handle this?" Mari asked Alain as they all rode back to the city. "We just acquired a sixteen-year-old boy."

"Do we want him living with us?" Kira's father asked.

"Yes," Kira said.

"No," Kira's mother said. "We'll find a good place. I wonder if Alli and Calu would take him for a while? Calu would love to pick Jason's brains, and their boys would be great companions. He could ride the train—"

"The train?" Jason said, looking alarmed.

"You are wise to be worried," Alain commented.

"The train," Mari said. "It's an easy ride between Pacta and Dana-lee."

"Danalee?" Kira demanded. "You want Jason to live in Danalee? That's almost as far from Pacta Servanda as Urth is!"

"Give or take a bunch of light years," Jason muttered.

"See? Jason agrees with me!"

"We could ask Asha and Dav to take him," Mari said with mock seriousness. "I'm sure that their girls Ashira and Devi would love to have a boy near their age staying with them."

Kira made a face at her mother. "Very funny. What is wrong with him staying with us?"

"You want him living with you as a brother?"

"No! Maybe. No. I don't know."

Mari spread her hands as if helpless. "If you'd rather he'd gone back to Urth…"

"I didn't say that! I just want a chance to know him better!"

Her mother smiled reassuringly. "We're not keeping you apart. We'll give you that chance."

Kira exhaled heavily, gazing morosely ahead. "All right."

"All right?" Mari said. "Are you serious? That's it?"

"I don't feel like arguing," Kira said.

Her mother made an exaggerated reaction of surprise. "You don't feel like arguing? Who are you? And what have you done with Kira?"

"She's still here." Kira rolled her eyes at her mother. "See? But Kira knows a little bit more about herself now. And she knows a little bit more about her mother, and maybe even understands her mother a little more."

Her father managed a look of interest. "You must tell me what you have learned. I have spent twenty years trying to understand your mother and am still far from knowing what I should."

Mari rolled her eyes at both of them. "I always treasure these family moments when my husband and daughter gang up on me. However, at the moment nothing can bother me. We were so worried, Kira, especially after your father had that vision of you being chased along the side of a mountain."

"I was what?" Kira asked.

"Being chased along the side of a mountain. You and Jason. You had your pistol in your hand. When did that happen?"

Kira turned a puzzled gaze on Jason. "When did that happen? Did that happen?"

"I don't remember anything like that," Jason said. "As far as I can remember you holstered your pistol after we got out of Kelsi and didn't draw it again until we were in Ihris."

"I checked it and reloaded the night before we got to Ihris, but I was sitting down near the fire."

Her mother grew suddenly intent and serious. "Are you certain? You were never running along the side of a mountain with your pistol in your hand? Not even once for even a very short time?"

"No," Kira said. "I would have remembered that."

"Alain!" her mother said to her father.

He shook his head. "It has not yet happened."

"You're looking at Kira now. How much older was she in your vision?"

Her father studied Kira. "Not much older. It will happen within a few years at the most. Perhaps much sooner."

"*What* will happen?" Kira demanded.

Her mother answered in a weary voice. "Whatever will lead to that vision. Your adventures are not over, young lady. The vision your father saw still has to happen. At some point, before you're much older, you're going to be getting chased through mountains somewhere."

Kira realized that her mouth had fallen open and snapped it shut. "Jason was with me? You said that, didn't you?"

"Yes, Jason was with you," Alain said.

"Why is someone going to be chasing us through the mountains?" Kira demanded. "What have I done? Or is it something Jason did?"

"It may be what you will do at some point in the future," her father replied.

"What is that? Don't I deserve to know?"

'We'll all find out when we find out," Mari said. "Can you imagine how I felt when soon after meeting your father he saw the two of us fighting in a battle together at Dorcastle someday? And married? All we know now is that if our daughter will be in that situation, it's because she will have a good reason, is trying to do the right thing, and will be able to handle whatever happens. Even if she meets a dragon or two along the way."

Kira gave her mother a worried look. "I've heard some things in the last few weeks. Do you think whatever happens will be about… about people thinking or hoping that I would take over the daughter's responsibilities some day?"

Mari sighed. "I've never encouraged that kind of talk. I've *dis*couraged it. But people cling to it. I'm sorry. I don't expect that, and I will never pressure you to do it. Though…you did good, Kira. If that happened, I think you'd be fine. But my goal is still to get things set up so this world doesn't need the daughter to resolve disputes. And making the position hereditary would carry all kinds of risks."

"I know about Queen Sien and Prince Tien," Kira said.

Her mother studied Kira. "You don't seem overwhelmed. The Kira I know would have curled up into a whimpering ball at the idea of taking on my job."

"The Kira you knew almost did just that the first time she heard it," Kira told her mother. "This Kira is…still well aware of how little she is suited for that role, but she's not going to freak out."

"That's my girl. You always seemed to think that having me as your mother was a curse."

"I did," Kira admitted. "There was a lot I wasn't seeing, or understanding. I am so proud and happy to be your daughter. The daughter of the daughter."

"Thank you, Lady Kira," her mother said, blinking away tears.

"Oh, don't you dare do the lady thing to me!" Kira reached across to grasp her mother's hand. "When we get home, can we talk? I need to tell you a lot more about the last few weeks, and I hope you can tell me more about…things that are hard to talk about."

"I'll try. Oh, Alli is going to want to talk to you, too."

Kira felt her blood chill, remembering events at the railyard. "About Gari?"

"Yeah. She's kind of upset. Don't worry. We'll face that lecture together."

"Let's not tell Aunt Alli about you and me aiming at each other."

"Stars above, no!" Mari said. "We'd never hear the end of it."

"Mother," Kira said, still holding onto her mother's hand, "we're plotting together!"

She heard her father speaking to Jason. "I hope you realize what you are getting into."

Don't miss the adventure that started
it all...

THE DRAGONS
OF DORCASTLE

PILLARS OF REALITY ❋ BOOK 1

JACK
CAMPBELL

NEW YORK TIMES BESTSELLING AUTHOR

About the Author

"Jack Campbell" is the pseudonym for John G. Hemry, a retired Naval officer who graduated from the U.S. Naval Academy in Annapolis before serving with the surface fleet and in a variety of other assignments. He is the author of The Lost Fleet military science fiction series, as well as the Stark's War series, and the Paul Sinclair series. His short fiction appears frequently in *Analog* magazine, and many have been collected in ebook anthologies *Ad Astra*, *Borrowed Time*, and *Swords and Saddles*. He lives with his indomitable wife and three children in Maryland.

FOR NEWS ABOUT JABBERWOCKY BOOKS AND AUTHORS

Sign up for our newsletter*: http://eepurl.com/b84tDz
visit our website: awfulagent.com/ebooks
or follow us on twitter: @awfulagent

THANKS FOR READING!

*We will never sell or giveaway your email address, nor use it for nefarious purposes. Newsletter sent out quarterly.

18918595R00199

Printed in Poland
by Amazon Fulfillment
Poland Sp. z o.o., Wrocław